Praise for Er

The Other Women

"This book is like a love letter to anyone with a broken heart. Erin Zak is telling you that you will get through it, and if someone breaks your heart, they were never worthy in the first place."—*Les Rêveur*

The Road Home

"Zak writes interesting, unusual, and unique circumstances in which the leading ladies meet but their chemistry is so awesome right off the bat that you are rooting for them all along…This is a wonderfully immersive read and highly recommended."—*Best Lesfic Reviews*

"Lila and Gwen have chemistry for days. They also have quick witty banter that keeps you on your toes. I love this angsty drama, it is just an amazing read. I could gush over this one for days, but I am just going to say don't deny yourself this one."—*Romantic Reader Blog*

Beautiful Accidents

"The main characters had so much chemistry I felt like I was right there with them observing every interaction. The attraction was so well written from their first meeting. The writing was engaging and well paced."—*Melina Bickard, Librarian (Waterloo Library, London UK)*

"*Beautiful Accidents* is an intriguing and exciting romance with real depth, and I really appreciated how romance is reframed as enrichment rather than sacrifice. Stevie and Bernadette never give up any aspects of their real identities to be together; Zak has created a pair of characters that are definitely going to stick with me." —*Beyond the Words*

"This book kept me engaged from beginning to end. I enjoyed the chemistry between Stevie and Bernadette."—*Maggie Shullick, Librarian, Lorain and Cuyahoga County (Ohio)*

"[T]his lesbian age gap romance book is [Zak's] best to date. This is an easy one to recommend to romance fans who like a lot of chemistry and some angst."—*Lez Review Books*

"[I]f you want big dramatic feelings, Zak is the way to go." —*Colleen Corgel, Librarian, Queens Borough Public Library*

"This book made my heart ache from the start. When Stevie sees Bernadette for the first time, her breath catches. Mine did too. The way Erin Zak describes reactions, both physical and mental, pulled me in absolutely. It's both wonderful and painful. It's what I'm looking for in romances. It's the best feeling."—*Jude in the Stars*

"Zak takes her time with the characters in developing them as individuals and allowing the relationship time to develop…This is a bit more of a mature romance in that there is unquestionably a connection but both characters recognize that with their lives at major turning points…that HEA isn't easy and compromising for the other person holds the danger of regret. There's drama, but not overblown—it's real, messy, and complicated with difficult decisions that have to be made."—*C-Spot Reviews*

Create a Life to Love

"Erin Zak does unexpected attraction and sexual awakening late in life really, really well."—*Reviewer@large*

"*Create A Life To Love* is a soulful story of how love can conquer all. I laughed, cried (sobbed) and got butterflies more than once, and did you see the cover art? Fantastic."—*Les Rêveur*

"This is officially one of my favorite books of all time."—*Maggie Shullick, Librarian, Lorain and Cuyahoga County (Ohio)*

Breaking Down Her Walls

"If I could describe this book in one word it would be this: annnngggssstt…If angst is your thing, this a great book for you." —*Colleen Corgel, Librarian, Queens Public Library*

"*Breaking Down Her Walls* had me completely spun. One minute I'm thinking that it's such a sweet romance, the next I found it sexy as hell then by the end, I had it as an all-encompassing love story that I just adored."—*Les Rêveur*

"I loved the attraction between the two main characters and the opposites attract part of the story. The setting was amazing…I look forward to reading more from this author."—*Kat Adams, Bookseller (QBD Books, Australia)*

"This is a charming contemporary romance set on a cattle ranch near the Colorado Mountains…This is a slow burn romance, but the chemistry is obvious and strong almost from the beginning. *Breaking Down Her Walls* made me feel good."—*Rainbow Reflections*

"If you like contemporary romances, ice queens, ranchers, or age gap pairings, you'll want to pick up *Breaking Down Her Wall*s."—*Lesbian Review*

Falling Into Her

"*Falling Into Her* by Erin Zak is an age gap, toaster oven romance that I really enjoyed. The romance has a nice burn that's slow without being too slow. And while I'm glad that lesfic isn't all coming out stories anymore, I enjoyed this particular one because it shows how it can happen in a person's 40s."—*Lesbian Review*

"I loved everything about this book…I'm always slightly worried when I try a book by someone who a) I've never heard of before; b) never published anything before (as far as I know). Especially if the book is in a sub-niche market area. But I'm quite glad I found my way to trying this book and reading it. And enjoying it."—*Lexxi is Reading*

"[A] great debut novel from Erin Zak and looking forward to seeing what's to come."—*Les Rêveur*

By the Author

Falling into Her

Breaking Down Her Walls

Create a Life to Love

Beautiful Accidents

Hot Ice Novella – Closed Door Policy

The Road Home

The Other Women

Swift Vengeance (with Jean Copeland and Jackie D)

The Hummingbird Sanctuary

Visit us at www.boldstrokesbooks.com

THE HUMMINGBIRD SANCTUARY

by

Erin Zak

2022

THE HUMMINGBIRD SANCTUARY

ISBN 13: 978-1-63679-163-0

This Trade Paperback Original Is Published By
Bold Strokes Books, Inc.
P.O. Box 249
Valley Falls, NY 12185

First Edition: April 2022

Credits
Editor: Barbara Ann Wright
Production Design: Stacia Seaman
Cover Design by Jeanine Henning

Acknowledgments

Whew! I don't know about the rest of y'all, but the past couple of years have really taken it out of me. COVID and politics and maintaining friendships and wearing masks and wondering if every little sniffle was going to be the dreaded virus. It was a lot! For a lot of us, aside from, oh, maybe Taylor Swift, writing during the pandemic has been really hard. (Also, thank you, Taylor, for putting out the two best albums of your career.) Everything about my writing habits had to change. It may seem dramatic, but it took everything out of me most days. But other days? It felt really amazing to write again, and to write for myself, once I got into my groove. In the end, I'm so very happy with how this story turned out. I really hope you enjoy visiting *The Hummingbird Sanctuary*. If I were to ever own and operate a resort, the sanctuary is what it would be like. Hard to believe a fictional place could mean so much to me, but it does. And it means even more to my characters.

I have to give a huge shout-out to my amazing editor, Barbara Ann Wright. Let me tell you, this lady knows how to deal with a broken author. She helped me so much, so many times, and I'm forever grateful to her. Much love to you!

And, of course, I want to thank Rad and Sandy, who continue to let me tell my quirky stories. It means the world to me. And to the rest of the BSB team—thank you so much for everything.

To my friends…you're all amazing. Jackie and Stacey, thank you for all the words of encouragement. Jean, thank you for slapping me silly a couple of times. And Anne Shade! Thank you for beta-reading for me.

To Gail. What a ride this has been. You have always been my rock, but even more so in the past three years. I'm so happy you married me.

Finally, to my readers. It always, always takes me by surprise that people actually read what I write. I wish I had a better way of saying that I love you all without it sounding so nonchalant, but it's the truth. I keep writing partly for myself, but also for you all. Thank you and enjoy your stay.

To the brokenhearted amongst us. Trust me, it gets better.

The Mesa County Times
April 1, 2022

"Dilapidated Old Resort Near Grand Junction Finally Booming"
by Cassandra Smith, Tourism Staff Writer

If you haven't had a chance to visit the Hummingbird Sanctuary yet, what are you waiting for? Not only is it this year's hottest destination for Coloradans, but it's also a top tourist destination for many others. When the new resort owners, Olive Zyntarski, Eleanor Fitzwallace, and Harriet Marshall, decided to purchase the abandoned property in Unaweep Canyon, they set out to build a getaway that would rival the most amazing resorts across the United States. A Native American term, *Unaweep* means "canyon with two mouths." Any newcomer to the newly renovated, refurbished, and renamed Hummingbird Sanctuary Resort will quickly find that there are certainly a lot more than two mouths escaping to the gorgeous territory.

The five-hundred-acre plot of land is home to ten buildings, a fifteen-thousand-square-foot living area for the owners, and a soon-to-be-open, state of the art event venue. All the structures are adobe style, with light brown stucco and wooden beams protruding. The landscaping is impeccable, not xeriscaped like many expect because of the dry weather conditions typical in Colorado, especially on the Western Slope. Instead, beautiful shrubbery and lush turf areas are spread throughout the property.

"After my husband passed away, I wanted to open a resort that caters mainly to women. I don't want to say we frown upon men being here because men are more than welcome. But everything we offer is specifically marketed toward women," explains Olive Zyntarski, dressed impeccably in a navy-blue suit with a fuchsia button-down peeking out. She has a floral scarf around her neck, tied delicately in a bow, bringing the entire outfit together. Olive, who moved her entire life from the bustling city of Chicago to chase her dream of being a resort owner, jokes, saying, "It wasn't easy, and there were definitely moments when we all wanted to kill each other, but that's what happens with friends. You love each other through all the ups and downs."

Eleanor Fitzwallace says she wasn't entirely ready to make a move, but Olive was persuasive enough that she decided to follow her best friend. "I'm forty-seven, and I've been in the marketing industry since God was a boy." She runs her hand through blond curled hair. "I left a great position at Synergy Marketing, one of the top marketing firms in Chicago, for this chick," she says, jerking her thumb toward Olive, then leaning into her with a gentle nudge. "The CEO at the time, Cecily Yates, was sad that I was leaving but was super excited for me to grow. The energy at Synergy…" She pauses. "I'm a poet on the side." We all chuckle. The mood is very easygoing with these women. "The energy there made it easy to want to be the best I can be. It made the decision to leave a lot easier, especially because the firm dealt mostly with casinos and the gaming industry. The jump wasn't big to come to the hospitality side of things."

And Harriet, who scolded me because she likes to be called Hattie, was an executive chef for Cat's Pajamas in Chicago. Her main reason for making the move? "They told me the mountains would seduce me."

"Were we wrong?" Eleanor asks, her hand out, a turquoise ring on her middle finger.

"Not one bit."

"Any particular reason you used hummingbirds as your mascot?"

They all grin. "Well, we all have lost our moms." The news that Eleanor shares is slightly shocking. I find myself pulled into the conversation even more. "When it came down to it, we wanted to find something that spoke about all of them without calling it the Mom Sanctuary."

"And," Olive interjects, "I'm originally from Colorado. Rangely, to be exact, which is literally a wide spot in the road. If you blink, you'll miss it. I grew up learning about all the wildlife. But my mother, as much as she loved a good bear sighting or a mountain lion, she was, at the end of the day, a huge lover of birds, especially hummingbirds. I learned a lot about them when I was growing up. They are said to bring good news from beyond."

"And a group of hummingbirds can be called a 'charm.'" When Hattie speaks, her brown eyes hold a lot of kindness. "Which, once Ollie told me that, I was all in."

"Right? It made it all come together." Eleanor places a hand on Hattie's.

"Everything here has a certain charm to it," Olive explains. "Our mothers would have been very proud of this place."

Many people are proud of the three women. Mesa County, in particular, has seen a huge uptick in tourism since the grand opening a little under three years ago on Mother's Day. The unveiling of the new event venue will happen on this year's Mother's Day, followed by a grand party for the guests. The event has been sold out for six months, and the rooms have been booked as well.

These women are doing everything right. And it shows.

You can head to their website to check room availability and their event calendar.

"Escape to the Hummingbird Sanctuary, where you're not only part of the family, you're part of the *charm*."

CHAPTER ONE

Olive

"Oh, holy *shit*. Snake!" I jump like a frightened cat onto a wrought iron chair on the patio behind the welcome building of the Hummingbird Sanctuary. If I were to make a list of things I cannot stand about nature, snakes would be at the very top. I cannot stand snakes. And they're everywhere in Colorado. Everywhere! Even, apparently, on the patio sunning itself like it paid the resort fee.

The chair wobbles, the metal clanging as the legs bob from side to side on the brick pavers, and a shudder runs through my body. Homemade nectar from the hummingbird feeder I'm holding spills down my arm and all over the ground. The only thing I was truly looking forward to today—putting up the very first feeder of the year—and now it's ruined. "Goddammit." I groan. I am a mess, and I feel my nerve endings rake against my skin, a physical manifestation of my sure brush with death. One more thing to add to the already jam-packed day on my plate. As if seeing a reptile I loathe isn't bad enough. "Oh God, Juan," I say as my very amazing director of maintenance approaches from the path to the maintenance shed. He's staring, wide-eyed, a smirk on his face.

"What's going on, Ollie?" Juan is loving this. He's choking on the laughter he's holding back.

"What's going on? Oh, I'll tell you what's going on. There's a freaking snake. Right freaking there." I point and gesture too wildly for my precarious position atop the chair.

"Okay. Just walk by it. It's more afraid of you than you are of it, *mi amiga*."

"Yeah, yeah, I could do that. And"—a weird strangled sound

escapes from me—"I'd love nothing more than to do that. But you know I hate snakes." A shiver sweeps through me like a zap of electricity. "What the frick kind of snake is that? Is it poisonous?" It slithers toward me. "Gah! Holy shit, it's huge! Get rid of it!"

Juan snickers. He's adorable with his perfectly manicured beard. I want to punch him, though, for no other reason than he's making fun of me. If I and the rest of the sanctuary didn't need him, I'd have half a mind to be pissed off at him. "I've never seen someone jump from seeing a snake before." He is going for sincere, but it comes out like an accusation. As if I should be able to control myself.

"Oh? You think this is funny, do ya?"

"Well," he says, clearly trying to keep a straight face. "It's not *not* funny."

"Juan, I swear to Christ up above, if you don't fucking get rid of that snake right now, you're gonna have to find another job."

"Sure."

"I am not kidding."

"Okay, okay," he says, his hands held out as if to tell me to calm down. "*Tranquila, tranquila.* You realize it's only a snake, right?"

"Exactly. It's a gross, disgusting snake. I think you should probably dispose of it. Right this instant." The feeder swings as I gesture, spilling more nectar. "Seriously, Juan."

"Olive, come on. It is not poisonous. It's a yellow-bellied racer, and it helps keep the other pests away. Like mice."

"I'd rather have a herd of mice."

"No, you wouldn't. I can promise you that. What do you want me to do with it?"

"I want you to kill it. But because you're such a nice guy, you won't do that." I groan again.

He shakes his head with a somber expression. "No, I sure won't." He wipes at his face with a handkerchief he pulled from his back pocket, clears his throat, then folds the red paisley material neatly and shoves it back into his dark blue Wranglers. He pulls at the brim of his ball cap, a gaudy thing with a gold mustang on the front. After about two weeks of working here, he stopped wearing the prescribed uniform and decided he looked better in his Wranglers, tailored black Polos that he took to get fitted, and whatever new ball cap he picked up.

Juan moves around the snake, and I adjust my stance, moving awkwardly in the chair, making it wobble all over again. "Whoa." I steady myself and thankfully don't spill nectar again. "As the director of grounds maintenance"—I point at him—"you're supposed to get rid of all the pests. *Rapido.* We have a busy day ahead of us, and we have an entire walk-through to get accomplished, and it's already ten after six."

"That's funny."

"What's funny? Hmm?" I hate being irritated like this, but if the shoe fits…

"Getting rid of pests? I've been trying to get rid of you since you hired me." He shrugs, nonchalant.

I roll my eyes. "Oh, that's rich. Real, real rich. Let's see if you find this one funny: I'm going to tell Harmony in the kitchen you have the hots for her if you don't act. Now." His eyes go wide. "Oh, not funny now?"

"Ollie, please don't."

"I won't if you get it out of my sight. Immediately."

He shakes his head and gathers the necessary tools from the golf cart. "He's cold. He should have slithered away by now."

I shiver again. The word slither makes me want to pass out.

He tries to scoop up the snake, and it moves, and because I'm a total wuss, I let out yet another bloodcurdling scream, which, in turn, causes Juan to start laughing. After a scuffle or two with the snake, Juan finally manages to get ahold of it with the tongs. He very carefully walks across the courtyard and into the brush, where he places it near the bottom of the sagebrush that lines the property. When he walks back over, he holds his hand out for me to take. "Is that better?"

I take his hand, step off the chair, straighten my navy slacks, and run my hands through my hair. I clear my throat and hand over the half-empty feeder. "Whew. Thank goodness we didn't panic."

"You're *loca* in the *cabeza.* You know that, right?"

"I'm sorry. I cannot stand snakes."

"I couldn't tell."

"Stop." I smack him on the arm before I let the fun facade fall away because it's time to get down to business. I take off toward the east side of the guest room buildings and wave for him to follow. "Come on. We have a lot more to cover."

I only have two speeds these days, fast and mega-fast. I've been working on slowing down during the walk-throughs because Juan accused me of rushing the journey. "Enjoy the world you've built," he often says. They are wise words. It's not hard, either. The mountains, the blue skies, the dry air. Being back in Colorado has been calming for me.

Trying to run a resort with three hundred rooms and twelve villas that have been at full capacity almost every single day since we opened wouldn't be possible without our amazing staff. We started with two buildings, one hundred twenty rooms, and four villas on opening day. Within a month, we had plans for three more buildings and eight additional villas to accommodate the demand. Juan, bless his heart, has been here every step of the way, helping me deal with the contractors, employee issues, any and all things, really. I've learned to listen to him. His knowledge is unmatched, and he, just like the mountain air, calms me. Little by little, I'm enjoying the world my friends and I have built. I'm working on trying to forget the past and letting go of the deep-seated guilt I am harboring. Guilt I can't seem to talk about to anyone. And it's becoming an issue, especially in the mornings when it's quiet, and I see my husband's face in my memory. His kind eyes and his sleepy smile. And I have to remind myself that he's not here to enjoy this. That this would have never been possible without him passing.

When we round the far side of the welcome building, I point out a few different plants, shrubs, and decorative grasses that are getting missed and need to be maintained by our lawn staff. I point to a few areas on the buildings where the paint has started to chip. "I emailed you the contractor's name and phone number," I say after I slide my cell phone back into my pocket. We start at the farthest side of the property where the villas referred to as nests reside. The nests are amazing. Everything inside is stocked as if it's a bed and breakfast. Renting a nest isn't cheap, but the technology inside is state of the art, and they have a tremendous amount of privacy, including a firepit and a hot tub. "Also, the nests on the far west side are getting neglected. Can you please ask your staff to pay extra attention to the weeds? I feel like after a rain or two, they'll be out of control."

"Absolutely. And I already called the stucco people, and they'll be out first thing Monday morning."

"Oh, Juan, what would I do without you?"

"You would have had to take care of that snake on your own."

I chuckle. "I'd still be on that chair."

At five after nine, Juan is already on his cell, letting workers know where they need to be. I take a stroll through the lobby of the welcome center. A dozen or more people are in the waiting area, checking out, and I cue my professional expression of gratitude for the guests. I love the people, but being *on* all the time is exhausting. The customer service part has to happen, but damn, some days I wish I had a clone to do this part, someone who doesn't feel so strange around strangers.

"Carol, Jane," I say as I approach a wonderful couple who stayed the weekend with us. "How was everything?" Twenty-five years together, and it was finally the right time for this pair to get married.

"Oh." Carol puts her hand to her bosom. "This was exactly what we needed. An escape."

"I cannot begin to describe how lovely everything was." Jane takes my hand. "You and your ladies have gone above and beyond. The one-bedroom nest was immaculate."

"And the private hot tub was exactly what the doctor ordered." Carol winked, and Jane shushed her with a playful wave. "We loved every second. We will be back."

"Thank you for choosing to stay with us to celebrate your love," I say with as much sincerity as I can muster. "Make sure you email Keri behind the desk when you make plans for your next visit. We'll take care of you." I turn and head to the next group of ladies, a foursome of friends who heard about us because of a celebrity visitor who posted about it on Instagram. "Ladies, how was your stay?"

"Holy shit," one says, followed by a gasp of air. "I can't even begin to tell you how perfect it was. Thank you for everything. We needed this trip more than you can even imagine. It was exactly what we hoped for."

"You have no idea how happy that makes me. I hope you took advantage of the pools and spa?"

"Best facial I've ever had," one says, followed by a long, luxurious sigh. "I don't want to leave."

No matter how many times I hear those words, I beam inside and out. "Please make sure you come back to see us."

"We'll be back. No worries there."

I wave as the four of them rush out to the black limo that will take them to the small airport in Grand Junction. There are days when I work hard to miss the check-out crowd, but every now and then, it lifts my spirits to know everything I've gone through is helping people in whatever capacity that happens to be.

"How has the rest of check-out been?" I ask as I head behind the counter to where Keri is standing. She's my customer service manager, and if Juan is my right hand, Keri is my left.

"Great as always." Keri turns, a grin spread across her thin lips. She's an adorable young woman with long dark hair she never leaves out of a ponytail. "Those four older women? I hung out with them last night at the lounge. I was in stitches. It was like *The Golden Girls*. Only thing missing was the cheesecake."

I can't fight my happiness, and it no doubt shows. I should probably be insulted because those ladies were more my age than the Golden Girls. "They were adorable, that's for sure. We've had quite a few women's groups as of late. I think the word is out that just because we're a quaint resort doesn't mean we aren't a little wild and crazy."

"Shocking that you're in charge of something this hip, right?"

"Oh, is that a zinger? Are you mocking me?"

"Only a little, Ollie." She nudges me. "You are a little tightly wound these days."

I scroll through the list of names for check-ins, expertly avoiding her comment, to see how the rest of the day will pan out. "Any complaints?"

"Uh, not today." She clears her throat. "In fact, every room has been a perfect temperature this time."

"Thank goodness for small miracles." My all-time favorite complaint was that it was too cold in the room, but she refused to turn the thermostat up. I almost decked the woman. "Let me know if you need any help for the three o'clock crowd."

"I'm sure I'll be fine. Sarah and Kara are on later to help out."

"Perfect. The dream team, right?"

"Absolutely." She places a hand on my arm, as if to urge me to look at her, so I turn. "I love working here. You know that, right?"

"I promise you, I know. You're part of what makes this place great. Thank you for all you do." As tightly wound as I appear, most days, I'm simply just trying to hold it all together. And I don't mean emotionally. I mean the actual resort. There's a fine line between being successful and being in way over our heads. And these days, I feel as if we are way too close to understanding the difference.

❖

After this week, Mother's Day weekend is right around the corner. Not only are we booked solid, but we're hosting a journalist from *On the Verge*, the newest and hippest magazine to burst onto the scene. The journalist, who has been heralded by her editor as the most talented and unorthodox writer on staff, will be here for four days with her closest friends. We've had A-listers at the property before. We had a slew of celebrity guests, as well as politicians and sports figures. But a journalist? Who's going to write an article about us? It's nerve-racking to say the least. Not to mention the fact that they're coming specifically for the grand opening of our new event venue, the Amphitheater. And if all of that isn't enough to handle, I also got a wild hair up my ass to change the menu, which will not go over well with Harriet. Thank goodness that as the Director of Operations at the sanctuary, I've learned how to delegate like a boss-ass bitch.

Eleanor, unfortunately, is going to hate me for delegating this one to her.

Dear, sweet Eleanor Fitzwallace, my very best and longest friend—and the sanctuary's Director of Marketing and Events Coordinator—is my go-to person to deliver bad news. She doesn't like that I put her in that position, but she is insanely good at it. She has this way about her that helps people not be angry. I haven't a clue what it is, but I swear to God, she could literally fire someone, end up crying with them, exchange phone numbers, and hug them as they leave. She's amazing with people, as if she was born to manage. In the fifteen years of our friendship, she has never lost her cool. It's a little strange. I thought for the longest time that she was taking something to help keep her even-keeled. But nope.

"Just vitamins," she told me one day when I finally worked up the courage to ask.

"Like, *vitamin* vitamins?"

"Yes, like B12 and Vitamin C, D3, a little biotin for my hair and skin. A turmeric supplement. What did you think I meant?"

"Oh, I don't know, like vitamin Klonopin."

She sails along, never bobbing, even in choppy water. And it's because of vitamins. Fucking vitamins. Maybe I need to start taking them.

I turn the corner into Eleanor's small office, the one with the best view on the property. She's so deep in thought that she doesn't notice me until I let out a heavy sigh after I sit in the comfy chair across from her desk. "You'll never guess what we have."

She doesn't look up. "What?"

"Snakes. We've got snakes."

She stops typing on her MacBook, spins in her chair, and peers over the top of her black-framed glasses. "Excuse me?"

"Snakes. We got 'em."

Eleanor is classically beautiful: high cheekbones; full, perfectly shaped pink lips; sea green eyes; naturally arched eyebrows; long honey-blond hair. Oh, and her skin practically glows. As if she's an angel or something. At forty-seven, she only has the slightest signs of aging, which seem to make her even more striking. "What the hell are you talking about?"

"There was a snake this morning on the patio out back, and Juan wouldn't kill it. He just set it free. Like some sort of good person or whatever."

"Was it poisonous?"

"A yellow-bellied something or another."

She blinks once, twice, a small smile now on her lips. "You sure he wasn't calling *you* yellow-bellied?" She squints.

"Touché."

"Olive, honey." Eleanor props her elbows on her desk, and her beach-waved hair falls over her shoulders. "You ever think about going to our on-site therapist? She might be able to help you."

"With what exactly?"

"This irrational fear of snakes. I think we should work on it."

"Excuse me? Irrational?"

"It wasn't poisonous. It's fine."

"Sure. You say that now."

"I'm sure Juan would have killed it had it been a bad snake. But it was a nice one. A nice snake that gets rid of unwanted critters."

"Oh, my God. Nice snakes? There's no such thing as a nice snake."

Eleanor sighs as she pulls her glasses from her face. There's something about the way she does it, as if she gives no fucks if her skin touches the glass and smudges it. That is a stressed-out sigh and an even more stressed-out action. "Is that all you wanted me for? To tell me we got snakes?"

Yep, and that's a stressed-out question and tone. "Whoa, whoa, what's going on?"

"Everything is fine."

"Um, yeah, I don't believe you.

"No complaints from the check-outs?" She's very skilled at subject avoidance.

I glare at her. "No. What is going on with you?"

"That's surprising."

I shake my head. "I'm as surprised as you are. Now answer my question."

"I mean, we have been working our asses off. Maybe we're finally at the point where complaints aren't as plentiful."

Okay, okay. We're playing this game. Got it. "From your lips to God's ears." I cross my legs and smooth a wrinkle in my slacks. "I guess there's nothing else to do today, then."

"Um, hardly." Eleanor swivels, takes a stack of papers from her desk, turns back, and plops them in front of me. "We need to discuss money."

"My favorite subject."

"Olive, we're in the red. Like, a lot. And since you don't want to hire an accountant, you're going to have to discuss this stuff with me."

"Discuss what, exactly?"

She rolls her lips inward and groans. "You overspent on the Amphitheater. By a lot. I need you to cut some of these expenditures. Not tomorrow. Not in a week. Now." She flips a few pages from the stack and points to a lot of numbers that sadly mean nothing to me. "I'm not trying to be a complete dickhead, but you've overspent by twenty-five thousand."

"What are you saying?"

She's staring at me. Unflinchingly. "How have you survived in life? How?"

"I had people to take care of the money for me. First it was Paul. Now it's you." I shrug. "Break it down to me in laymen's terms."

She blinks. "We're broke. We don't have a dime to our name. You spent the last of our nest egg on that fucking venue." She points in a furious manner out the window toward the now finished Amphitheater. "If this doesn't bring in the money you think it will, we will need to have a very, very, very hard conversation about our next steps."

I can tell by the heat coursing through my body that my face is probably red. Not with anger. But with fear. "You're saying this could ruin us?"

"I tried to tell you that when you were in the planning stage. But you wouldn't listen." She's standing now, pacing the small space between her desk and the window. "All you kept saying is, 'Make it bigger. Make it better. Make it grander.'" Her arms flail around her in big sweeping motions. "You have got to start listening to me. When I say no, you need to say okay. If you don't want to understand the money aspect, then you need to listen to me. For fuck's sake, Olive."

"You're not fun when you get like this." I try to lighten the mood. "Excuse me?"

"You know we'll be fine. It'll be fine."

She shakes her head as she props herself against her desk. "You don't get it, do you?"

"I get it. I do. But I'm not worried."

"You used to always worry. In the past, you were the one I was saying we'd be fine to. And now you're all easy breezy? Why aren't you worried now?"

I am. I'm very worried. And I have been for months. It keeps me up nights. This place is my everything. "Maybe because of the publicity?" I lie. "*The Mesa Times* article came out this morning. *Fast Company* article comes out the beginning of next week. Hattie has the interview with *Foodie Delight* and the Food Network early next week. And lest we not forget the most important one, *On the Verge* will be here Thursday to interview you, me, and Hattie. We are going to be fine." I hope I sound convincing because, believe me, I know the money issues have been plaguing us. We dumped a lot into this place. And only within the last year have we really seen any sort of profit. I may act stupid, but I'm far from it. I read the reports she gives me. But one of us must not let the worry show. If we both lose our shit, it won't work. She knows that. Or at least, I hope she does.

Her chest rises and falls with her breath. "You need to promise me you'll stop spending."

"I promise." And then I remember why I'm there in the first place. "Except for this one thing."

"I'm going to murder you."

"Listen, listen." I slide to the edge of my seat. "It's not a huge deal. But I have been thinking a lot, and I'd like to…" I gather all of my courage. "Change the menu for the weekend."

"I wasn't kidding. I'm going to murder you."

I stand in front of her and grab her hands. "I get what you're saying. I promise, I will rein it in. I swear on everything. But this is a huge weekend for us. And I want it to be flawless."

Eleanor sighs. "Fine."

"No, Eleanor…" I stop the argument I was prepared to make. "Wait. *Really?*"

She nods. "But only because if this doesn't work, I get to move back to Chicago." A small upturn in her lips happens, and I know she's joking. Only slightly.

"Not funny." I squeeze her hands. "And…do you think you could talk to her for me?"

"You are going to be the death of me." She purses her lips, a low grumbling coming from deep inside her. "What do you suggest I say to Hattie when she threatens to quit?"

"She won't."

"Yes, she fucking will." Eleanor pushes away from her desk and moves around me to the door. "The last thing I need is for you two to be fighting when we're trying to fucking run a calming and relaxing resort."

"I don't understand why she isn't happy here."

"Because, Olive, you boss her around. Like she's a child. You don't let her run the restaurant like you told her she'd be able to do. And you control everything. Right down to the menu, which is her pride and joy."

A puff of air passes through my lips. "I do not."

Her eyes are wide, and her mouth falls open. "What do you call this?" She turns and exits her office. "You do the same thing to me, but I've learned how to tell you to fuck off without it affecting our friendship."

I can barely contain my eye roll. "Keep it up, and I'll find another marketing person."

"No, you won't," Eleanor shouts from down the hall before she disappears.

It's a good thing I love her so much. Actually, it's a good thing she loves *me* so much. I can be a real pain in the ass. Hard to handle. Difficult. Mean. Bitchy. Bossy. All the words that would have never been said if I was a man. I'm a perfectionist and driven to the point of madness some days. The idea that something I have poured my entire soul into could fold with one false move keeps me up at night.

The Hummingbird Sanctuary is my pride and joy.

My reason for living.

I cringe at my thoughts as I sit at my desk.

My reason for living? God, Olive, you need to lighten up.

The sanctuary is important, yes, but not focusing on anything else for the past five years hasn't been great, considering that the rest of my life stalled once the purchase of the sanctuary happened.

Who am I kidding? My life stalled the second I got the phone call from an ER nurse at Rush University Medical Center.

Before the Hummingbird Sanctuary, my husband was my sanctuary. Until he wasn't.

Time was supposed to heal the gaping wound left behind by the death of Paul, the gaping wound from the lies I told myself and the guilt that has manifested, running as far and wide as the Rockies.

I am going to find a way to get past it all. Leave the self-deprecating thoughts behind me. Carve out some happiness for myself in my very full life. How can I expect women, in all walks of life, to come here to the sanctuary to fix themselves if I can't do it here, too?

It isn't easy to think about being truly happy again. I play off my sadness well most days. Eleanor seems to be the only one who questions me, and I try to wave off the concern. I am fine. Everything is fine. I can handle all of it. The guilt. The sadness.

That is all a lie. I haven't been handling anything. My brain is a professional gravedigger, burying my feelings deeper and deeper and covering them up. It'll get better, won't it? It has to. I have heard people my entire life say the loss of a loved one never heals. It gets less raw. How about the loss of two loved ones? Two holes remain now, where feelings have been buried. My mother. My husband. I'm worried my loss will permanently be a gaping wound. And nothing will fix it. That's also a lie, isn't it? Because the sanctuary will fix it. It has to. I will do whatever it takes to save this place, even if that means throwing myself into every aspect, including the dreaded money aspect. I refuse to let another thing I love be stripped away from me.

CHAPTER TWO

Eleanor

"You've got to be kidding me?" Harriet Marshall is irritated yet defiant, mad as a wet cat, yet outwardly cool as a cucumber. Her bright white chef's jacket, a stark contrast to her dark brown skin, has not a single stain. Under the edge of her chef's hat, however, her forehead is beaded with sweat. She is two seconds from either screaming and punching a wall or completely breaking down.

I know a couple of things about Harriet Marshall: she is loyal to a fault, even when she *should* walk away, and if provoked, she will not back down. Probably why she's such a phenomenal chef. She doesn't put up with anyone's shit, and she never leaves until the job's done. She would have made a fantastic spy or assassin.

I force myself to hold back the happiness tugging at my lips as I imagine Harriet wielding a gun instead of a butcher knife.

"What the fuck are you smiling at?" Harriet's hands are on her hips.

"I was imagining you as Tom Cruise in *Mission: Impossible*, and it made me happy." And that's when Harriet's pissed-off facade cracks. "Y'know, killing people for the greater good. All that shit."

"I swear to God herself." Harriet's lips tighten together, and she shakes her head. "You are the fuckin' worst. You're a professional subject-changer, aren't you?"

After a shrug and a roll of the eyes—because Harriet is right, I am a professional at changing the subject to keep things less tense—I lean against the counter in the large industrial kitchen of the sanctuary's newly rated five-star restaurant, Bird's Eye View. "Shouldn't an outstanding chef like yourself be able to roll with the punches?"

"Hey, hey, listen here, lady, I can roll with the punches." She pats herself on the chest, puffing it out in a proud manner. "I can handle a change in plans. I'm a professional and have been doing this for a very long time. A change in the menu isn't an issue except for the fact that, y'know, we are in the middle of East Jesus, Nowhere, not a body of water in sight, and instead of special-ordered mussels, I'm going to have to order Atlantic scallops. Instead of a fuck-ton of broccolini, I need seventy-five pounds of asparagus. I mean, the list goes on and on. I can handle all of that." Harriet's hands wave in the air to denote her point. "The plan change is never the problem, and you know it, Ellie."

"I know. I know. I told her she needs to lay off."

"That won't make it better." Harriet shakes her head. "All I want to do is run this restaurant. That's all. Why won't she let me fucking do it?"

"She can't let go of the reins, and I don't know why. Except when it comes to the goddamn money. She's hands-off with that part until it comes time to spend it."

"I try to see where she's coming from. But it's hard, y'know?" Harriet mimics my position against the countertop, removing her chef's hat and wiping her brow with the back of her hand. "What are we gonna do?"

"We're going to get through this weekend. That's the number-one thing." I place my hand on her shoulder and give her a gentle shake. "And you're gonna try to get laid. How long has it been now? A day and a half?"

"Oh, you're a fuckin' comedian now?"

"I'm here all week, folks. Try the mussels. Oh, wait. I mean, *scallops*. Try the scallops. And tip your servers."

"You are such a fucker." She chuckles, and I feel better in an instant. "It's been two months or more, to be honest. Longest stretch I've ever been through."

"Celibacy looks good on you, though. You have this real pent-up glow about you."

"I swear, if I didn't need you as a salve for my sanity, I'd drive you to the middle of nowhere and leave you for dead."

"Unfortunately for us both, I'd find my way back, I'm sure."

"We both hate our jobs. Yet we stay. Why?" She looks at me, her eyes seemingly searching for an answer she knows I don't have. "This place." She sighs, a deep sigh that lets me know she doesn't actually hate her job any more than I do. "I want Olive to realize that I know what the goal is, and I get what the plan is. If only she would trust me enough to let me execute my side of it, y'know? I understand what makes a restaurant memorable and exciting. We have that *something* that pulls people back time and time again. I am that something." Her eyes are sparkling. "Me. Harriet fucking Marshall. Creative, original, ground-breaking, not afraid to come up with new recipes. But Olive fucking Zyntarski changing the menu on me at the last minute shows me that she doesn't trust me."

"She does trust you, Hattie."

"No, she doesn't."

I want to keep arguing, but it's hard to argue when I agree. "No, she doesn't, does she?"

"She treats me like a child, like her child. My mama is already gone. I don't need or want another one. And it's starting to drive me absolutely bonkers. Why did she beg me to leave my restaurant in Chicago if she didn't want to trust me to do the job? I mean, it's not like I don't have ownership in this. I put a lot of money into this place, too. I own twenty-five percent like you. I have a lot at stake if this doesn't go well."

I understand all too well what she is going through because there are times when Olive's overbearing tendencies are almost too much for me to handle. I pull a breath in and hold it for a beat before I say, with as smooth and calming a voice I can possibly muster, "It's fine."

She huffs. "I hate you."

"Hattie, honey, it's fine."

"Ellie, honey, it's *not* fine. Trust is a big deal between business partners, but it's especially big between friends."

"I'm telling you right now, it *is* fine. It has to be." I push away from the counter and close the distance between us. I am a good three inches taller than her, especially in heels, so I put my hands on her shoulders and ask her to look at me. "Handle it instead of trying to fight it. Okay?"

"Because I'll never win that fight, right?"

I chuckle. "No, not necessarily. But it's not the right time to go to war. Is this the hill you want to die on? Maybe? But not today. Not tonight. And especially not next weekend. You and I will have a meeting with Olive when the time is right. She's only trying to make sure this all looks good for that stupid interview with that journalist."

"Dammit." She lightly jerks herself away and takes a deep breath. I watch as she holds it for a few seconds before she breathes it out through her nose, nostrils flaring. "This better be worth it, Ellie. I was pumped to debut that new mussel recipe."

"Well, your scallop recipe is to die for, so fucking kill it, and stop being such a dick."

"You are lucky I love you."

I place a hand on her bicep and squeeze. "I'll let you get back to it since, y'know, you have to go place a new order."

She groans as she turns, her shoulders pulled back, her head held high. "Yeah, yeah. Tell Olive drinks are on her tonight." She heads through the stainless-steel labyrinth, presumably to her office.

"Whew," I say under my breath and heave a sigh of relief as I make my way through the restaurant. I push through the front doors and into the beautiful spring day in the Rockies. The clear blue sky against the Uncompahgre Plateau is striking. The view is one of the few things that grounds me these days. Sure, business is booming. Sure, everything *seems* to be going smoothly. Sure, I don't have bills or personal issues or anything else I had back home in Chicago. And I don't want to toot my own horn, but I'm brilliant and gifted, and I understand the marketing world better than most. But dammit, if there aren't moments when I feel like the entire world is closing in around me. These money issues are so much to handle, too. It's not as simple as some would think.

You've got to spend money to make money, right? It's unfortunate that little tidbit is what Olive decided to take at face value. I know dealing with the ups and downs of a fluctuating market are all part of the package when owning and operating a business, especially one in the hospitality industry. But I didn't realize how quickly it can get out of hand. We're so deep now. I don't even know when we'll come up for air.

She just doesn't get it. And explaining it doesn't work. If it does, she's not being honest with me, and that's even worse. She's not the only one who's in this mess. We all are.

The suffocating madness of possible mediocrity has taken up residency in my mind, peeking its head around the corner, taunting me. I left Synergy with so much support. For months, I dreaded the idea of telling them I was leaving. And within two minutes of starting the conversation with Cecily, I wondered if I was making the right choice.

Impending doom simmers inside me at the nagging suspicion that maybe I didn't.

And to top all of that off, on the horizon, looming, is the meeting

Harriet and I need to have with Olive. The more of a micro-manager she becomes, the harder she is to work with. She was wonderful in the beginning. The honeymoon phase. We all three wanted the same thing: for the sanctuary to be successful.

We have succeeded at that part. The sanctuary is successful. But it feels as if one false move will topple what we've built, and that frightens the shit out of me. It needs to frighten the shit out of Olive, too, and for some reason, it doesn't. Does something big have to happen, something that will test us all, in order for each of us to realize how delicate the sanctuary is?

These are the moments when I regret leaving Chicago. When I wonder what it's going to take to wake us all up. What's it going to take to wake myself up? If I love this place as much as I say I do, then I need to fight for it, right?

Or is it my love for Olive that keeps me here?

I refuse to believe it most of the time because did I really leave everything behind for a woman who will never feel the same way about me? The truth is so much harder to admit than it should be. I hate the admission, though. It makes me look weak, like a homeless puppy who follows around the person who fed her scraps. It isn't an out-of-control love. It's something that exists. And against my better judgment, I have never tried to stop it or find a way around it or through it. I simply love her. Unconditional and pure, constantly burning, a candle with a never-ending wick and just enough oxygen.

Stop obsessing, Eleanor. It's not worth it. There are more important things than Olive to obsess about. I close my eyes and breathe the crisp mountain air deep into my lungs. The weeks before summer hits hard like a sledgehammer are my very favorite times in the Rockies. Life has started to blossom in every aspect of the word. These are the moments when the possibility springs to life that maybe I can figure myself out and start trying to blossom in my own right.

Maybe.

Just maybe.

Or maybe not.

"Your usual, Elle?"

The sound of Heidi—the bartender at the Feeder, our craft cocktail lounge and wine bar—snaps me out of my thoughts. I nod, and she gives me a seductive glance in return, her eyebrows rising slightly. She, for some reason, is the only person who calls me Elle. Everyone else uses Ellie because that's what Olive and Harriet call me. I don't correct her, even if I probably should. The nickname gives us a familiarity we simply don't and shouldn't have. But correcting her isn't worth the hassle. If she wants to have a special nickname for me, I guess I'll allow it. Let's be real, she's cute enough, and I'm lonely enough.

I'm sitting next to Olive, who is in some type of mood. I'm assuming it's the impromptu money meeting we had earlier, but who the hell knows? Her moods are all over the place some days. Diagnosing every shift would be like trying to herd squirrels. I used to try and try until she'd get angry at me.

Now?

Now I wait as patiently as possible for my old-fashioned. She's not the only one who is allowed to be in a mood. And after the day I've had, I need a drink desperately. If stress were electricity, me crunching numbers, working on the new marketing pieces, organizing all the ins and outs of the grand opening of the Amphitheater, all while not having any actual idea if this place will survive, would provide enough electricity to power a small country.

Olive is swirling a Berkeley Estate Cellars chardonnay in her glass as if she's letting it breathe. She's not a wine snob, even if she tries to play one. She used to drink Kendall Jackson or Fetzer all the time. Now, whenever we meet for drinks, she tries a new chardonnay. I'd love to say it's because she's daring and likes to live on the edge, but I'd be lying. It's because Harriet gave her shit and told her she needs to branch out. She thinks trying different chardonnays is branching out.

Deep, deep down, I realize this is the reason I can't get past my feelings for her. She's predictable, comfortable, and stress-free. Our relationship is a dance we've been rehearsing for the past fifteen years.

When Heidi finally sets my drink in front of me, I wait a beat before I pick it up. I don't want to seem too eager. When I was growing up, my parents would get a drink at a restaurant or after a long day, and the *ah* that they would let out after the first sip was something I did not comprehend at seven.

At forty-seven, I completely understand.

"Everything okay, Elle?"

Heidi's staring, piercing in the weirdest of ways. I hate when she stares. I hate it because I secretly love the attention. "Everything is great."

"You haven't taken a drink yet. That's not normal." She's bracing herself on the reach-in cooler. The evening uniform is usually blue button-downs, a bowtie, and jeans, but for some reason, she's wearing a black tank top, and it's cut just low enough to accentuate her cleavage. Just low enough to cause a wave of heat to wash over me. She's young, with blond hair, short and bobbed, and is super petite. She's not my type. Because my type is apparently older, curvier, and, the most important difference, not interested.

I finally take a sip and bury the urge to say *ah*. It is exactly what I needed. And Heidi, aside from being very cute and very hard to resist, is a wonderful mixologist. "Thank you," I finally say.

"Is it good?" Her eyes are locked on mine.

I break contact because my vagina simply can't handle it. "You know I enjoy the way you make them."

"A lot of bourbon and a little dash of love." Her eyes flit from me to Olive, then back to me. She winks before pushing herself from the cooler and heading down the bar to wait on another guest, her ass swaying back and forth. *Back and forth.* I need to get laid. I raise the lowball glass, shake my head, and take another sip.

"Have you slept with her?

I turn to Olive, whose face is twisted in disdain. "Ex*cuse* me?"

"You heard me. Have you slept with Heidi?"

"Olive, are you kidding me?"

"I could see the way she was eye-fucking you. I'm not blind." She sighs, drinks her wine. "And the way you were undressing her with your eyes."

I want to say it's not really any of her business who I fuck, but I can't. Instead, I simply say, "Don't worry. I'm not fucking our insanely hot bartender."

"Well, if you decide to, remember, you shouldn't shit where you eat."

"Christ, Olive, that's graphic." I shrug. "I mean, I wouldn't mind eating her."

"She's not on the menu." Olive motions to Heidi. "She is half your age. And isn't she straight? She has a boy she goes on and on about."

"Who knows? Kids these days. They're all fluid. And all the chicks in my life have said they're straight at first. Every last one of them."

Olive goes to sip her wine, then pulls back and looks at me. "Seriously? All of them? How many?"

I glance at the bronze ceiling tiles and do a mental tally. "I think twelve?" I breathe in deep and let it out slowly. "Curiosity kills my pussy."

A laugh pours from Olive's mouth. "You are ridiculous. How do you not know the exact number?"

"Well, as you are very aware, Natalie was bisexual." I spin the ice ball in my drink with the swizzle stick before I take another sip. "I cannot believe she divorced me to be with my brother. Of all the kicks to the cunt I could go through, that one I was not expecting."

"Oh, come on," she says, followed by a groan. "You know how I feel about the c-word."

"I mean, how else would you describe that? I don't care that she's a bisexual. I mean, I've been attracted to men, but my fucking *brother*?" I take another sip, hold it in my mouth for a beat, let it burn my tastebuds, then swallow. "I mean, she said she was straight when we met, but I don't think she is. Who knows? Thirteen is my lucky number. Maybe I should say fuck it and count her?"

"Damn." Olive raises her glass. "Cats land on their feet, right? You and your resilient pussy."

I mimic Olive and clink our glasses together. "I don't know about resilient." I glance at my drink, then down the rest of it before motioning to Heidi for another. A silence has fallen between us. Not a comfortable one. It's a weird one where I can feel that she wants to say something, but she's either too stubborn or too proud to bring it up. I'll have to drag it out of her. I've played this game a million times. She thinks she'll win, but she wants to talk. She always does. But for some reason, she's too afraid to let it all out. "You gonna tell me what's going on or…"

I continue to eye her, her button nose, her high cheekbones, her rounded jawline, her blue eyes as she stares at her glass, the stem held gently between her forefinger, middle finger, and thumb. The first time I saw Olive at an event in downtown Chicago, I was taken with her. I had recently broken up with a girlfriend, and because I'm a little too clingy in relationships, even when I'm unhappy, my entire life felt as if it was spinning out of control. And in walked Olive, with her gorgeous long brown hair and her curves and wonderful personality. She had my attention and my time from the word go. As the years went on, our friendship became one of the only things I could rely on. And I never stopped seeing her as this beautiful spirit that I was somehow lucky enough to find.

Even as she lost her mom and her husband and her weight fluctuated and she sank into a depression I didn't know if she'd emerge from, I stayed by her. The obvious sadness from everything she has gone through still lurks beneath the surface. There is something lovely about that sadness, that emotion, that darkness. It gives her a deepness I feel as if only I am privy. It makes me sad, yes, because I miss her lighthearted spirit. But she needs time. And I'm giving it to her, even though it's becoming more and more obvious that time isn't healing the wounds as it should. If anything, time seems to be shards of glass, and they keep cutting deeper and deeper into the gaping sore.

"Or should we continue to sit in silence?"

Olive finally cracks and the corner of her mouth tugs upward. "Silence would be weird, wouldn't it?"

"Mm-hmm." I lean into her with my shoulder, and her perfume, Ralph Lauren Blue, stirs. "Talk to me. Tell me what's going on in that head of yours."

She acts as if she didn't hear the question for a good four seconds. She finally snaps out of her reverie and lets out a breath. "Just the money talk from earlier."

"Sure, sure." She acts as if I was born yesterday. There's a difference between stressed Olive and pensive Olive. "Tell me what's really going on."

"Shouldn't the money be what's bothering me?"

"Absolutely." I lean harder into her. "But that's not it. I know you almost better than I know myself."

"I can't argue with that, sadly."

"C'mon, talk to me."

Olive's sigh is almost unnoticeable, and I feel more than hear her gentle inhale and exhale. "I'm sick of talking about him."

"Talking about it is how you heal. Isn't that what your therapist said?"

"I'm...sad. Five years and I still have all this...*guilt*."

Guilt? That wasn't the word I thought she was going to use. "Because you're living your life? And he isn't?"

She doesn't answer right away. She sips her wine, stares at it, opens her mouth as if she's going to say something, but she closes it and clamps her jaws, the muscle flexing beneath her pale skin. "Yeah. That."

"Did something happen that made you start thinking about it all again?" I wait for her to look at me. She will, eventually.

And when she turns her head, her eyes are filled with tears. "I've been writing my speech for the dedication of the event venue, and

I…" She swipes at the couple of tears that have escaped. "I'm okay. I promise."

"It's okay if you're not okay. You know that, right?"

She looks away, lifts her wine, swirls the remainder, then finishes it. "It's been five years. I've got to get over it eventually."

"Olive…" I stop, bite my tongue, and remind myself I only have a small idea of what she's going through. I've had to bury people, namely my beautiful mother, but I've never lost a significant other to death. I want to tell her she may never get over the death of her husband or her mother. And that it is okay. But sometimes, reminders aren't helpful. They're hurtful. And the last thing I want to do is hurt her.

"I'll be fine."

"Of course you will be. You're the strongest woman I know."

She lets out a puff of air before she accepts a fresh glass of wine from Heidi. She thanks her, then looks at me. "If I'm the strongest woman you know, you clearly need to get out more."

"You're the one who made me move to the middle of fucking nowhere."

"Maybe you should have stayed in Chicago."

Yikes. That was below the belt. Probably true, but still. "Whoa, whoa, whoa." I swivel on my barstool. "What the fuck is that about?"

Olive's shoulders fall. "God, Ellie, I don't know. I don't know what's going on with me."

"Y'know, I love you more than anything, and I'm always here for you. You need to remember that when you start going to this dark place."

"I'm sorry." Olive swivels toward me. Our knees bump before she steadies herself on the rung of my stool. My mind is hyper-focused on the feel of her leg between mine. "You are amazing, and I love you, and I'm sorry. I…I feel like things are happening at the speed of light, and I'm having the hardest time trying to keep up. Like, I'm running a marathon I didn't train a day in my life for or something."

It's great when friends, without an ounce of struggle, can understand each other. In this circumstance, on the other hand, I happen to hate how much I get her. All I want to do is help her. Hold her. Take all of that *trying* and calm her fears. And I simply can't.

"Hey, ladies," Harriet's voice slices into my foolish thoughts as she slides onto the stool behind Olive. She has a black baseball cap on and her glasses. She looks dead tired. Staring at a computer screen placing orders does that to her. She orders an Acqua Panna, then turns to us. "Hey, now. What is going on? What'd I miss?" She leans in closer. "Did someone die?"

"I mean, yeah, five years ago." Olive turns to face Harriet, whose expression is now filled with regret.

"Shit," she whispers.

"I'm having a moment." Olive leans back so she's pressed into Harriet's side. "Another moment in a long string of them. I'm sorry. It was a bad joke."

"I gotta say, I'm the first person to laugh at an inappropriate joke, but that was in poor taste." Harriet wraps her arms around Olive's shoulders, hugging her from behind. She holds eye contact with me as if silently telling me she is relenting and giving up the control she so badly wants. At least right now.

We're all messy. Each of us has skeletons that rear their ugly heads from time to time, and we get to help each other deal with the bad things. The beautiful part is that we also get to celebrate the good things, the fun things, the things that make us keep going every single day. The momentous occasions that slam into us since we bought the sanctuary. Great things have happened. When the bad sneaks up in the dark and tries to scare us, we help each other by turning on the lights. Not much is as scary in the light as it is in the dark. And together, I feel as if we can conquer anything.

Except my inability to get the hell over Olive.

Dammit.

I'm such an idiot.

CHAPTER THREE

Harriet

The restaurant is packed, and on a scale of one to ten, excitement-wise, I'd say I'm at about eleven. I'm so jazzed, I can barely stand it. We're on a forty-five-minute wait for the bar alone, completely booked with reservations, and it's only seven o'clock. I love it when it's busy. There's nothing better than the adrenaline that comes with performing, and this is most definitely a performance. Some people love being onstage. Some people love singing or dancing. Some people love acting. I love to pack a restaurant, make food, and listen to the guests say, *oh my God, this is good*, and *I feel like I've died and gone to heaven*. Or the best one yet is when they don't say a word. They look at the person they're with, drop their shoulders, hands on the table, still gripping their silverware, and chew. Silence can be the best compliment.

I'm the executive chef, yes, but I'm also, for all intents and purposes, the general manager. I have an incredible sous chef and kitchen manager, which makes it possible for me to manage the restaurant. My post at the back of the dining room gives me the best access to see how everything is flowing. How are the servers doing? Are the bussers doing their jobs? What about the bartender? Is she in the weeds? Who do I need to help? If there's one thing I've learned about flow, it's how important it is in a restaurant. If things can flow properly, that's half the battle. A restaurant that flows is as amazing as smooth jazz. And there's nothing I love better than smooth jazz.

I also really love being able to study the guests. I want to know what kind of people are eating at my restaurant, what foods are they enjoying, and does the entire experience make them want to come back for more. I make rounds a couple times throughout the night and speak with the tables to check their temperatures. It's personable, and I like that, even if I'm not all that personable in real life. It's all part of the performance. I get paid to perform, and I will never not make it Oscar-worthy.

As Amber, one of my newest servers, bursts through the swinging kitchen door, I take one look at the plated lamb shank on her tray. "Amber, whoa, whoa, chica, what's this?" I stop her before she gets too far away. "This doesn't have the correct garnish, and the cream sauce is everywhere. Were you tested on which garnish goes with each dish?" Her eyes have glazed over, and she blinks a couple times before she gives me a pained expression. My blood starts to boil. "Seriously?" She goes to answer, and I raise my hand to stop her. "Never mind. Give me this, you go deliver those drinks." I spin back toward the kitchen, plate in hand. As soon as the door swings to a close, I shout, "Harmony?"

"Yes, Chef?"

"Can you please take a look at this?"

My sous chef and kitchen manager peers through the racks from near the stove. Her face falls. "For fuck's sake. *Jessica.*" She's shouting, and I am all for it because I shouldn't be the only person pissed off by the presentation. "You cannot let a plate like that out of this kitchen. Are you hearing me?"

"What are you talking about?" Jessica rounds the corner, and her eyes almost bulge out of their sockets. For good reason. "Crap. I'm sorry, Chef. And Harmony. I'm sorry. That's my bad."

"Where were you?" I'm glaring at Jessica. If my eyes shot laser beams, she'd be decimated. "You cannot leave this post unless you tell someone where you're going. You know this. We've had this conversation a hundred times."

"I'm sorry. I really am. I had to pee. I've been holding it for the last hour. I'm sorry."

I set the plate down and slide it under the heating lamps. "We all hold our pee, Jessica, sometimes all damn day." I sigh as I make eye contact with Harmony. "Remake this, please. And Jessica?"

"Yes?"

"Did you take care of your business?"

She bounces on her toes. "Yes, Chef. I am truly sorry."

"Please. Stop apologizing, and, next time, let us know. You have a headset for a reason."

I hold back my normal head shake because Jessica is a hard worker, and I've almost gotten her to the point of being a fantastic coordinator. Almost. She's too flighty, though. And apparently, has a child-sized bladder.

After I move out of Jessica's way, I stand back and observe. The line is a mess, but we're two people short. I need to find replacements fast, replacements who show up for work. Working in this industry is interesting, to say the least. In my twenty years in the restaurant industry, in some way, shape, or form, I have worked with every single type of person. Lazy people, perfectionists, punctual people, people who are chronically late, old, young, and everything in between. For some, this is only a job to make some quick cash. They're working through college or bartending on the side to save for a car. And then there are others where this is their career. They're lifelong servers or managers, and they love the business as much as I do; those are my favorite people to work with. They take it seriously.

My favorite employee, Glenda, has been working in the business since she was sixteen. And she's the best manager I've ever hired. She's never late. She never calls off. She does all her side work. And she knows every single job on the floor, from bussing tables to bartending to helping in the kitchen when I need her. She can do it all.

"Chef, we have a bit of an issue out front."

I don't look at Glenda as she approaches because I know what it's going to be. "Lamb shank?"

"Yeah."

"Taking too long?"

"Yep."

"It wasn't plated correctly."

"Great." Glenda groans. "What are we going to do with Jessica? She can't keep making these rookie mistakes."

"I have no idea."

"I know a guy."

"I want this place to be run by women." I look at Glenda, at her blond hair pulled back into her signature low ponytail. She decided to get bangs about three weeks ago and hasn't stopped bitching about them since. She has them pulled back with a bobby pin tonight. She's close to fifty, but she looks not a day over forty. When she first applied, I remember thinking I was either going to love her or hate her. Thankfully, I love her. And she's quickly become my right-hand woman.

"Hell, it's not like we can't boss boys around."

"True." I'm grateful for her sense of humor during stressful nights such as this one.

"Sometimes you gotta roll the dice, Chef."

"Yeah, yeah."

"Anyway, can you please come speak to the guest?"

"Is it anyone we know?"

"Yeah," she says followed by a sigh. "It's everyone's favorite curmudgeon, George Redden."

"Fuck."

"I know." Glenda pushes away from the counter. I follow, giving myself a pep talk the entire time. "It's never nice having to deal with a regular," she says as she pauses to let a busser pass. "It's not your night. Sorry, love."

As I approach the table, I can tell this isn't going to be fun. George makes eye contact with me, and my stomach ties into a knot. This is my least favorite part of the job. Obviously. "Mr. Redden, good evening. I want to apologize for the wait on your lamb. I spoke with the kitchen staff, and it should be out momentarily."

"Listen, Mrs. Mitchell—"

"Mr. Redden, please, Mrs. Mitchell was my mama. I told you that you can call me Hattie."

"Well, Hattie, I want to tell you how much I love coming to this restaurant."

"He really does, my dear," his wife, Martha, says, as she lays a warm hand on my arm.

"Thank you, sir. And Mrs. Redden. I'm very glad to hear that."

"But…"

"There's always a but, isn't there?"

Martha chuckles. "Mm-hmm. You get used to it with him."

"You two," George says with a gruff tone. "I want my damn meal, that's all."

"George, do not use that tone with Hattie." Martha points at him. "You don't get to treat people that way. Ever."

I want to thank Martha. I want to hug her. I can't even begin to count the number of times I've been treated like shit by someone at a dinner table. Is it because I'm a woman? Is it because I'm Black? It's probably equal parts of both. "Mr. Redden, again, I apologize. I promise you, this meal will be comped. Fully." As soon as I finish my sentence, his meal is delivered by Glenda. She has Amber following with another drink for him, a whiskey, neat. She knows the way to his heart.

"Here we go, Mr. Redden." She places the dish in front of him, and his frown is immediately turned upside down. He's the literal definition of hangry.

"Thank you, Glenda. And Hattie, I should apologize to you. I get a little mean when I'm hungry."

I place a hand on Martha's shoulder, and squeeze gently before I leave the two of them to their meal. Glenda is behind me, and I only stop when she grabs my wrist. "You handled that beautifully."

"As always."

"As always, indeed." Glenda doesn't drop my wrist until I look her in the eyes, nod, and accept the compliment. She knows when I'm being fake, so it has to be real. "I'll handle any other issues up here, Chef."

"Thank you, Glen." And I turn and retreat to the kitchen where I can ride the asses of my staff in peace.

❖

My new year's resolution was to stop casually sleeping with people. Actually, my exact words were, "I'm going to stop fucking around with people I barely know." I felt like maybe I was becoming someone I didn't recognize. I've always been the sort of person who doesn't want anything long-term when it comes to relationships. I want to have fun and have sex and leave. That's all.

I am a weak, weak woman, though, and I didn't succeed in the beginning.

January is a hard month in the restaurant biz. It's not a good excuse, but it's true.

February isn't easy either.

March isn't any better, typically, but for some reason, I started to take myself seriously. And now I'm two months into my search for life's meaning. Sounds like some mythical quest. I guess to a certain extent, it is. I love my job, even when everything in me wants to hate it with the burning passion of a nine-hundred-degree brick oven.

And I love my friends, even when everything in me wants to scream at them that I'm a grown-ass woman.

But a part of me is missing. I don't know what it is or how to fix it. I simply knew it was time to make a change when the loneliness I was trying to squash was present even when someone else was in my bed.

For as long as I can remember, release has been very important for me. When I'm stressed? I seek that sweet release. But now, instead of throwing myself into the arms of someone, anyone, I try to remind myself of how far I've come.

I have known what I wanted from a very young age. And I never, ever, have any doubts about what my path should be. I've known since I was twelve that I wanted to be a chef. From the very first minute I made eggplant parmesan with my grandmother, I knew. It was as if the food called to me and said, "Hattie, girl, you gonna be a chef."

I never looked back. I took every single cooking class I could. Every single class my parents would permit. And even some they didn't know about. Being driven at such a young age had its ups and downs. Supportive parents are lovely, but not all parents support their children a hundred percent of the time. Well, maybe some do. But mine, as supportive as they were, wanted me to be realistic.

I get it now. But as solid as my foundation is and as hard as I worked and as much as I have to show for it, I still look back and think they were trying to hold me back for all the wrong reasons. Telling me it's for my own good only worked when my own good was actually *bad*. My own good was so good.

A lot of people have called me cocky. Conceited. It took me a long time to learn to use that to my advantage. I was twenty-five the first time I ran a kitchen, and the feeling was incredible. I was indestructible. And I have been riding that feeling ever since. I am indestructible. I am formidable. I am a fucking hot motherfucker with an amazing head on my shoulders, rock-solid fashion sense, and a tight little body. I may be conceited, but every part of me is something I fought tooth and nail to attain. I am who I am, and there is nothing anyone can do to change me.

I set an open bottle of Purity Wine, their red blend, on the ground next to the Adirondack chair where DeeDee, my lovely sixty-five-year-old friend, as well as my favorite winery owner, is sitting. I sit next to her, admiring the fire. I sip from my glass of red and sigh. It's delicious. It's not too heavy, not too dry, with the right amount of raspberry and licorice. It's interesting and heavenly, and I could drink the entire bottle myself.

DeeDee hasn't moved, her eyes still closed, and I wonder what's going through her mind. She owns Purity Wines, and through the numerous tastings I've done, we became fast friends. Now she's a regular, and joining her on the back patio of the Feeder is a usual occurrence. Tonight feels different. I'm filled with a weird giddy happiness I haven't felt in a while. I thought tonight would be a shitshow because of my morning, with the menu change and my feelings about Olive being an overbearing asshole. But it wasn't. I'm finding a way to deal with the stress, and it feels very good. Eleanor was right when she told me to handle it instead of fighting it. I'll never tell her that. And having a very busy restaurant is not a bad problem to have. And the better we get, the more word spreads, and the more crowded we are.

The sanctuary sits between two small towns, all within about thirty minutes' driving distance. And the restaurant and lounge are open to anyone, regardless of if they're staying at the sanctuary. It's the only accommodation that's open to the public. Olive and I went round and round about that. I wanted it to be open, and she wanted it to be exclusive. I understood why, but at the end of the day, the restaurant and the Feeder make money. And considering our money woes, taking the business away wouldn't be wise. And since it's slim pickings in the two closest towns, letting the public enjoy the restaurant and lounge has been a wise business decision, one that Olive refuses to admit. Whatever. It's fine. I take it as a win every time she updates us on the profits coming in from the restaurant. Like I don't fucking know.

The fire roars in the outside fireplace on the patio, and I can tell that DeeDee is at peace for the first time in a long time. She's been through a lot in the last six months. Her husband, Earl, passed away at the beginning of December, and she had the hardest time adjusting. I mean, for good reason. But it's hard to see someone I've grown close to having such a difficult time. It's strange because I have never been a person who wants people in her life. I'm a loner by nature.

The firelight is dancing on DeeDee's reddish brown skin. The sun is harsh in Colorado, but she doesn't look like she's aged at all. Her natural beauty is refreshing. "What're ya thinking 'bout?"

"Wondering if Earl is happy, wherever he is."

My heart clenches. Her sadness has that effect on me. "DeeDee," I say quietly. "I'm sure he's at peace."

"Oh, I know he is. He wouldn't have it any other way." She takes a breath. Her hair is long, with more salt than pepper, and braided. She pulls it over her shoulder most of the time, complaining about it and how she is one step away from cutting it off. She is stunning, even with the years and years of stress stacked on top of her. Her eyes slide open, she picks her glass up and holds it out for me to refill. I do before she looks at me over the top of her bifocals. "The kitchen fell apart on you tonight?"

I chuckle. "Is that why you stayed? I thought for sure you'd have gone back to the winery."

"I hadn't seen you in a few days. Figured you'd need the venting session."

I chuckle. "You know me so well."

"Olive still being a pain?"

"Absolutely." The very mention of her name has me thinking about how badly I love her and hate her at the same time. "She's a complicated woman."

"Aren't we all, my love?"

"So very true." I lean forward and rest my elbows on my knees. Peering into the fire is calming after tonight's performance.

"Any beautiful women traipsing into your life? Or beautiful men?"

"Jesus," I say through my laughter. "You really do know me."

"Well, two years of being a regular at the most expensive bar in a ten-mile radius has its perks. Besides, you know my children live too far away to hound." She's right. She has taken me under her wing for as much her benefit as mine. But she's also someone who nudges me to take chances.

"You want the truth?"

"I do."

"I haven't slept with anyone in two months."

She gasps. "Two *months*?" She stands and places her hand on my forehead. "Are you okay, honey? Do you need to go to the hospital?"

I roll my eyes as I sit up, straighten my back, then glare at her.

"Okay, okay, tell me the details. What's going on?"

After letting out a deep sigh, I relax. She's teasing, but this new leaf I'm trying to turn over hasn't been the easiest. "I mean, you know how I told you I'd been lost? Floatin' around, not sure what to do or where to turn? Like, you know, I want this restaurant to be the best it can be. And I'm sure it will be because, like, hello? It's me. I'm running it, and it's gonna be great. But…" I let my shoulders fall. "It's lonely here. And flitting around like a literal hummingbird from one flower to the next is not getting me anywhere."

"What you're saying is, what used to work for you no longer works?"

I shake my head. "Not like that. Like, *it* works. Y'know what I mean? Like, it *works*. But I'm not into it. I want to, I don't know, like, visit only one flower. If that makes sense?" I'm trying hard not to be crass. I could very plainly say I am ready to stop fucking people simply because they look at me with *fuck me* eyes.

"Thank you for censoring yourself, dear."

I chuckle before I drink. "This whole new chapter shit hasn't been super easy."

"Writing a beginning is never easy." She clears her throat, and it prompts me to look at her, at the way she's lightly swirling the wine. She watches the deep red liquid with something akin to admiration. "Look at those legs," she whispers, then sips once and again. "I feel once you start, you'll find the words will start to flow."

"God, I hope so."

"Is this like, an itch that needs to be scratched, or are you not interested?"

"Oh, I'm interested." I laugh, and so does she. "I'm trying, y'know?" I breathe deep, then let it slowly out. "I met someone tonight who I would have gladly taken back to her room. I swear, it's like recovering from coke and like, everyone has it and wants to give it to you, but I'm like, nah, man, I'm cool. But I'm not cool."

"Are you trying to tell me you're a sex addict? Or a coke addict? I'm confused."

"Neither." We laugh together again, and I try to gather words that don't make me sound like a complete asshole. "I need to figure out if I want to be with someone or if I'm totally fine only being with me. Does that make sense?"

"Honey," DeeDee says softly, and I feel her hand on my back, the palm, the fingers, the heat from her. Her touch is comforting in the best of ways. "It makes perfect sense."

Thank God because I wasn't about to try to explain it any further. Too many words. Too many emotions. Too many feelings. It all adds up to too much mess that I don't want to deal with. The people I keep close know me well enough to understand all of that. I am lucky in that respect. Otherwise, I'd be even more alone, I fear. And while I may enjoy being alone, being isolated is not good for me.

CHAPTER FOUR

Eleanor

At first, we were skeptical about living together on site because it sounded like a recipe for disaster.

"The cabin is fifteen thousand square feet, Ellie. If we don't want to see each other, we don't have to," Olive said the night before we moved in. "And besides, we always said we wanted to form a commune. This is the perfect opportunity."

"Commune?" Hattie said. "Um, I'm sorry, but I am not going to be celibate."

"What are you talking about?"

"Isn't a commune where nuns live?"

"That's a convent, you asshole."

And we all descended into laughter.

I asked the most important question. "Okay, what happens," I started as we stood together on the steps, "if one of us meets someone?"

"And what? Wants to get married and move out?" Harriet's face twisted with disgust.

Olive shook her head. "I am never getting married again."

"And I don't do long-term," Harriet said with a shrug.

"I don't want to get married again, either."

And we hugged and cried together.

Things haven't changed much, which is surprising and nice. Well, aside from the moment two years ago when I brought home a nine-month-old golden retriever puppy from the shelter a couple towns over. Little Lizzie is her name, and she is the cutest, most lovable pet I have ever had. Her previous owners ran over her paw, and it never healed right. So I have a dog with a limp, and I love her more than I can express.

She's my companion these days. And that sort of companionship is all I keep telling myself I need.

I stare at the cup of tea I made after returning from the lounge. I was headed for the wine when I decided I didn't want to have a hangover tomorrow. The tea isn't cutting it. It's exactly how my life is these days: lukewarm and boring. I want so badly to mix things up. To find someone other than my friends to laugh with. To maybe have sex or at least make out with someone.

God, it's been far too long since I've kissed anyone.

I think I'm at three years now.

Three very long, long, long years.

Everything in me wishes I was exaggerating. I had a quick fling with an employee. She was straight, and I was in no place to start an actual relationship. We lasted a summer. She left to go back home to Maine, and I went about the rest of my life. I never told a soul, and I do not include her in my tally of sexual encounters.

"What in the world are you thinking about that you're crying into that dumb fucking tea?"

The voice startles me, and I snap my gaze onto Harriet as she breezes into the room, her maroon shirt unbuttoned, her black-tie loose around her neck, a white tank top clinging to her rock-hard body. She discarded her shoes at the door and is barefoot in black skinny slacks.

She strips her black blazer off before she bends to greet Lizzie. "Seriously, what are you thinking about?"

"Oh, y'know, how pathetic my life is."

She pulls an already open bottle of white wine I eyed earlier from the left side of the industrial-size refrigerator. She yanks the cork with her teeth and spits it out onto the large center island. It bounces a couple times before it falls to the floor. She raises the bottle to me and winks. "Salut." And she drinks directly from the bottle, one, two, three giant gulps before she smacks her lips together. "Ah, that's exactly what I needed."

"You are literally the most ridiculous person I've ever met."

"If you had to deal with that fucking piece-of-shit restaurant staff we've managed to hire this season, you'd be the same fucking way. I swear to Christ above, some of these fuckers have never worked in a restaurant in their entire lives."

She spins and easily pops onto the granite counter next to the refrigerator. She pulls her legs up and crosses them, her head bobbing to the jazz I have playing in the background. She has no filter with her mouth or her body. She's completely comfortable in her skin. It amazes me. Or maybe I'm envious. I don't know. Probably the latter. I wish I had one-tenth of her self-confidence.

"Seriously, Ellie, the newest server doesn't even know how to carry a tray. A tray. I shouldn't be the one worrying about that." She's animated and angry, and before long, she's finished the rest of the bottle and is sliding from the counter to get another.

"You're drinking this with me. Ditch that fucking dumb fucking tea, and let's go in the hot tub."

It's the best idea she's had in, oh, who the hell knows? "That sounds like an amazing plan. Let me go put my suit on."

"Fuck the suit. Let's just go in."

I spin around. "You're out of your goddamn mind. *Hell* to the no. I will not be going anywhere near you in nothing but my skin. And you know guests can easily wander onto our property."

"I still think we need the electric fence."

I shake my head as I leave the kitchen and climb the stairs to the second floor, Lizzie hot on my tail. She never lets me out of her sight when I'm home. It's one of the things I love about her.

❖

"This is the best thing we did," Harriet says softly after I step into the hot spring water.

"You're so right." I submerge to my neck and lean against the slanted side. I take the wine and take a sip without a single hesitation. "Fuck the hangover. This tastes way better than Earl Grey."

"What's going on with you?" She knows me well. Sometimes too well. "Is it still Olive?"

I sigh. Is it still Olive? Isn't it always? "No, of course not."

She lets out a puff of air. "Sure."

"Don't, please." I sip my wine again. A white blend from Napa. My friend Jeremy brought bottles when he stayed at the sanctuary a couple months ago. He was the *only* man that weekend, and while he was devastated to know he wouldn't find a like-minded gentleman, he was elated at the end because he was the most popular person the entire time. Every woman at the sanctuary knew him, knew his name, and passed him around like a traveling therapist. It was the first time our on-site therapist wasn't booked solid. Jeremy is good during a breakdown.

And a lot of women who stay with us are either recovering from, going to have, or are in the middle of a breakdown.

"Baby girl, you gotta find a way around those feelings for her. You know that, right?"

Once again, I sigh. "That's not it. I'm in a rut. Like, it's been forever since…"

"Yeah." Harriet's tone is drenched in understanding. I can hear Van Morrison from the outdoor sound system over the bubbles of the hot tub. Him singing "Days Like This" while I slow danced with Natalie is all I can think of.

Harriet clears her throat. "You've had the opportunity."

God bless Harriet. She knew where I was going, and it's always refreshing to not have to have the entire conversation because the entire conversation about my nonexistent sex life is embarrassing. "It's hard when the feelings aren't there."

"Not for me."

"You will catch feelings one day, and you'll see what I mean."

"Ugh, *catch* feelings. Sounds exactly like the type of disease I do not want to get anywhere near." Her words are pointed, but I hear the slight waver, the way her voice snags the tiniest of bits.

"Can I say one thing?"

"Say away."

"I don't think I'm in love with Olive like I used to be. I feel like that has faded. I don't know what else to do with the feelings other than, like, box them up and put them on a shelf or in the recycling bin or something. You know what I mean?"

"Mm-hmm."

"I'm lonely." My volume is soft, but dammit if it doesn't sound as if I shouted from the top of the highest peak.

Under the water, Harriet's toes press against my right shin. It's comforting; no other touch could be in that moment. The sliding glass door opens, and my heart falls a notch.

"Hey, you two. Room for one more?"

We both turn to Olive as she glides through the door in her bathing suit. She has a glass of red wine and, regardless of how hard I try to get past whatever I have for her, *she still looks beautiful*. "There's always room for you."

Olive slips into the warm water and slides next to me on the ledge. "What's going on? Did I interrupt?"

"Just Ellie being all sad because she drinks way too much hot tea for a woman her age. You're not seventy-five."

My laughter feels forced. Probably because it is. For half a second, I thought she was going to out me to Olive. It's not like Olive doesn't know. She just doesn't *know*. I've never said it, but I have no poker face, and Olive has been an expert in Eleanor-ology since the second we hung out together. "Very funny," I say. I want to kick her, but her sly grin across the tub is enough for me to forgive her.

Madonna's "Like a Prayer" is playing now, and Olive is humming away. "Remember when we all went to see her at the United Center? How stoned you got, Hattie?"

"Sweet Jesus. I've not been that high in quite some time. I don't even remember half the concert. What was I thinking?"

"For some reason, you thought that joint from the people next to us was a good idea." I roll my eyes. "And you had like fifteen beers. How did we even afford that?"

"I kept getting free ones from that guy Joe." Harriet shrugs. "What are ya gonna do?"

"I wish I had pictures of that evening. I think you threw up in the bathroom, didn't you?"

"Oh, yeah." Harriet shakes her head. "I was sweating profusely. Even my elbows were sweating. I had sweat marks on the knees of my jeans."

"Shut up, did you really?"

"No lie."

"It's almost like that time you had us take Molly," Olive says. "I think someone tried to make out with me."

"It wasn't me," I say. "Shockingly."

Olive nudges me. "You've only tried two times." Her tone is sincere and nice, and it causes my throat to tighten.

"Two times too many."

"When did we take that? Was that at the Taylor concert?"

"Hell, no." I lean forward and try to distance myself a little. She's touchy-feely when she's drinking, and I don't think it's on purpose, but tonight is not the night for me to stay calm, cool, and collected. I'm about two seconds away from becoming too emotional to deal. "I am alert during Taylor Swift concerts. I'm not missing a thing."

Harriet huffs. "Fuckin' Swiftie."

"Whatever. You loved her *Reputation* tour." I splash her. "Admit it."

"Never." She winks.

"I think it was Lollapalooza when we saw Florence + The Machine." I think back to that day. It was right after I found Natalie with my brother, right before the world's quickest divorce. I had one of the best times of my life that day and night. The Molly might have had something to do with it. "I was jumping around during 'Dog Days Are Over' and almost sprained my ankle on this chick next to me. I ended up making out with her. Remember that?"

Olive's puff of air is oddly telling, and I feel it in my stomach. "Pfft, no. I don't."

"Oh, I do." Harriet smacks the top of the water. "Olive, remember when you told that guy you hoped he got a yeast infection in his dick because he was peeing on that sign instead of going into the Port-a-Potty?"

"My God. Why do I do drugs? I turn into such a jerk." Olive sighs before she continues to enjoy her wine.

"Well, to be fair, we don't do drugs, plural. And pot is legal here. So we're good."

Olive's low throaty chuckle is perfect. "So very true."

"And it calms my anxiety." I raise my glass. "To legal pot."

"To legal pot," they both say, and we all descend into laughter.

❖

I drank entirely too much wine. And the hot tub was a bad choice. And now the room is spinning and spinning, and, *oh God, I think I'm gonna be sick.*

I open my eyes and stare at the ceiling, trying to find my bearings. I told them both not to open another bottle. But did they listen to me? No. Did I listen to me? No.

I will for sure be hungover tomorrow. I was looking forward to not being hungover as I drank that damn Earl Grey. I was going to go running on my favorite trail. I was going to sweat and feel the earth beneath my feet and remind myself that I am a strong independent woman who doesn't need anyone. I have an amazing vibrator and my hands. I'm fine.

I hear a small knock on my door and see the light from the hallway. "Who is that?"

"It's me."

Olive. Of course. She's going to come and lie in bed with me. I don't know if I can handle that tonight. I don't know if I can handle her tonight. The bed dips, and I hear her sigh as she pulls the covers up over my shoulder. *Fuck.* "What are you doing?"

"Are you okay? You were pretty tipsy."

I take a deep breath and push it out. "No. I feel like I'm going to be sick."

"Roll over. I'll rub your back."

Why is she so fucking nice to me when I really need her to be a giant jerk? I do as she says and roll onto my stomach. Her hand lands softly on my back, and within seconds, my body starts to calm. I both hate and love how she affects me. "Thanks." It comes out as a whisper, but she smooths her hand back and forth before she continues to the small of my back.

It's interesting, the stuff she and I have gone through. Heartache, loss, happiness, love. And I will be there for her no matter what and vice versa. But every now and then, I want us to fight and scream and tell each other to fuck off. If for no other reason than we need to. It doesn't make sense. None of it does.

How can I be so in love with someone who, for so long, hasn't been able to love anyone else? Maybe she loves me enough to know I need her tonight, though. She loves me as much as she can, and that's all I'll ever get from her.

But I'd give anything for more. For all. For every last part of her.

My tears are making the pillowcase wet. I need to get over this.

I need to get over *all* of it, every last part of her. Deep inside, there's a part that thinks I can do it. I'm almost there most days, nearly to the top of a mountain, or at least I think I am, but I get to that next level and realize there's another hundred feet to climb. So I start climbing. And then bam…there's another fifty feet. And then a hundred. And then I realize I'm climbing the world's only peak that never ends. It's great. Oddly like that candle with the never-ending wick.

"You can stop," I whisper, hoping she can't hear the emotion in my voice.

"I will soon."

I want to ask why she does this. Why does she never have a problem giving me the attention I need but nothing else? It's frustrating. I hate her for it. But I also love her way too much to ever hate her. She's the best friend I've ever had. And she's the only friend I have never wanted to lose. If I came clean and told her everything, I would lose her. Unless…she knows. And doesn't care. Or maybe she knows and does care but doesn't want anything? How can we have been friends this long, and I have no idea if she knows or not?

Oh, I know. Because I will never speak to her about it. Ever.

Her hand starts to move slower and slower, and I realize she's falling asleep. Us sleeping in the same bed is a normal occurrence. Happens about twice a week. Sometimes three times. And each time, my anxiety keeps me from getting a good night's sleep. Tonight, though? I will sleep. Thanks to my good friend, wine. I hope I don't dream. I talk too much in my sleep when I'm drunk. Way too much. *Ugh.* There's the anxiety. Great. Just great.

Fast Company
April 2022

"Who Says You Can't Reinvent Yourself?"
by Jennifer Lyndy

In today's day and age, more and more people are finding that loyalty to a company is yesterday's news, and staying at your first job is for the birds. In the world of marketing, which seems to get smaller and smaller the longer you're invested in it, if you want to move up, you need to be prepared to move on. That wasn't the case for the talented Eleanor Fitzwallace, Director of Marketing and Events Coordinator at the mega-popular Hummingbird Sanctuary, Colorado's newest, hippest, and trendiest mountain getaway.

Not your typical mountain resort, the Sanctuary, as it's lovingly referred to by the co-owners, Olive Zyntarski, Harriet Marshall, and Eleanor Fitzwallace, you won't see a ski lift to the top of the nearest peak. You won't rent a cozy mountain chalet. You won't be surrounded by families in a lobby with a massive fireplace roaring away at six hundred degrees. Instead, you'll find a gorgeous, stress-free escape marketed entirely toward women.

"How did you all come up with this idea?" I watch the question wash over the three women as we sit comfortably on the back patio of their immaculate on-site residence. They're running a mental relay race. Who's going to get the hand-off?

"Well," Olive starts as she places her mug on the wooden table. "As an older woman who, unfortunately, has suffered a lot of loss in her life, I've had to reinvent myself. We all have. Things popped up, happened, forced us in a direction we either wanted to go or didn't. And as far as this place? I dreamt of a place where I could retreat with my girlfriends. Y'know, a place that was gorgeous, affordable, all-inclusive, and not on a beach. Where it wouldn't be about anything other than us and our time together. I didn't start off thinking it would be geared toward women, though."

"Oh? That's interesting."

Eleanor raises a hand, taking the imaginary baton. "Yeah, that was my idea."

"Makes sense, since she's the big ol' lesbian out of the three of us." Harriet Marshall is next with the baton.

"Guilty." Eleanor pushes a hand through her hair. "The reinventing yourself thing that Olive touched on? That's true. I wanted to take this position, not only because I was ready to have more responsibility, but because I wanted to do something that mattered to more than only me. I wanted to do something that mattered to a lot of people. Something that would make a difference. I believe the sanctuary does that. We make a difference in people's lives. In women's lives. I have been in the hospitality world for what seems like forever, and ninety percent of the time, it feels like all we do is market everything toward the man and then the woman. I wanted to market to women. Sure, we get husband and wife couples and husband and husband couples, but for the most part, this is a place where you can get away with your girls. Where you can laugh and be loud and drink, and you're safe and respected. I wanted it to be that way for a multitude of reasons."

"Which are?"

Eleanor clears her throat as if she's asking permission to just handle this interview, and Harriet and Olive give her the stage. "Listen, as women, we know what we want most of the time. I think a lot of our insecurities exist because we're given too many choices, and in the end, we have to be the ones to make up either our own mind or the mind of some man. I say 'some man' with as much love as possible. The point I'm trying to make is, women make so many decisions all the time. But here? There are so few decisions for a person to have to make. What wine to drink? What meal to eat? What do you want to do to relax? Sure. Those decisions exist, but they're going to lead to you having an amazing time. I'm all about making everything as stress-free as possible. Ladies will not experience decision fatigue here. Ever."

"And it seems like it's working?"

"Oh yes. We've been booked for as long as we've been open. Right now, we're booked clear into next year. A few sporadic weekends remain, but ultimately, there's no room at the Sanctuary."

"You're doing something right."

They give each other smiles, then shrugs. Reinventing yourself comes with a lot of courage, class, and stability. If I can say one thing about these three women, it's that they're most definitely doing it right. And Eleanor? Keep on marketing the good life to as many women as possible. We all deserve to feel less fatigue in the decision department. *Yawn* Including myself.

CHAPTER FIVE

Olive

I never thought I'd say the words "I'm running out to the helicopter pad," but I say that entire sentence frequently. I didn't think we'd ever need to use the pad. I guess a part of me didn't want to assume things were going to go as well as they're going here. When I was younger, I was an optimist. As I aged, that faded. I tried to get it back, the spark, the desire to assume good things were going to happen instead of constantly fearing the bad. I guess it all came to a head when Paul passed. Or maybe right before that.

I stand inside the small shelter we built to get out of the blazing sun. I'm still shocked at how warm it's been for the first week of May. The feeders are attracting more and more hummers throughout the property, and I couldn't be happier. Everything looks great. The ground crew stepped up their game in the last week, too, which is fantastic. I need every aspect to be in order for this trio of women. I'm nervous about their arrival. If things don't go perfectly, I fear the journalist from *On the Verge* won't be writing a glowing article.

I can't even think that way right now. I need to be positive instead of letting my pessimism get in the way.

The sound of the helicopter is getting closer and closer. "This is it." This *is* it. And it's going to be great. I can feel it. And I'm not saying that to psych myself up. I really do feel it.

The blue and silver helicopter floats over the top of the Uncompahgre Plateau. The colors are a beautiful contrast against the red of the rock. I pull my iPhone out and snap a few pictures, making sure to choose the wide-angle setting like Eleanor taught me. She's the real photographer. All the pictures on the website and the marketing pieces were all taken by Ellie. She has an eye, part of the reason I needed her to make this leap with me and open the resort. The other part is because I don't feel as off-balance when she's around. She helps ground me in a way I will forever be thankful for. I don't tell her that enough. I probably should. I don't tell anyone what they mean to me. I didn't before Paul's death and now—

"Hey, want some company?" Harriet says as she walks up next to me.

"Hey there."

She leans into me, and I can smell her cologne. It's lavender and chamomile, and I love how it smells on her.

"I'd love some." Damn, she looks great. She dressed up on purpose. I did, too. I don't wear dresses often. I'm a bigger girl, and my thighs constantly rubbing together, sweating…I hate it. I hover between a sixteen and an eighteen most of the time. I seriously think I went from being in a kids' size six to a fourteen in women's and never looked back. My mom was a fantastic cook, and my grandmother as well. There was food in front of me at all times. Truthfully, my weight has never bothered me. Not even when I was made fun of in middle school. Free Willy was never a fun nickname, but I shrugged it off and realized that people overcompensate for their own issues at a very young age. My weight is part of me, and as much as I would love to look rail-thin, deep down, I'd feel uncomfortable. And of all the things I am pessimistic about these days, my body and my beauty aren't one of them. It's the only exception I give myself.

So I wore a dress today. I wanted to look great. I wanted to play the part of the resort owner and operator who looks as great as the rest of the place, who fits in, who shines. Also, I finally found ladies' boxer briefs, thanks to Harriet, and my thighs no longer chafe when I wear dresses. I've never been happier. The spring navy wrap-dress I bought at the beginning of April accentuates everything I need it to. Three-quarter-inch sleeves, low-cut but not too much, and it falls right below my knees. Taupe open-toed heels, red polish on toes and fingers, gold jewelry. I look good. Period.

And Harriet, in her skinny navy slacks, French-rolled; men's wing tips without socks; and short-sleeved yellow button-down with tiny pink and purple birds all over it looks incredible standing next to me. "We make quite the welcoming committee." I put my arm around her waist, and she stands a little straighter.

"We are both fine motherfuckers."

"You're right, we are."

"I'm right about a lot," she says and the air of cockiness that usually accompanies those words is missing, and this time, they're dripping with defense.

"Yes, you are." I squeeze her. "The restaurant brought in a lot last night." Most of the times, the restaurant is our saving grace.

She beams. "It was a great night."

"Scallops were delicious."

"They're no mussels." She looks at me, her left eyebrow raised slightly. "But yeah, they were good."

"I need to thank you. You know I have a hard time giving control away. I'm working on it. I promise."

"Will you do me one thing?" She's practically shouting now that the helicopter is ready to land. I nod as I pull my hair to the side and hold it from blowing everywhere. "Please trust me. I know what I'm doing."

"Hattie," I semi-shout as the helicopter's engine shuts off. I glance at the aircraft and reach to hold her hand. "I love you, and I do trust you. Okay?"

"Okay, boss." She squeezes my hand, and we take off to welcome our important guests.

"Hello there," I say as they disembark, "welcome to the Hummingbird Sanctuary. My name is Olive, and this lovely person next to me is Harriet. We are very excited to have you all."

"Olive, hi, I'm Mabel Sommers from *On the Verge*."

I take Mabel's outstretched hand and make sure to firmly shake it. The one thing I've learned throughout this entire process of buying, renovating, and running the sanctuary is that a firm handshake is the only way to go. Anything else and it's uncomfortable. Too limp? Weird. Too sweaty? Gross. Too long? Inappropriate.

Firm and quick. Get it over with.

"Ms. Sommers, thank you for wanting to write about our lovely resort. I am honored."

"Please, I insist you call me Mabel." Her voice has a hint of a Southern twang, and I wonder where she's from because it can't be Los Angeles, where she and her two friends flew in from. She adjusts the wide-brimmed Panama she's wearing and pushes her long, wavy auburn hair over her shoulder. "And these two behind me who haven't said a word are Sunny Micha, up and coming actress, and Judy Pilson, a producer for *The Sandy Show*."

"Whoa," Harriet breathes out. "Like *the* Sandy Shields? Dyke extraordinaire? Olive, Sandy is like, Lord of the Dykes." Harriet chuckles. "That's amazing."

Judy leans into view. "Yep, Lord of the Dykes herself." She laughs. "I'm going to have to text her that one." She slips her phone out of her back pocket and starts typing with her thumbs.

"Holy shit, you're texting her right now?" Harriet takes the three steps to Judy like a flash. This whole routine is very familiar. I've seen Harriet in action more times than I'd like to admit. "Oh my God, she's texting Sandy fucking Shields. This is the coolest thing ever."

"Welp, I can assure you," I say, followed by a nervous chuckle, "we have seen celebrities before and aren't complete idiots all the time."

And then Sunny moves into my view. She pushes her hand through her short dark hair, and it falls right back where it was, shaggy and across her forehead. She's wearing a brown tweed blazer, sleeves rolled up over her elbows, over a cream-colored cotton shirt, and her hands are shoved into the front pockets of her skinny dark jeans, holes ripped into the knees. She's the epitome of cool. If cool wore men's brown boots and looked like that, she'd be the picture next to the definition in the dictionary. "It's okay, Olive." A smile spreads across her full lips. She's wearing red lipstick, and for some reason, I can't pull my gaze away from her. "Judy gets this all the time."

I'm embarrassed. Who knows why? Maybe because my mouth has gone instantly dry. I can't find my voice? Am I having a stroke? I'm trying to be professional and impressive, and it's not working. I wish I could take a page from Harriet's book, who is never nervous in front of people. But here I am, fumbling, nervously chuckling, staring, wondering if I am going to freak them all out. I'm still not talking. I need to respond. *Respond, Olive, respond!* "It's nice to meet all of you. If you'll follow me to the welcome center, we can get you checked in. No need to bring your bags. We'll have those delivered to your rooms."

"Lovely," Mabel says softly as she starts to follow. I feel her fall in step next to me, and as we're walking, I can hear Harriet's barrage of questions to Judy. I should have had Eleanor out here. She would have been much better at all of this than I am. I have never been this off my game before. What is wrong with me? Why am I fumbling? "So, Olive, can you tell me a little bit about the grounds?"

"Well, we have around five hundred acres of land. The actual livable property is around ten buildings. I'll most definitely be available to give a tour if you'd like. We can go into the amenity buildings, and I can show you a couple rooms since you'll all be in a nest."

"And what about you? Anything you want to share now about yourself?"

"Oh, goodness. I'm the most boring out of the three of us, I can assure you."

"I doubt that." Sunny's words, the softness of them, the low volume, as if I was the only one who should have heard them, make me pull my shoulders back.

"Well," I start, clear the weird emotion her words caused to rise into my throat, and then finish with, "I'm a widow at fifty who runs a very successful resort with her two best friends. I guess that is pretty interesting."

"You're right about that," Mabel says with a gracious tone. "I'm sure there are a lot more details you're leaving out. We have time, though." She's dressed in a black David Bowie T-shirt, tied in a knot at her navel, with a long, flowy floral skirt, and black and white checkerboard Vans that have seen better days. She is so Boho chic that I can hardly handle it. She screams laid-back and fun. I thought she'd be stuffy and strange, journalistic in a bad way. I find myself kind of wanting to get to know her. Isn't it supposed to be the other way around? "We have guest room buildings scattered throughout. And this is the welcome center." I open the large wooden door and hold it as Mabel walks in. I feel the weight of it lighten and glance over my shoulder. Sunny has her hand above my head. My eyes are drawn to her forearm, to the tattoo of a geometric human heart.

"Go ahead." Her voice is smooth, like the worn handle of the door.

I move before I allow myself to linger too long. "Please, right this way." I cross to the check-in counter where Keri is waiting like the true professional she is. "Keri, this is Mabel, Sunny, and Judy. Would you mind?"

"Absolutely not a problem."

"Okay, you're in good hands with Keri. She'll make sure to get everything taken care of."

"Awesome, thank you, Olive." Mabel places a hand on my forearm. "Can we meet up in about two hours? Drinks? I'd love to chat with you and your partners."

"Our cocktail lounge is right through there."

"Perfect. I'll see you then." She gives me a smile before turning to Keri.

"Hello, ladies, how was your trip?" Keri's customer service voice is warm and welcoming, which gives me the exact right moment to take my exit. As I turn to leave, I make eye contact with Sunny. "Have a gun time. Wait, I meant to say, have a good time, but then thought fun would be better so I said fun and good together," I say, and *why don't I sound even more like an idiot?*

Sunny shakes her head as she chuckles. "You have a gun time, too."

I turn away as quickly as possible and rush away even faster. When I round the corner, I lean against the wall and take a deep breath, closing my eyes to help calm my nerves.

"What the frick is going on with you?" Harriet's voice sounds far away even though she's standing right next to me.

"I have no idea."

"Are you nervous? I've never seen you like that before."

"Yeah, tell me about it." I sputter a little and open my eyes. "I swear to God, I was having a stroke or something."

"Ollie, that's a serious thing to say. Are you okay? For real?"

"Yeah, yeah, I'm okay." I take a deep breath. "I think the nerves are getting to me. That's all."

"Mm-hmm." Harriet leans against the wall next to me. "You gotta settle down. You know what you're doing. We all do. Remember, we are the experts here. Not them."

"You're right." She is. But I don't have the words to tell her everything that just went on with me when I saw Sunny. I don't know how to explain it to myself.

Chapter Six

Eleanor

"She wants to meet with all of us? Now?" Lucky for me, I couldn't go out to meet the helicopter earlier due to a meeting with the marketing staff. Thank God. There are days when I do not want to be the face of this place. I don't mind it most of the time, but my performance tank is empty now. And I have no reserves. I peer into my reflection in the mirror in my office. My long-sleeve black button-down is sheer enough that my black lace bra is visible. I hope Olive doesn't fuss about it. She's stuffy sometimes, and I get I'm supposed to look professional, but something about these visitors makes me want to look professional *and* sexy. Is that wrong that of the three of us, I want to be the sexy one for once? I apply my favorite light pink Lancôme lipstick. I have about ten of them scattered around my life. One in every room I frequent. But dammit if it didn't take me ten minutes to find this one.

"Yes, she wants to chat with us over drinks."

"I have Lizzie with me." I look over my shoulder at her as she snoozes next to the couch. "She was strange at home, so I brought her in."

"That's fine. She'll behave."

"Uh, yeah, because she's the best dog ever," I say with the sweetest voice I have, and Lizzie perks up. I find Olive's eyes in the mirror. Her hair looks perfect, and her makeup is flawless, but her expression is pained. "You okay? You seem off your game a little."

"Tell me about it," she replies with a grimace.

"She stroked out at the helicopter pad," Harriet explains.

"I did not stroke out."

Harriet shakes her head. "You're the one who said you thought you were having a stroke."

Olive's shoulders fall. She breathes out and shakes her hands. "God. It was weird. I don't know, Ellie. I am a mess today."

"Great."

Harriet is leaning against the windowsill with her arms crossed. We make eye contact, and she raises her eyebrows, and her eyes get big. Whatever Olive did was something I shouldn't have missed. Which means I'm super happy I did miss it. Witnessing Olive when she's awkward is a lot to handle. I hate watching anyone squirm, but Olive? It's like torture.

I fluff my hair. I don't miss the Chicago humidity at all, but the dry air wreaks havoc on any sort of curl I do. "Okay, how do I look?"

"Amazing." Olive sighs. "You literally do not even need to try."

"Olive, what is going on with you? You wanted this article. You set it up. Now you're a hot mess? I'm sorry, but no. That's not allowed." I smooth my hands over my stomach and down the side of my skinny black slacks as I close the distance between us. "You are our leader." I put my hands on her arms, bend a little, and look into her blue eyes. "Be the leader."

She gently pulls on the gold hummingbird charm hanging from the long chain around my neck. We all have them and make sure to wear them on important days. Olive's is on a shorter necklace, and Harriet's is on a bracelet. "Okay," she finally responds.

"No, not okay. Say it. You're the leader."

"I'm the leader."

"Say it again."

"I'm the leader." That time is much more forceful. "I'm the motherfucking leader."

"Exactly!"

"Okay, come on, we're going to be late," Harriet says, swiftly ushering us from my office.

As we're walking down the hallway to the Feeder, I realize something. "Who are we meeting again?"

"The journalist," Olive answers.

I sigh. "I mean, what's her name?" I ask as I turn into the Feeder and pull on Lizzie's leash. She sits right next to me, and I pat her head. I notice Heidi perk up when she sees us walk in, her lips turning upward into a grin. I lift my chin to acknowledge her. "Is anyone going to answer me?" I turn, and my eyes land on wavy auburn hair, a skirt, a David Bowie shirt, a fucking hat. *Oh, Jesus Christ.* I'd know this person anywhere. Why is she here? Why is Mabel fucking Sommers here? This is not okay. Not at all.

"Olive, Harriet, great to see you again." She's holding her phone and a key fob and the realization slams into me like a ton of bricks.

"Holy shit," I say softly. At least, I thought it was soft, but they all turn, and I have to wonder. Lizzie heads over to Mabel like she's been in my life for forever. I'm betrayed by my own dog.

"Ellie?" Mabel has finally seen me, and she blinks rapidly, as if the more she does that, I'll simply disappear. She squats to say hello to Lizzie. "Who is this beautiful pooch?"

"What the hell are you doing here?" I ask and adjust my stance.

"Ellie?" Olive has her hand on my back.

"This is...we, uh..." My face is on fire. My palms are sweating. I shake my head again. "Um, we, uh, we went to high school together." I can't take my eyes off her. The look of shock is enough of a hint that she never put together that Eleanor Fitzwallace is the same Ellie Thomas from Maine East High School. The same fucking person.

"We sure did," Mabel says with a voice coated with fake enthusiasm. She stands from petting Lizzie. "How are you doing?"

"Well, I mean," I say as I hold my arms out and turn from side to side. "I'm doing very well."

She smiles. The same smile that used to leave me breathless as a baby lesbian high schooler who had no idea what was happening to herself and could never mention it for fear of being ostracized. "You look...wow." Mabel pauses, her voice breathless. "Great. You look really great."

Harriet, in true Harriet fashion, takes charge. "Let's all have a seat and chat," she says and maneuvers us to a table near the windows. It's a perfect spot with great light. Where I can sit and stare at Mabel and hope with everything in me that this is a bad dream. A nightmare.

Olive has her hand on my hip and holds me back, spinning me toward her so she can laser me down with her glare. "Are you going to tell me what the hell's going on?"

"It's a long, long, long story."

"That you will be telling me." She gives me a gentle pat on the hip before she brushes past me and sits. I roll my eyes, then turn to see the seat they saved me, the one next to the only person who ever truly broke my heart. My high school crush. My old best friend. Mabel fucking Sommers.

I need to start asking more questions—something along the lines of, oh, I don't know, *what is the person's name?*—before I agree to anything else at the sanctuary.

The interview turns out like every other interview we've done. I'm not impressed. The same stock questions. The same boring answers.

How did you all meet?

How did we come up with the idea?

Who found the property?

Yadda, yadda, yadda. The whole thing is causing me to be super on edge.

I excuse myself and head to the bar, where I slide in between two stools and get Heidi's attention.

"What's up, babe?" She looks adorable today. But why wouldn't she? The daytime, light blue, floral bowties and suspenders over the navy button-downs look fucking good. Harriet knows how to pick out great uniforms.

"Can I get another round for the table?" I glance over my shoulder and notice Lizzie has her head in Mabel's lap, and she's getting the attention she clearly loves. I want to call her a traitor.

"For sure." Heidi flips a mixer into her left hand. "You okay? You seem more on edge than normal."

"Than normal?" I sip on my freshly delivered glass of sauvignon blanc and eye her over the top. "What's that supposed to mean?"

"Oh, Elle, you know what I mean."

Her coy banter is usually fun, but right now? It's stressing me out something fierce. "Heidi, I literally cannot do this right now." I shake my head and breathe out a deep breath before I say, softly, "I'm too fucking stressed out."

"Hey?" Heidi's voice is quiet, and I look up at her. "Are you okay?"

I make eye contact. And all my mind's eye can see is Mabel. It makes me want to cry. "Nope," I finally respond.

"You know I can help with that stress, right? No strings…"

I chuckle. I wait for her to chuckle in return, but she doesn't, which causes me to chuckle again. Taking Heidi up on her offer is so tempting, so very tempting. I need the release really, really badly. But "no strings" will turn out poorly. We'll sleep together, and it'll be great, and I'll take the no strings seriously, and it'll break her heart. This isn't my first rodeo. I take a gulp of wine before I slide the tray with the drinks from the bar top and carry it to the table. Harriet takes her tequila, neat, then hands Olive a glass of wine. That leaves me to pass Mabel her water. When I do, her fingers brush mine. Because why not? Why not make me spin even more out of control? Perfect.

"I think it's my turn to ask a couple questions." Olive goes to drink. She pauses and motions to Mabel and me. "Seems to be a story here."

I glare at her. She's going to regret this. "There's no story at all. And honestly, I have to leave. Now isn't the best time—" I go to push my chair away but am interrupted.

"Sit down, Ellie." Olive's voice is braided with intrigue and irritation. "And tell us how you two know each other."

I roll my eyes. I'm going to kill her. "It's not a great story. We went to high school together. The end." I stand. "Again, I apologize for being abrupt. I have a mountain of paperwork I need to get through before the event this weekend." I turn to Mabel. "Please forgive me. You three can continue without me, I'm sure."

It's the rudest I've ever been. I can't help it. I am ready to have a full-blown panic attack. I never freak out in public. But I never thought I would see Mabel again. I never wanted to see her again, let alone have her sitting next to me at the bar I own, asking me questions about my success. I would have been a lot happier if I continued without being forced to think about her again.

And think about her I am. Dammit. She looked amazing in that stupid skirt and T-shirt. Like, how the hell does she get away with looking so casual yet appearing so professional?

I am out the door of the Feeder with Lizzie in tow, ten steps from the exit of the welcome center before I hear Harriet shout my name. I don't stop. I'm not stopping for anything.

When I push through the doors, I make sure to quicken my pace. I have longer legs than Harriet. Unless she starts to jog, she's never going to catch me.

"Ellie, for Christ's sake, slow the hell down." She is jogging. I can tell by the way her shoes are hitting the concrete. When she finally catches up, she shakes her head at me and points. "What has gotten into you? Having both you and Ollie freak the fuck out on me is not at all how I saw this day going."

"Nothing is wrong. I needed to take a walk. I'm fine."

"Sure. Sure." Harriet has her hands on her nonexistent hips, and she's giving me a look that says she doesn't believe a word.

"I promise. Everything is fine."

"You are a horrible liar. You know that. Why are you trying to lie to me now?"

"Because. I don't want to talk about it, okay?" I spin to leave and notice Mabel walking toward us. "Fuck," I say under my breath. "Hattie?" I grab Harriet's thin forearm. "Don't you have something super important to show me? Like, anywhere? Somewhere other than here?"

"Uh, no, I don't. You are being fucking weird."

"Yes, you do. I'll go with you." I grab her with both hands now and pull her in the opposite direction of where we were originally headed. I am pleading with her with my eyes. *God, Hattie, don't make me spell it out.*

"Ellie, stop." And then Harriet finally gets it. "Oh. I see."

Mabel pulls up right in front of us. I make eye contact with her, and before I can let my heart make any further decisions, I look away. For some dumb reason, I let my head, which I normally hold so high, fall the tiniest of bits. I feel defeated, deflated. I can't do this. I can't.

"Ellie?"

Her voice is too much for me.

"Mabel, hi. My apologies, but I have to monopolize Eleanor's time."

Mabel's brow is furrowed as if she is all too aware of the fact that her reappearance in my life has caused me to spiral out of control.

"We have some important marketing things to, y'know, like, make decisions about or whatever." Harriet's very sincere "So sorry" at the end of her sentence is all I hear as she escorts me away from that total fucking train wreck. I wish I could get my shit together so I didn't have to be whisked away like the fucking lunatic I am. Harriet leads me right back to the welcome center and through the back hallway to my office. She sits me in the chair across from my desk, then closes the door. My legs feel all wobbly, and I thought for sure I was going to pass out.

"Thank you," I whisper. I'm embarrassed, yes, but also, my entire body feels how it does after a bout with the flu. I am burning up as if someone cranked the heat to eighty-five. My brow is sweaty. My arms are achy. And I'm nauseated. I lean down, prop my elbows on my knees, and cradle my head. You'd think I was hit by a Mack truck. But no, I was slammed into by something far worse. Twenty-nine years of repressed feelings careening out of control.

There's a gentle knock at the door, then it opens, closes, and I hear Olive's footsteps, feel her hand on my shoulder and smell her perfume.

"I'm sorry." My hair has fallen over my shoulders. "I just...I couldn't...I had to get out of there."

"Shh." She kneels next to me, her knees cracking on the way down. "You're okay." Her soothing tone is exactly what I don't need right now, but it still helps. I wish it didn't. But damn, it does.

"I can't talk about this now. Please don't make me."

"Babe, we are not gonna make you talk about anything you don't want to. When and if you feel comfortable, you know we'll listen." Harriet is sitting on the rug now, too, leaning against my desk, her knees bent. She reaches out and holds my hand. "We got you."

I don't know what I did to deserve these two women in my life, but I have never felt more thankful than I do right this instant.

CHAPTER SEVEN

Olive

Eleanor's breakdown dampened our spirits a tad. The desire to know what threw her over the edge is strong, but I'll respect her wishes and allow her to tell us when the time is right. But damn, I have never seen her like that before. Not even when she caught Natalie in bed with her brother. She was sad, sure. But this? I've never seen her this messy, and our friendship has spanned fifteen years, with every single type of emotional up and down a person can think of. We've helped each other through the death of parents, failed relationships, work stresses, a divorce, the death of my husband. It's been a long, winding road with a lot of debris.

Clearly, something very big happened between her and this Mabel woman.

The way her face fell when she saw who was doing the interviewing, I thought she'd seen a ghost. And not a friendly Casper ghost. More like something out of *The Conjuring*.

A jolt of chills shoots through my body. I don't want to even think about those scary movies Harriet makes us watch. She won't do it alone. I spend most of every horror movie hiding my eyes. I watched *The Blair Witch Project* without covering my eyes and couldn't stop seeing a big hairy witch standing over me for the next three weeks. No, thanks. Not again.

It's after seven o'clock now, and it's almost time for us to do our rounds at the Feeder and Bird's Eye View. I'm hoping Eleanor has calmed down. As I take in these final moments of peace in one of the Adirondack chairs on our back patio, I see a doe and her fawn walking across the east side of the field behind us. She stops and stares, ears perked, as if she can hear me breathing. She's in protection mode as her fawn munches away on the new berries of one of the crab apple trees. I feel the emotion in my throat. Why does this move me?

She eventually starts to walk away, her little one following close behind until they disappear into the sagebrush and tall grass. My heart is full, and for some reason, I feel very alive. More than I have in years.

"You ready?" Eleanor asks, and it yanks me out of my thoughts.

I push up from the chair and smooth out the wrinkles from the white linen shirt I've changed into. I decided on jeans because one full day in a dress is enough for now. "I sure am." I wait a beat as I study Eleanor in the entryway of the sliding glass door. "You sure you want to do this?"

"I'm sure."

"Okay. Hattie said she'd meet us at half past seven, as long as the kitchen was cooperating." I follow Eleanor into the house, watching her like a hawk, trying to gauge her mood. The urge to push her into spilling her guts is palpable. I want to know. No, I *need* to know what the hell happened between the two of them. I'm not sure why I care so much. It happened in the past, and it was way before I knew Eleanor. Maybe it was seeing the way she was taken off guard so easily, so quickly. I'd never seen her so vulnerable before. A little like the fawn from earlier, yet unlike the fawn, no one was there to stand in protection mode. Should I be the one who protects her? Is that what I'm feeling?

Our walk to the restaurant is very quiet. She's not okay, and she's pushing herself. The last thing she ever wants to do is make us look bad. And she never wants to disappoint me.

"I'm a little subdued tonight. I apologize." Eleanor's voice, low and gravelly, as if she's been crying, breaks through the quiet.

"You don't have to come. I don't want you to think that it will reflect poorly on us or anything."

She lets out the smallest puff of air. "No, it's fine. I'm fine. I need to put on a brave face."

I slip my hand into the crook of her arm. She looks sharp tonight. Her hair is pulled back into a messy low ponytail, and small locks around her face are free. I'm impressed with her makeup, as well. Simple and fresh. There's something about how her eyebrows are shaped that makes me jealous. She has never over-plucked in her entire life. And she's wearing a black V-neck shirt under her blazer, untucked, with dark blue jeans and Frye black booties with a decent heel. I remember the day she bought them. She was beaming with excitement. It was as if she was a kid again. She's still wearing her hummingbird necklace, too, but she's paired it with a couple other gold chains, one she wears often with a gold pull tab from the top of a can. "Well, you *look* amazing."

She breathes deep in the warm glow of the well-lit walkways. "Thank you, as do you."

How can someone I know everything about feel like such a stranger? I don't get a chance to respond as we approach the restaurant. There're quite a few people hanging around the doors, which is a good sign for business, but I'm wondering how the kitchen is handling it.

"They're fine."

"Who is?"

"The kitchen. The staff. Don't worry. Let them handle it. Let Harriet run her show."

"How did you—"

"I felt you tense up the second you saw the people." She sighs. "You're very easy to read."

If only I could say the same about you. "Oh, okay, Miss Fancypants." I roll my eyes as we squeeze through the crowd. I say hello, shake some hands, give hugs to a few regulars: the part of the job I really hate but seem to excel at these days. Getting out of my comfort zone has been an issue for as long as I can remember. The mountain air, the kindness of people, and the fact that if this all fails, I'm fucked, has a lot to do with me working to ditch that comfort zone.

When we get to the bar, we're met by Glenda. "Busy night tonight," she says with a nod. "We are totally handling it. I promise."

"Do I look like I don't think you are?"

"No. But you normally do, so I'm being proactive." She laughs, and then her eyes perk. "Eleanor! Honey, I haven't seen you in forever." She throws her arms around Eleanor and hugs her for a few seconds. "You look absolutely phenomenal. What have you been doing?"

"Stressing out. Worrying. Not eating. Y'know, the usual." Eleanor shrugs. "But thank you. I needed to hear that."

"Anytime, hot stuff. If I wasn't happily married, you'd have to fight me off with a stick."

"Please, I'd welcome it with open arms, my love." Eleanor's smile is the first genuine one I've seen since the breakdown. "How's everything else going?"

"Great. The VIP threesome is enjoying dinner."

"The VIP threesome? Is that what we're calling them?" I shake my head. "I don't know if that's appropriate."

"What else would we call them?" Glenda asks. "It works, and you knew who I was talking about. Oh crap, gotta go. Deb, get them a drink." She motions to us as she speed walks up to the front of the restaurant.

"Old-fashioned? Vodka soda? What are we having?" Deb asks while she wipes down the bar top.

"Vodka soda with a lime for me." Eleanor leans against the bar. A few people are seated along it, but they're far enough away that we can take in the sights and sounds without bothering anyone.

"I'll take a tequila sunrise," I say, and Eleanor snaps her head toward me. "What? I thought it'd help me loosen up."

She smiles for the second time tonight, the crooked one this time. The smile I have grown to love over all these years. "You're the boss." When our drinks are delivered, we thank Deb, then raise them toward each other.

"To our moms." I watch the toast wash over Eleanor's face. The three of us have that in common: the loss of a mother. It's something that brought us closer together. There are a lot of people in our lives who don't understand the pain of losing a mom. Not even my brother truly gets it because he and my mom weren't close.

"I'm going to go check in with Hattie. You okay?" Eleanor pushes from the bar. "Thanks for getting me out of the house."

I fight the desire to stop her and simply nod as she turns and walks away. Yeah, I'm going to have to push her a little harder to tell me what's going on. And that will not go over well.

As far as the restaurant is concerned, though, things are going over very well. I make a mental note to tell Harriet what a great job she's doing. She knows her shit. There has to be a reason why it's difficult for me to trust my business partners. I trust them explicitly when it comes to being my best friends. Why should partners be any different?

"Hello there, gorgeous. What can I get you?" Deb's asking as she leans closer to hear whatever the guest says. She's one of the best bartenders I have ever seen. She and Heidi share the load of shifts, which is great for us.

"May I please have the Añejo Suerta tequila? Chilled, please. No rocks."

I do a double take at the customer. "Oh my God, Sunny, hi." *Oh my God.* "I mean, hi. Hi there." I roll my eyes at myself.

"I didn't mean to startle you," she says as she leans against the bar. There's something about her that gnaws at me. Not in a bad way. In a

"I want to get to know her" way. Is it her self-confidence? Or that she's an actress? Or is it that she's like me, curvy and not bone-thin but holds herself so very well?

"It's not a problem at all. How are you? How has everything been?"

"It's been amazing. I am thoroughly impressed." She threads her fingers through her dark hair. She's standing a hell of a lot closer than she was earlier in the day, and I notice a smattering of freckles across the bridge of her nose and cheeks. "I, uh, have no idea how I'm going to occupy my time, though. Mabel plans on taking in all the different amenities. I sort of, y'know, just wanna chill."

"Just wanna chill, hmm?"

She nods. "Yeah, like, I have been filming a movie for the past three months. I'm eager to take a breath."

"That is exciting." I take a sip of my drink and realize Deb did not go light on the tequila. The strength makes me squint. I glance over to Deb, and she gives me a thumbs-up, snickering the entire time. "I'm sorry. Deb is trying to kill me with this drink."

After Sunny gets her drink, she gracefully sips it, then, eyebrows elevated, asks, "Do you mind if I join you?"

The only response I have is to shake my head. She sits, swivels toward me, her knees pressing lightly into my thigh. "So," I start, finding my voice that is situated directly behind my nerves. "Tell me about this movie?"

"Well, I mean, I play a nonbinary character who is trying to figure themself out. Part of the reason my hair is short now." She motions upward. "I don't know. I may keep it this way. It's incredibly easy to maintain."

"Yeah, you look great. Not that I would know what you look like with long hair. Not that it would matter either way." I cringe. "I'm sorry. I'm unnerved by you for some strange reason." *Christ, Olive.* Did I seriously admit that out loud? "Hey, Deb?"

She zips down the bar. "Boss?"

"Remind me to fire you for making this drink strong enough to kill a person."

"Will do!" She salutes and heads back, chatting it up with guests.

"It's the tequila, I promise. I am not usually this, um…messy?"

"Don't worry, Olive. I am finding it insanely endearing." Her posture as she sits is impeccable. Back straight, shoulders pulled back, one hand holding the glass, the other draped on the back of her stool.

"How long have you been acting?"

"About ten years. I started in my mid twenties after grad school and haven't stopped. I was in a bunch of off-Broadway plays in New York City and then auditioned for a movie about two years ago. Moved to LA and haven't looked back."

"Off-Broadway in New York *City*? Not a different city?"

She graciously laughs at my poor excuse for a joke. "Sorry, it's a habit."

"I'm only kidding." I reach over and place a hand on her knee, then realize what I've done. I pull away. "What movie were you in? I feel bad admitting I never saw it."

"Don't be. Oh, man, it was seriously the smallest role. In a movie called *Bewilderment*. I was a server at a restaurant."

"Okay, wait, I've seen that movie. How come I don't recognize you?"

"Phone?" She has her hand held out, so I pull my phone from my wristlet and slap it into her hand. "Passcode?"

"Nineteen eighty-nine."

"Whoa, whoa, whoa. Please tell me you're a Taylor Swift fan."

"Guilty," I answer.

Sunny's demeanor is so refreshing. Light, airy, as if she's tried every other way of living and has settled on easy-breezy. She's tapping through to get to the YouTube app, then holding the phone up. "Here you go."

She comes on the screen in a café uniform, long brown hair pulled into a braid over her shoulder. "Holy shit. That's you."

"Guilty," she echoes me from earlier. "Told you I had to cut all my hair off."

"I can't decide which I like better." I look at her. "I think the short."

"That's good because it's going to take forever to get back to that length." She hits the power button on my phone and hands it back. "So, Olive, tell me about you."

My cheeks fill with heat. The last thing I want to do is talk about myself. I want to learn more about her. I want to know her. "Why don't we skip me and keep discussing you?"

"You know all there is to know."

"I highly doubt that. How do you know your travel companions?"

Sunny glances over at the table where Mabel and Judy are seated. "Judy is my ex-girlfriend's ex-girlfriend."

"Whoa, that's a lot."

"Yeah, the LGBTQIA+ degrees of separation are intense." She chuckles, takes a sip, then sighs. "After their breakup, she moved to LA to produce for *Entertainment Tonight,* which is when I met her. I was on *ET* for another small film I did that stirred up some Oscar buzz. Then after that, she was handpicked to be the producer for Sandy Shields."

"That's exciting."

"Yeah, I think she's over it all. If she could retire, she would. She's done, y'know?"

I want to say I know because, wow, do I know. But I don't because admitting how stressful the sanctuary is to one of the people who has Mabel's ear? Probably not a good plan.

"And Mabel? Well, I met her at a bar one night in New York, and we hit it off, and that was that. She was there doing a story for something, I can't even remember what at this point, and I was getting ready to move to LA. She said to look her up, and I did, and we've been friends ever since."

"It must be fun, the three of you all so important, traveling together."

"Oh, honey, we are far from important. I'm a B-list actor, Mabel is a journalist, and Judy is a producer."

"Nice try." I tilt my head. "You took a helicopter in. You're far from a nobody."

She shakes her head, a small smile etched on her lips. "None of us drive. We're from New York, LA, and Chicago. I mean, I think Judy might have driven before her divorce, but she doesn't anymore."

"I guess that makes sense." I take another drink. The ice has not melted enough, and it's still too strong. Too much tequila causes me to make poor decisions. And I'm flirting with those right now. There's a part of me that wants to pry and see what I can find out about Mabel. Will she tell me why Eleanor freaked out? Does she even know? "Can I ask you something?"

"Sure, what is it?"

I pause. Do I want to do this? "What's up with Mabel and Eleanor?" Welp, there it is. I am disappointed in myself, but the look on her face is telling me I'm right.

"Hmm." She purses her lips, a clear indication that I have overstepped the bounds. Bounds neither of us are fully aware of or even want to acknowledge yet. "Sounds like something you should probably talk to your friend about, don't you think?"

"God, yes, you're right. I apologize. I'm telling you, this drink, it's making me say stupid things."

"No need to apologize. I'm just…I'm not the person who gossips. Ever."

Something about the way she says that makes me want to tell her all my secrets. I trust her. And I barely know her. It's an odd feeling for me. I don't trust often, and when I do, I typically get hurt. "That's a great trait to have."

She leans forward. "Doesn't mean I have never gossiped before in my life, though, so yes, I can see why you want to know what went on with them."

"I'm glad to know I'm not hallucinating."

"You are definitely not." She messes again with the front of her hair, pushing her bangs away from her face as she looks over her shoulder. She has earrings I didn't notice before. Tiny gold studs. Why am I finding her earrings interesting? Hell, why am I finding her ears interesting? "Well, I guess I better get back to my friends. They keep glaring at me."

"Yes, I'm sure you're missed." I occupy my eyes with the mirror behind the bar where I can see both of us perfectly.

She slips off her stool, and her body presses against my side. "Let's do this again."

I am rendered speechless. I can only nod as she excuses herself and makes her way back to her seat. I blink a couple of times, place a hand on my chest, and feel my heart thudding. It's been a hot minute since I've felt this way.

And it scares the holy living shit out of me.

CHAPTER EIGHT

Harriet

"It's time to get out there and mingle a bit with the guests. Are you coming or what?" I unbutton my chef's jacket and drape it over the back of the chair behind my desk. "Do I look okay? I didn't plan on being in the kitchen at all tonight."

Eleanor has been camped out in my office since she and Olive arrived an hour ago. She nods. "You look great. I love those salmon-colored pants. And great call on the black penny loafers."

"The black shirt and polka dot tie isn't too much?" I push the sleeves up over my forearms, then loosen the tie. "I feel stuffy."

"You look great. I don't know why you're fretting." She stands and walks over. "I think I'll hang back as you mingle. Olive will go with you."

"Girl, I hope not. You should have seen her earlier. I can't even believe how nervous she was. Like, next fucking level. It was weird."

"I don't know if I've ever seen Olive nervous." She stares into the distance as if recalling a memory. "Yeah, no. I haven't. I don't even know if I'd be able to spot it."

"I swear on every pair of shoes I own, you'd be able to spot it. A fucking NASA satellite spotted it, I'm sure." I pull her from the chair and out of the office. "You can mingle with me, y'know. You're good at this. Outgoing, fun, you get the guests excited."

"Oh, Hattie, I'm not feeling it tonight."

"Okay, okay. I'll stop pestering you." We both approach the bar and find Olive tapping away on her phone. She's always working, even when she should be relaxing. She needs to learn to take a break. Or at least take a breath. "Ollie, you're with me tonight. Let's go mingle."

Olive raises her eyebrows. "Um, you think that's a good idea? I mean, after my horrible display earlier?"

"You're fine. And Ellie doesn't feel like it." Olive digests that comment. She won't stand for Eleanor not being on her A-game for much longer. She doesn't ask much of us outside of our roles, but Eleanor is the people person, so her not wanting to do the part is not gonna fly. "Let's go. Then we can get out of here and go back to the house and chill the fuck out." I say the last part under my breath as Olive slips off the stool. She places a hand on my back, and we take off to the first table.

"Hello, hello. We wanted to stop by and ask how everything was tonight."

The guests are eager to answer. They go on and on about the food, which I'm thrilled about. And they also compliment their server, Amber. She needed to step up her game from the other night, so it eases my mind that she came prepared tonight. The next five tables are the same with all good things to say. One man even said he wanted to stay forever simply because he wants to have the scallops every night. Believe me when I say I got a very long stare from Olive, complete with a very cocky grin.

We approach the VIP threesome. I'm drawn to Judy, and there is not a bone in my body that understands why. She is not at all my type for a woman or a man. She's older than me, she's blond, she's thick, and she's straight. But I am giddy with nerves. "You gonna hold it together?" I ask Olive as we approach.

She rolls her eyes before she greets the table with a very lovely, "Good evening, ladies. You all look absolutely amazing. How is everything?" Her voice is smooth, with no hint of nerves, and finally, I am able to take a breath.

Mabel is the first to answer. "I cannot even begin to describe how delicious this buffalo steak is. I am in awe of how tender it is. Absolutely marvelous."

I am beaming, feeling the pull in my cheeks and jaw as if I've eaten something sweet.

"And the scallops? To die for." Sunny's eyes are on Olive. My senses perk. "The best I've ever had."

"Did you hear that, Hattie? The best she's ever had." Olive grins once more at me, but it's more of a smirk than anything else. "Thank goodness you decided to change it up."

I want to kick her right in the ass. "Of course," I say. "Scallops with roasted garlic cream sauce is a favorite recipe of mine. I had a feeling it would go over well." I take a chance and place my hand on Judy's shoulder before I ask, "How is your bourbon-brown-sugar glazed salmon?"

She looks up at me, into my eyes, when she says, "It is the best I have ever had in my entire life." Her voice, the way the words sound coming out of her mouth, has me feeling some type of way. Excited about being alive. Her eyes are the most intense blue I have ever seen. All I want to do is swim in them for days and days. Skinny-dip. *Goddamn.* She finally breaks our gaze when Mabel starts talking.

"Listen. I wanted to see if I could get solo time with each of you. Olive, then Harriet, then Eleanor. Would that be something we can set up?"

"Absolutely." Olive is much more laid-back than she was earlier, and it thrills me. "Here's my cell. You can text when you'd like to meet. Sound okay?"

"Yes, that works well."

Judy is tracing the stem of her empty wineglass with her index finger. She has dark, cherry-colored nail polish, and all I can think about is her dragging her nails down my back. My libido hasn't been this raring to go in quite some time. Keeping a lid on things maybe wasn't the best course of action. I'm my very own pressure cooker. "Well, we'll let you all finish up. I am very happy to hear that you've enjoyed yourselves." I place a hand on Judy's shoulder again and squeeze lightly before I walk away.

The rest of the evening goes well, I feel accomplished and excited, and even though I am ready to go home, I let Olive and Eleanor drag me over to the Feeder for one more drink. They've ordered meals and had Glenda walk them over in carry-out containers. Now they're sharing, and I'm waiting with as much patience as possible for them to tell me what they think. Not that I need their approval. I like getting my ego stroked. And I'm not too proud to admit it.

Olive moans around a mouthful of food, her hand held up as a cover. She places another bite into her mouth, chews, swallows, then sighs. "This, all of these tastes, are exactly why I wanted this to be the dish this weekend. God, Hattie, this is incredible."

I'm shocked by her compliment. Olive doesn't hand them out very often. It's best to receive it without a lot of fanfare. "Thank you," I respond, holding back my happiness. "And Ellie? How's the lobster à la vodka? Good? Bad?"

Eleanor places her fork down, wipes her mouth, and looks at the ceiling as if searching for what she wants to say. She is one of the only people I got nowhere with. Not because I didn't try. She denied me every time. She is beautiful, even when she's not trying. Looking back on those failed attempts, I'm grateful we were never ruined by my stupidity. It was a blow to the ol' self-esteem, that's all. "You know how most vodka sauce has that weird pink color?" she asks, and I don't move for fear that she's going to say she likes that weird pink sauce. "Well, I hate that weird pink sauce, and I'm madly in love with this. Why haven't you made it before? And the lobster pieces? God. I don't want to stop eating."

"That is exactly why I love cooking. I'm a legal drug dealer."

"This is true," Eleanor says with a chuckle. "I'm thankful you don't charge us because I'd probably need a loan shark."

I'm leaning against the bar next to her. She seems to have calmed, and I wonder if the old-fashioned she's drinking has anything to do with it. I cannot wait to get back to the house and feed her some more alcohol so she'll tell us why she broke down earlier. "I'm glad you both like the meals. I plan on making the vodka sauce a permanent fixture."

"And the garlic cream?" Olive leans forward. "Because it's amazing, too. Ellie, you gotta try it." She has a piece of scallop on her fork, and she holds it up for Eleanor. The two of them feeding each other makes me want to smack them. Olive has no idea how much Eleanor loves her, and Eleanor has no idea how to tell Olive to stop. It's a swell spot for me to be in. I'm constantly waiting for them to have a blowup. I pray to God it never happens.

"I'll put it in the rotation."

"Also, and I'm not trying to be a bitch." Olive pushes Eleanor, and she leans back. "Can you please not sleep with Judy? I saw the way you were looking at her. I don't want to fuck this article up."

I blink once, twice, then lick my lips. How do I play this off? "What are you talking about? I'm not going to try to sleep with a straight woman this weekend."

Olive lets out a huff.

"What?" I narrow my eyes. "What is going on?"

"I don't want to tell you." Olive leans back and puts another bite of scallop in her mouth.

"Ellie, what the fuck is she talking about?"

"Ha! You think I have any idea? I've steered clear of that group and plan on doing that for the remainder of their visit." Eleanor brings her drink up and takes one sip, then another. Olive sighs as she places a hand on Eleanor's thigh, right above her knee.

"I don't want to throw you off, but Mabel would like to interview us all separately. I told her that would be fine."

Eleanor leans her head back and makes a nauseated groan. "Olive, I swear to Christ, I am going to murder you in your sleep tonight."

"That's dramatic." Olive pushes her meal a bit and props her elbows on the bar. "Are you going to tell us what happened with you and Mabel, or are we going to have to accept you acting overly neurotic this entire time?"

"Fine." Eleanor shakes her head, takes a deep breath, and gathers… something. Not sure what. Is it courage? It doesn't matter what she says. We will never judge her. I don't know why she seems ready to combust. "When we were in high school, we were very close. I don't even want to say best friends because it was more than that. We did everything together. We had sleepovers and a group of friends we hung out with, and it was amazing. I loved high school because of Mabel. She was my everything." She bites her lip, and my heart breaks for her. "Then senior year, she started dating Bobby Lee. And everything stopped."

"You're not saying you're still angry at this chick because she got a boyfriend?" Olive's words aren't necessarily accusatory.

"No. When I say we did everything together, we did everything together. Including—"

"Sex?" I ask.

She nods.

"Like, more than once?"

She nods again.

"Wow." I'm surprised but more that it happened numerous times. Mabel looks like a total straight edge.

"Yeah, then Bobby happened. She pretty much stopped speaking to me, and one day, I came to school, and everyone knew, calling me a dyke and a carpet muncher, and I…well…I was devastated." Her face is completely devoid of emotion except for the tears welling in her eyes. She's staring straight ahead. It'll take but a gentle nudge to get her to cry. And that is the last thing any of us wants. Especially her.

"You don't need to interview," Olive says matter-of-factly.

Eleanor chuckles as she fans her eyes. "I'll pull up my big girl panties and do it. I will. It's been a slap across the face, seeing her again. I forgot how much it messed me up. And then there she was. In that skirt and hat and…it's hard to explain."

"I get it," I say as I place a hand on her forearm. "It's hard seeing you every day after you denied all my advances." And the three of us burst into laughter.

"I hate you," she says as she wraps her arms around me. "I hate you so much."

"Ditto, baby. Ditto."

"Olive?" Heidi breaks into our conversation. "There's a call for you from Keri at the front desk. She says a guest is asking for you."

"Oh. Hmm. Okay, tell her I'll be right there." Olive shrugs. "Wonder what's going on." She rushes toward the check-in counter as Judy walks into the bar in her black skinny jeans, brown booties, and jean jacket. I didn't notice her outfit earlier. She is so fucking hot. I want to stare at her for hours.

"Well, hello there," I say under my breath, and Eleanor turns.

"You are awful." She chuckles. "Olive literally said seconds ago that you can't sleep with her."

"But Ollie ain't my mama." I smirk. "I'm gonna go talk to her."

"Great. I'll stay here and ward off Heidi's advances as best as I can."

"Good plan." I squeeze Eleanor's arm and casually make my way to where Judy has found a seat. She's next to the large overhead door, open tonight to let in the cooler air. "Fancy seeing you here."

She shrugs. "Figured I'd come sample the craft cocktails. Anything you'd suggest?"

"The Honey Paradise is great."

"Done. I'll take that," she says to Heidi, who rushed over as soon as Judy sat.

I flip a chair around and straddle it across from her at the small table. I cross my arms, prop them on the chair back, and lift my chin. "Tell me, Judy, what's your story?"

She leans back and lays her hands in her lap. Her shoulder-length blond hair is in waves, and her bangs are swept gently to the side. I am mesmerized by her beauty, her cute nose, her jawline, and the line of her neck. "I doubt you have the time for my story."

"I'd clear an entire calendar for you."

Her left eyebrow rises slightly higher than the right. I've impressed her. And I am thrilled. "What do you want to know?"

"Everything."

She finally breaks eye contact, and I miss the weight of her gaze. "Well, let's see. I hate peas."

"That's a shame."

"And don't get me started on people who don't use their turn signals." She sighs. "I was married for a very long time to a man. And I left him when I finally came to terms with the fact that I like women."

My heart leaps into my throat. I swallow, but it doesn't move.

"I have two kids." She pulls her shoulders back.

"Okay."

"Does that scare you?"

"Nope."

"And I was a news anchor on an AM radio station for a long time. I eventually moved to a producer role. Then I was offered a job in LA, so I moved, and here I am. Not super exciting."

"On the contrary, I'm definitely excited."

"Oh? By which part?"

"That you like women."

"I had a feeling."

I rest my chin on my forearms and narrow my eyes. "Bi or lesbian? Not that it matters. I am simply intrigued."

"Lesbian. Fully. Late in life, yes, but I am not going back to men." She reaches up and messes with the necklace under her white shirt. "What about you?"

"I do enjoy men from time to time."

"Interesting."

"Is it?"

"I thought for sure you were only into the ladies."

"Well." I shrug. "I thought for sure you were straight."

"Can't judge a book by its cover." A few seconds pass before she says, "You are an exceptional chef."

I am so sweaty. So, so sweaty. Thank God I am wearing a black shirt, or my pit marks would be very visible. "I owned a restaurant in Chicago for years."

Her eyes light up, and she leans forward. "Really? Where?"

"Cat's Pajamas in Old Town."

"Shut up. I used to go there all the time with my best friend," Judy muses. "What are the odds?"

"Wait, are you from Chicago?"

"I guess my years of keeping my Midwestern accent at bay have finally paid off." She licks her lips. They're full and look delicious, and *I am so fucking horny*. I need to calm down. "But, yes, I was born and raised there. In Bucktown."

"I'm from the South Side."

Heidi finally delivers Judy's drink and apologizes profusely. The bar is getting crowded. She should have help on its way from the restaurant. I start to worry a little but am pulled back to the conversation when Judy says, "I was at WGN. In the news department."

"Wait a second, were you on in the mornings with Kathy and Judy?"

"Oh God, did you hear me? I was the news anchor for a long time until their contract wasn't renewed. That's when I moved to producing."

"I used to listen to them all the time when I was in college."

"It's a small world." She finally takes a sip. "This is very good." She takes another. Her lips against the glass…And another. It's as if she's watching my reaction to her reaction, and it's too much for me to handle. "You came up with this recipe?"

I nod.

"You're good."

"Thank you," I say, my voice softer than normal. Her fingers on the stem of the glass have caused me to forget how to breathe.

"Harriet?"

I swallow the lump in my throat. "Yes?"

"Do we need to get out of here?"

"Yes." And I stand and grab her hand, practically pull her from her chair, and lead her as quickly and nonchalantly out of the bar as possible. I keep my head down. I don't want to make eye contact with anyone. Especially not Eleanor. And as we move through the back lobby of the welcome center, Judy pulls on my hand.

"In here," she whispers and pushes through the door to the unisex bathroom. "Anyone in here?" We wait a beat, two, and when no one answers, she clicks the lock. Her hand is still on the door when I place a hand on her cheek, her neck.

"Is this okay?"

"Probably not. But I don't care." She grabs my shirt and pulls me into her, her lips crashing into mine. She kisses me in a way I didn't even know was possible. I am not leading at all. It's a new role for me. Even with men, I lead. It's who I am. But with Judy? Holy shit. She spins me around and has my back pressed into the door and is kissing me as if this is the last kiss we will ever experience. Her lips are exactly how I imagined them. Soft, full. I slip my tongue into her mouth, and she greedily accepts it, moaning against my mouth. The sound reverberates, sending a zip of chills throughout my body.

"Goddamn," I say into our kiss, and she giggles as she bites my lower lip.

"I've wanted to do that since I saw you." Her voice is muffled against my cheek as she places kisses along my jawline to my chin. "You are so fucking hot."

It's my turn to giggle. My cheeks fill with even more heat, and I lean my head back on the door. "I am completely thrown by you right now."

"I guarantee you, with absolute certainty, this is not the only time I will throw you."

I lean forward to kiss her again. Her tongue presses against mine, and I bite down gently, then allow it entry into my mouth. She moves with me, every part of her, her hands, her hips against mine, but especially her lips. And I cannot get enough of them. I could kiss her all night long.

I plan on it.

CHAPTER NINE

Eleanor

"Heidi, did you see where Hattie went?" I lean against the end of the bar and look around. "I went to the bathroom, and now she's gone."

Heidi stops shaking the martini shaker and glares at me. "Are you kidding me, Elle? I've been swamped since the second you all came in here. I'm not paid to be Hattie's babysitter."

"Hey, pump the brakes there, missy." I hate confrontation, and I certainly don't want to mess up the easy camaraderie I have with her, but she shouldn't be talking to me like that. Regardless of how important she is to my fragile ego that needs every single boost she so generously hands me.

At this point, I just want to go home. I don't want to be a boss right now. I've wanted to go home since before we walked into this bar, and now I'm all by myself, and with every second that passes, my anxiety is climbing and climbing, and I'm getting more and more nervous about the possibility of running into—

"Shit. Fuck. Damn." My stomach falls into my ass. Mabel is walking into the Feeder, beelining toward the bar, determination on her face. It's way too late in the evening for that level of determination. What is her deal? Is she that hard up for a drink, or is she, like me, wondering where the fuck her so-called friends are? I'm frozen in place. The way her auburn hair has fallen over her shoulder in gentle waves, the way she seems unaffected by everything around her, the way her body has matured. She hasn't changed at all, yet she has changed completely. She had self-esteem, even when being bullied in middle school. And now she looks like she knows she belongs in any room she enters, any circumstance she experiences, any encounter she's involved in. Back then, I was in awe of her. But right this second? She's driving me bonkers.

I finally realize that she hasn't seen me. I yank myself out of my memories and duck as far out of sight as possible, hoping the large vase of flowers at the end of the bar will help hide me. I do not want to talk to her. Not tonight. Not tomorrow. Not ever. Up until ten hours ago, I was happy not thinking about her ever again. And now she marches in here and takes up space in my brain all over again and never even bothered to check to see if there was a vacancy.

Which there is, but whatever. That's not the point.

"Hi, can I get a vodka soda with a lemon?"

I roll my eyes. The only guest at a craft cocktail lounge to get a fucking vodka soda. And with a lemon? Who the fuck drinks it with lemon? I'm irritated, and none of what is happening should have anything to do with me. This is how much her presence has affected me. If I had a clear shot at an exit, I'd have already taken it. She is still standing, head down, scrolling on her phone. She looks up when her drink is delivered, says a way too pleasant thank you, then goes back to her phone. The drink sits, untouched, for what seems like forever. I can't stop remembering the very first time we got drunk together at her parents' house. On Boone's Farm strawberry wine. And I threw it all up. *Ugh.* The very thought of the sugary "wine" makes me gag.

Her phone starts to ring.

I'm annoyed. *Turn your fucking ringer off.*

She doesn't answer it and continues to type. Since she's so important, I'm sure she's taking notes about this dumb fucking article she's writing. I'm the only one listening to my stupid inner banter, but I need to make sure every eye roll is out of my body. What could she possibly have to take notes about right now? Some super-secret issue she's had while here and now she's going to bash us? Or maybe she hated her meal? Or maybe she's a vapid jerk who can't remember anything and must write it all down? Who knows? I don't want to know, that's for sure.

The only thing I *want* to know is how this got past me. How was I immersed completely in my work that I didn't ask questions? How did I not know she was a journalist? How did I not know she never changed her name to Lee when she and Bobby married? How did I lose track of her?

What am I saying? I didn't keep track because she broke my

fucking heart. That's why. *Shit, shit, shit.* I'm a mess. I need to get out of here. She's on her phone right now. Perfect time to escape. I gingerly take a step, and she doesn't notice. I take another step. I'm almost home free. And then I hear, "Elle, babe, where you going? You haven't even touched your last drink."

My shoulders fall, and the air and blood seem to drain from my body. *Heidi, you asshole, why did you have to ruin my plan to flee?* I don't realize how close I still am to the flowers, and I hit them, cause the vase to wobble, and nearly knock the entire thing over. I lunge and steady the giant vase and take a deep breath. "*Fuck.*"

"Fuck is right. You klutz," Heidi says. I manage to contain the glare I want to give her. It's not entirely her fault. At all. It's mine. I'm the idiot who has no spatial awareness. And I'm the idiot who can't woman up and leave the bar without feeling anxious.

"Once a klutz, always a klutz, hmm?"

Mabel's voice slices into my awareness. I don't want to look at her, but I do. Reluctance doesn't help the way seeing her is making my heart feel. I smirk because answering her is too much for me.

"Ellie, look," she starts and takes a step toward me. I step back. I don't need her to be close. Her face falls as I reinforce my already erected walls, sturdy and strong, and nothing is going to breach them. Especially her. "I wanted to say that I'm sorry. I didn't...I didn't realize you were..."

"A part of this?"

The tilt of her head and scrunched face makes my stomach twist. "I didn't do my research, I guess."

"A journalist who doesn't do her research? Makes me leery to read the article. Hopefully, you do your research *this* time." Inwardly, I cringe. I'm not a mean person, but sadly, one of my best and worst qualities is that I never keep my mouth shut when given an opportunity to shoot a person down. For someone who hates confrontation, my smart mouth still gets the best of me. And this time, my poisoned barb strikes its target. I didn't realize witnessing the direct hit would make me feel this bad. Seeing a shitty comment make her expression shift and falter causes me to feel exactly how it used to in high school. Except now, I'm the one being the jerk. Not some dumb jock I thought I was protecting her from.

"I'm sorry either way."

"Okay." I make myself stop looking at her, stop looking at her in her navy tweed blazer and floral shirt tucked into her high-waisted jeans. She looks amazing. Still. And it makes me mad at her. And so very sad.

All over again.

"Do you think we could talk?"

My first instinct is to say yes. It's what I do. I let people explain. It's a blessing and a curse. But when it comes to her, I've conditioned myself to say no to my instincts. "There's not a lot to *chat* about." Again, her face falls, along with her shoulders. "Try to have a good time while you're here. Okay?" I drop the words and rush past her.

My stomach is upset, and my hands are cramping. I have no idea what is happening to me. The only thing I do know? I'm never going to the Feeder again.

CHAPTER TEN

Harriet

If someone asked me ten years ago if I thought I'd ever sneak back into my own house, I'd have laughed at them and said I'm a grown-ass woman, and I can do what I want.

Yet, here I am, hand on the door, hoping to God that Olive and Eleanor are asleep because if they are, I won't have to answer any questions about where I ran off to. It's a struggle to come up with yet another lie they won't believe. And if I have to hear "Look what the cat dragged in" one more time, I swear, I'll scream. Like, let's be real, right? I was out with someone, and I was making out with someone, and it was maybe the hottest make-out session I've had in, oh, I don't know? For-fucking-ever? Why can't I say that?

I close the door behind me, the latch clicking as silently as possible. The light over the stove in the kitchen is on, and I realize I'm holding my breath. What the hell is wrong with me? I have one hand on the wooden banister to climb the stairs when the light in the sitting area clicks on. Sigh. I knew I wasn't going to escape. I just knew it.

"Well, well, well."

I release the air I've been holding. "Please don't say it."

Olive, sitting in one of the three chairs, her feet on an ottoman, a book closed on her lap, shakes her head. "Oh? Whatever do you mean?"

"Come on, Ollie." I sigh again as I drop my shoes. Defeated and worried, I plop onto the chair near her. "It's too late to be coy."

"Or is it too early to be honest?" She pulls her reading glasses from her face. This whole exchange reminds me of coming home to my mama, and I'm hating it and secretly kind of loving it. But only because it makes me miss my mama's laugh and her wide grin.

"Look what the cat dragged in," I mimic her perfectly.

"I was not going to say that."

"Sure."

"But now that you mention it, look what the cat dragged in."

"I hate you. You know that, right?"

"But I love you." She places her book and glasses on the side table next to her chair. Her movements hold many unsaid emotions. Disappointment. Irritation. Fear. As if single-handedly, I could fuck up the entire sanctuary simply by being me. "You're not doing anything with anyone you shouldn't be, right?"

"My God, can you *not* act like a parent to me for like, oh, I don't know, twelve seconds?" I let out a groan. "I'm allowed to sleep with whomever I want."

"You slept with someone tonight?"

"Who *slept*? I mean, come *on*." Her mouth falls open, and my hands shoot into the air. "I'm kidding. I promise." I lean back into the chair and prop my bare feet on the ottoman. She pushes her foot forward and touches mine.

"I worry about you."

"You mean to tell me this has nothing to do with me sleeping with guests?"

"Well," she starts and shrugs. "I want us to seem professional. You know what I mean?"

"Like how stupid you got when you saw Sunny for the first time? That was *super* professional."

She breathes in through clenched teeth, and a miniscule laugh escapes. "Touché, pussycat. That was good."

"And also true." I shake my head. "I want to find someone, Ollie. Just once, find someone who I want to love. Is that so bad?" I watch her, watch my words wash over her clean face, and see her eyes fill with tears. I feel sad for being brutally honest on this strange, strange night.

"I want you to find someone, too."

"Then you have to stop policing the people I sleep with. I would never stop you from loving someone again."

The way her face changes makes me wonder. There's something there, something right beneath the surface, something I have wanted to ask her about but have never dared to do so. She had such a different marriage when I first met her. Everything about her was different. Their love for each other was unlike anything I have ever seen before. I don't know how to describe it other than to say I never wanted to be in a marriage like theirs. "Thank you," she whispers. "I hope I can find it, too. Find love, I mean."

"You will." I go to stand when she leans forward.

"Be careful, okay?"

"Always."

"And please, God, don't fuck this shit up if you're going to start chasing Judy. Okay?"

Busted. "I would never."

"Never fuck it up or go after Judy?"

"Fuck it up." I wink as I lean down and kiss her cheek. "Love you, Ollie. Go to bed."

"I love you, too." She's smiling. I can feel it in her cheeks.

As I climb the stairs, I think back to the way Judy kissed me… to the way she tasted…to the way she softly asked me to take her somewhere we could kiss and kiss and kiss. I collapse against my door after I shut it and slide to the floor. Never would I have thought I'd be giddy over kissing someone for hours. God, it was amazing. I did as she asked, and we found the most secluded fireplace on the property. And we looked at the stars as we lay next to each other, holding hands, tracing our initials in the bare skin of our forearms, and she told me about her kids, and I tried to remind myself that she isn't *forever*. She is *for now*.

But maybe she could be.

The Foodie's Delight Magazine
The Food Network
May 2022

"Soul in the Form of Food"
by Jason Adams

I don't know how I would describe the cuisine at Bird's Eye View, even if I had a gun to my head. I'd probably say it's a little bit of everything, but where the general manager and executive chef Harriet Marshall shines is her Italian and Mediterranean dishes. Not to mention the bar's extensive whiskey and bourbon selection and phenomenal wine list.

As a newcomer, I was a little worried that as one of the only men on property, I would stick out like a sore thumb. Boy, was I mistaken. I was welcomed with open arms, and the hospitality was top-notch.

Harriet Marshall, who insists on being called Hattie, is a maniac in the kitchen, and I was very honored to be able to join her for the creation of three dishes: seared scallops, hickory-smoked venison steak, and my personal favorite, blackened mahi-mahi.

The scallops were cooked to perfection. A sear on the outside, served with roasted garlic cream sauce and asparagus. I can't describe the garlic cream sauce without using the words "authentic, amazing, and savory." I saw God in this dish.

The first thing I thought of was Bambi, but once I was assured that the venison was farmed appropriately, I was a little more at ease. And woo, am I glad. I've never tasted a more tender cut of venison in my life. And the fingerling potatoes and creamed spinach were a wonderful touch from the richness of the meat. A+ for sure.

When I stepped out of my vehicle and walked into the resort, the last thing I imagined was that the seafood in a very land-locked restaurant was going to be good. I could not have been more wrong. Just like the scallops, the mahi-mahi was seared to exactly the right temperature. The fish was moist, the flavor was out of this world, and the handmade lemon hummus and fresh pita bread that accompanied the feta, tomato, and cucumber salad was out of this world.

I've never been so stuffed. Or so happy.

Harriet Marshall was born and raised in Chicago, Illinois, where she learned to cook in her grandmother's apartment kitchen. She lovingly referred to the old one-bedroom as "the best-kept secret in all of Chicago." Hattie learned the tricks of the trade and decided at a very young age to pursue a career as a chef.

"At first, I dreamed of being a pastry chef, but I hate chemistry and math, and that's what I feel like baking, at its very core, is. It's science. Cooking, though? That's an art. And deep down, I've always been artistic, and I've always wanted to color outside the lines. Sure, you can't take out salt if you add too much, but that's part of the learning curve. I love it."

And thank heaven she does. The Hummingbird Sanctuary is very lucky to have Hattie and her crew. They bring life to the resort that you don't experience in other places. The food has soul. The food has personality. And it's clear how much it all means to them all, but most importantly, Hattie.

"Seriously, Jason," she says to me, a hand on my forearm, "Finding peace here in the mountains isn't as easy as they tell you it will be. But finding peace here in the kitchen?"

I know what she's going to say, but I let her finish.

"Finding peace here is like discovering yourself and being happy with the discovery every single day. And I'm grateful for that."

Listen, Hattie Marshall, so are we.

Visit www.thehummingbirdsanctuary.com to check availability.

CHAPTER ELEVEN

Olive

"Okay, Keri, there should be a couple contractors on property today. I'm not happy that they couldn't come until now, but we'll deal with it."

Keri, the only twenty-five-year-old I've met who doesn't use her phone for everything, is scribbling notes into a planner. I have oodles of respect for her, probably more because of her reluctance to rely on technology. I've never relied on people as much as I rely on her and Juan. It's scary sometimes, but lately, I try to remind myself that it will not get any better or easier, and it's okay to delegate and trust those people.

I haven't been burned yet.

"Do you have anything else for me?"

Keri thumbs through her notes, a few Post-its, and a small spiral notebook. "Yes. I have a few complaints."

"Great." I wait for her to hand over the slips. I read the first one. Loud banging on the wall all night long. Room D121. "Did you look into this?"

"Yes. The room next to this, D119, has a newly married lesbian couple."

"I wonder why there was banging?" My eyes widen as it hits me. "Oh. Oh! I get it. I guess we can't really tell them to keep it down."

"I mean, I guess we could, but I doubt it'll go over well," Keri says while laughing with me. "And the other one is about the air-conditioner in room E215. I already have Juan's guys on it."

"Wonderful." I take a deep breath as Keri's demeanor changes from fun and sweet to *let's get back to business*. She is exactly who I need in my life. "Keri, what would I do without you?"

"You'd be very, very busy."

"You are so right. Thank you, seriously. Thank you for being exactly what I need at the exact right time. I don't think you understand how important you are."

She tilts her head. "You realize you don't have to keep thanking me, right? That's what the paycheck is for."

"I think it's important to tell people when they're important in my life." I didn't get to with Paul, even if I was miserable and ready to get out, *and apparently, so was…*

A wave of emotion slams into me, and I grip the counter behind the check-in desk to steady myself. "Anyway, I'll get out of your hair. If you need me, I'm going to meet with Ellie and Hattie about the final touches for the event on Sunday."

Keri doesn't seem to notice my slip, thankfully. No one notices the quiver of emotion in my voice anymore. I've been keeping a lid on my emotions for far too long to be a novice at this game. We say our good-byes, and I head over to the Feeder for brunch with the girls. It's still early enough that it shouldn't be too busy.

Eleanor and Harriet are sitting outside in a sunny area on the back patio. It's another gorgeous day in the valley, so I'm glad they chose an outdoor table. I make sure to pass by the bar where I can say hello to Serenity, the morning barista and bartender, as I walk through. "How are you doing, Serenity? I feel like I haven't seen you in a while."

"Yeah, I had to take the last two weeks off to finish up school."

"Junior year, right? Next year is your last?"

She grins. "God, yes. I cannot wait."

"And how did the semester go?"

"So freaking good. I checked my grades this morning, and I got straight As. I literally worked my ass off, but it was worth it."

I reach over the bar and grab her hand. "I am proud of you. That is great news. Cause for celebration, y'know. You'd best be here on Sunday."

"Oh yeah, I'll be here. The girls and I reserved a nest for the weekend. That way, we don't have to worry about drinking and driving."

"That's a great idea. And make sure you come have a drink with us later. We'll be around, I'm sure. And tomorrow night, we're having a little get-together at the residence. You're all invited. Tell the girls."

"Oh wow, okay. That's amazing. Thank you."

"Bring your suits. The water is perfect." I wink at her, then tap her hand before I head outside to my meeting.

As soon as I approach the table, Eleanor and Harriet stop whatever they're whispering about, which means they're talking about me. They act as if I don't know them like the back of my hand. I'm sure it's probably about my protective mothering attitude toward Harriet last night. And every night. I need to stop. It's become a bad habit. I'm sure a sliver of it relates to our age imbalance, but I long to see her happy.

Being the only woman of this group who is fifty-plus is difficult to navigate. Things like being a protective mama bear and only a tad overbearing are annoying, sure, even if it is an instinct I never thought I'd have. And smaller things like, oh, I don't know, hot flashes, hormone imbalances, and irregular periods? Yeah, those seem like small potatoes when you're still in your prime, and you've never had to throw the covers from yourself in the middle of the night because you're positive you're going to combust. Little do they know that my mood is continuously hanging on the thread of whatever my body is deciding to do for the day.

"Ladies, good morning." I pull out a chair, sit, and welcome the mimosa Eleanor passes me. She never skips a beat when it comes to alcohol.

"Please don't say a word about how you don't drink while working. I think we all need these this morning."

"Okay. Um, what's going on?" I peer at Eleanor over the top of my glasses and over the champagne flute. "You look like death warmed over, by the way."

Eleanor rolls her eyes. "Gee, thanks."

"What's going on? Are you getting sick? You know you being down and out during this won't be a good thing." I reach for her forehead, and she smacks my hand away.

"I'm fine. I don't have a fucking fever. I didn't sleep. And I'm stressed."

"Hmm." That's strange. She always sleeps. Aside from me, sleep is Eleanor's very best friend. "About the event? Or…"

"Obviously, the event." She drinks the rest of her mimosa, grabs the bottle of Prosecco from the chiller on the table, and fills her flute. The tiny splash of orange juice she tops it with makes me cringe. I pray she doesn't get sloppy. "What?" she asks. "I'll be fine."

"*Okay.*"

"Stop," she says, and there's almost a growl at the end of it. That is definitely unlike her. Eleanor does not get angry with me. She never has. "I'm fine. I...I need to relax."

Harriet, who is watching this whole display from behind her clear-framed glasses, looks as if she didn't sleep much, either.

"And you? How are you?" I ask.

She shrugs. "I'm good. Just, y'know, chillin'. Hangin' with my homegirls. Havin' brunch, drinkin'. It's a beautiful day."

I peer at her harder. Her eyelids look like they weigh ten pounds apiece. "Are you *high*?" She looks away while trying very poorly to hide a sheepish grin. "Hattie, you're high as a goddamn kite, aren't you? *Great.* The two most important people at this goddamn resort, and you're both a hot fucking mess."

"God, *Mom*, yes, I'm ripped," she finally says with a huff. Her tone causes my mouth to fall open slightly. "Y'know, Ollie, you're gonna have to get off our dicks, okay?" She motions to her and Eleanor. "I needed to relax. Ellie needed to relax. We work our fucking asses off for this fucking place. And you fucking know it."

"Wow." I am offended, don't get me wrong, but the truth in her words slices through my annoyance like a cleaver. She's been right a lot these days.

"Yeah. Calm the hell down, okay? It's Friday morning, and we both need you to be cool today. Every day, really, but especially today." Harriet fidgets with the black baseball cap she's wearing, takes it off, then puts it right back on, this time backward. Fidgeting is one of the other reasons I knew she was stoned. She does this every couple of months, goes on a mini bender with marijuana. She'll be fine. This weekend, for some reason, feels so absolute, as if it's do or die. And it scares me that we aren't all on our A-games. But maybe she is. She never hasn't been. And the same goes for Eleanor. I take a deep breath and nod at Harriet, telling her I hear her.

She folds her arms and props them on the table. "I'm super stressed as fuck about the event. And about every other little thing going on here this weekend. But maybe you could, oh, y'know, maybe fucking trust us? I mean, for fuck's sake, Ollie."

I am holding on to the wow I so badly want to say and remind myself that these two are the only reason everything here runs smoothly. But I'm still taken aback by Harriet's tone. And by the phrase: "Get off your dicks, hmm?" I look at Eleanor, then Harriet.

"Yeah, you got a problem with that?" Harriet is staring at me, both eyebrows raised to her hairline. This may be the first time I have ever seen her mean business when speaking with me. As much as it's a smack in the face, it's also strangely refreshing. "Drink your mimosa and order, please." She motions to Glenda, who is now standing next to us, prepared to take our orders.

"Glenda? What are you doing here? I thought Coryn worked the morning shifts on the weekends."

"Called off." Glenda shrugs. "She mumbled something about being bitten by a snake on a hike yesterday. I don't know. I don't ask questions."

"Goddamn snakes," I mumble, and Eleanor snickers. "I'm telling you, they're the devil."

"Let it go." Eleanor shakes her head, then orders French toast, bacon, scrambled eggs, and hash browns. She doesn't miss a beat before she ends her order with, "I'm stressed. Let me eat."

I order oatmeal and fruit, and Harriet orders eggs, hash browns, and biscuits and gravy. She points at me. "I'm stressed and high. Let *me* eat."

"You two are going to be the death of me." But I drink my mimosa as Glenda walks away, even though it is only a glass of champagne with a dash of orange juice. "Let's discuss the event."

"Can I say one thing before we get all up in the final stages of this"—Eleanor moves her hands wildly in the air, her numerous bracelets clinking—"discussion?" She waits for us to give her our attention. "There is this cloud hanging over us since these three chicks came into our lives, or in my case, *back* into my life, and I am not okay with it. My chakras are all off, and I am just…" She takes a deep breath and exhales. Even looking tired, she is still a sight. She's wearing a Jurassic Park T-shirt under her black blazer, and I wonder if she meant to dress casually today or if she truly was so tired, she rolled right out of bed and threw on a jacket. Either way, she still looks fantastic. "I'm having a hard time dealing with the weird vibes." She takes another deep breath. "Can we discuss this? I feel it's far more important than the event at this point because I'm telling you right now, if I don't find a way to calm the hell down, the event is not going to go well."

She's being dramatic. It's part of her charm. Her stress is manifested in drama. And that's fine. But I am picking up a different type of drama today. Who am I kidding? It's not *some reason*. It's Mabel Sommers. I am starting to realize that this woman has a stronger pull on Eleanor than her story from the other night alluded to. "Okay, what would you like to discuss?"

"Oh, I don't know, what's going on? I mean, are we all fucked-up by these vibrations, or is it only me?"

"Ellie, baby," Harriet starts, "I think you need to take some deep breaths and chill out. You're the first person to remind me that the universe puts things, people, in our paths. How we choose to deal with the obstacle is on us."

I place a hand on Harriet's arm and squeeze. "That was exactly the right thing to say."

"Yeah, man, I pay attention to this shit now. All this energy and universe and vibration bullshit. Hell, I am the most Leo y'all ever met, right?"

"Yes," Eleanor and I say in unison. It's funny, too, because I never paid much attention to any of this stuff either before I met Eleanor. She is very in tune with celestial bodies and people's emotional energies, and when something is off, it affects her a lot more than it affects anyone else. Or she at least acknowledges it more than anyone else, which is one of her most endearing qualities.

"Listen, Ellie, I have to say this." I gather all my courage. "I know you don't want to talk about this, but do you think maybe you're allowing Mabel's presence to affect you a little too much?" Her face twists. "No, seriously, listen to me. You're not the same person you were in high school. For Christ's sake, *look* at you. You're gorgeous, your hair has never looked better, and you don't look a day over forty. You're running a very successful business with your best friends. And to top all of that off, you are in the best shape of your life. Why don't you flaunt that a little, hmm? I happen to know that Mabel is going on a biking excursion today. Why don't you go with her?"

"Oh, hell to the no." Eleanor shakes her head vigorously.

"Stop frowning like that. You look like an upside-down kidney bean," I say, and Eleanor flips me off. "I'm being serious, Ellie. You're always telling me to lighten up. Well, now it's time for me to tell you the same thing. Lighten up. You are amazing. Maybe let her see that?"

"And you dress fucking cool as fuck." Harriet raises her glass. "Thanks to my influence, but whatever."

"You do not dress me," Eleanor says, followed by a small laugh. She's staring at the table as if she's afraid to make eye contact, afraid that it'll admit defeat.

"Either way, you look cool all the time."

"She's right about that. You're amazing. And you deserve to be okay. And this? Some chick from high school coming back into your life who treated you poorly? It shouldn't define you."

She sighs, her gaze still glued to the table.

"I'm being serious, Ellie. I think you need to focus on the fact that you're fucking fantastic."

"And," Harriet starts, raising a hand slightly, "you're allowed to forgive her if you want to. You've outgrown the person you were, what? Nineteen years ago?"

I glare at Harriet and shake my head. "Jesus, math is not your strong suit, is it?"

"Try twenty-nine years," Eleanor says, finally lifting her head and letting out a guffaw.

"What*ever*. Holding on to all this shit is toxic. And probably why your world feels all wonky."

"I can't believe you listen when I talk about all this stuff." Eleanor blinks a couple times. "I figured you both thought I was a weirdo."

"Well, we do think you're a weirdo." I pat her leg, and finally her eyes lock on mine. There's something about this look that makes my heart ache, as if a part of my world that has been forever off clicks into place. The knowing look is unnerving. It's as if she's figuring something out that I'm not privy to. "But it doesn't mean we don't love you and value every single thing you say."

She looks away, pulling in a deep breath and straightening her jacket and spine, a look of defiance on her face. "Looks like I'll be getting that chance to forgive and move on a lot sooner than I thought." She raises a hand. "Hi there, ladies. How are you this morning?"

Sunny, Judy, and Mabel—in all their California freshness—are strolling up to the table. My eyes are drawn to Sunny. The grin that spreads across her lips when our eyes meet causes my hands to ache. A look like that would make me break eye contact in the past for fear of nerves taking over my body. I don't know if I'll get over how easy-breezy this woman seems at all times. I find myself intrigued by her, yes, but also so very envious.

"Why don't you join us?" I ask, and Eleanor kicks me under the table. I hold back the yelp as well as the glare I want to give her. "We can pull a table up and put them together."

"Oh no, we don't want to be any trouble. I'm already all in

y'all's business more than I'm sure you'd like." Mabel's answer is too rehearsed, as if she knows she's not wanted.

Eleanor groans softly before she stands and says, "No, it's fine. Sunny, help me with the table?" They place a table at the end of ours and grab chairs. My heart beat quickens as I wait for how the seating arrangement is going to unfold. As if I'm watching the season finale of my favorite television show or something. *Who will end up next to whom? Who will come out of this alive? Or who will fight to the death?*

Eleanor moves her mimosa, scoots one seat over, and opens the space next to me; Sunny sits without a second's hesitation. Judy sits next to Harriet. And they're both fools if either of them thinks I missed the hand Judy placed on her shoulder. The gentle squeeze, the way her touch lingered for a second too long. It's as obvious as a two-by-four to the face that they've done something. Whether it be kissing or fucking, I haven't figured out yet, but there's a definite simmer. And Harriet's *fuck me* gaze is enough of a giveaway.

Eleanor's eyes are still on me when I finally look at her. The side of her mouth ticks upward before she turns her attention to Mabel. She's giving in. I can see it as plain as day. And the part deep, deep inside me that is afraid of everything, of losing her, of losing Harriet, of losing the sanctuary, clenches its teeth.

"I cannot get over how beautiful the grounds are, Olive. You've all done such a marvelous job." Mabel sips a cappuccino as we sit together after brunch. The conversation is light, easy, fun. Almost. I mean, if a group of six women who are all clearly fighting battles inside themselves can have fun together.

"Thank you. Our maintenance director is the reason everything looks great all the time. He and his team are the hardest workers I've ever met."

"Wow." Harriet shakes her head. "Thanks." Her tone is very sarcastic, and I love her for it.

"You know what I mean."

"Sure," Eleanor adds as she narrows her eyes.

"Oh, stop. Both of you. Honestly, Mabel, these ladies are the reason the entire place works, and they know that. I am forever grateful for them both." Harriet is beaming. And Eleanor's cheeks fill with a lovely blush. I'm not the only one who seems to notice Eleanor's lovely blush. Mabel's eyes are glued to her. I want to hate her. She hurt Eleanor. She hurt Eleanor much more than I know. I'd heard about the high school heartbreak because Eleanor shared some of her past with me. But I never knew about being outed, about being the butt of the jokes, about being alone and scared because of fear. Fear really does control so much in our lives.

They're discussing something about marketing. Eleanor mentions the local print shop we use for some of the guides and brochures. Judy is talking to Harriet about Sandy Shields, which gives me a small amount of peace, even though I am still worried Harriet will fuck this up by breaking Judy's heart. I take a deep breath and pull myself from my thoughts. My negative thoughts that are taking up way too much space in my brain.

"You okay?"

My attention snaps to Sunny, to the softness of her voice. "Yes. Yes, of course. Why?"

"You were super deep in thought."

It's my turn to blush. My cheeks, my neck, filling with heat under her microscope. "Oh gosh." I am such a dork. "It's just nice watching us all having fun. That's all."

"Mm-hmm."

"What's the mm-hmm for?"

"You all do not strike me as ladies who don't have a lot of fun."

"You'd be right about that." I find myself feeling the need to explain. "Lately, things have been hectic. And letting loose is the first thing to go when stress settles in. Y'know?"

Sunny's arms are folded and resting on the table. She shrugs nonchalantly. "I mean, don't you think you should relax into this place a little? It's your pride and joy, right?"

"Absolutely."

"And you've done a fantastic job."

"I like to think so."

"Sometimes, letting go and realizing that things will unfold as they should is the best thing you can do for yourself."

I let out a laugh, and she blinks rapidly. I am being so rude. "I'm sorry. I don't mean to…I just mean…your wisdom seems beyond your years."

She licks her full lips. "This may sound strange, but I like to believe I've lived a lot of lifetimes before this one."

What the fuck is she talking about? "Oh?"

"I don't know if brunch is the right time to delve into the deeper meaning behind karma and reincarnation," she says softly, another shrug following her smooth as fuck response. "But I promise you, I will leave you a little more enlightened than when I found you."

Something about that answer makes my entire body flush with heat. I'm thankful my hair is pulled back because my first instinct is to hide behind it or fidget with it, run my hands through it, or rip it all out because *what the fuck is going on with me?*

"Can I ask you something?"

I cannot find my voice. I couldn't if someone paid me to. I can only nod.

"Will you do dinner with me?"

No. No. *No, I will not.* I can't. I cannot tell Harriet not to mess around with Judy and then go to dinner with Sunny. That's not fair. "Yes," I say softly. *Goddammit.* I'm such a hypocrite. Harriet will murder me. The number of times I told her to stop messing around with guests, and now, here I am. But wait…I don't plan on messing around with Sunny, do I? This is only a strange attraction. I don't want to kiss her or have sex with her. Do I?

Harriet pulls Sunny's attention away with a question. As nonchalantly as possible, I study her, her lips, the way she speaks, the way she licks her lips before she answers Harriet's questions and looks at the sky as if the answer is floating around in the ether, and she needs to grab the words and polish them up before responding. She is a cool breeze on a hot day. She is the embodiment of warmth at the same time. And I want to learn from her. Her who is half my age. Her who is nothing at all like what I thought would startle me awake after all these years. And I don't mean since Paul passed. I'm talking about in my entire life. Wow. That's a long time to have been asleep. And here I am thinking that Sunny Micha is my alarm clock? That's dramatic.

"Okay," she says as she nudges my leg under the table. "Back to business. Do you want to meet me or…"

"Can you come to me?" I'm trying to be quiet. "I can cook for you."

"Oh?" Sunny smiles. "I can do that. Yeah."

"Great."

Great.

Fuck.

Harriet is going to murder me.

Maybe it's time for me to stop fearing the what-ifs and immerse myself in the what is. I am in need of a change, after all. I have been for quite some time. Sunny Micha may not be the answer, but she seems to have the study guide to the test. It can't hurt to get outside myself, to figure out what has been happening inside myself, to take a second and relax into this place.

I hope this doesn't backfire.

CHAPTER TWELVE

Eleanor

Being told by the woman I can't stop harboring feelings for that the *other* woman who broke my heart deserves forgiveness is quite the blow. There are moments in life when I wonder if I'm being punked. The last twenty-four hours has been one long string of those moments.

And now, as I stand next to Mabel and she signs consent forms for the mountain bikes we'll take on the trails, the only thing I can think is that this is going to end poorly. Not that I'll fall off the bike because of my clumsiness; that doesn't scare me. It's all these emotions and feelings coming back to haunt me after years and years of getting over them.

After years and years of *burying* them because I never got over them if they're—*she's*—still affecting me.

Mabel is finishing the paperwork after getting the entire explanation from the excursion staff. Erica and Thomas know who she is, so they go above and beyond. I'm proud of them. As director of events, excursions fall under my realm. Hearing them being overly hospitable with guests makes me beam with pride.

"If you have on shoes that tie, please make sure to tuck your shoelaces. We don't want them to get wound up on the pedal," Erica explains. "It's happened way more times than you'd ever think possible."

Mabel scoffs. "Yeah, I learned my lesson at a young age, didn't I, Ellie?" The memory of a twelve-year-old Mabel getting her shoelaces caught in her bike on the way to the ice cream shop floods my mind. I haven't thought about that day in forever. Hell, I haven't thought about her in forever. These memories are starting to take a toll on me, leaving me breathless and aching, like I'm running a marathon. "Thank goodness you were there to help me."

"Ms. Fitz, you and this nice lady go way back, eh?"

I perk at my name. "I'm sorry?"

"You know her? Like, you two went to school together?"

I force a smile and try to remain professional. "Yep, sure did."

"That's awesome. I bet you have some really great stories about Ms. Fitz, don't you?"

Mabel nudges me with her elbow. It's gentle, and for some reason, it calms me. I don't want it to calm me. I want it to piss me off. But, *sigh*, it doesn't. "Yes, yes, I do."

"There will be no telling of stories, children." I roll my eyes, wave off Erica and Thomas's laughter, and head over to the equipment garage where Andrew is waiting. He's just as thorough as he explains the bikes, as if we have never ridden before, and even goes so far as to remind us not to use the front brake when going downhill.

"You'll flip right over the handlebars. Trust me. It doesn't feel good," Thomas says while rubbing his shoulder.

"He flipped the other day," I explain, and Mabel's eyes widen. "It was funny once I found out he was okay."

After we each secure our helmets, I glance at Mabel, at the way the black helmet can barely contain her auburn hair, and something inside me shifts. She's focusing on getting the strap on the helmet adjusted. I want to help. I want to stop her, tell her I got it, and *help*…But I don't. I can't. I'm frozen in place and time, as if I'm still the embarrassed high schooler who's brokenhearted and humiliated.

"You ready?"

She doesn't answer, but she mounts her bike and gives me a thumbs-up. I take off toward the best trail for biking. It's paved part of the way and a little dicey in a couple areas, but overall, it's perfect, especially for a novice.

It's also hard to have a conversation when mountain biking. That is the only thought that keeps me balanced. I'm going to be leading, her following, and me hoping she doesn't try to discuss anything. I'm doing this because I'm trying to be the gracious host. That's it.

Strangely enough, this is exactly how we were in school. I led, she followed, and I hoped every single day that she didn't try to discuss anything. She was as nervous as I was back then. It was easier for us to solely exist side by side, on the school bus, on the playground, eventually in high school, in band, in drama, in speech and debate, in my bed, in hers...

I hope she knows better now, but who knows? She's been pretty brave so far. It's not out of the realm of possibility that she'll continue that trend.

Do I know better now? Doesn't fucking seem like it, does it? My brain seems ready to forget the heartache she caused, and my heart seems ready to forget the anxiousness she *is* causing.

After about twenty minutes of climbing, the trail flattens out, and it's not as uphill and difficult. I glance over my shoulder, expecting to see her lagging, but she's keeping up. I'm impressed. The altitude normally winds people who aren't from around here, but she's doing great. There's a scenic overlook on the right, so I ride over and stop. It provides an amazing view of the entire property. Definitely something she should see. I slide my pack from my back and pull my camera from the case. The quick look through the viewfinder practically takes my breath away. This place is beautiful. I wonder how we got this lucky with the property. The price was a steal, and after the old owner's widow met the three of us, the sale happened immediately, especially when we told her our plans. Her name was Mary, and she was wonderful to us. Her kind heart is part of the reason we often think everything happens for a reason.

Mabel pulls up next to me, steadies herself, feet on the ground, and starts to drink from her CamelBak. Sweat is rolling down over the side of her face to her jaw, down her neck, to the band of her black sports bra under her light pink tank top. She managed to pull her hair into a messy braid over her shoulder. It's much longer than it was when we were in school, but the color is exactly the same, and it reminds me of happier times. Times when we used to laugh so hard our sides ached, and the only scars we had were from bike rides and not broken hearts.

I pull my camera up and casually find her through the viewfinder. She's staring over the valley, sun glistening on her sweat, and I snap a picture. She doesn't budge, as if she's used to being the object of someone's obsession. Her comfort makes me self-conscious. I'm giving in way too quickly.

I hate how much I still want her, even through all the shit that happened and regardless of all the time that has passed. Most people wouldn't want to relive their high school years, but I'd give anything to turn back time and have those stolen moments together again. In my bedroom, under the blankets, giggling, holding hands, kissing, discovering what we both loved and hated. She didn't seem to hate anything we did, though. And I loved her so very much.

"God, it's gorgeous." She's breathing heavy but nothing crazy. Just enough that the rise and fall of her chest is mesmerizing. "I knew Colorado was going to take my breath away, but damn. It's more than I imagined."

I'm frozen. For the first time ever, my heart is holding me back, and my brain is the body part not cooperating.

"Everything about this place suits you."

I should say that I agree. Because I do. I may miss Chicago, but the calmness of these mountains is part of why I've been able to get a handle on my depression, my anxiety, my inability to love myself. But I can't answer. The blue of her eyes is too, too much, and her smooth voice is too, too much, and if I have to look at the sweat glistening on her shoulders for one more second, I may have a full-blown panic attack. I make myself look completely away, over the scenery, the mountains, the valley, the green of spring before summer's drought robs everything of its lushness. I snap another picture before I put my camera away, occupying my hands because otherwise, she'll be able to see their slight shake.

"Ellie?"

"What?" I'm working overtime to avoid eye contact. When we were younger, her eyes grounded me, calmed me, but right this second, they will be the death of me.

"I am so very sorry. For everything."

"Mabel," I say and groan. This is the last fucking discussion I want to have. Or maybe I do? I can't decide, which is also infuriating. A part of me wants to yell and scream at her and tell her how badly she fucked me up. And another part, albeit small, wants to act as if I have recovered and barely remember what happened. "We do not need to rehash the past."

"Yes, Eleanor, we do." She dismounts, kickstand down in an instant, and comes to stand in front of me with the front tire of my bike between her legs. She wraps her hands around the handlebars. My gaze is pulled to her hands, to the white knuckles. She's not wearing any jewelry. Something about her hands naked like that makes my knees weak. "I fucked up by telling him anything about you...without also telling him about me."

My heart is begging me to look at her, but I can't. I won't.

"And Bobby and I didn't work. We married and divorced almost in the same year, but you were gone, and I couldn't…I couldn't bring myself to admit I was wrong." She stops talking, and her hand is on my face, then two fingers on my jaw. "Look at me, please."

I can't. I won't.

"Ellie, please." The pressure is gentle, but it's pressure, and I crumble too easily under pressure, especially when it comes from her, so I give in. "I didn't tell everyone about you. I promise. I didn't find out who did until a few years later, but I swear to God, it wasn't me."

"Stop."

"I will not."

"I don't care what happened." The lie burns my tongue as it escapes into the space between us.

"You do care, though." She smiles, a smile that is sad and knowing, and it makes me angry that all these years have passed, and she still fucking knows me. I thought I had changed. I thought I had left parts of me to die in the past. "And I care so much about you. I did then. I do still."

"I'm glad you *care* about me."

"You are such a stubborn ass."

"I am? What about you, Mabel, hmm? You admitted that you never told me the truth because you couldn't admit you were wrong. Sounds pretty fucking stubborn to me. And petty, to be honest." I jerk my face away and dismount. I walk away after propping the bike up with the kickstand.

"Don't you think it's petty to still be so hurt over something I did in high school? In high school, Eleanor." She's standing next to me now. As if I need her to be close to actually hear her. "I was young and stupid and scared. Can you please see that? I was frightened. Of my feelings for you, of my lack of feelings for Bobby, and it snowballed, and that was it. I wish you could see that. I wish you could stop acting like I wanted to hurt you."

"But you still hurt me."

She sighs. "I'm sorry about that. I am. I don't…I don't know what else to say. I was hurt, too, though. You don't seem to care about that."

"Pfft. Why the hell were you hurt?"

"Are you kidding me? You are kidding, right?"

"No, Mabel, tell me. Why the hell were you hurt?"

"Because I loved you, Eleanor. And I was so scared that I broke you instead of being honest with my family, with myself. God. Ellie. I just…I was eighteen."

She's right. Goddammit, I hate when she's right. But being right can't be all that matters, can it? Right or not, she still fucking hurt me. And I cannot let an *I was so young* argument make it all better. Or can I? Because life is too short, and I'm getting too old, and shouldn't I be letting go of all these fucks I seem to give?

Suddenly, she laughs. It's small, and it really has no place in this conversation, but for some reason, it fits. The same way we fit all those years ago. "Will you please admit that you still have feelings?"

It's my turn to laugh. "You're out of your goddamn mind."

"Well, y'know what? I do. And I'm not ashamed to admit it. I'll shout it from this mountain if you need me to."

My mouth drops, and I gape at her looking out over the valley, over the resort, chest puffed with determination. And I'm slip, slip, slipping down the mountain of my hatred, right back into her, into this, whatever this is between us that has never gone away. How can so many years pass, and all of this still exists?

"I think I always have. It took me a long time to understand that what we had when we were young, when we were in fucking high school"—she huffs—"was the most important relationship I have *ever* had." She closes her eyes, pulls a breath into her lungs, and holds it for what seems like forever. "I've never been able to replicate it. Those feelings."

It takes me a couple seconds to finally realize why none of my relationships ever worked. Why I held on to an attraction to Olive for way too long. Why my marriage ultimately failed. Why nothing has ever worked the way I wanted. "We've both changed a lot since then, Mabes."

She nods, her eyes still closed. "But we're both the same." Her eyes open. "Aren't we?"

"But I hate you," I say softly.

"I know you do."

"Why are you doing this to me?"

"The same reason you've haunted every single one of my thoughts for as long as I can remember." She chuckles. "I guess I'm returning the favor."

I look away, to my feet, to my legs, to make sure they're still there because I cannot feel them.

"Listen," she starts, then lets out a low groan. "I did not plan on running into you here. I was as surprised as you were. But I will say this, with all the certainty in my world, I have been trying to find the right time to look you up, to tell you how sorry I am, to tell you that I fucked up. Life has always gotten in my way. And fear. Fear that you'd never forgive me, so why even try? But seeing you…Ellie, I'm done trying to hide who I am."

"And who are you?" I find my courage. "Hmm? Who are you, Mabel Sommers?"

"You really want to know?"

"I do," I whisper.

"I'm a lesbian, Ellie." She pushes out a little grunt. "God, it's so hard to say but feels so good once I do it. And"—she pauses—"I'm in love with you. Still. Always. Seeing you again…" She pulls in a sharp breath, and her eyes fill with tears. "You still have this." And she places her hand over her heart.

Fuck. How do I tell her that she had all of me before she broke me? How? How do I tell her it's too fucking late, and I'm beyond repair now? That we are beyond repair? I want to scream at her. I want to tell her to leave me alone. But most of all, I want to tell her that I still love her, too, and all of this is too fucking scary to comprehend.

"Please don't lock me out. Give me a chance." Her trembling hand is the only indication of nerves.

"A chance? For what?"

Mabel shrugs. "To fix everything I did wrong? To make it up to you? To tell you everything that has happened since high school? I don't know, Ellie. I…I want to fix this." She motions between us. "To fix us." She breathes deep before she lets out a loud "I am in love with Eleanor" into the valley.

As fast as humanly possible, I have my hand over her mouth. "Stop, oh my God, stop."

She's chuckling, and it fills my heart. "I told you I'd shout it from the mountain."

"How do you know I'm not in a relationship?"

Her face falls. "I didn't…Oh God, I didn't even think…Wow. What is wrong with me? Why wouldn't you be in a relationship? I mean, look at you."

That comment makes me feel good because, *yeah, look at me.* I have leveled up since high school. I am finally beautiful. Even when I don't feel it or believe anyone who tells me. I figured out makeup and my hair, and I take care of my skin, and I know how to dress, and I stopped fucking caring what other people think about me. I look back at the young girl I was in high school, so nervous and afraid of what was happening inside my body. I want to hug her and tell her that it'll be okay. That one day, she'll look at herself in the mirror and feel good. I wait a couple seconds, let the embarrassment flood Mabel before I start to laugh. "I mean, I'm not in a relationship. No worries."

She gasps and smacks me on the arm. "You jerk."

"You sort of deserved that."

"I did. You're right."

She leans into my shoulder again. Her skin is very warm from the sun. I'm going to regret this. I can tell. There are warning flags and past experiences and those damn memories shouting at me to *stop, apply the brakes, for God's sake!* But the part of me that wants to get past *everything* tells me maybe it's okay to have some regrets, to ignore the flags, to speed around the corners of whatever is happening. What's not okay is to never do anything because I would regret that even more.

After we came back down the trail and turned everything in, I felt a mixture of every single emotion. I was having a hard time trying to process. It was like my worst nightmare. I've put a lot of thought into what would happen if I had the opportunity to stand up to her. In every single reenactment, it never happened like this. I'm always screaming and telling her how much I hate her for ruining my life, for making me feel like something is wrong with me, for choosing a boy over everything but especially over our friendship. And she cries, and I feel good about myself because finally, I'm able to get it off my chest. And I have closure, and I'm on cloud nine, head high, nothing in the world getting in my way.

But that was not at all how it happened, and my brain has been playing catch-up with my heart ever since. And I'm spent. Truly and utterly spent. I could blame the ride because it was strenuous. But I've done that ride a hundred times, and at forty-seven, I'm in the best shape of my life. Even better shape than when I was seventeen and starting varsity volleyball and basketball and throwing in shot put and discus.

Jesus, I am such a lesbian. How did I not know that about myself sooner than the first time my lips touched Mabel's?

Sitting and poring over the latest marketing plan is the only thing I can think to do to try to occupy my mind.

And big surprise, it is not working.

At all.

Every time I read a line, my brain zips right to Mabel telling me she's a lesbian, too. That she's in love with me, still. And that she wants to fix us.

I stare across my office, out the window, and chuckle. "How the fuck did this happen?" My voice sounds loud in my office, even over the radio. *Gotta stay guarded, Ellie.* I have to figure out a way to keep this wall up that I have taken an insane amount of time and effort and hate-filled confrontational reenactments to build. Piece by piece, every single brick started with Mabel. Even my divorce ultimately stemmed from my inability to get over her.

I am so confused and worried, and my anxiety is off the fucking charts. My heart hasn't stopped fluttering like one of our many hummingbirds since the second I laid eyes on Mabel. And now? *Christ.* That hummingbird might as well be on a full cup of coffee.

"Hey, Eleanor?" Keri is standing in my doorway, hands on her hips.

"Hey there, what's up?"

"You have someone here to see you. I know you said no visitors, but she's pretty…um…bitchy." She whispers the last part, and I can't stop my chuckle.

"Well, great." I look at myself, at my workout apparel. "Send her in, I guess." Why the hell do I have a visitor? "Wait, Keri, who is it?"

"One of the VIP threesome ladies."

Mabel. *Shit.* "What the fuck?"

"Do you still want me to send her back?"

"Sure." Send her back. Send back the one person I do not want to see as I'm sitting here freaking out about her. Sounds like a fabulous idea. Add salt to my wounds. I wish I was an oracle or something so I could see the future and know whether I'm going to survive all this. I hate surprises. I'm one hundred percent the person who looks up spoilers for TV shows and reads the last page of the book before I start. I want to know. I've had enough heartache in my life that if I can spare it now, I'm going to do it.

Of course, *The Handmaid's Tale* is still my favorite book. And that book is one heartache after another. And the same with *The Seven Husbands of Evelyn Hugo*, my other favorite. Hmm, maybe I enjoy heartache more than I think. I'm a masochist. Perfect.

I go over to the door, peek out. It's not Mabel. It's Judy, and my anxious brain flips a U-turn and starts freaking out about everything in a different capacity. And I have no idea why. Catastrophic thinking is my best friend, apparently.

"Hi, Eleanor. I'm sorry for barging in here. And being pushy. Your front desk clerk was probably ready to throttle me. But I need to speak with you."

Oh, yes, pushy is the word she used. "Okay."

"Do you mind if we chat? I have...I..." She's fumbling all over herself, and it makes her sort of...endearing? "I want to chat. And I'm not sure who to chat with."

"Chat?"

She sighs. "I'm messing this up, aren't I?"

"You're fine," I say. "Settle down and come in." We sit opposite each other on the couch and chair. Patience is not my strongest suit, and I realize I'm bouncing my foot.

"Are you from Chicago, too?"

"Mm-hmm." I cross my legs.

She motions to the Griswold jersey hanging on the wall behind me. "That is worth a pretty penny."

I don't respond. She's not looking for a response.

"And that Cubs picture of the sign after they won the World Series? That's such a great shot."

"Thank you. I actually took that."

"You did?"

I continue to observe her observing me through the story my office tells. My skin is crawling. I don't like being under a microscope. Ever. But I don't know how to speed up this conversation without sounding as bitchy as I'm sure she sounded earlier. What is it about this weekend that has us all acting like we've recently discovered the most ridiculous things about ourselves? Before she leans back into the chair, she removes her over-the-shoulder bag. She starts wringing her hands, which is only causing me to be more nervous. "Judy?"

"Yeah?"

"You wanted to chat?"

"God, yeah," she says, followed by a soft groan. She looks a little older than me. Maybe early fifties. She's striking, and even though I can tell she's seen some stress in her life, she has this aura that screams, *I'm ready to take a motherfucking breath.* I see why Harriet is taken by her. She pushes her fingers through her bobbed, wavy blond hair. It messes her bangs up, but she doesn't seem to mind. "I have a couple things to talk about."

"I don't want to sound rude, but you're really freaking me out."

She sighs. "I'm sorry. I knew I shouldn't have done this, but I can't talk to Mabel, and Sunny is, well, out there, flitting around like the free spirit she is." She groans, a grimace forming on her face. "But I think I might be developing feelings for Harriet, and I think maybe you can see it, and I'm worried, and I don't know what to do."

I push out a chuckle that is drenched in relief. "Christ," I say and breathe out all the stress I was clenching between my teeth.

"I'm sorry."

"First of all, please stop apologizing." I go to my small refrigerator and grab two White Rascal Ales. "Second, have a beer and try to relax."

She takes it, and her shoulders slump. "Thank you." She opens and sips in one fluid movement, as if it's a magical courage elixir. "I needed this."

"Same here." I laugh again. "Now, tell me what's going on."

"Okay, so…" She pauses. "Wait, are you busy? Do you even have time for this?"

"I'm gonna kill you."

It's her turn to laugh, and she nods. "Sorry." She shakes her head. "I'm having all these feelings for Harriet, and I don't know what to think or how to feel about it all."

"Are you straight?"

"No, not at all."

"Then what's the problem?"

"I don't normally do the whole one-night stand thing." Judy sighs, then drinks again. She tells me how good the beer is before she adds, "I'm not in a great spot for a fling."

"That makes sense why you'd be nervous, then." I lean back on the couch, pull my legs up, and stretch them out. My knee and ankle pop. I am getting so old.

"When I was married to a man, I fell for this younger woman who I mentored. She was lovely and wanted me to run away with her, but I have kids, and that wasn't feasible. So I stayed. And at the time, I was also fighting feelings for my best friend and neighbor. Then her husband died, and I thought, maybe I'll finally work up the courage to tell her. And then I found out she was dating a woman, and the woman ended up being the same one I had my original affair with."

I blink once, twice, three times before I ask, "What?" Is there something about me that says, *please tell me all your secrets?*

"It sounds convoluted."

"It sounds like a movie to me. How the hell did you handle all that?"

"Oh, I didn't. I hit on Pam and tried to ruin their relationship, and it was the most ridiculous thing I've ever done." Her head is down, her voice shaking. "So very stupid. I was a mess, Eleanor. A hot, hot mess."

"Then what?"

She takes another drink, then wipes her lips. She's growing on me. In a good way. And I'm happy I'm not the only hot mess at this resort. Or in my office. "I ended up divorcing Tom. He was strangely okay with everything. My lawyer said it was one of the most amicable divorces he's ever handled."

"Must have meant it was truly over, hmm?"

She nods. "I dated this woman, Sydney, off and on for a while. She was lovely, but I was offered a job in LA, and she didn't want to go. I moved, and Tom was okay with me taking the kids."

"How old?"

Her eyes soften, and the smile that spreads across her lips is obviously one she reserves for her children. "One is in college, one is getting ready to go to college, and the other is starting high school."

"Man, you were busy."

"Yeah, I guess so."

"What's the problem now?"

"I'm afraid I'm going to fall for her."

"In five days?"

Her eyes start to fill with tears. "Yes."

"Wow."

"Yeah."

I gather all the wisdom I have. It's not much, but I feel like I know Harriet better than most. "Let me give you some advice. Harriet is a complicated woman. She has never…man, how do I say this without it sounding awful? She hasn't settled down until recently. She is constantly moving, like a shark."

"That sounds terrifying."

"No, no." I wave a hand. "I don't mean—*ugh*—that's not what I mean. She's not one who has relationships. I'm not saying she never will, and between you and me, she has always been a little like a player. But—and I mean this—she has been in a different spot in the last year or so." Judy is hanging on every word, as if at any second, I'm going to say something that will send her running for the mountains.

She blinks a few times, then her mouth pops open. "That's it?"

"Yeah, I guess so." I feel bad. "I know you're looking for some sort of sign, right? I wish I could point at something and be, like, 'There it is. The sign you are looking for.' But Harriet is not that person."

"That's not really advice."

It's as if she's reading my mind. "Okay, what about this: enjoy the ride because we are all searching for something. She is. You are. Hell, even I am. So keep your eyes open and go with the flow."

"That's…that's exactly what I was looking for."

"Was it?"

"I would have rather you said that she's head over heels for me, so go for it, but that's not realistic, is it?"

"I'm sorry. It might not end how you're hoping, but I don't know. No one knows what the future holds. But we all know what's in our hearts, don't we?" I swing my legs around and plant my feet on the floor. "If you can handle anything other than falling in love, then maybe it's worth a shot? Even if you just have some fun."

Her expression brightens. "I could try that." She lifts her beer to me as if to offer a toast. "Thanks."

I clink mine against hers, and she drinks. "Is that really all you came to chat with me about?" I may be an anxious mess most of the time, but I can read people's energy. She has something else she wants to say.

"Well, I mean, also Mabel."

"I had a feeling."

"Please be careful with her."

My gut reaction is to be a complete dick and say something like, *me be careful with her?* But I don't. "Any particular reason other than hurting her would be awful?"

"She's…" Judy stops, seemingly to gather words. "She's not nearly as put together as she lets on."

"Okay."

"And she hasn't shut up about you since we became friends forever ago."

I'm intrigued. "Oh?"

She nods. "I feel like you're the one who got away."

"She pushed me away."

Judy shrugs. "No one is perfect." She's right, and all I can do is stare. "Well, I'll get out of your hair." She stands and grabs her bag. "Thank you for this. I didn't think you'd allow me to word vomit all over, but you did, and I cannot tell you how grateful I am."

I walk her to the door. "You're welcome. And if you need any more chats, I'll be around."

She leaves, her head much higher than it was when she arrived. I hope I didn't say too much about Harriet. It's nothing she wouldn't say about herself. Either way, I'm nervous that maybe I should have kept my mouth shut. There's something about helping other women not get their hearts broken that speaks to me, though. Must be my love of spoilers.

CHAPTER THIRTEEN

Harriet

Being interviewed is one of the few things in this world I don't particularly love. There's something so impersonal about the process, which should be the opposite. But it's not. At least in my limited knowledge, they haven't been personal. Maybe I should be happy about that. I don't exactly love sharing the deep side of myself. I'm a surface person. What you see is what you get. Sure, I have feelings, thoughts, and a heart, but I want to be as authentic as possible. If that means I don't hold back, and I say things I shouldn't, or I always keep my feelings intact, well, that's just the way it is.

When Olive first told Eleanor and me that we would have a journalist here to do a story on the sanctuary, I thought she meant some small-time person who worked for a tiny news outlet. We've had those types here already. I'm prepared for them.

But no. This one is big-time. Even more big-time than the interview I did for the *Foodie's Delight* magazine. That was one of the few times I let a little more of myself show than normal, which made sense since cooking is where I bare my soul.

Mabel Sommers, as big-time as she seems, is for sure one of those journalists who is going to scrape the surface. Sure, she writes for *On the Verge*, and that is a great magazine with a lot of very talented writers. But come on. She's a white LA journalist who broke my best friend's heart when she was a young thing, and now she's gonna come in here and want to write some exposé about the sanctuary? Hell to the no.

Needless to say, as I'm tying my apron in the restaurant kitchen, I'm also trying to keep my skepticism reined in. Mabel requested my specialties. I told her, "Everything is a specialty." Anytime I can toot my own horn, I'm one hundred percent going to. I don't need a long, drawn-out invitation. At the end of the day, I love to show off.

"What are you going to make for me?"

She's sitting on a stool, out of my way but close enough that she can see everything I'm doing. Through all my suspicion, I can see why Eleanor is still taken by her, even if she doesn't want to admit it. Mabel is beautiful. She is unique looking, with beautiful blue eyes and auburn hair, which does not fall into the category of *Eleanor's type*. It makes sense now that she chases blondes because the two women who have effectively stopped her in her tracks are both brunettes: Olive and Mabel.

I want to shake her some days and tell her to get the hell over Olive. Then I heard about Mabel, and I wanted to shake her even more. But now, as I'm looking at this woman, I want to know why the fuck she broke my best friend. There are two sides to every story. I'm sure she has one.

"Prosciutto-wrapped shrimp skewers with lobster risotto and grilled teriyaki filet tips with pancetta-wrapped asparagus on a bed of ramen noodle *aglio e olio*."

Her eyebrows rise, and I'm pleased with the menu I've prepared.

I get started, skillet on the stove to sauté onions and garlic for the risotto. Once the onions are translucent, I toss in a healthy spoonful of garlic and cook the heat out of it. It smells delightful. I pour the arborio rice into the sauté pan and expertly flip it, allowing it to brown nicely with the onions, garlic, and butter. Once it's ready, I pour pinot gris over it and let it simmer until the wine has almost evaporated. I ladle a few spoons of my signature vegetable stock into the mixture. As the risotto simmers, I slice the cooked lobster into hearty pieces and wait a few minutes for it to be completely ready.

Now it's time to prepare the steak, and the grill is piping hot. I use tongs to spread the marinated filet onto it, watching as the fire starts to lick it.

My mouth is watering. I hope Mabel's is, as well.

After three minutes on the one side, I flip the steak. I want it to be medium-rare when I pull it off, then it can rest and cook to a medium temperature. A couple more minutes...I squeeze the meat with the tongs. "Perfect." I pull the meat from the heat and plate it, placing a precut piece of foil over the top.

I pre-wrapped the asparagus with the pancetta and the prosciutto-shrimp skewers, so I pop them from the fridge under the counter and place the asparagus on the grill. I do the same with the shrimp. I don't want either to get away from me. After a quick check on the risotto, which is ready, I stir in the lobster and freshly grated Romano cheese, then place a nice serving on the middle of one of our square plates.

The shrimp skewers are ready. I place them gingerly on top of the risotto. I made a lovely tomato-basil cruda earlier for the finish. I spoon it over the top, wipe the plate, then place it in front of Mabel. I spin and grab the bowl of ramen noodle *aglio* I made earlier. I take the steak, slice it, then plate it on top of the noodles, as well. I use the juice from the drippings and drizzle it over the meat, which adds an amazing teriyaki juiciness to the noodles that have garlic and olive oil already all over them. Then I place the pancetta-wrapped asparagus over the top. I wipe the bowl, impressed with my presentation, and place it in front of Mabel, too.

"Wow."

"Thank you."

"You are very impressive to watch." She picks up her fork. "May I?"

"Absolutely."

She removes a shrimp from the skewer and takes a bite. From the pop the shrimp makes, I can tell that they're perfect. "Holy shit," she says around a mouthful, her hand over her mouth. "This is incredible."

"Try the risotto."

She takes a healthy forkful, a piece of lobster perched on top of the creamy risotto. She places it in her mouth and chews, chews, then swallows. She does it again. Chews, chews, swallows. Then again. When she's done, she lets out a crazed cackle. "I am in love."

"Try the other dish."

She shakes her head. "No. I want to eat all of this."

"No, no. That's not how this goes."

She grumbles. "Fine." She cuts the asparagus in the bowl, then takes a couple pieces along with a piece of steak and a forkful of ramen. When she places it in her mouth, she closes her eyes, and the moan she releases could be easily misconstrued. "Ermygosh," she says, her mouth still mostly closed. I start to laugh as I watch her swallow, then load up another forkful. "This is incredible."

"Thank you."

"You're good. Like, really, *really* good." She takes a bite of the ramen and steak, again closing her eyes and moaning. "I can't get over how good this is."

"Ramen isn't only for poor college kids."

"That's for sure. Goddamn." She takes another bite. There's something genuinely satisfying about watching someone enjoy the food I've prepared. It's not erotic, but God, sometimes it's borderline. I can't put a name on it. I feel accomplished. Like I'm flying high, and nothing can bring me down. "Where did you learn to cook like this?"

Oh yeah, the interview. *Ugh.* "My grandmother was probably my most prolific teacher. I learned every dish she made by the time I was ten. And then culinary classes. And for a while, I lived at home after college and made my mom whatever she wanted."

"What is your favorite thing to cook?"

"Probably breakfast. I don't know why, but it's very calming for me. I think maybe because it's, like, the easiest thing to make. I can't fuck it up. But it's also what you cook for someone you're hoping to impress." I realize I've said too much. I wave my hands. "Off the record."

She laughs while holding another forkful of risotto. "This isn't that kind of interview, Harriet. I'm truly interested." She eats. "And I'm not letting any of this go to waste."

"You're a trip. You know that?"

She nods enthusiastically.

"Can I ask you a question?"

"As long as I can answer between bites."

"Okay," I say, followed by a chuckle. "This may sound weird or forward, and maybe you don't even want to talk about it, but, like"—I lean into the counter with my hip and fold my arms—"can you tell me your side of what happened between you and Eleanor? Like, between you and me and the food." I motion to the food, and she swallows what's in her mouth in a very cartoonish way. All that was missing was the *gulp* sound.

"Yeah, so…" she starts, fidgeting with her fork. "I guess you could say…" And she flips the fork across the kitchen. She gasps. "Oh, for fuck's sake. I'm an idiot."

I let out a whooping sound that is so loud, Glenda peeks her head around the corner of the office. "Everything okay?" she asks.

"Yes, yes, everything is fine." I pull a fork from the holder next to the shelves and hand it over. "You okay?"

She nods. "You want me to be honest?"

"Has anyone ever answered that with 'no, please lie to me'? Seriously?"

She shakes her head. "I was afraid of being a lesbian. I chose a safe boy over her and completely cut her out of my life, then that boy, along with a few other people, ended up telling everyone about her being a lesbian, and the entire school ostracized her."

"Fuck."

"Yeah, not my proudest shining-star moment. That's for sure." She sighs, and her shoulders fall. "I hate myself for doing that to her. I lost a lot of time with her because I was a fucking scaredy-cat." After a couple of deep breaths, she finishes with, "I'm the one who's supposed to be asking you questions like this."

"The revealing questions that make you feel like shit? No, thank you." We both let out light chuckles, completely in agreement. "She's fine now. You know that, right?"

"I do. We talked." The straight face she's trying to hide is telling.

"Everything went well?"

She nods.

"Great."

"Now, my turn."

"Fine."

"Tell me what is going on with you and Judy."

Well. Didn't expect that. I open my mouth to say something, but I'm speechless. "Um…"

"Yeah, that's what I thought."

"No, I mean, nothing." My voice cracks. *Christ.* I clear my throat. "Nothing is going on."

"It's good to know that the three of you are fantastic business-women but horrendous liars." She smiles, her eyes twinkling.

The black floor mat is all of a sudden very interesting. I take a deep breath. "I don't know what's going on." My fear of being too transparent has me frozen. "I like her, though. She's…" I shrug. "She sort of flipped my world upside down."

"She does have a way of doing that to people."

Mabel's simple shrug and tone of voice is intriguing. "What do you mean?"

"She breezes into your life, and the aura that surrounds her is truly remarkable. She is sunlight and happiness personified."

"Wow."

"Yeah." Mabel picks up her water, but before she sips it, she says, "Don't you fucking hurt her, or I'll murder you with one of your own kitchen knives."

"Ditto with Eleanor."

"Deal." She extends her hand, an olive branch level truce, and I accept. Then we continue our conversation as she finishes most of both meals. She can put the food away. She's so thin. I wonder what she does to work off those calories.

❖

Before I left the restaurant at seven, I checked in with the staff. Harmony was prepared, and Jessica was doing much better as the coordinator. Glenda was there, all smiles, of course, and Heidi was on her game. She made me a new drink. It was Absolut Vanilla, X-Rated vodka, strawberry puree, topped with champagne in a glass with a raw sugar rim. Beautiful and pink, she called it Escape.

"For Mother's Day," she said, kindness all over her face. "And we can use it again during October for Breast Cancer Awareness and donate all the profits to research."

"I love the way you think," I said before I left, carrying my drink and feeling better and lighter than I have in months.

While I was making sure all my ducks were in a row, I shot a text to Judy. I was hoping she'd respond, and maybe we could find a way to hang out. I check my phone as I'm walking to the residence and see that she finally responded.

I would love to get together. What time are you thinking?

I can visualize the way her eyebrows rise at the end of her question, and *fuck*, I am grinning. I can feel it in my cheeks. *Would eight work? I can whip us up something to eat.*

You want me to come to you then?

That's a loaded question. *Absolutely.*

I'll see you at eight.

My heart is fluttering, and I try to remember the last time I felt like this. I don't think I have ever felt like this before. There is something about the way Judy makes me feel that doesn't seem like it will ever be replicated. I should probably tell her that. I should tell her how I have never wanted to settle down before, and now I keep picturing myself with her in a week, in a month, in a year, and that is not normal for me. Will it freak her out to know this is all brand-new? Will it freak her out to know this isn't a fling?

Hell, it's freaking *me* out to know this isn't another notch in my headboard. I've never been in love. Not once. Not even when I was a kid trying to figure myself out. I don't know if that means something is wrong with me or not. I'm thirty-five and have never felt the rush of looking at the person I'm with and thinking I would die for them. Is love something I should have felt before?

Sex, on the other hand, I've obviously felt that before. Way too many times to count. I don't know what it is about her or why there is this pull to her, but it's causing me a lot of inner turmoil, and I wonder if this is worth it. All these feelings and shit? That's too much for me.

I mean, isn't it?

When I think about kissing her, though…

The feel of her lips and the way she was so sure of herself and the taste of her breath and tongue. Wow. I just…*wow*.

She is, by far, the most incredible person I have ever met. I want to know everything about her. I want to sit and talk to her for hours, days, *hell*, the rest of my life.

Once I get to the house, I go into the kitchen and pull the crab cakes I premade from the freezer. They pan-fry nicely, especially when frozen. They stay together better and don't dry out. I also throw a small frozen bag of the roasted red pepper sauce into a bowl with water to defrost. I'll serve them with a small arugula, roasted mushroom, and truffle oil salad, and it'll be delicious. I am giddy with excitement as I fly up the stairs to change.

Olive said she was going to be working late, and Eleanor texted that she was going to meet Mabel for a drink, then added a rolling eyes emoji for good measure. There are moments in our friendship where I want to throttle her because she has this stubborn streak and holds grudges. She's such a Pisces, as she makes sure to remind us at all times. Artistic, funny, loves her naps, and will cut someone right out of her life if they become too much for her to handle.

In the time I've known her, she has cut out a couple people. The most notable was Natalie. But even then, she can't quite seem to get past it completely. On the one hand, she's easy to read; on the other hand, she's a mystery. Her even allowing Mabel to be near her is shocking. I want her to be careful, but I'm also glad she's going to try to forgive. Forgiveness is all we can control. And sometimes, it's the best thing we can do.

I take a look at myself in the mirror and lift my chin. I look good. Casual in jeans and a white T-shirt, but good. I want Judy to see that I'm easygoing and carefree and that I am ready and willing to see where this goes.

Hattie, come on, get your head in the game. It's too soon for those kinds of thoughts.

I have twenty minutes to start whipping together the impromptu dinner. I hope she enjoys it. The doorbell rings as I'm on my way to the kitchen. As I approach it, I take a deep breath and put on my best game face. "You got this." My whisper sounds loud, even over the volume of the music playing. Wait. I don't remember putting any music on.

Weird. I open the door and, "Sunny? What…what are *you* doing here?"

"Yeah, hi. I, um, I'm supposed to be meeting Olive?"

"Oh, you are, hmm?" What the actual fuck? Olive is meeting with Sunny? And I'm not allowed to do anything with Judy? I hear a small gasp behind me, a gasp that can only belong to… "Olive, Sunny has arrived." I'm glaring at her now, and she knows. Oh, she knows how mad I am.

"Sunny, hi," she says as she rushes up to us. Her voice is breathy, and she bounces on her toes a couple times like a teenager. "Come in."

"I had no idea you were using the house to entertain tonight since, y'know, you said you were working late in the office," I say.

"Can you please excuse us for one second?" Olive closes the door behind Sunny and ushers her to the kitchen. "I'll be right with you." She rushes back to me and pushes her hands frantically through her hair. "Hattie, please don't be angry with me."

"Too late."

"I'm a hypocrite."

"Ya sure are." I realize I'm tapping my foot when I hear the sound of it on the tile. "Can you explain to me how you can tell me to lay off Judy, but you're going to meet up with Sunny? I mean, seriously, explain it to me."

"Please keep your voice down." She wraps a hand around my wrist and pulls me outside on the patio. She's pleading with her eyes. "This is not like me, you know this. But there is this pull to her I haven't felt before, and I think I need to figure out what this means." She pauses, and her shoulders relax as if she's done fighting with me. "I didn't know what to do except to explore it."

It's hard to be mad at her after that explanation. "Why didn't you explain it like that to me instead of lying? You know you always get caught when you try to lie."

She shrugs.

"Olive, I am never going to be mad at you for following your heart. Or your vagina."

"Hattie, oh my God." Her words are whispered but she chuckles at the end.

"I'm serious. You've got to stop being closed up about what's going on inside you. Because lying to me? Of all people? Come on. Girl, that's dumb."

"God, I had this weird feeling you were going to find out."

"It's because I'm clairvoyant. You may be the mother figure, but I'm able to read you like a book." I fold my arms. "And you, you sneaky bitch, you were so nervous at brunch."

"Was I really? That's embarrassing."

"Well, I hate to break it to you, but you're going to have to share the kitchen."

"What? Why?"

"Because I invited Judy over."

"Hattie. I specifically told you that you're not allowed—"

I glare so hard that she immediately shuts up.

"I mean." She clears her throat. "That you are more than welcome to share the kitchen with me."

"That's what I fucking thought."

"Hattie, seriously, you're okay? You're not mad?"

"I'm not. But you've got to tell Eleanor because if you don't, Olive, I swear to God I will."

"I promise. I will." She pulls me into a hug. "What are you making for dinner?"

When I try to pull away to glare at her again, she holds on even tighter.

"I love you."

"Girl, you are very lucky that I love you, too."

When we walk back inside, I see Judy has arrived. The look on her face says she knows exactly how I'm feeling about the company. It'll be fine. We'll have a good time. But I wanted it to be just us. And after I see her in black jeans and a denim button-down, sleeves rolled, buttons unbuttoned just far enough, I am very sad that I won't be able to grab her and kiss her right then and there.

She seems a bit more nervous than normal as she swipes her bangs to the side. I want to ask if she's okay, does she want to talk, run away together, anything. I'd do it if she asked. She walks over and gives me a hug. "I see we have to keep our hands to ourselves?" Her whisper is perfection against my ear.

"Yeah, but damn," I say as I pull back to take her in. "You look fine as fuck." Her hair is pulled back, and I can't stop admiring the line of her jaw.

"So do you," she says softly. I won't last long without kissing her. I'm hoping Sunny and Olive find a way to get out of here.

"Don't you need to give Sunny a tour?" I ask.

Olive gets the hint and turns to Sunny. "Come on, I'll show you around."

And as soon as they're out of the kitchen, Judy has her hands on my face and is pulling me into her. Kissing her is becoming a drug. I cannot get enough of the taste of her lips and saliva and tongue. She is so fucking good at this. I want to ask how many people she has kissed, but that would mean I'd have to answer the same question, and I don't know if I even have an idea. It'd take some tallying, for sure. My twenties were wild.

When she releases my lips, she sighs. "I could do that all night."

"Fuckin' preach."

"Maybe we should cook, eat, and then go back to my room?" Her simple one-shoulder shrug is adorable. "Would that be something you'd be interested in?"

"Do we even need to cook and eat?"

"I'd love to say no, but I have a feeling you'd get into even more trouble. And"—she runs her hands up and down my arms—"I function better with food in me."

"Holy fuck."

"Come on." She pulls me to the island. She pushes her sleeves even farther up her arms. "I'll be your sous chef."

"Hottest sous chef I've ever had."

"Try to keep your hands to yourself." Judy winks before she goes to the sink and washes her hands. In that instant, she could literally do anything, say anything, and I'd be all in. I wish there was a way to explain to my own brain how it's possible to be enamored with someone this quickly. I need to stop questioning it. I need to go with the flow. I need to find a way to stop staring at Judy's ass in those black jeans, or I'm going to combust.

"Come over here and wash those hands." Her voice breaks into my dirty thoughts, and I clear my throat, do as she commands, and hope to God we move as perfectly together in the kitchen as we have since we met.

CHAPTER FOURTEEN

Olive

"Honestly, Sunny, I'm a giant hypocrite. I didn't tell them because I get on their cases about not sleeping with guests, and I knew they'd take it wrong."

Sunny's eyebrows rise. "You think we're going to sleep together?"

My entire body flushes, and I feel as if I'm going to faint. "Wait, no, that's not what I meant. I only meant that I don't like it when they fraternize."

"Mm-hmm."

"I promise. That's all I meant."

"Sure."

I playfully slap her arm. "I know how to put my foot in my mouth, don't I?"

Her lighthearted chuckle is charming. She places a hand on my back as we stand in the middle of the theater room. "May I ask what exactly it is you're looking for?"

"Ha!" I say and realize seconds later that she isn't joking. "Oh, you're serious?"

"Yes."

God, she's intense. "Y'know, the usual. Happiness, good friendships, a great bottle of wine." I force another laugh. "Um, yeah, so, I'm not," I let out a small groan, "uh, I'm not exactly sure…what I'm looking for."

"That's not a bad thing."

"I'm fifty years old, Sunny. I should know what the hell I'm looking for in life."

"Putting a time limit on things is a great way to drive yourself insane."

Her wisdom astounds me. "True. God, that is so true." Memories float around me, ones where I'm supposed to be happy, but I'm just not. "There are moments, especially recently, where I don't…actually know *who* I am." The way my heart sinks after the confession is almost too much for me. "Wow. I don't have any idea why I'm being this honest with you." It feels as if I've opened the floodgates. "I have to say this," I say softly. "I was married to a man for a very long time. And all throughout our marriage, I…" Words fail me as I look into her deep brown eyes.

"You what?" Sunny tucks my hair behind my ear, then trails her index and middle finger down my jaw to my chin. I lean into her touch, into the soft pads of her fingertips, into whatever is happening between us that is causing my mind, body, and heart to short-circuit.

"I have never shared it with anyone." My stomach is rolling, my palms are sweaty, and I realize yet again how powerful fear is.

"Not even your husband?"

"Especially not him."

"Are you sure you want to tell me?" She gives me a very small smile. "I don't want you to do anything you aren't ready for."

"That's just it," I say softly. "There's something about you that makes me feel safe."

"That's good news."

Maybe I should abort this mission? I can leave it at what I've already said and move on. There's nothing holding me back now, right? Except there is. And it's the same fear that has held me back my whole goddamn life. "I might as well spit it out. You see, I have never…that part of me, the drive, the desire…for, um, sex…it's never been there."

She places a hand on my arm. I can feel the heat radiating through my entire body. "You remind me of me."

Deflated. I feel deflated. "Sunny, I just shared something super intense about myself. You're…I mean, that's sweet of you to say, and I see what you're doing, but I'm not nearly as amazing and put together as you are."

She leans against the back of the row of theater chairs. "I'd like to tell you something. If you don't mind."

"Of course, please."

"It took me quite a few years to figure out what I want in a relationship, if I even wanted to have one. A lot of trials and tribulations and therapy, honestly. I finally figured out that I want that companionship. I want to be with someone. But I don't necessarily need to be with them. Do you know what I mean?"

"I understand." *No, you don't, Olive.* "I lied, I don't. What are you saying?"

Sunny's eyes lighten as she says, "I'm asexual. I meant that you remind me of me because I used to feel the same way before I figured myself out." She leans a little closer. "I wasn't trying to be sweet, although I do think you deserve the sweetness."

"Oh." My brain has stalled. What has happened? I went from being attracted to this woman, to understanding her on a weird level I didn't know existed, to being completely confused by her. "You're asexual?"

She nods.

"And you're saying you think maybe I am?"

"It's a possibility."

"But I like sex."

"So do I."

"I'm so confused."

Sunny's lighthearted laughter is perfectly timed. "Understandably so." She slides down the back of the chair to the floor, where she sits cross-legged and pats the spot in front of her. I let out a puff of air and do as requested. "Let me tell you a bit about me…"

Sunny launches into a history about her life, her love life, and the reasons she identifies as asexual. I am enthralled and hang on every single word she says. There's a realness about her in these moments, even more than before. It's as if she had a filter on her, and now, I'm seeing her as she's meant to be seen. No filter, no Photoshop, completely fresh. I'm moved by her. I'm moved by her ability to be emotional and caring and at the same time, truthful and raw.

"In the end, I know I want that romance and that push and pull of desire. But I don't need that physical connection." She has a hand on my knee when she finishes with, "You have all the answers. You just need someone to ask the questions."

"Well, shit." My voice comes out as a strained whisper. "Wow."

"Is this the first time you've thought about being asexual?"

I nod. "I guess I need to do some research, hmm?"

"Google is a great research partner." She places a hand on my cheek. "As am I."

"Yeah, I'm gonna have to research how to handle feelings like this first. I don't think you'll be able to help me with those."

"Listen, our bodies are complicated. Every person is different. And I think it's perfectly fine to take as long as you need to get to a point where you can figure it out, waiting until you're given the tools to understand why you feel certain things."

"Does this make you not want to talk to me anymore?"

She laughs, and it's such a lovely sound, one that calms me in a way I never expected. "On the contrary, my love. It makes me want to get to know you even more."

My love. My heart starts to race. "Really?"

"Absolutely." She cradles my face, her thumbs gently stroking my cheeks. "You tell me what you want, when you want it, and I'll do my best to accommodate your desires."

I lunge and wrap my arms around her, and she does the same. I don't know what any of this means or how to feel about it, about myself, about her. I'm glad I told her what I've been feeling. I still don't know what asexuality entails. Maybe I fall on some sort of spectrum? All I know is that I have been so afraid to say anything for so many years that finally getting it out in the open is like being able to breathe again.

Now I need to find a way to tell my friends.

❖

"Dinner was absolutely amazing, Hattie."

"Yeah, it did turn out, didn't it? Not bad for an impromptu dinner party." Harriet continues handing me plates, and I rinse them. "So." She clears her throat. "Sunny, hmm?"

I roll my eyes. "We already discussed this."

"I am simply happy to know you're not as straight as I thought you were. Or as straight as you said you were."

"I think I lean more toward bisexual than anything. I find the company of women far more enticing than men."

"Yeah, but there's like, the dick thing."

"Oh my word, Hattie."

"I'm only saying." She pushes playfully into my shoulder. "It's kinda fun to see you having a good time."

"Are you saying I wasn't having a good time before?"

"That's exactly what I am saying. Sure, occasionally, but joy never seemed to reach your eyes. Being happy about life has a way of affecting a person's entire being. But so does sadness."

I finish the final dish and close the dishwasher, letting her words wash over me. I don't want to react because *obviously* I've been sad. I lost my husband in a motorcycle accident. A motorcycle I told him he didn't need. A motorcycle he needed to wear a helmet with. A motorcycle that barely resembled a motorcycle in the end.

"Even if none of us has any success in the love department, at least we're getting back on the horse."

"Hattie?"

"Yes?"

"Did you ever get off the horse?"

"As a matter of fact, yes. I did." She leans against the concrete countertop and folds her arms. "I haven't slept with anyone in quite some time. I don't even remember the last time. That's how long ago it was."

"Hattie?"

"Yes?"

"Do you ever remember the last time?"

"Fuck you." She chuckles. "I am not heartless. I never wanted to be tied down...before. And now, things are different."

I lean my backside against the space next to her. "You are an amazing person. I've always admired you. Your ability to know what you want even when it seemed like you had no idea. Your version of what you wanted was so different from what other people's visions were for you. And I love that you were like, nope, fuck that."

I feel her take a deep breath, the way her shoulders move up, then down with the deflation of air. "Now I have no clue what I want."

"Wanna talk about it?"

"Not really. Is that okay?"

I nod and lean into her. "Can *I* talk about something?"

"You never need to ask."

"I think I might be asexual. Or something kind of like that."

"Wow," she says, and her face softens. "Okay."

"Just okay?"

"It is what it is, Ollie," she says softly, kindness and understanding all over her expression. "You are the only person who knows your story."

"So you still love me?"

"No, absolutely not," Harriet says, followed by a laugh. "But only because you are the world's biggest hypocrite."

I hang my head in shame. "I didn't see this coming."

She pushes off the counter. "The best things in life are often the ones we don't see coming." She places her hands on my shoulders and squeezes. "Either way, you are figuring shit out, and that's all that matters."

"What about you?" Her facial features shift from encouraging to weirdly hopeful. "What are you figuring out?" I want to pry. I love hot gossip, even if it's about one of the people I told her to stay away from. I can't say a word about that now. I don't plan on sleeping with Sunny, but hell, I certainly didn't plan on getting this close with her, either. There has to be a reason this is all happening this weekend. The one weekend that requires all of our attention to details, and not a single one of us can find a way to focus on those oh-so-important details.

"I think I'm figuring out how to love someone other than myself."

"Wow."

She rubs my shoulders one final time before she leans in and kisses me on the cheek. "I'm going to go. Good luck tonight."

"Hattie."

She raises her hands in the air and snickers as she's walking away. "I'm only saying!"

All these emotions coursing through my body are a lot to deal with. In one breath, I have no desire to sleep with Sunny. I love talking to her, learning about her, hearing about the way she thinks and why she feels certain ways about life, love, the pursuit of happiness. Her voice is soothing, silvery, like a cloud bringing a desperately needed rainstorm. And she is handsy when she speaks. A simple hand on the arm, a light touch along the back of my hand, or when she casually stroked the side of my neck as we sat on the bench swing together.

With another breath, I imagine her taking my clothes off, touching my bare skin, looking at me as if I am the most beautiful person in the entire world. But is that something she wants? Or wants to help me out with?

I don't know why I never desired sex with my husband. I loved Paul so much. But in the last four years of our life, something shifted, and I could never put my finger on what.

I make a mental note to google everything. Asexuality, bisexuality, followed by *when does perimenopause typically start* because I am having way too many hot flashes to be considered normal.

Unless they're because of Sunny.

Which is possible.

Confusing as fuck.

But possible.

CHAPTER FIFTEEN

Harriet

We're acting like teenagers, Judy and me, and it is so much fun. As we rush to the nest she's sharing with Mabel and Sunny, people are milling about everywhere: groups of women around fireplaces, couples chatting in secluded areas, laughter and live music coming from the Feeder's patio. Everything about the night is perfect. Even dinner with Olive and Sunny turned out okay. I tend to let things go instead of allowing them to fester. Life is too short to hold on to animosity.

We push inside the front door of the three-bedroom nest and quickly climb the stairs two at a time. I'm holding Judy's hand as she fumbles with her bedroom door. When she finally throws it open, the door bangs into the wall, and once we're inside, the return motion causes it to latch behind us. The lamp is on, and I can smell her perfume the second we enter. She smells like spring, like honeysuckle and jasmine, and I have found it intoxicating since the second I got a whiff. It's taking everything in me not to spin around, strip her down, and take her right now with her back pressed against the door, her leg hiked up over my shoulder.

She breezes past me and flips her sandals off. I follow her lead, toeing off my Air Jordans. She very slowly pulls on the elastic band holding her hair back until it's free. The way the blond falls around her face, her bangs, everything, I need to kiss her. My stomach aches just thinking about it. She moves her hands to her button-down, her fingers working to unsnap each closure. My mouth has gone dry. I blink a couple times to make sure I'm not imagining this. Am I dreaming?

When the shirt comes open, I realize that, no, I am, in fact, not dreaming. She slides it over her shoulders, down her arms, and drops it to the floor. Her black lace bra is not at all what I pictured, but I am so okay with it. Her stomach is flat, but there are light stretch marks. I want to touch her. I want to do so much to her. She starts to walk toward me, breasts bouncing lightly with each step. She holds her hand out, and I put mine on hers, palm to palm. She pulls carefully on me before her free hand starts messing with the hem of my shirt. I take the hint and pull it over my head. I never wear a bra, and they're not big, but the look on her face makes me feel like I'm the best she's ever seen.

She licks her lips. "You're so fucking hot."

"Yeah?"

She turns her back to me. "Will you undo mine?"

I run my fingertips across her shoulders, down her shoulder blades to the clasps on the black lace. I bend my head and kiss her shoulder as the bra goes limp. She slides it off, and I see goose bumps erupt all over her shoulders and biceps. I can see her profile, and on her face is some trepidation that didn't exist moments earlier. "You okay?"

"I want you to know that I understand this might not go anywhere. That this might be a one-time thing."

"Wait…wh…what?" I'm suddenly finding it very hard to breathe.

"I don't want you to think I don't know what this is."

"Judy." I turn her. I'm beside myself with worry, fear, with more apprehension than I've ever felt. "Have I done something to make you think this, whatever is happening between us, is anything but extraordinary?"

She doesn't respond, just licks her lips, and tears surface in her eyes.

"Talk to me, please."

"I, um, I had a conversation about you, and I was told to maybe apply the brakes…because this wasn't going to end how I wanted. But I'm okay with that." She takes a deep breath, then folds her arms across her chest to cover her bare breasts. "I feel stupid saying this because, what? Am I sixteen or something? But I can't help this. I really like you, so I'm preparing myself."

"I'm sorry, but what are you talking about? Who said you need to apply the brakes or that I'm going to hurt you?"

"Does it matter? I'm wondering if I'm strong enough to be a one-night stand. I don't…I don't know if I am."

"Judy." I put my hands on her shoulders, then slide them softly to her biceps. I hold on to her tightly. "This is not a fling for me. *You* are not a fling for me."

"You're not a player?" Her tone comes across as accusatory, but I'm hoping it's not how she meant it, and it's all in how I'm hearing things.

I swallow the lump in my throat. "Judy."

"Please tell me I'm different."

"You *are* different. My God." I pull her into my arms and hold her as close as possible. "You have turned everything in my world upside down." She's crying. I can feel it in the way she's shaking. She takes a ragged breath, and before another second passes, she's sobbing into my shoulder, and I'm baffled about what happened and how we went from all of that to all of this in less than a minute. I also want to kill Eleanor because she's the only one who has ever referred to me as a player.

"Come here." I lead her to the bed and lie next to her, pulling a blanket up over our nakedness. Silence has plagued our conversation. I need to know who she heard that from. All knowing will do is lead to me being pissed off, of course, but I don't care. "Who said that I was a player?"

"Does it matter?" She runs her right index finger from my earlobe along my jaw. I am going to devour her.

"I think it does," I answer, chills erupting all over my body.

"But aren't you?"

"In my past, yes. Don't tell me you didn't have a time in your life when you were a little on the wild side."

"Aside from now, you mean?"

"Yes, aside from now."

She grins, and I find it hard to focus on anything but her lips. "When I was married, I had an affair with a woman. Her name was Kate. Well, Kathryn, but Kate to me. And she was everything I thought I wanted in my life. She was perfect. Until I couldn't bring myself to leave." She takes a deep breath. "And she ended up with my best friend, Pam, who"—she pauses, laughs, groans—"I also had feelings for. If I didn't have a wild side, I definitely have, at the very least, a crazy streak."

"Don't say that. You're far from crazy. Love makes people do the damndest things."

"It really does." She wipes a tear and sniffles. "I dated this woman, Sydney, Kathryn's friend, for a while, too. But I don't know, it never felt…" She looks at me. "Like this."

My heart clenches. My stomach is in knots. *Please don't say what I think, hope,* want *you to say.* It's too soon, too much, and too fear-inducing for my unqualified heart. Even if I do want it and need it, and fuck, I want her so much, I can barely handle this. Is this what taking things slow feels like? Because my body is on fire. And my brain is hating me. And my heart is the last one taking a test I didn't even know we had to take.

"I hope that doesn't scare you."

I won't lie when I say I never thought I'd be feeling this way over a white woman. Not for any other reason than I pictured myself, if I ever did settle down, with a person who looks a little like me, at least in the skin department. *Jesus, calm the fuck down, Hattie. Settle down? With Judy? Stop, stop, stop!* "Um—"

"I can tell by the look on your face that it does." She rolls to her side and props her head up. Her hair is all messy and *dammit, focus, Hattie.* "It's okay if it does. I'm not exactly handling it well. Christ, I've only known you for thirty-eight hours."

"Thirty-nine," I correct her, and her face softens. "This is all new for me. That's all."

"Which part?"

"All of it." I roll onto my stomach and pull a pillow under me to prop myself up. "I don't do serious. I do casual. I don't take it slow. I race to the finish line. And I don't ever feel like this."

"And how do you feel?" Her voice is a whisper, and it sounds sexy as fuck. She starts to run her short fingernails over my back. That's it. I'm putty in her hands.

"I don't think I can put it into words yet." I take a breath. "Is that okay?"

She runs her finger down my side to the waistband of my black jeans and pulls me closer. I can feel her bare skin against mine. "Yes," she whispers against my ear and with the same seductive tone, "Are you going to fuck me tonight or not?"

My attention snaps to her. "Seriously?"

"Yes."

"I thought we were going to take it slow?"

"Who the fuck said anything about taking it slo—"

I lunge to cut her off and capture her soft, full lips. She giggles into the kiss.

"Thank you," she says against my lips.

"Don't thank me yet." I maneuver myself and engage fully with her, with her intense kisses. She is a phenomenal kisser. She takes her time, doesn't rush, even though there has been urgency since the beginning, as if our bodies and souls know we need to get this out of our systems, or neither of us will be able to focus on anything else. Her lips have a purpose, and it's not to *only* kiss me. She is seducing me with every single flick of her tongue, every nibble of my lips, every breath she takes, every nudge she does against my nose, every kiss she places down my jaw, down my neck, and *goddamn*, when she bites the soft skin of my pulse point on my neck.

Fuck, I wish I could have Alexa call me an ambulance because I'm near death, I'm sure of it.

She's in control, too, which I am fucking digging. In almost every sexual encounter I've had, I am the one in charge. Most of the time with men, I'm glad about that. I should be the one in charge. If I say something isn't good, then they need to stop. But sometimes, with women, I love to lie back and let someone control me. Right this second, that's exactly what I want. I want her to lead the fuck out of me. She must read my mind because she pulls away, rolls me onto my back, unbuttons my jeans, and starts to pull them down. She runs a finger along the waistband of my Calvin Klein boxer briefs before she practically rips them from my body. To say I'm turned on would be the biggest understatement of the year. I'm ready to explode. She stands and unbuttons her jeans, pushes them over her hips and black hipster panties. I push myself up onto my elbows.

"Fuck, you're hot," I say softly. She goes to kneel on the bed, and I stop her. "What about your panties?"

"Um…" She blushes. "Aunt Flo is here with me this weekend."

"That bitch."

"Tell me about it." She shrugs. "This is the first period I've had in, oh, I don't know, almost six months."

"Why she always gotta ruin shit?"

She finally straddles my hips, all while laughing with me. "Doesn't mean I can't show you the benefits of settling down with someone like me."

"Oh? Is that so?" I'm still laughing as I lean back. She takes each of my hands and braces them above my head. Her breasts are right above my face. I latch on to one of her nipples. She shrieks. "Too tender?"

"No, God, that felt good." She leans closer. and I do it again. She still has my hands, so I can't touch her, but I make sure to show as much attention as possible to each breast as she gives me access. I fucking love tits. And Judy's are fucking magnificent. There is something goddamn erotic about nibbling on a nipple until it's erect, about kissing the soft flesh, about running my tongue along the bumpiness of the areola. And Judy's hips grinding into me as I do it? Yeah, well, that's a sweet bonus.

She releases my hands finally as she leans up. She raises her hands, pulls her hair tie off her wrist, and hastily ties her hair back into a messy ponytail. "If I told you that going down on a woman is one of my favorite things to do, would you be excited by that?"

I blink once, twice, three times before I look to the ceiling. "Thank you, dear baby Jesus."

She chuckles, and her breasts move with her laughter, and I think to myself that I am falling for her. I am falling for this woman on top of me. This completely unexpected breath of fresh air. "I figured you'd be down with that."

"I am very down with that. Very, very, *very* down with that."

She moves down my body, spending plenty of time on each of my breasts, then lightly places kisses on my sternum, stomach, each of my abdominal muscles, my tattoo that says *never forget your worth* in my mother's handwriting on my hip, the scar on my thigh from a paring knife I accidentally dropped. "I want to know about all of this," she says against my scar, then lightly runs a finger over the tattoo. "Later."

I can't fight a nervous laugh. I never sound nervous. "Okay," I finally answer. "Later."

"You good?"

I raise my head. "I am. I don't know why I'm nervous, but I am."

"You sure you're good?"

"I promise you. I am good." I reach down, and she grabs my hand as she settles between my thighs. I prop myself up on my elbows again, our hands breaking apart, and lock my gaze on her as she leans forward and kisses my wetness. Watching someone go down on me is one of *my* most favorite things to do. And I can see exactly why she said this is one of her favorites. She is good, like, *holy shit* good. She has two fingers inside me, her mouth on me, and I am enjoying every single sensation, riding every single wave.

"You're drenched," she says before she puts her mouth back and starts to flick my clit. She doesn't break eye contact, and I only do when the feeling is so good that I have to lean my head back and moan. I spread my legs wider as she thrusts into me. I am so close. So, so close. She slows her licks and continues to thrust. Even with men, I don't typically get off with penetration, but whatever she is doing has me riding the wave still. It feels fantastic.

"Judy, fuck, I am so close." Like a flash, she moves, and she's next to me, her face near mine, her fingers still inside me, moving at the perfect rhythm.

"Come for me," she whispers against my lips. I collapse onto my back as my orgasm starts at the top of my head and rushes through me. It doesn't stop. It continues as she thrusts softly, her fingers curled. With every thrust, another shockwave hits me. Without warning, she pulls her fingers from me to massage my clit. And within an instant, I have another full-blown orgasm slam into me. I grip the comforter and wait for it to subside.

Breathless, my eyes clamped shut, I say, "Holy *hell*." I hear her chuckle. "That was…wow."

"Not bad, hmm?"

"Wow." I feel a small kiss on my cheek. "Yeah. Wow." I take one last deep breath and peel my eyes open. "Is it your favorite because you leave people completely fucking breathless?"

"Duh," she says with a wink.

"I want to get you now." I roll to my side, my legs still shaking. "I want to return the favor."

"Give me one more day. Okay?"

"Deal."

"In the meantime," she says as she kneels and rolls me onto my stomach. "Let's get you again."

"I don't know if I can."

She has her breasts on my back, her lips on my ear, as she says, her voice low, throaty, "I guarantee you, I can get you again."

"By all means, have at it, my love." I feel her breasts down my back, hard nipples dancing across my ass before her fingers slip into me from behind. I spread my legs a little to welcome her. She places a kiss on each of my ass cheeks, her fingers not moving. I lift my ass a little to give her a better angle, and I hear her low sexy chuckle. And she starts to thrust lightly because she must know I'm slightly sore. She's hitting that same spot again, and I can feel it building.

"Get on your hands and knees," she instructs, and I do exactly as I'm told. She has her free hand wrapped around me now, and she's massaging my clit. I am never going to want to have sex with anyone else ever again. She's ruining me. She is doing everything I love. She's taking charge. She's going down on me, she's fucking me from behind, she is everything I want in a sexual partner. What the fuck is happening to me?

I lean back onto my knees, and she braces my body with hers. She pulls her fingers out and massages me a little more before she says against my ear, "Will you ride my face?"

Yeah.

One of two things is happening. Either I have died and gone to heaven.

Or...

I met my soulmate.

Whatever the case may be, I want to fucking marry this woman right now.

CHAPTER SIXTEEN

Eleanor

I'm meeting Mabel for drinks. I didn't want to, and I tried to skirt the invitation a couple times, but she's persistent. And I'd really like to know how people keep finding me in my office, the one place I never allow guests.

First Judy, then Mabel. I tell Keri, "That's it. I don't want another person to know where I'm located."

She laughs at me. "Yeah, okay."

I roll my eyes as I leave the building and finally head home to change from the same workout clothes I wore to go mountain biking. I shower and throw on a thin black sweater and jeans. My favorite jeans, my lucky jeans. Not that I'm trying to get lucky. I'm just trying not to be *un*lucky. I let my hair air dry.

In the past, I got to the point where I stopped trying so hard, and that was when everything fell into place, my hair, my body, my life. I am not trying too hard tonight. Simple makeup, lavender-rose perfume, gold necklace, my usual beaded bracelets. I look like I'm going for drinks with a friend. And that is all I'm doing.

I may say that a thousand times, yet here I am, sitting at the bar of the Feeder and wondering if I'm the only one thinking this is drinks with a friend. Also wondering if I'm that early, or is Mabel late?

"Okay, why do you look even hotter than normal?" Heidi hands me my usual old-fashioned. "Are you trying to get me to sleep with you finally? Because it's working."

My cheeks are on fire as I take a sip. "You wish."

"Damn, girl," Heidi says, pushing the sleeves of her navy shirt up her arms, then straightening the clip on her floral tie. "Only woman I'd ever sleep with, and you're gonna play hard to get?"

"Get over yourself, Heidi. I always look this hot."

"Actually?" She pauses and narrows her eyes, studies me, and I am at an insane level of discomfort. I'm trying to play with her, but she's on the A team, and I'm used to riding the bench. "You do always look this hot." She leans closer, her breasts right below my eye level. "I'm staying here this weekend. Y'know, if you get a wild hair and want to…" She raises her eyebrows.

"You couldn't handle me." My voice isn't supposed to sound so low and sexy, but it does, and I see the desire start at her eyes and wash over her. Next thing I know, a jacket is being draped over the stool next to me before I feel the owner's hand on my back. I give Heidi one final look before I turn. "Mabel, you made it."

"Am I interrupting?" She's giving me a look that says she is fully aware of what she's doing and what she's interrupting.

"Not at all," Heidi says with a grin. "What can I get you?"

"Vodka soda with a lemon."

"Oh yes, the lemon girl." Heidi's tone isn't exactly friendly, but she gets busy making the drink nonetheless. "Double?"

Mabel is standing very close. Her hand is still on my back, still warm, still pressed firmly. "Yes, please."

I'm taken aback by this display. "Are you marking your territory, or what?"

She's staring at Heidi. No, she's boring holes into Heidi, and I want inside her mind. When her drink is delivered, she sips, all the while keeping her not-kind glare. I'm torn between being turned on and being scared. Also, slightly offended. I'm not a piece of meat. Or a fire hydrant for her to pee on.

"Hey," I say, and it takes one beat, two, *three*, before she finally stops the stare down. Her eyes look brighter than normal tonight. It must be the cerulean tank she's wearing. "Stop."

"Stop what?" But defensiveness is written all over her face.

"I'm not interested in her."

"You're allowed to be, though."

She's got a lot of nerve. "I know. But I'm not. If I wanted to sleep with her, I would have already."

Her expression softens. She has done nothing but age well. She's gorgeous. Even more than in high school when I thought she was the most beautiful girl I'd ever seen.

"What?" I ask because her gaze is intense, and it's causing me to perspire.

She drinks from her double vodka. Her hand is still on my back. "You've really grown into all this."

"All what, exactly?"

"Your beauty." She finally moves her hand, then pulls out the stool where her jacket is draped and sits. "You want to stay here at the bar, I presume?"

"You're ridiculous."

"Whatever do you mean?"

"Do you think anyone can hold a candle to you?" It's her turn to blush, and *fuck*, she can wear that flushed look well. "Stop, okay?"

She seems like she might protest, then relents with a simple nod. "How was the rest of your day?"

That's better. "Well, I finished the final touches for the event on Sunday. I met with my staff to make sure they were all on the same page. I'd like for them to enjoy it, I learned that from my old CEO in the city. She was cool about things like that. If the staff can enjoy the events, they'll look forward to them instead of dread them."

"You stayed in Chicago?"

"I did. I never thought I'd leave, actually. But here I am."

"Leaving was the best thing I ever did." She seems to realize what she said as soon as the words leave her mouth. "I don't mean—"

"It's fine, Mabel." I shrug. "We both needed to figure ourselves out." I watch her take a breath. "Things didn't work out with Bobby, hmm?"

She shakes her head with a look of regret mixed with sadness. "Not even a little bit. I tried, but it was a flop from the start. I don't know why he thought things were great. They weren't. At all."

"Why did you marry him, then?"

"Who the hell knows?" She lets out a lighthearted laugh. "I guess I was hoping I would grow out of—"

"Being a lesbian?"

"God, yeah, I guess so." She's picking at the napkin under her drink. "Little did I know that I would never grow out of it."

"It's a lifetime phase."

"Tell my mom that." Her voice shakes, and I can see plain as day the scared teenager who broke my heart for no other reason than the fear of disappointment. "She's much better now, more supportive. Even belongs to a PFLAG chapter."

"How the hell are your parents, by the way? Betty loved me."

"Yeah, she loved you until she started putting together why we had so many sleepovers."

"If only she knew how happy I made you."

"Oh, I told her."

I practically choke. "What?"

"Yeah." She sighs. "End of senior year when we weren't speaking…" She trails off, eyes on her drink, stirring it with the straw. "I was such a mess. Trying to love Bobby. Trying to understand why my parents were okay with me marrying him at such a young age. I told Mom that I wasn't happy, that I was happier when you were in my life." She shakes her head, the emotion bubbling to the surface in her voice. "The marriage didn't last long."

"What happened?"

"Nothing, and yet, a thousand little things." She lifts her head, and she is no longer sad but proud. "I ended up applying to be a transfer student to NYU's journalism program. I got in, and I never looked back." Her face softens. "Except when I thought about you."

"Mabel," I whisper.

"I lied earlier when I said I was going to look you up. I knew you were in Chicago. I knew you graduated with honors from Northwestern and then top of your master's class at U of C." She seems nervous. She thinks I'm going to be mad at her, and I probably should be, but I'm honored. And why? Why does it feel amazing to know she kept track of me? When she's the reason I was so brokenhearted to begin with? "The only thing I didn't know was that you were here. Why change your name to Fitzwallace?"

I shrug. "I needed a change. And Eleanor Fitzwallace has a nice ring to it."

"Ellie?"

"What?" I am exasperated by the questions. "I don't know, okay? It's my mother's maiden name and…it was easier to move forward with a brand-new name than to go back to one that had nothing but pain associated with it."

"Wow."

"Well? Are we being honest here, or should we lie to each other? Contrary to popular opinion, you're not the only person who has broken me." I empty the last swallow of my drink and motion for another. Thankfully, Heidi is hovering like a vulture. The fact that these two women—one who wouldn't give me the time of day when I was a kid and the other who won't give me the time of day now—are both acting jealous makes me want to laugh. And scream. Life has a way of dishing up some interesting things to digest.

"You're right. I don't want to start with lies." She places a hand on my knee. "I want to tell you something."

"Oh God."

"No, it's not bad. I mean, it's not good, but it's not bad." She takes a sip, lips wrapped around the biodegradable straw. Every fiber of my being wants to be that straw. "You know how everyone bullied you your senior year?"

"Nope. We are not doing this."

"Ellie, please."

"Why do you keep wanting to talk about this shit?"

"Because I need to tell you this." Her hand lands on my forearm, and my eyes are drawn to her fingers, the gold ring on her index finger, the manicured nails, and my heart clenches.

"Fine."

"When I was at NYU, I ran into Jessalyn. Remember her?"

"How could I forget? Queen of the mean girls."

"Yeah," she says, followed by a sigh. "Well, I stupidly went for drinks with her, thinking things would have changed."

I hold my hand up. "You're telling me I'm supposed to believe she got into NYU?"

"Hell no." She laughs. "No. She was there on vacation with some of her rich bitch friends. I don't think she made it to college."

"I was going to say. Anyway, carry on."

"She started going on and on about Bobby and how she's been spending time with him. And then she admitted to pulling the information about you from Bobby while we were in school. Apparently, he could never stay away from her, even when he and I were together." She sighs as she stirs her drink slowly. "I wish I wouldn't have thought I could get past…"

"Mabel?" I say, and she looks over. "We need to move past all of that. Okay?"

"You're not mad at me?"

"I've been mad at you for years. I'm ready to stop."

Her deep breath causes her chest to rise and fall. Her eyes are red-rimmed, as if she's seconds from crying. At the bar. With Heidi only ten steps away. "I cannot begin to tell you how relieved I am." Her voice is barely above a whisper.

"Listen," I start and prop my feet on the rung of her stool. My legs are brushing hers, and there is something so erotic about the sensation that flares inside me. "I've grown since high school. And that includes realizing that everything happens for a reason. Natalie leaving almost killed me. But then this place happened. And I found solace in things I never thought would be comforting."

"Like?"

She seems to be hanging on every word, and the glee of witnessing that spurs me on. "Like the mountains. Nature and seeing wildlife when we drive east to go skiing or hiking. I've seen a mama bear and her cubs, and I realized that life, in all its uncertainties and misgivings and ups and downs, has gone on. Even when I didn't think mine could. Hell, even when I didn't want my life to go on, it still did. And I'm really glad."

"How is this possible?"

The microscopic attention would normally have me feeling very self-conscious. But not now. No. Now it is giving me courage, fanning the long dormant flame inside me called hope. How much longer can I go without throwing gasoline on the fire by kissing her? "How is what possible?"

"You, you're the same, yet you've changed, and I'm having the hardest time figuring out which is worse: the fact that I have always been in love with eighteen-year-old you or the fact that I am falling even more in love with the forty-seven-year-old you."

"Mabel," I say softly. "You still don't know me well enough to say that."

"Do you still love *Star Wars*?"

"Duh."

"And Princess Leia?"

"And Carrie Fisher, God rest her soul." I rest my hand over my heart.

"Not surprised. Do you still love pink Starbursts?"

"Absolutely."

"Do you still…" she says softly, then pauses as she pushes her hair over her shoulder. I want to run my fingers through it, to pull on it until she leans her head back and exposes her marvelous neck. "Watch reruns of *The Facts of Life* and laugh, even though you've seen all the episodes at least three or four times?"

I chuckle. "Still ship Blaire and Jo, too."

"Do you still squirm when your earlobe is sucked?"

My entire mouth goes dry. *Jesus H. Christ.* And I can't even describe the sensation in my vagina. I am a pile of nerves. I can only nod because I'm sure I still squirm, but it's been a hot minute since anyone has done that. I never do certain intimate things with anyone else because it's too much for my fragile heart to handle. That's one of them. I don't let anyone near my ears.

"Do you still moan when the back of your neck is kissed?"

And that's the other. "What are you doing?" The deepness of my voice shocks me.

"You're the same," she says. "Yet you're much more than I ever imagined."

I've had intense eye contact with women before. Hell, I've even had my share of intense eye contact with men before I finally freaked out and remembered I don't want dick. But what's currently taking place is some of the most powerful I have ever experienced.

It's only when Heidi swoops over and asks if we need more to drink that we both look away.

There's live music outside on the patio. I take my drink and tell Mabel to grab hers so we can go listen. It's been a while since I've been able to relax and listen to any sort of live music. And maybe it will fill some of these silences instead of us filling them with longing stares.

The band consists of a lead singer, Talula, and her guitarist and pianist, Taryn. The aptly named The T's are very talented, and I look forward to these warmer nights when their music floats across the resort grounds.

We find an empty bench near a fireplace, and my heart warms when Mabel props her feet next to mine on the small footrest. I'm holding my drink for dear life because my hands don't seem to be working properly. Feeling like this causes such love-hate emotions. On the one hand, I love being near her and knowing, for the first time in forever, that my heart does still beat, even if it's seemingly only for her. On the other, I hate knowing that in a couple days, she'll be gone again, and I'll be left wondering if this was a blip on her radar or if it meant as much to her as me. She's the one who started it. She apologized. She pursued me, said she is still in love with me.

I'm along for the ride now, and the thought of this car careening over a cliff because neither of us is paying attention makes my stomach ache.

Talula starts singing "A Sorta Fairytale" by Tori Amos, and her name instantly makes sense.

"What are you smiling at?"

"Nothing," I say too quickly. Then I lean closer. "The lead singer's name is Talula. Tori Amos sings a song named 'Talula.' Just made me happy."

"This song reminds me of us," she says quietly. "It always has."

"Love and loss yet not being able to put it back on the shelf?"

She nods.

"Tell me about New York."

A smile stretches across her lips, and I find myself breathless in its wake. "Best years of my life. Did a lot of soul-searching. A newly divorced twenty-one-year-old living on her own for the first time. Things got a little wild."

"I can only imagine."

Mabel sinks down and leans her head back. Her profile, with the light of the fire flickering on her skin, is giving me much to think about. Namely, how did I remember what she looked like yet forgot how gorgeous she is? She tells me about her apartment, a small one-bedroom she sublet from an artist who grew pot, and the whole place reeked. "The smell never went away. Probably didn't help that I also started smoking weed that year."

"You did not."

"Oh yes. I was nervous at first, being on my own. Because you know me, straitlaced and such an introvert."

"You're kidding, right?"

"What? You don't think I'm straitlaced?"

"Absolutely not. Or an introvert. You're the most outgoing person I know."

She shrugs, and a look of pride floods her features. "Yeah, you're probably right. Anyway, I met a group of women at this granola-y coffee shop. They were amazing. And I remember confiding in one of them about…you."

"Man, you had it bad, didn't you?" We both chuckle, and she smacks me lightly on the leg.

"I did, yes." She sighs. "I still do."

The fire has her attention, and I find myself missing the intensity of her gaze, yet I am thankful for the reprieve. "Anyway, she helped me see the error of my ways."

"You're saying that you slept with her."

Even in the amber light of the fire, I can see her cheeks redden. "Yeah, I slept with her."

"And?"

"It was good."

I raise my fourth old-fashioned to my lips, arch an eyebrow, and say softly, "Good, hmm?"

"Yeah, it was really, really good."

I chuckle at how nervous and excited she is. "I'm glad."

"Yeah, so then I got a job at the NYU newspaper, *Washington Square News*. I worked my way up to editor in chief my senior year and then soon after, got a permanent job at *On the Verge*. I was doing freelance articles for a bunch of different publications. The editor job helped put me on the map. Then I moved to LA, and I've been there ever since. I can write from anywhere, and they have pretty much allowed me to do whatever I want as long as I clear it first."

"Tell me how you stumbled upon the sanctuary."

"You should have gone into journalism. You're pretty good at these questions."

"It helps that we have almost thirty years of material to go over."

"True, true." She takes a deep breath and launches into a story about Amanda Perry, one of my favorite actresses who has visited the sanctuary, and how Judy met her on Sandy Shield's show. "I knew I needed to come check it out." She shrugs. "I try to write my stories about women empowering women. And that's exactly what this place does."

"You're right about that." I lean forward and prop my elbows on my knees. Talula is singing "I Will Remember You," and I'm trying to keep myself grounded because I'm very tipsy, and Mabel is, well, she's very perfect. And Sarah McLachlan's lyrics bring me right back to Mabel, right back to her arms and her lips and how I made her listen to *Fumbling Towards Ecstasy* because I couldn't handle how my young gay heart felt during every single song.

"May I ask you a question?"

I chuckle. "Do you ever ask if you can ask before you ask?"

She presses her leg against mine, and my breath hitches. Talking, smiling, laughing is one thing but touching? I don't know if I can do this while feeling this drunk. *Shit, I went from tipsy to drunk in record time.* Her being so completely at ease in her skin is unnerving in the best ways. She has grown into her body, but damn, it's more impressive how much she has grown into her soul. She is exactly how I pictured her as a kid.

"Only when it really matters," she says.

Fuck. What is she planning on asking? "I guess you can, then."

"Why are you single?"

I take a deep breath and let it out before I lean back. "That's not the question I expected."

"What did you think I was going to ask?"

An inebriated cackle bubbles from my throat. "Oh, I don't know. Maybe how I became rich and successful or why I'm the most amazing woman you've had the pleasure of knowing. Something I could bullshit my way through." She seems to have found humor in my explanation. "Not why I'm single. Because I really don't know why other than…" I pause. Talula's voice is filling the silence with their rendition of Taylor's Swift's "Wildest Dreams," Taryn seducing the ivory on the piano and Talula caressing every word as if she was born to perform. This song is fitting, this night is a dream, and I'm remembering every single thing about our past and now our present, and it's almost too much for my soul to handle. "I was married for a minute. About three years."

"That's quite a bit more than a minute."

"Yeah, well," I let out a shaky breath and allow myself to feel the feelings—the despair, the hatred, the abandonment, the guilt—I've been holding back for so very long. It's quite the package, and I feel it sitting on my chest, on my throat, as if I'm wrapped too tightly in blankets. My breath is shallow, and I scold myself because if I don't get a grip, I'll have a panic attack, and that's going to be real attractive. *You haven't seen me in years, Mabel, but I'm a certified anxious asshole now. Lucky for you, you really dodged a bullet!* I hold a breath and concentrate on it, on the fact that I have survived a lot in my life, and I'm beautiful and kind, and goddammit, I am not what my past has made me feel like. I am more and better. "It's hard to talk about." I shake my head, focus on the crackling fire, the hint of blue, the reds, the orange, and yellow.

"You don't have to tell me if you don't want to."

"It's not that." I shrug. "Y'know, I spent a lot of years healing from, well, y'know." I hear her breathe out, an almost silent acknowledgment. "Nothing prepared me for my wife to, uh…" I sigh. "Her name was Natalie, and she was great. Until…" I take a drink. "I found her in bed with my brother."

She gasps. "With Ethan?"

I nod as I take another sip.

"Wow."

I sigh. "Yeah."

"Holy *shit*."

"Yeah."

"That was not what I expected."

"Yeah, me, either." I chuckle at the irony. "Men seem to always fuck up my relationships."

She raises her glass; her left eyebrow quirks a tiny bit before she drinks. She discarded the straw when her last refill was delivered, claiming she'd eat the ice to stay sober. We all know that doesn't work. Either way, I'm happy that I get to witness all of this, including and especially the droplets of condensation as they run over her full bottom lip. She licks it after she drinks. "I should probably be getting back to my nest."

"Yeah, me too. I'm going to be worthless tomorrow." I raise my glass to the fire, then drink the last swallow.

"Thank you, Ellie. For tonight. For doing this with me. I don't deserve it."

I place my hand on her arm before she stands. I want to tell her to stop, to let it go, to move forward with me because that's what I want to do. I want to get past it all. But I'm four drinks in and two seconds from making a very bad decision. "I'll see you tomorrow."

She looks as deflated as I feel as she stands and heads to the doors. I should walk her back to her nest. It's on the way to the residence.

I shouldn't follow her.

No, I should follow her and kiss her.

I shouldn't have stared at her longingly.

I should have kissed her.

I shouldn't have touched her like that.

Fuck.

I should have kissed her.

The Grand Junction Gabber

"Events Around Town"
by Sheila Wilson

Greetings, Coloradans! It's been a gorgeous spring, and thankfully, we still have quite a few days left before the summer's dry heat settles upon us like a blanket. This weekend is Mother's Day. Hopefully, you already have reservations made so you can treat your mom or mom-in-law to a lovely brunch or dinner.

If not, here are a few events that are taking place this weekend.

Mooney's Place:

Mooney's will be hosting a pancake breakfast this year benefiting the Ronald McDonald house. Tickets are $60 and can be purchased at www.MooneysPlace.com/pancakebenefit.

Jack and Diane's:

Another great spot for brunch, but this is brunch with a twist. The buffet has waved good-bye, and this year, Jack and Diane are trying family style. Reservations are not needed but are strongly encouraged.

The Hummingbird Sanctuary:

The Western Slope's most popular resort is having a huge party to celebrate the grand opening of their brand-new event center, the Amphitheater. Live music, a fantastic menu, and a toast to the mothers in our lives. Be there or be square, as our parents used to say. Unfortunately, the event is completely sold out, but if you're lucky, there might be a cancelation or two due to inclement weather over the Front Range. Check it out by giving the Sanctuary's website a visit: www.TheHummingbirdSanctuary.com/2021events.

Have a great weekend, y'all!

CHAPTER SEVENTEEN

Olive

Not only have we tainted the journalist so that there's no way on earth she can write an unbiased review, but I've also gone against everything I believe about not fraternizing with guests, and I've given Harriet free rein to go off and fuck one.

What has happened to me? Who am I becoming? A bisexual, asexual woman who has no idea what that truly means? And Google did not help clear up anything. The research I did until three in the morning only confused me further. I am in over my head. Why can't I just *want* sex? That'd make all of this much easier.

I guess I don't *not* want sex. I don't desire it. I don't think about it when I'm by myself. I don't masturbate. I don't pine for people. Maybe that's a little bit of a lie. I do pine. I don't pine sexually. I pine romantically. I want Sunny to romance me. I want Sunny to wine and dine me and tell me all her secrets and hold me and tell me how beautiful I am and be happy with my curves and not expect me to lose weight.

That's kind of all happening, though.

Ugh, I don't know. I want to rewind all of this and go back to being sad and unhappy. At least then, I sort of understood the meaning behind it all. Or I thought I understood. But I guess, ultimately, I was wrong about that, too.

I was unhappy for years. I was sad for years. I got used to dealing with both simultaneously. Losing Paul emphasized each, and I learned more and more how to handle the two symbiotic emotions leeching on to me.

I lean against the floor to ceiling windows in the kitchen and stare out across the valley to the mountains. It's slightly overcast, and the forecast calls for a storm. We need the rain, but Mother Nature better not do anything even remotely close to rain tomorrow.

Eleanor has made sure all the t's are crossed and the i's are dotted. And I'm on this whole new level of trust with Harriet. I know everything will go smoothly. Then why do I feel so stressed out?

Could it have anything to do with the fact that I'm having all these weird feelings for a woman I barely know?

Sunny was too perfect last night. She answered every question I asked. And when I said my neck was hurting, she had me sit in front of her, and she rubbed my shoulders. And I felt cared for. I can't remember the last time I felt that. I'm the one caring for either Eleanor or Harriet. But Sunny, she cared for me. She cares for me.

She told me about her parents and how supportive they are. She went on and on about the pain and suffering of auditioning for role after role. And my favorite part was when she described, in great detail, the way certain actresses look in a picture and how it's nothing compared to the way they look in person. I couldn't stop smiling, even when she asked me questions. I answered with a smile on my face. I never willingly answer things about myself. But her kind words and her lovely voice made it easier.

I'm so confused.

I hear footsteps behind me, and Eleanor appears. She's all wild-haired, pajama top cockeyed. She doesn't acknowledge me. Not until she has poured herself a cup of coffee and taken that first sip will she acknowledge me. She may love me, but she loves coffee even more. If I didn't know better, I'd say she looks like she might be fighting a hangover. She takes her coffee with two creams, and once she's done stirring, she takes a sip. She doesn't blow on it. Always amazes me that she doesn't burn her tongue.

"Good morning," she says with a wave. She shuffles to the island and slides up onto a stool. She props her elbows on the island, keeping the R2-D2 coffee mug at nose level. She is inhaling the scent as if it's cocaine. "How'd you sleep?" Her right eyebrow is naturally arched more than the left, but she is most definitely arching it on purpose now.

"Great. And you?"

"Great." She sips her coffee. "You were up late. I saw you outside with Sunny when I got home."

"Yeah, she didn't leave until around one."

"What's going on there?"

I try to swallow the lump that appears out of nowhere. "What do you mean?" My voice sounds strained. I sit on a stool two down from her. Maybe if I'm far enough away, she won't be able to read me like a book.

"You like her." She shrugs. "It's fine. Don't lie about it, though."

"Whoa." I set my coffee on the island. "Okay, then."

"Why would you lie? You act like I don't know you." She has a point.

"True."

"What's going on?" She still hasn't looked at me. Eleanor always looks at me. It's one of the things I love about her: unwavering eye contact.

"I could ask you the same thing." I wait for her to respond, but she doesn't. She keeps her eyes forward. "Why won't you look at me?"

She lets out a puff of air, then laughs so hard she has to set her coffee down so she doesn't spill it.

"What's so funny?"

"Nothing, Olive. Nothing is going on. I don't want to look at you today. Is that so wrong?"

"Eleanor?" I'm getting irritated. And kind of hurt.

She sighs. "I assumed you just didn't like women."

"What are you talking about?"

Finally, she lifts her gaze to me, and her eyes are filled with tears. "Not that you just didn't like *me*."

"Ellie." My voice is gone. I open my mouth to speak, and nothing comes out.

She shakes her head, wipes her tears, then picks her coffee. She closes her eyes as if she's savoring the taste.

"Do you—"

"Yeah, I do. I always have." After a shrug, she says, "It stings. That's all."

"I…I'm sorry, Ellie. I am."

She chuckles. "Don't be sorry. I should have let this go a long time ago. I came home last night feeling pretty good after immersing myself in the pain of my past, and there's you and Sunny on the swing, and everything slammed into me." She has her hand on her chest above her heart. "I didn't expect it, for whatever reason. And everything seemed final."

"Would it make you feel any better if I told you Sunny is helping me unpack a lot of feelings I've been having?"

"No," she says, followed by a strained huff.

I take a deep breath and let it out. "I feel like I'm flailing and falling, and I'm not quite sure where I'm going to land."

She blinks rapidly as if computing what I've said and how to respond. "I'm beside myself right now."

"What do you mean?"

"Olive, I've been here for you through every single thing you've gone through. But Sunny is helping you unpack some feelings? Sunny? Fucking Sunny?"

"Whoa."

"Yeah, whoa. I'm just…wow. I guess I'm super glad Sunny arrived. Right in the nick of time."

"I do not deserve this." I'm done with this conversation, and an abrupt exit from the island should be enough of an indication. But it isn't. Apparently.

"You know, I would have caught you wherever you landed, not because I've been in love with you for years but because that's what best friends do. We catch each other."

"Yeah? Okay, fine." I place my mug on the concrete countertop a little too harshly because it makes an awful noise. "You wanna catch me? You think you can handle anything I throw at you?"

"Fucking try me." Her nostrils flare. Shit. She's really mad.

I take a breath, "I was going to divorce Paul," I say as I breathe out, sounding as if I'm rushing through a horrible secret, which I am, but this is not how I wanted to tell anyone this. Especially her. *I am awful.* "I had the papers drawn up and everything. I was leaving. I needed out."

She blinks once.

"And then he got into the…accident."

She blinks again.

"And he died. And I inherited everything. And when I say everything, I mean everything. All of his parents' money that they left him. All the insurance money. Literally, every single thing. And then, as if all of that wasn't bad enough, the guilt of knowing I wanted out but ended up with more money than I knew what to do with, I…" *Oh God, there's no going back.* "I found a note. And it turns out, it might not have been an accident." Can I sound any more heartless? When actually, I am still wrecked. I still hear him, feel him, smell him. And even if I wasn't in love with him any longer, I loved him with everything in me. And finding that note…

She blinks once more.

"Goddammit, say something." I want to strangle her, but that would defeat the purpose.

"Uh."

"Something more eloquent than that, please."

"You didn't let me finish," she says, anger and distrust dripping from her words. She stands so quickly that the stool almost topples, and she paces. "I don't even know where to begin. What the *fuck*, Olive? What the actual fuck?" Her hands are locked in her hair at the scalp. "Why would you keep this from me? From Harriet?"

"I don't know! Okay. I don't know." I have no idea what else to say because I'm ashamed to admit that I don't have a good reason.

"Olive, seriously? Something more eloquent than that, please."

It's my turn to roll my eyes. "I am being as eloquent as possible. What do you want me to say? I was devastated. And scared."

Eleanor purses her lips. "When did you find the note?"

"Three weeks after his funeral." The admission makes me want to vomit. "I finally broke down and started going through his clothes. And it fell out of the pocket of a pair of slacks. I don't know when he wrote it. It could have been weeks before. Who knows? The only person who knew is gone, and I was stuck cleaning up the mess of a failed marriage and a life I didn't love, all the while suffering the loss of a man I didn't know if I could actually live without." My legs are going to give out. "I'm just gonna sit here." When my butt hits the floor, I slump against the cabinets. "They said it was an accident. I didn't...I would have never thought..."

Eleanor is kneeling in front of me before I can get another word out. "Stop. Stop talking right now."

"Ellie, I thought it was an accident. Everyone did."

"Listen to me. You need to keep your mouth shut about this, do you hear me?" Her hands are on my face, on my cheeks and she's tilting my face upward. "Olive, honey, do you hear me?"

I can only nod. My head feels fuzzy. My arms and legs are filled with static. Within an instant, everything fades to black.

CHAPTER EIGHTEEN

Harriet

I've captured Judy for the afternoon and decide to sweep her away to wine tasting at Purity Wines. DeeDee normally brings the wine to me, her favorite line being "Have wine, will travel." But I liked the idea of showing Judy a little bit of the Western Slope, especially since they didn't drive in. She's busy looking out the window, and I'm busy trying to occupy my mind. As the hours since I met her pass, I am more and more captivated. In the past, the idea of being captivated scared the holy living shit out of me. I will never understand *why* it scares me. My mother and father were a very amazing couple with a terrific relationship. He'd hug and kiss her, and she'd playfully dodge his compliments, and honestly, they were exactly what I thought I'd find when I grew up.

After losing my mom, my dad refused to remarry. "Vivian was the love of my life," he said one day as we made bread together in the kitchen of their tiny South Side apartment. "I can't even imagine trying to replicate what we had."

Olive's father was long gone before her mother passed. Sixteen years old and she was left trying to figure out how a man who was supposed to love her unconditionally could up and leave without a second thought. She doesn't speak about it much. The couple times she brought it up, we were a few bottles of wine in. I think the memory is too much.

Eleanor's dad found someone almost immediately. Hank referred to this new woman as his "lady friend." Eleanor referred to her as *the stand-in*. She was devastated after he remarried. If I were to bring it up today, she'd still be upset by it. I used to tease her that she was more upset about the inheritance. That goes over very poorly. "I don't give a flying fuck about his money, Hattie," she finally said to me one day. "I care because the legacy of my mom is gone. Her memory is diminished. He doesn't even have a picture of her up any longer."

Needless to say, I stopped teasing after she said that to me.

The importance of the memory of a loved one never being tarnished or fading is something I didn't understand until I lost my mom. I was young. Too young to go through it alone. I guess that's part of the reason why God brought Olive and Eleanor into my life. I was never alone in my grief.

"Colorado is gorgeous."

I glance out the window at the mountains. "It really is."

"I'm sick of LA," she says softly. "I love my job. Don't get me wrong." She sighs. "I'm so...bored."

"I understand that." We sit quietly, the scenery passing by, listening to Sam Cooke's "Bring It on Home to Me," and I want to tell her this is my most favorite song ever. I can hear her humming along, and it makes my heart happy. "You like this song?"

"I love this song," she says, placing a hand on her chest. She leans her head back. "This has forever been one of my very favorites."

I swallow the large lump that has taken up residence in my throat. "Mine, too," I try to say around it, but I need to clear it. "Yeah, mine, too."

She chuckles and puts a hand on my thigh. "You're nervous. Why?"

"Am I that transparent?"

"Yes, my love, you are." She squeezes my thigh gently. "I am shocked at how quickly I have been able to get to know your little mannerisms."

I keep my eyes on the road. I can't look at her right now. I'll crash. "Like what?"

"Hmm." She takes a breath before she rubs my thigh. "You bite your lip when you're contemplating saying something. I haven't figured out if you don't *think* you should say whatever you're thinking or if you don't *want* to say it." She's still rubbing my thigh. "And you have this cute little one-shoulder shrug when you say something you absolutely want to say." Her hand is much higher now. The placement is holding all my focus. "And you lick your delicious lips right before you kiss me." Yeah, I'm gonna crash. "And when you're flustered, you blink a lot." She laughs, and I realize I'm doing it right now. "See?"

I shake my head and release a strained sound. "Yeah, you do know me pretty well."

"I pay attention to the things that intrigue me." She's right below the crease between my hip and my thigh and slides her fingers along the fold in my pants. "Almost thirty years of being a journalist has taught me to pay attention."

"I intrigue you, hmm?" I finally glance at her, and our eyes meet. I've only seen love in a gaze like that once before, and I ran exactly twenty-seven seconds after.

"Every single thing about you." Her voice is soft, her tone determined, and I bite my lip. Damn, she's right. "What is it? What do you want to say?"

I breathe out, eyes on the road again, and shrug. "I am intrigued by you, too." I can hear the way her lips separate, the sound of them turning upward. Goddamn. I'm so turned on. "Enamored with. Captivated by." *In love with.*

"I can tell."

"Good."

❖

"We get most of our wines from them. They're an estate winery."

Judy leans onto the wine tasting bar next to me. "They grow all their own grapes on land they own?"

"Yes, exactly. How did you—"

"Did you forget that I live in California? Wine is our passion." She leans into me playfully. "And I'm a wine snob."

"Great. I promise that this wine is great. I'm one test away from being a master sommelier."

"Wow, I had no idea." She pulls back. "You're even hotter now."

My entire face fills with heat, and I start to fidget, pushing up the rolled sleeves of my light blue floral button-down, popping my knuckles, anything to ground myself at this moment. I'm walking this fine line between being completely out of my element and being comfortable with all the flirting, the staring, the touches, the compliments. How am I supposed to handle this? "Well, thank you," I decide to say after I bite my lip because what the fuck else should I say? Let's go fuck in the bathroom? Because that's what I want.

"You made it," DeeDee shouts as she approaches.

"Hi!" My voice cracks. *I am not smooth at all.*

DeeDee stops, narrows her eyes. She knows. She knows almost instantly. I'm both impressed and stressed. "And you brought someone."

"Yes, DeeDee, this is Judy. She's—"

"A friend," Judy says, cutting me off, and reaches to shake DeeDee's hand. "A good friend."

"Well, it's lovely to meet you, Judy. I'm DeeDee. I own Purity Wines."

"You have a beautiful winery. I'm in love with this building. The stonework is remarkable."

"Thank you. My late husband and I designed everything here."

"Oh, my condolences," Judy says as she lays a hand on DeeDee's shoulder.

"Thank you, dear. It's okay. I'm surviving. And this place is thriving," she says and waves in a sweeping motion around the packed tasting room. "Let's head outside to the tasting area. I pulled a bunch of wines already, and it's a gorgeous day for an afternoon buzz in the sun."

Judy laughs, and I try to join in. I'm having second thoughts. I should have come by myself or had DeeDee to the resort or something. I'm sweating and breathing heavy, and sweet Jesus, am I going to have a panic attack? Everything has changed since meeting Judy. She's clearly interested. Why am I so nervous? Is it because I'm afraid of falling for a woman who lives in LA and has a career and is more than likely not interested in a long-distance relationship?

Whoa, Hattie, chill the fuck out.

"Hey, calm down." Judy's voice is soft, caring, but also worried.

"How do you know that I'm not calm?" My question is with awe more than anger. I'm genuinely curious.

She runs her hand to the small of my back, then around to my hip. She slips her hand into the back pocket of my Levi's. "I have to prove it again?"

"Yes. I need to know."

"Your entire posture changed." She stops before we get to the outdoor tasting area and adjusts my straw trilby. "Whatever you're thinking and feeling? I can assure you, I'm feeling it, too." She pulls her tortoiseshell sunglasses down her nose. "All of it."

"Okay." I hope I sound convinced.

"Enjoy this time with me." She pushes her glasses back and grabs my hand. "Show me the beauty of Colorado wines."

I let her pull me toward the tasting area and shrug off as much uncertainty as possible. I have got to get my head on straight. There's no reason for me to be so in my feels when I have no way of knowing what the future will hold.

And besides, watching Judy taste wine will be the highlight of my life, I am sure. Might as well enjoy the fuck out of it.

CHAPTER NINETEEN

Olive

Well, I certainly managed to put another nail in this coffin, didn't I? I wake up on my bed after my apparent fainting session with Eleanor. My head is killing me, and the only thing running around my mind is how I can't believe I finally told someone about Paul.

"Hey," Eleanor says softly from the other side of my bed. "How you doing?"

"Ugh," is all I can respond with.

"I'm being serious. Anything hurting? Do we need to call the doctor?"

"No. I'll be fine." I reach for her, for her hand, for anything, and as soon as I grab her, she pulls away. My heart clenches. "Ellie…"

"If you're okay, I'm going to get out of here. I have a lot to think about. A lot. I'll check on you later."

I rise up on my elbows and again, sadness and regret plague me. She's almost to the door when I ask, "Are you mad at me?"

She stops, hand on the knob. "I'm not happy with you. But I'll get over it. I always do."

And she leaves.

She leaves.

I'm left lying there, my heart racing, my head fuzzy, my nerves shot. What am I going to do? Mabel has requested a one-on-one to ask more questions about the resort. I relented only when she said she would come to me. I don't want to talk to her. Of all the times that I don't want to be around anyone else, this is at the top of the list. I can't get out of it, either. What am I going to say?

"Oh, sorry, Mabel, but I just came clean about the fact that I may have committed insurance fraud. Can we reschedule?"

I pull myself together, shower, get dressed, and hope to anyone listening that I can get through this. When she arrives, she promptly slips her brown booties off at the door. She's armed only with a leather journal and a pen. She always looks as if she breezed right in from LA. I wonder if she does that on purpose or if the years she's spent there lend themself to her like an old friend, encouraging her to be classy and cool all at the same time.

"I cannot thank you enough for doing this. All of these tiny one-on-ones can seem a little daunting. They really help me get to know you and the other ladies."

Her constant thanking is exhausting. "It's not a problem at all. Come with me." I motion for her to follow and take the long way around to the kitchen so she can get a feel for the residence.

Once we reach the entryway to the kitchen, I hear a gasp. "Wow," she whispers. "This place is amazing."

That reaction thrills me. "We made the decision to go all out since we were going to be living together full-time." I glide over to the wine cooler and slip a bottle of chardonnay from the rack. I offer her a glass, and she accepts with vigor. I uncork and pour into my favorite glasses. "Should we take these to the patio?"

She sips and pauses, seemingly allowing the taste to wash across her palate, then answers with a firm, "Absolutely."

She's right behind me as I open the sliding glass door and head outside. The mountain plateau gets great afternoon light. There's a large umbrella shielding us, and I've already moved a table next to her chair for the wine. When she sits, she pulls her legs up and sits with them folded as if she's a pretzel. Her not being stuffy is very calming and makes me happy. Being asked questions is hard enough, but when the person asking is a giant pain in the ass, it makes it even worse.

I take a sip. *God, it's such a magnificent wine.* I'm a huge fan of this chardonnay from Napa Valley over the one from Purity Wines, but I will never tell Harriet. She'd kill me. Her partnerships with the local wineries are very important.

"You have opened a wonderful resort, Olive. I hope you know that." Mabel's voice brings me back to the patio. She seems as if she's in her element like this, a glass of wine, her journal, her feet pulled up.

I prop my feet on the square pillow ottoman in front of my chair. "Your opinion means a lot to me."

"I keep thinking something will happen that will make me go, oh yeah, this is exactly like every other resort. But even small things like getting more towels has been enjoyable. Everyone goes above and beyond. Is there something in the water? Do you drug us?"

I snort. "My word, no. We do not drug anyone. Although, weed is legal here, so maybe I should consider having a dispensary."

"That's not a bad idea at all." She leans back into the cushions and sighs. "There is nothing better than a glass of wine and a mountain view."

"That's very true." Is this how the whole night is going to go? Just a bunch of small talk? It's skirting the territory of uncomfortable. But at the same time, it's nice not thinking about everything that happened earlier, and I hate to admit I am kind of enjoying myself. "You had questions for me?"

"Not necessarily. A few. I enjoy getting to know the people I'm writing an article about. Is that okay?"

"It's a little unorthodox."

"Yeah, I, um, I don't do things like everyone else." She has her hair in a ponytail, and she's wearing a cream, cable-knit sweater with yoga pants. The weather is perfect, but a crisp breeze can rush through the valley every now and then. She must have done her research before she packed. Obviously. She's a journalist. "I'm having such a remarkable time discovering the hidden gems here."

"I often say Colorado has its own soul."

"How so?"

I swirl the wine, stare at the way it creates a tornado in the liquid gold. "It's almost as if it has its own heartbeat. There are moments"—I pause, take a deep breath—"when everything lines up perfectly. The weather, the conversation, the company." I shake my head. "Damn, maybe I am high right now. I sound like it."

Mabel's small chuckle is cute. I join in, and she lets out a long sigh. "I can see what you mean. Everything has been…lining up… since we arrived, hasn't it?"

"It certainly has."

"You think that's the soul we are feeling?"

"Mm-hmm."

We sit in silence for two or three minutes. It's a little after five. A couple more hours and our home will be filled with the staff, all invited to enjoy a night of fun before tomorrow. The party has been planned for weeks. The restaurant staff is handling every detail, and for some weird reason, I'm not nervous about it. I'm looking forward to showing the staff how much I appreciate them. I'm looking forward to seeing them have a good time. I'm looking forward to the karaoke Eleanor insisted on and the free bar Harriet made me agree to.

Ugh. Eleanor.

That's going to be a problem. This whole weekend has gotten out of hand.

"What is your favorite thing to do out here? On the Western Slope?"

Oh, good. A question. "I love kayaking." I motion to my body. "Sometimes I'm a little self-conscious, but I manage."

"Hey," she says in a very soothing voice.

"It's okay. It's easier to call it out before someone else does."

"I think you're gorgeous. I see you for what you are. A beautiful woman who is running a multi-million-dollar business."

A multi-million-dollar business that is one false move away from closing. My eyes are stinging with tears. *Get your shit together, Olive. You cannot cry right now.* All I can say is, "That means a lot." It comes out as a whisper because if I say it any louder, I will cry.

Silence falls upon us once more as we both stare across the property. These are the moments when I can feel the soul of Colorado. Because instead of feeling guilty about Paul, I am thankful I was able to take the money and do something amazing with it.

"This place really is a sanctuary," I say, breaking the silence. "Women from all over come here, and we give them time and space to grow into whatever they want or need to be. We offer this gorgeous land as a place to heal, too. It has been the best experience of my life."

"I'm sure you've been able to meet some really inspirational people."

"And some really interesting characters, as well." We both laugh. "I'm thankful. Y'know what I mean? Because I knew after my husband passed that I needed to heal, and I wanted to do that with other people, with my best friends. And they wanted to come along for the ride." I take a deep breath. "It's been a dream come true."

"You're a remarkable woman, Olive." Her eyes narrow. "Sunny is very taken with you."

I pull a sharp breath in. *Sunny.* I haven't thought about her since this morning, since I blew up my friendship with Eleanor. "She is an amazing person."

"It's interesting."

"What's that?"

"How the three of us have paired up with the three of you. I did not intend for that to happen." She shrugs. "I'm supposed to stay unbiased."

"True."

"When I interviewed Meryl Streep the first time, it's not like I was unbiased. I fucking love her."

"Who doesn't?"

"I mean, right? Like, how could I remain unbiased?" Mabel drinks her wine, then sighs. "Do you hate me because of what I did to Eleanor?"

I run a hand through my hair and shrug. "Yeah, sort of."

"Yeah." She sighs again. "Me too."

"It was a long time ago, though." I place both feet firmly on the patio pavers and lean forward, propping myself up with my elbows on my knees. "You were young. So was she. People do stupid shit when they're young."

"I think she's forgiving me. I hope so anyway." She readjusts her legs into the chair instead of folded beneath her. She is sitting cockeyed, head leaned on the cushion as the sun starts its descent behind the mountains. I'm amazed at her flexibility.

"Are you going to hurt her again?" I ask, barely above a whisper.

She answers with a quick, "No." Matter-of-factly, as if she's been thinking about it for far too long. "I will never hurt her again."

"See what I mean about the soul of this place?"

She doesn't speak, just hums a soft, "Mmm." She seems as if she gets it. And she better never fucking hurt Eleanor again.

"Am I interrupting?" Eleanor's voice startles me, and I find myself filled with immediate dread.

"Absolutely not," I answer, hoping the slight quaver in my voice doesn't betray me. "Join us. But grab another bottle of wine." She retreats to the kitchen, and I turn to Mabel. Her expression is flooded with relief and excitement. "This okay?"

She nods emphatically. "Yes."

Eleanor reappears, holding another bottle of the delicious Napa chardonnay. She has already pulled the cork and tops me and Mabel off before pouring herself a glass. She slides between the chairs and sits on the ground in front of Mabel's chair. Not mine, as she normally would. She leans back, her knees bent, and sighs. "Everything is set for tomorrow."

"I cannot even begin to thank you for handling it all today." I squeeze her shoulder.

"Oh, I know." Her tone is still peppered with anger. Not enough for anyone else to notice. Just enough for me to feel sick to my stomach because of it.

"How long have the two of you been friends?" Mabel asks.

Eleanor answers first. "Fifteen years. Long time."

"Going on sixteen."

"Almost old enough to drive."

"Dear God, don't let us wreck this car now." I'm trying too hard, but I need her to know I'm not going to roll over and give up. "That'd be our luck."

"Wouldn't it?" she says with a wry smile. She's so much more relaxed than she was two days ago. Her hair is down and pushed to the side. No beach waves. Just natural. Even her clothing is relaxed. A simple black T-shirt, ripped jeans, black Dr. Martens. She makes relaxed look great. Is this new demeanor because of Mabel? Or is it because the most stressful event we've thrown is almost over? Or did she decide to say fuck it after I told her and is going to leave? Oh no… *oh no, oh no, oh no.*

Mabel runs her fingers over Eleanor's shoulder, rests her hand for a couple of seconds, and runs her fingers through Eleanor's hair. The way Eleanor closes her eyes and leans into Mabel's touch is almost too much.

Within seconds, the uncomfortableness has me standing. "I'm, um. I'm going to, um, go. Yeah, I'm gonna go. You two, um, you two have fun." After I've fallen all over myself, I leave. The uneasiness is making my skin crawl.

I'm halfway out the front door when I realize I'm still holding my wineglass. For half a second, I think I should take it back. It's one of my favorites. But I don't want to go anywhere near them. I close the door and start walking. I have no idea where I'm going. I just need to get away.

As I round the edge of the property, I steer toward a bench. I sit, take a deep breath, and ground myself. The last three days has been midlife-crisis material, and I need to get my bearings.

"Get moving, Olive," I say softly. "Get back, get ready for the party, and stop living inside your head."

Being hard on myself is a skill I've mastered over the years. It's part of why I'm successful now. Or at least, that's what I tell myself.

Paul used to tell me all the time that I needed to calm down, take a breath, and relax. I used to get so angry with him. "Don't tell me to calm down," I would say, even less calm.

He was great at butting in and giving advice, even when sometimes, it was the worst advice ever. I've been thinking a lot about him lately. In more of a "wow, I wonder what things would have been like if I had been able to talk to him" way.

Maybe I couldn't because I wasn't ever *in love* with him.

The thought stops me in my tracks.

If I was never in love with him, and I stayed to *stay*…that makes everything hit a little harder. That makes my sadness and his depression and my irrational fears and his inability to love me and my disgust at having sex with him and his possible suicide…

What the heck do I do now?

When I get back to the house, I can't even go talk to Eleanor about this new revelation. Not only is she furious with me, she's probably going to leave the sanctuary. She's going to leave me. My stomach ties into a knot. I can't do this without her. She's my whole world. She's the only person who understands me and loves me unconditionally.

Oh my God.

Am I in love with Eleanor?

I fall face-first onto my bed and let out a bloodcurdling scream into one of my pillows. I am such an idiot. I am not in love with Eleanor. If anything, I've kept a wall up when it comes to her because I don't want to hurt her or ever fuck up our friendship.

Looks like I went ahead and fucked it up anyway.

My brain is running at full speed, and I need to stop, to settle it down. I truly need to find a way to shut it off and let this evening happen.

Tomorrow is one of the most important days this resort has seen. The Amphitheater will allow us to do many more events and put us on the map as a wedding venue. Everything that has happened is good.

Even if I feel like I'm on the verge of a nervous breakdown.

All of this is good.

Isn't it?

CHAPTER TWENTY

Eleanor

I have literally no idea how I got stuck behind the bar mixing drinks, but here I am. Despite my love of alcohol, I hate bartending.

I slide a dirty martini across the counter to Keri. "Anything else, miss?"

"Oh, Ellie, you funny lady, you're dying to get out from behind there, aren't you? Do you want me to take over?"

"Jesus Christ, yes. Do you mind?"

She motions for me to leave. She pulls a Corona Light from the beer cooler and opens it expertly, and after pouring it into a clear plastic cup, hands it to me. "Here you go."

"That looks lovely," I say as I squeeze a lime into it. I take a drink, then hand it back. "Pour a little Bacardí Limón in there."

"Oh, a hard Corona. I like your style." She stirs it gently, then hands it back.

I eagerly take a drink. "Ah, that's perfect. I'll get nice and loaded early and be perfectly fine tomorrow."

"Has that ever actually worked?"

Suddenly, Heidi slides into my line of sight wearing a dress she has absolutely every right to wear. "Holy fuck," I say as she approaches. She looks ah-mazing. And the expression on her face says she's going to see how long it takes until that dress is on the floor. I've seen this scene a thousand times. I regret letting her hear me because the look she gives me is very telling. I clear my throat and straighten, pull my shoulders back, and hope I don't look as taken as I sound. "Welcome to the party. Keri is apparently our bartender."

"Deb will be here shortly to sling drinks." She pushes her bobbed blond hair behind her ear and shrugs a bare shoulder. It's far too chilly for that dress. But she's pulling it off expertly. And I hate her for it. I needed her to try months ago. Now I want her to back off because jealous Mabel is not something I enjoy seeing. And once she arrives, she'll most definitely be jealous.

"Awesome. I'll leave you two to it, then."

I give Keri a look, and her eyes are as wide as saucers. Oh, she fucking knows. The moment I don't want Heidi is the moment she decides it's game on. It's just my luck. I feel a hand on my arm as I try to move past Heidi without touching her. She's gripping my bare forearm, right above my bracelets, and I gulp before I glance at her. "What's up?"

"You're not going to hang out with me?"

"I have to mingle." I hold my beer up as I shrug. "You know how it is when you're the hostess with the mostest."

"Come back when you're done?"

"A hostess's job is never done." I wink as I escape, taking a long drink on the way. This drink is going to get me very tipsy, very fast, and I'm in desperate need of it. I need the peace a nice buzz brings.

At least, that's what I tell myself.

Sounds pretty convincing, too, when I'm halfway in the bag.

I can't stop thinking about Olive and what she told me. I'm not a coroner, so I have no idea what goes into all of that, but wouldn't they know if it wasn't technically an accident? There would have been an autopsy. And that note could have been from forever ago, and this was indeed exactly what it looked like.

Right?

I shake the memory of Olive collapsing onto the floor from my mind. I've been looking for a way out of this mess with the money and the micromanaging and my inescapable feelings for Olive. This is it. Here is my door. I'd be an idiot to not walk through it. I can go back to Chicago and get my old job back in a heartbeat.

Across the patio, my marketing staff, Sondra, Celine, and Delia, are mingling, and they wave at me to come to them. I make my way over, sliding between a few employees making their way to the bar.

"Ellie, you look so great!" Sondra throws her arms around me and practically takes the wind from my lungs. She's drunk. When she pulls away, she cackles. "Oops, I'm drunk. I've not had anything to eat."

"I told her like, oh, I don't know, seventy-five times, to lay down a bread base. But does she listen? No." Celine rolls her eyes, then drinks her champagne. She's the classiest person I've ever met under the age of thirty. She comes from money. A lot of it.

"I did lay down a bread base," Sondra says, a hiccup following her slurred words. "I just don't believe in taking it easy when the alcohol is free. And hey, I get to enjoy tonight after the nonstop graphic design *genius-ness* I've done to prepare for the event tomorrow."

"Eleanor, did you see Heidi?" Delia asks, then playfully pushes me when I flip her off. "Girl, she's on the prowl for you." She points, left eyebrow arched, lips puckered. "You know that, right?"

"Ugh, don't remind me," I say as I lean against the rock retaining wall. "I swear to God, I don't know what I did to deserve that."

"I thought you were crushing on her?" Sondra asks. "Or did you finally get past it?"

"Listen, you three think you know me so well—"

"We do," Celine says. "You're an open book. Especially when it comes to women."

"I do not remember the part in the employee manual that says you're allowed to speak to your boss this way." I glare at them.

"Oh, sure." Sondra rolls her eyes. "We'll start respecting you *now*. Right this instant."

"You're all fired."

Delia gives me another playful push. "You know we're ragging you."

"Yeah, yeah, I know."

"Besides, we all are fully aware that you've got your eyes on that hot little journalist."

I choke on my drink. I cover my mouth and cough a few times. "What kind of drugs are you on?" A couple more coughs. "I do not have *my eyes* on anything or anyone." Cough. Cough. "Especially that journalist." I pray the coughs make me sound convincing.

Sondra pats my back. "We need a medic?"

"I'm fine."

Sondra leans closer. "In case you haven't noticed, this place isn't as big as it seems. It's like a small town."

"What are you saying?"

"Delia saw you having drinks with her the other night. It's cool. We get it."

"Rumor has it you two used to go to school together." Celine's eyes are wide.

"This isn't any of your…I mean, it's not like any of you need to…

It's that…" I look at each of them, all of their stares are glued to me, each of them poised to drink, on the edge of their proverbial seats. I groan, then let out a sigh. "Yes. God. We went to school together. We grew up together. There. Are you happy?"

Sondra nods. "So? Tell us about her?"

"Yeah, dish the dirt. Spill the tea." Celine waggles her eyebrows.

"Oh, hell to the no." I shake my head. "I will not be spilling any tea tonight. Or any night, for that matter. We knew each other. We still do, and that's that."

"You don't want to sleep with her?"

I almost choke again. "Stop, please?"

"Come on. You know we're rooting for you. We'd never want anything bad to happen. It's been fun seeing you sort of, y'know, out of your element."

"What does that even mean?" I glare at her.

"It means you've been especially on edge. Not in a bad way, just, y'know, jumpy."

"I have not been jumpy."

"There she is," Celine says, and I whip around, only to see that I've been had. I fell for the oldest trick in the book. I groan before taking a very deep breath and letting it out slowly as I turn. Celine clears her throat as she places a hand on my shoulder. "You were saying?"

"That I hate you all. Listen, I'll tell you this and only this."

"We're listening," they say in unison.

I lean in, motioning for them to do the same. "You're all fired."

They start to laugh, and Delia smacks me on the shoulder. I wink at Celine, and she rolls her eyes before I walk away. This tiny part of me did want to stand around and talk about Mabel. I knew if I started, I wasn't going to stop. It's odd how she's managed to take up so much space in my brain again without really trying. It shouldn't surprise me because she has always taken up space in my brain. Like the way she used to smile when I said something stupid. Or the way her laugh sounded when we stayed up way too late watching *Xena: Warrior Princess*. Or the way her fingers felt when she memorized every inch of my body. Or the way she gasped when I touched her in the exact right way.

The beer is no longer going down as well as I was hoping. But bourbon is for bad choices, and vodka is for even worse. I'm at an impasse. Wine will give me a headache. Maybe I should calm down and not drink. What a fucking concept.

Employees are mingling everywhere. I am pleased everyone came instead of saying they'd be here and then not showing up. That's how I was when I was their age. Well, most of their ages. We do have a few people who aren't in their twenties. But we snagged the majority right out of college. I enjoy how young they keep us. It's never a bad idea to stay close to the younger generations. I may not be a millennial—or is it generation Z—but keeping things trendy is doing wonders for us. I told Olive I would never work for a place that wasn't hip. She made fun of me for months. Until the last article that came out, which praised us for how "hip and trendy" we managed to make the sanctuary. I rubbed that in her face for quite some time.

And now I get to decide if I'm going to leave and let Olive take this ship down with her. Or if I'm going to stay and hope for the best.

Someone sits next to me, and an arm finds its way around my shoulders. I look over to see that it's attached to Harriet. Within seconds, my stress level subsides. I take a deep breath and kiss her on the cheek. "I have never been happier to see you."

She breathes out a small chuckle. "Wanna get high?"

"What is it?"

"A nice, mellow edible." She places a square gummy in the palm of my hand.

"Fuck, why not?" I pop it into my mouth, chew, chew, chew, and swallow. "Better than getting drunk, right?"

"Yes, and baby girl, you need to cool your jets. You look like you're gonna fly off the handle at any moment. This"—she motions to me, toes to head—"is *not* you." She rubs my back, and I shake my head as I look at the ground. She has no idea why I'm struggling. I'm sure she thinks it's about Mabel. She'd be furious to learn the truth.

I want to tell her. I want to spill my guts and tell her everything Olive told me earlier, and I want her to join me in solidarity and be mad at Olive for lying to us for as long as she has. But I can't.

Olive is sitting next to Sunny across the patio, a look of pure enjoyment written all over her face, and I hate how much I want to go over and hug her. Tell her I could never be mad at her forever. She's too important to me. And deep down, I am way too important to her.

Resilient.

Goddammit.

I lean into Harriet. "This weekend has been so fucked-up."

She lets out a puff of air and adjusts her trilby. She's so stinking cute. "Listen to me, okay?" Her arm is still around me, holding me close. "You are much more than all this. And Ellie, baby girl, you are way more than your past. We all see that. And you need to, too."

"Thanks, Hattie," I say softly. "Tell me, how are you doing with everything?"

Without a second's hesitation, she says, "I think I'm falling in love with Judy." Her voice is feather soft. I can barely hear her, yet the sincerity smacks me across the face.

"Are you serious?"

She nods.

"Hattie, what are you going to do?"

"I haven't the fucking slightest." She drinks her water.

"Wow."

She pulls me a little closer. "I do know that whatever happens, we will all be okay."

"You're sure?"

"Nope," she says while chuckling, and I can't help but join her.

The sight of Mabel getting a drink catches my eye. "Why a lemon?"

Harriet lets out a huff. "What are you talking about?"

"Mabel. She drinks her vodka soda with lemon. Like, why a fucking lemon?"

"Is that edible hitting already?"

"I guess." I grab her hand as she goes to stand. "Don't leave."

She sits back down. "What?"

"Don't, like, run to LA with Judy or something. This place will not work if we both leave."

"Whoa, whoa, whoa." She puts a hand on my face. "What do you mean?"

I swallow the emotion that has bubbled into my throat. "Just, don't leave. Please." The guilt of us both leaving would be too much to handle.

"You need to pump your brakes, sis. I am not going anywhere. Okay?" Either she is high and doesn't understand what I'm saying, or she truly thinks I'm worried she's going to dip out on us, on the sanctuary, on everything we've built together.

I nod.

"Don't worry. Okay?"

I nod again.

"Let's go get our girls."

"What do you mean *our* girls?"

She tilts her head. "You think I'm stupid?" She pulls on my hand, and I stand. "And we both know Sunny and Olive got something goin' on, too, which, I mean, whatever, right?"

"Yeah, yeah, yeah." I can't fight her any longer. And I don't want to, but that little voice reminds me about how I cried on my bed after Mabel broke my heart, saying, don't dive in without knowing what waits below. Please God, don't let my heart get broken again by the same person. In the same lifetime.

In another lifetime, sure. But not this one. Again.

CHAPTER TWENTY-ONE

Harriet

Yeah, I'm in love with Judy. Every single time I look at her, I find myself hoping for more and more time with her. She leaves on Monday, which means I only have thirty-six hours with her. That's not enough time.

She has her hair pulled up now. It was down when she arrived, but since we've moved from a classy party to the six of us awkwardly hanging out, sitting in the hot tub and swimming in the pool, she has pulled it up with a scrunchie. And her jawline, her cute nose, the way she leans her head back when she laughs, all of her has my complete attention. I want to lick her jaw, nibble on her neck, plant my face in her amazing cleavage.

"Hattie, honey, are you okay?"

"What?" I ask, but I'm in the zone, and it feels amazing.

"Are you okay?" Olive is submerged to her chin, her hair in a bun, her glasses discarded because of the steam.

"I am very okay." I'm still a little high from the edible I smashed with Eleanor, who has handled herself incredibly well. I'm surprised. She doesn't partake on the regular. Whenever she does, I'm impressed with how well she does. Olive, on the other hand, never partakes. Except tonight. She did, as did Sunny, and both were high as kites for quite some time. They seem to be on the back end now, but watching them figure out how to sit in a hot tub without floating was fun.

Judy only took a small piece, saying she wasn't a huge fan. Mabel said, "Absolutely not." As if I offered her cocaine or something. That may be the reason Eleanor sobered up.

"Very okay, hmm?"

Judy's question is whispered, and the sound of her voice makes me want to kiss her. I want to grab her and make out with her, have her straddle my lap, and let me finger her right here. "So very okay," I say softly as she slides her hand over my thigh. Her fingers graze the edge of my trunks, and I move the tiniest amount to loosen the material against my skin. Her finger slips under, and she grazes my pubic area lightly, never taking her eyes from mine. If she keeps doing this, I'm going to ask Olive and Sunny to leave, or I'm going to whisk Judy away to my bedroom. Neither sounds like a bad option.

"Well, Sunny and I are going to go join Mabel and Eleanor in the pool."

Did Olive read my mind? I don't even look at her as I say, "Sounds good to me." As soon as they're out of the water, Judy leans over and has her hand under the waistband on my shorts. Her fingers slide between my folds and find my clit easily, as if she's done this a hundred times and knows me by heart.

"I want to fuck you," she says against my ear before she pulls my earlobe into her mouth and bites it lightly. I am in heaven. Her fingers are rubbing my clit at the perfect speed, weight, everything. I'm ready to come within seconds, and as I close my eyes, she says, "Look at me." I do as she says. She has me right where she wants me. "I love watching you unravel." And that does it for me. I'm coming, and it's one of the most intense moments of my entire life.

"Judy," I whisper. "I still haven't…with you."

She squeezes my hand. "We have time."

"No, we don't," I say softly and close my eyes. I will start to cry, and I am not the person who cries. Not even when my mama passed did I allow people to see me break down. But something about Judy is making me want to share all those parts. The sadness. The fears. The insecurities. The tears. All of me.

"Hattie." Judy's voice is next to my ear. "Look at me." A part inside my heart says that I will do anything she says because I *love* her. "This crazy beautiful thing between us is never going to run out of time. Do you hear me?"

I nod.

"No, Hattie, baby, you have to *hear* me." She places her wet hands on my face, the soft pads of her thumb stroking under my eyes. "You are not a fleeting moment for me. You, God…" Her voice snags, and tears well in her eyes. "You make me feel things I thought I'd never feel again. Things I've only ever felt with the first girl I was with. And I've been chasing that feeling, and dammit, I found it, and I am not going to let this go."

I try to nod, but she's holding my face, and the pressure smushes my cheeks, and she chuckles. "I hear you. And, Judy?" Her eyes are lined with pink from crying. Seeing her like this makes me want to see her joy, her sadness, and everything in between for the rest of my life. "I love you." She blinks, and more tears fall. And my heart starts to beat more rapidly. "I've never loved anyone, and it scares the fuck out of me."

She lets out a tear-soaked whimper. "Hattie." The way her mouth wraps around the sound of my name causes my heart to hitch. Her saying my name is all I ever want. "I love you, too. And..." She pauses and sniffles. "It also scares the fuck out of me."

"I guess that's good, right?"

"I don't know, is it?"

"I've always said, if it doesn't scare you, it's not worth it."

"And you're worth it." She sniffles again. "I can't believe this has happened."

"Fucking tell me about it." I laugh, and she does, too, and *holy fucking shit, I want to spend the rest of my life with this woman.*

How the fuck did this happen?

And how do I make sure it never stops happening?

Olive

For a thousand reasons. For a million reasons. None of this makes any sense.

Three women, with seemingly nothing in common, find each other and start the sanctuary. Then they all happen to fall for these three ladies, who also don't seem to have much in common. Except they all clearly love women. And even, maybe, a little bit, love us.

I'm spiraling. I do not understand how any of this happened.

And yet, here we are.

The three most important guests at the sanctuary this weekend, and they're literally in our home, in our pool and hot tub, and almost in our pants.

I chuckle inwardly. I'm not wrong, though.

"What's so funny?" Sunny's voice breaks through my thoughts.

"Oh, nothing," I lie. "I've had such a nice weekend." Except, of course, for the part where I may have ruined my friendship with one of the most important people in my life. Y'know, nothing major.

Sunny's smooth laughter is calming in exactly the way I need right now. "That's good because so have I."

"I'm sure the other shoe will drop soon enough."

"Why don't you try not thinking the worst this time?" she asks, and I have to force myself to not start listing off a litany of reasons why I'll never be able to do that.

"She will forever be a pessimist." Eleanor's tone is apathetic. Her words, coupled with the tone, hit me square in the chest. Regardless of the fact that she's not wrong, it still hurts. All of it.

"I'm hoping I've helped a little in that aspect," Sunny says with a gentle look of concern.

"You think you're the only one who can help her?" Eleanor asks, and next to me, Sunny stiffens. "I've helped her." Is that jealousy in Eleanor's tone? Or is that anger?

"Ladies," Mabel says softly. "Calm down."

The air has stilled around us. Eleanor and Sunny are two seconds away from facing off in the middle of the pool. I finally find my voice. "Eleanor is right. She has always helped me see the good in things." Silence fills the air, and for half a second, no one else exists in the world but Eleanor and me.

A small part inside me clicks into place.

The corner of Eleanor's mouth ticks upward the tiniest of amounts. My pulse has quickened over the course of the last twenty seconds as the conversation from earlier slams into me, and I realize I'm gripping my plastic cup.

"You two must have quite the past."

It's hard to breathe under the weight of the realization that I may lose Eleanor forever because I was too scared, too embarrassed, too stupid to confide in her. "We do, yes. She's been the most important person in my life for a very long time."

"We've definitely had our share of tough times," Eleanor says. The harsh truth associated with her words sits like an anvil on my chest.

"But we've *always* gotten through them, Ellie." My addition to her statement is another truth, but will it weigh as much?

"That sounds really nice, actually," Mabel says, followed by a stupid dreamy sigh. The urge to tell Mabel she had her chance to have all of that with Eleanor, but she fucked it all up, is as strong as it has ever been. Fortunately for us all, I am no mood to be confrontational.

Eleanor, who has barely moved a muscle, finally clears her throat, then takes a deep breath, causing ripples throughout the warm water. The ripples remind me of my inability to tell the truth, small at first but immeasurable near the end. An ache settles inside my throat. "Yeah, I guess you're right," she says, and even though her tone is soft, it was harsh, as if she doesn't believe it any longer.

"Oh, come on," Mabel leans into Eleanor, whose piercing glare is beginning to make my stomach ache. "I'm sure you two have the best of friendships. Trust and caring and love. All the good stuff."

Eleanor huffs before she shakes her head and finally looks away. I miss the weight of her stare, even if it was filled with the heft of hostility. "You'd think, wouldn't you?"

"Yikes," Sunny whispers. "Well, I'm going to get out and dry off. Olive, why don't you join me?"

Only seconds pass, but they seem to stretch on for hours as I wait, gauging Eleanor's headspace, her reaction to me getting out of the pool. My organs feel like knots. She's done with me. "Yes," I say softly. "I'll join you." I want Eleanor to look at me. I'm willing her, begging her to look at me.

But my efforts are futile.

❖

Eleanor

Olive and Sunny deciding to get out of the pool is the highlight of my evening. Where the hell does Sunny get off thinking she's the key to Olive's happiness? Come the fuck on. She's too much for me. And Olive buying into that bullshit is also too much. Too much for my heart, my mind, my soul.

My stupid sensitive soul.

This is all Olive's fault. She's the one who accepted the proposal to host a journalist from *On the Verge*. She might as well have said, "Sure, visit and write an article where you'll run into the chick whose heart you broke when she was eighteen, and she can't get over it. Come on down. And while you're at it, bring a curvy, hot, trendy queer woman who will get me to realize I actually do like women because my best friend, who's been in love with me for years, hasn't been enough to convince me. Should be a great time."

I'm going to blame Olive for everything. Fuck off, Olive. Fuck all the way off.

And while I'm handing out fuck-offs, I want to tell Sunny to fuck off, too. She has a lot of nerve to swoop in here with her stupid cool style and just, oh, y'know, steal the one constant in my life.

The only constant heartache.

Come on, Eleanor. Get your head in the game. Olive is never going to be what I want her to be. That much is clear. And now? All this new information? I don't know if I can get past her lying about all this.

And Mabel? I can't even begin to figure out what the hell is happening with her. Are all these feelings for her because I'm lonely? Or because she's familiar yet different? Or because she's not Olive?

This, right here, is why I don't like taking edibles. My mind questions every single thing. Like why is the water so warm? What in the earth causes hot springs to be hot? And why am I mesmerized by the way the steam dances around Mabel's face? I want to be the heat from the water, causing her to sweat.

Breathe, Eleanor. Breathe.

"What is going on with you?"

My attention snaps back. Mabel's still lounging with her head back, but she's looking at me, and I hate her eyes because I love them too much. Even in the patio lighting, I can see the blue and remember how she looked under the white sheet of my bedroom at six in the morning as we promised to never stop loving each other. "Are you struggling at all with whatever is happening between us?"

She lifts her head. "Absolutely."

"Okay, good. I don't want to be the only one wondering what the hell is going on."

"I can guarantee that you are not the only one who's nervous about it." She clears her throat, which means there's more coming, and I don't know if I want to know what she's going to say. "Ellie?"

"What?"

"I never stopped loving you."

I let out a sigh, but it sounds like a groan, and anguish floods my body. "We lost so many years."

"Oh, Ellie, I would have never become the person I am today if I hadn't broken you. I would have never realized how I needed to change and accept who I was. You know that, right?"

Small hairs have made their way out of the yellow scrunchie holding the mass of auburn away from her face. The humidity has made them curl, and all I can think is that I want to kiss her. I want to love her for the rest of my life because I wasn't allowed to love her for the beginning and middle. "I know," I say. She rests a hand on my knee. "I think about all the shit we've both had to go through."

"Makes what we have worth it, don't you think?"

"Please don't hurt me again." I'm ashamed of myself for even saying that, but if I didn't say it, would I have ever learned my lesson? "I won't survive it."

"I won't." She pulls her hand from the water and places it, dripping and warm, on my face. "You are the loveliest part of my days. I don't want to lose you or this feeling again."

"Letting go of my hatred for you has been the hardest, and at the same time, the easiest thing I have ever done."

"Yeah, I know," she whispers. "Can I..." Her voice breaks, and I lean forward and kiss her like I'm drowning, and she's my life preserver, and her lips taste like home and feel like cotton candy, and I wonder if I'm still high or if this is how kissing was supposed to feel. I want to crawl inside her, curl up and live right next to her heart as it beats like mine. She's smiling into my kisses, and I hear her say, "Kiss you," and my sensitive soul rejoices.

I manage to find a way on top of her lap, straddling her. Our lips never break contact, and when I feel her hands on my hips, heat flares inside my chest like a fire on the verge of raging out of control. "I've missed your kisses," I say against her lips.

"Ellie?"

"Yeah?"

"Can we stop overanalyzing this and get on with it?"

Her bluntness has me chuckling. "Good idea." And I lean to kiss her again as she slides her hands up to my waist. Her thumbs press gently into the sides of my breasts, and the urge to give in completely is strong. She bites my bottom lip, and I grip her face with care as I deepen our kiss. My brain is stuck between this moment and the first time she kissed me as we sat on the old burnt-sienna-colored couch in my basement, watching *Jurassic Park* for the hundredth time. She was wearing Vanilla Fields, and I was so in love with her. When she leaned into me, my entire world seemed to right itself, as if I had been living before that moment like a planet off its axis. And then I was fixed, able to spin correctly, orbit the sun without fear that I was going to crash and burn.

She breaks from our kiss. "This may be a little forward, but can we take this—"

"Upstairs to my room? Yes. One hundred percent yes."

A giggle bubbles from her as she pulls me back into her. "I've missed you more than you know," she says softly before kissing me again.

And I've missed her.

I've missed this.

I've missed *us*.

CHAPTER TWENTY-TWO

Harriet

Well, it's four in the morning, and we haven't slept at all. I've had all-nighters before, but holy shit, this was next level.

Judy is the best I have ever been with. Not only is she completely free in bed, but she is entirely comfortable in her own skin. I never once felt out of place or like I was doing something wrong. Always before, there's been a moment, a very small moment, when nerves flare inside my chest. But I never once felt nervous with her.

I roll over to look at her wrapped in my white sheets. Her eyes are closed, a small grin stretched across her swollen lips, and my breath catches. I love her. And she leaves tomorrow.

My mind flashes to her riding my face, to the way she moved against me, to the way she was pinching her nipples, and the way she tasted as she came. The memory of her asking me to love her forever has tears welling in my eyes. Dammit, I can't believe how this woman has gotten inside me.

And her whisper-asking if I had a strap-on?

Lord have mercy on my soul.

I absolutely do have one, lucky for her. And lucky for me, she let me fuck her three times in three different positions, and I swear to the heavens up above, I came every single time: up against the wall, straddling me on the edge of the bed, from behind.

Every muscle in my body is sore. Muscles I didn't even know existed.

I slide my index finger over the sheet, the outline of her nipple, and when it instantly hardens, I find comfort in the predictability.

"Hattie," she whispers, her eyes sliding open. "You're not sick of me yet?"

I shake my head as I pull the sheet down and move so I can latch on. I suck, then bite, and she breathes in through clenched teeth.

"That feels amazing."

"I want you." My words are muffled against the soft skin of her breasts. I brush my fingers over her smooth side, hip to thigh, and dance my fingers across her skin until she moves the perfect amount, giving me access to her wetness. When I find it, she pulls in a sharp breath. "Are you sore?"

"Yeah," she whispers, "but I want you, too."

I lean into her, place my lips on hers, kiss her deeply, passionately, as she rolls onto her back, and I slip my fingers inside. She moans into the kiss. I'm in awe of her, of how much I love doing this, of everything that has to do with her. "I love you." The words come out against her lips, and within seconds, she has her head arched back, her lips out of reach, her neck exposed, and she's coming, moaning my name, whisper soft.

"Fucking *Christ*, Hattie." Her thighs begin to relax around my hand. "Goddammit, I love you, too." She lets out a giggle that warms my soul. "That's, like, my fifteenth orgasm."

"Sixteenth."

"You kept count?" She picks her head up. "Like, seriously?"

I shrug. "Yeah."

"You are incredible." She places her hands on my face and pulls me into her, her lips finding mine with ease. "I don't want to leave you. I want to stay with you forever." Her words are said between kisses, between breaths, and then between sobs as she starts to cry.

I smooth my thumbs over her cheeks, over the tears as they fall from the corners of her eyes and run down to her hairline. "Let's not freak out yet."

"We should have thought about this before—"

"Before what?" I ask. "Before our eyes met and I felt that instant connection to you? You think a conversation about why this wouldn't work would have made a difference?"

She shakes her head, a small chuckle escaping. "No, it wouldn't have."

"We will deal with it. Okay? Whatever it takes." When I stop talking, she runs both hands down my back and drags her nails lightly across my bare ass. Goose bumps erupt all over me, and the grin that appears on her lips is magnificent. "You're incorrigible."

"I'm a horny middle-aged woman. You should take advantage of this. There aren't many of us left."

"Oh, so you're an endangered species?"

She nods. "Yeah, and you're getting to witness me in the wild."

"In your natural habitat, hmm?"

She pushes me and with one fluid movement, has me on my back and is straddling my hips. "I think it's my turn to fuck you with that strap-on."

A zip of electricity shoots through me. Her? Fucking me? With a strap-on? "Sign me the fuck up," I say with a chuckle as I point to the bedside table and prop myself up on my elbows. She dismounts me, slides across the bed, and stands. Her sliding the harness up her legs, then adjusting the tightness and maneuvering the dildo into position as if she's done this a hundred times before, is one of, if not the, sexiest things I have ever seen in my entire life. I'm full of questions, but I decide to hold them in. I am not ruining this moment by asking where the fuck she learned to fuck a woman with a strap-on. After all, she didn't ask me.

"How do you like it?"

"How do you think I like it?"

"From behind."

Another zip of electricity courses through me. "You'd be right."

"I think you like to move back and forth while I stay in place."

I nod. "You'd be right again."

"Which means you control the fucking." She wraps her hand around the purple dildo. "Because you love to control everything."

"You know me well," I whisper because I honestly cannot find my voice. The way she's speaking about me is such a turn-on. And watching her standing there with the black straps of the harness in stark contrast on her pale skin, the dildo eager and waiting, I wonder if I'll ever be the same after her, or has she managed to change every part of me forever?

She kneels on the bed and moves closer on her knees, her breasts bouncing with the movement. She stops when she gets close enough to touch, reaches up, and resecures her hair. While she does that, her breasts are practically ordering me to play with them again. "May I ask you a question?" Her voice is softer than before but still full of determination.

"Absolutely."

"Would you mind if *I* controlled the fucking?"

My mouth goes as dry as a four-hundred-degree oven. I shake my head because of course I don't mind, but holy fuck, she communicated her desires. That is a first for me. I didn't realize how much I needed that in a partner until she said it. She leans down and kisses me, and within seconds, I hand my entire body over to her. She kisses my chest, breasts, stomach, and every single part of me. She is driving this car, and I am so okay with being her passenger.

"Roll over," she says softly, and I do. I feel her hand on my back, in the center, then both hands on my sides, then she kisses each ass cheek and drags her nails down the backs of my thighs, my calves. "Get on your knees." Her gentle yet firm commands are a dream come true. She reaches between my legs, palm flat on my stomach, then drags it down to my wetness and slips her fingers inside. I'm sore, but something about being sore *and* being fucked is my jam. Clearly, I'm enjoying myself because I'm dripping. I can't see what she's doing, which would have made me nervous in the past.

"Are you ready for me to fuck you?" she asks.

"Yes, God, yes." I barely recognize my own voice. I feel the tip of the dildo against me, and it slips easily inside. I moan. "Judy."

"Are you okay?"

"Yes. Yes, yes, yes." I'm trying not to sound needy, but she cannot stop. I do not want her to stop. Her hands are on my hips, and she pushes harder. This is when I would typically take over and control the fucking, as she politely put it. But I said I'd hand over the reins and let her do as she pleases. And am I glad I did because the way she moves in and out of me hits my G-spot just right, and it feels fan-fucking-tastic. I have had G-spot orgasms before but never like this. Never with a woman. She's moving at the perfect speed, the perfect intensity, the perfect everything.

My orgasm builds and builds, and when it hits, it hits hard. I can't hold in my moan, and when I say her name way louder than I should, I hear her chuckle. I'm still coming, and knowing she's loving every second of this is making it last even longer. She thrusts into me a few more times, the last time holding steady, and my arms start to shake. I can't hold myself up any longer. I collapse, and somehow, she manages to collapse with me, the dildo still firmly inside me. I'm shaking, I'm near tears, and I'm completely fucking spent.

"Are you okay?" Her voice against my ear is lovely.

"I am very okay," I answer, and I'm breathless.

"You were so loud."

"Well, you were fucking me the best I've ever been fucked. What did you expect?"

"Oh?" The surprised tone of her voice is endearing.

"My God, yes."

I feel her move. The dildo shifts, causing a moan to slip from my mouth, and she says against my skin, "I'm going to pull out." The second she's no longer inside me, I miss the sensation of her filling me up. She plops next to me on her back, and when I turn toward her, her entire body is on display, her breasts, the strap-on, all of it. I make a point to memorize this moment. The way the early morning light has started to sneak in my windows. The way gravity pulls her breasts the tiniest of bits to the sides. The way my skin looks against her pale white skin. The way her small hoop earrings managed to make it through the entire night without being ripped out.

Every.

Single.

Detail.

"I love you," I say as quietly as possible. "So much."

The grin that spreads across her lips makes my hands ache. "I love you, Harriet Marshall." She rolls, kisses my arm. "I love you more than I have ever loved anyone in my entire life. And…" The way she pauses gives me pause, but she needs this moment, or at least I think she does. She doesn't finish for the longest time. I give her what she needs. I'll give her whatever she needs. "And I think we should get married."

I let out a laugh. "Judy." But I see in her eyes that she is completely serious. "Judy?"

"I want to marry you." She blinks once, twice, then shrugs. "I want to spend the rest of my life with you."

My brain is short-circuiting. I am searching for words, for anything, because I can't *not* say anything. "Judy," I finally say, "baby, what about your kids?"

"Two are in school. And my youngest will go wherever I go."

"But…but what about you? Your job?" Ugh, I'm stuttering. I'm freaking out. Oh God.

"I'm ready to retire. I'm ready to stop being this person. I want to be who I am when I'm with you."

"Are you…are you *serious*?"

"It's crazy." She purses her lips, and it breaks my heart to see the way her features tighten, as if she thinks she needs to start playing it off as a dumb joke, something said in the heat of the moment, a string of words that shouldn't be taken seriously.

"No, Judy, are you serious?"

She sits up, leans forward where I can't see her face any longer. I move, too. She's still wearing the strap-on, and the dildo is staring right at me.

"It's hard to take you seriously when the dildo is looking at me like that."

She finally laughs, the tension breaking. "I guess I should take it off, huh?"

"Probably." I put my hand on her arm as she starts to get up. "Wait. I haven't answered you."

She smiles, but it doesn't reach her eyes. "It was stupid to say all that. I mean, who are we trying to kid, right? Neither of us wants to be married. I don't want to get married again. And you've never even met my kids. It was only, like, a heat of the moment thing. The altitude got to me. The high of fucking you." The chuckle that follows is one that sounds like she's trying way too hard to hide her true feelings. My heart is breaking. "I was kidding. Don't worry about it."

I know she wasn't kidding. She knows she wasn't kidding. And it's the first time since we met that the air between us is filled with awkwardness. I don't know what to say. We've known each other for less than a week. I do stupid things from time to time. I jump too quickly and take chances when I probably shouldn't. But I am not the marrying type. I am not the person who settles down.

Even if it's who I find myself longing to be.

❖

Eleanor

I should have never let Harriet pick her bedroom. There are six in this house, and she had to pick the one down the hall from mine. I swear to God.

Mabel found the sounds of Judy and Harriet's animalistic sex *very* funny. I told her that when you hear it as often as I do, you tend to stop finding the humor in it.

When my alarm goes off at seven, I reach over quickly and turn it off. I stopped using my cell phone as an alarm clock a while ago. I read an article about disconnecting at night from technology and how it can help anxiety. Oddly enough, it seems to work.

Last night was a different story. I barely slept. And not for the same reason Harriet and Judy didn't. Mabel and I stayed up for most of the night talking. And kissing. A lot, *a lot* of kissing. Some of the best kisses of my entire life. Like, sensual, amazing, deep kisses where I forgot where I ended, and she began. Kisses that made it very difficult for me not to rip her clothes off and devour her. But we had real discussions about life and love and the future and where we both see ourselves.

But yeah, ultimately, we kissed a lot.

It was like old times, giggling about how cold her feet are and letting her play with my hair, which now includes a head massage I was not anticipating but thoroughly enjoyed.

But the kissing. God.

I look at the ceiling and pull a deep breath in. I hold it for a few seconds, focus on the air filling my lungs, focus on the ceiling, on the way the light has filled my room. When I let it out, I glance next to me. At Mabel Sommers in my favorite worn-out Star Wars T-shirt. At her auburn hair and the way it dried from the pool into messy curls. She's sound asleep, even slept through the alarm, which isn't surprising; she literally has not changed since high school in that aspect.

She's on her back, barely moves, doesn't snore, doesn't even seem to breathe. I was in awe of that when I was a kid because I used to move all over. Hell, I still do if I don't relax properly before bed. And at two in the morning, my brain loves to remind me of some of my most embarrassing moments. Like the time when I ran into a flagpole while I was onstage to accept an award in high school. Or the time I split my pants as I did a cartwheel down the hallway.

Or the time I walked into school, and every single student knew I was a lesbian, and I found cut-outs of scissors everywhere for weeks on end. I didn't even get to come out of the closet for the first time. I was pushed out of it.

My stomach still twists when I think about it. And here I am, allowing the woman who essentially outed me and didn't stop any of the bullying right back into my life and my heart.

I shake my head. I'm not that same scared girl who didn't know what she wanted or who she was. I am Eleanor Fitzwallace, and I am a force with which to be reckoned. I am strong. Beautiful. And completely regressing. *Stop, Ellie. Stop.*

I freeze when I feel Mabel roll onto her side, facing me now. Her eyes are still closed, still barely breathing. Mabel *fucking* Sommers. What am I doing? Why am I doing this with her again? She's leaving tomorrow, and we both know long-distance doesn't work. And I don't even know if I want to be with her. For the first time in forever, I'm ridiculously confused about what I truly want. I can leave here if I want to. I can go where Mabel goes. I can be that person.

Or I can stay. With Olive. In a friendship that will never be everything I need even though it's so much of what I want.

Get out of my head, Olive. I'm lying here with Mabel and thinking about my dumb loyalty. And speaking of being dumb, how did two grown women, both half-naked, not sleep together? What does that mean? Should it mean something? We weren't ready is all I can come up with.

"Are you watching me sleep?"

Her voice startles me, and I breathe out the air I sucked in. "You scared the hell out of me."

Her eyes slide open. "I could practically hear your brain overthinking." She licks her lips, her very swollen lips. "We didn't sleep together because I don't want to rush this."

Okay. That's fucking weird. "That is not at all what I was thinking."

She lets out a very small puff of air. "Sure."

"I swear," I lie. "Is that really why?"

"I knew I was right." She pushes my hair behind my ear. "I love you, Ellie. But I don't know if you're there yet." She runs her index and middle finger down my jaw. "I know you too well to not also know that you're still wondering why you're doing this and if you're doing the right thing."

"Am I that transparent?"

"No," she whispers. "You're perfect." She leans forward and places her lips on mine. Her nose nudges mine as she deepens the kiss, her tongue pushing into my mouth, and she slides her hand to the back of my neck. She presses her fingers into the base of my skull. She knows exactly what I love, which, oddly enough, is not the same as in high school.

I moan into her mouth. It makes me happy that I sound this good because I can only imagine how good I'll sound when we finally fuck. All of a sudden, she's straddling my hips, our lips only breaking apart once, and it's when she reaches for the hem of the T-shirt and pulls it up and over her head. My mouth starts to water. I prop myself up with my elbows and take in her bare breasts, her dark pink areolas, her small nipples. She leans down, hands on my face, and kisses me again.

"Is this okay?" she asks between kisses.

"It's more than okay."

"Take your shirt off." She rocks backward a little and pulls me forward, her hands on the hem of my sleep shirt. She's yanking it off as if our lives depend on this, and it's a little manic, considering what we discussed.

When she starts kissing me again, I pull away. "Are you sure you want to do this?"

"God," she breathes out. She places her hands on my breasts, and I hold back the gasp from her slightly cold touch. "I have never wanted anything more."

"Okay, because moments earlier, you were saying—"

"I know what I said." She rolls each of my nipples in between her forefinger and thumb, which causes me to lean my head back. A low moan pours from my mouth. It has been entirely too long since I've been touched, and it's been even longer since she's done this to me, and the sensation is almost enough to make me orgasm on the spot. "And I know what I want."

"Jesus Christ," I whisper as she tweaks my nipples again. If there is one thing I absolutely fucking love more than anything else, it's my nipples being played with, and she is doing exactly the right thing. "What is it that you want?" She does it again and gets me to moan louder this time.

"I want you to unravel beneath me." She kisses me, bites my bottom lip, then moves her hands to my neck, fingers pressing again into my skull.

"Mission fucking accomplished," I say into her kisses as I wrap my arm around her waist. I easily maneuver and flip her over. She's so light, and I'm stronger than her. When I get her onto her back, she gasps, then lets out a low growl. "What? What's wrong?"

"That was fucking hot."

"Honey, you ain't seen nothin' yet." And I lean down to capture one of her nipples in my mouth. I feel her push forward, her back arched, and I continue to lavish each breast with attention. I love playing with breasts as much as I love my breasts being played with. I'm going to make sure I savor every last inch of Mabel's. From the small areola to the taut little nipple to the gentle curve down to her sides. She is enjoying every second of this. As am I.

Her hands are on my face now, and she's pulling me up to her. "I want your lips on me." She kisses me deeply, and I let my hand wander to her black panties, where I slip my fingers under the waistband. She's completely shaved, and yeah, that manages to turn me all the way on.

"Take them off, please." She's being very forward. It's refreshing. I do as she asks and yank the panties down her legs and toss them over my shoulder. "Take yours off," she says.

I stand and slowly push them over my hips, my thighs, one leg at a time until she's groaning for me to hurry up. I kneel before her and push her knees apart. She giggles at me.

When I ask what she's laughing at, she says, "I cannot begin to tell you how excited I am to feel your mouth on me." I bend down and put my mouth directly on where she's glistening. She tastes amazing. I take my time, tasting every fold, pushing my tongue inside, listening to her moaning, saying yes, telling me how good it feels, how much she's missed me. When I find her clit with my tongue, it takes no time at all to get her to the brink. I push two fingers inside as I lick her, and she moans my name. Not just Ellie. No. She moans, "Eleanor," and I almost combust. She's so close, so I curl my fingers and thrust softly as I keep the intensity steady on her clit.

"I'm going to come," she whispers, and two seconds later, she does. She moans and grabs a pillow to cover her face, shouting into it. I keep pushing and pulling as she rides out her orgasm, my tongue never stopping, and when her hips come off the bed, it's obvious I'm doing an incredible job. When she finally returns to the bed, she clamps her thighs on my head.

"Hey, easy there, killer."

"Ellie. What the fuck was that?" She's breathless, panting, and I beam with pride.

"That was…" I crawl up next to her. I drag my very wet fingers up her stomach, over her sternum, and she takes my hand and puts my fingers in her mouth, sucking each one. *Holy fuck.* "That was, um, almost thirty years of practice."

She places my hand on her chest and covers it with her own. "You are definitely not the same person."

"I'm assuming you aren't, either."

"You ready to find out?"

"Abso-fucking-lutely."

Mabel starts to move, but there's a knock on my door, and she freezes. Her eyes are as big as saucers.

"Eleanor, are you two getting up? Breakfast is ready," comes Olive's voice through my door.

Mabel collapses on the bed as I try to stifle my laughter. "I swear to fucking God," I say softly. "Olive, yes, we will be down shortly."

Mabel sighs. "So now what?"

"We pick this back up later. Is that okay?"

"Aren't you ready to combust?"

"Yes." I nod. "I am literally going to die."

"Well, then." She slips her hand down, down, down, until her fingers are dipping into my wetness.

"Mabel, I don't think I can—oh, my God. Fuck." She pushes a finger inside, then another.

"I'm sorry, what were you saying?"

I let out a strained groan. "Shut up."

"Let's get you to come," she whispers as she thrusts into me lightly, just enough that I'm starting to get close. She pulls out and finds my clit as if she still has the map to my body memorized. Her fingers are rubbing with the perfect intensity, and I feel my orgasm building and building. She presses a tiny bit harder. "I want to hear you," she whispers against my ear, and her lips close around my earlobe, and her teeth bite into the soft flesh. And, well, that fucking does it. My orgasm rips through me, my entire body shaking, and I feel a cramp start to build in my calf.

Once it passes, which seems to take forever, I let out a ragged breath. "I'm like a teenage boy. I'm sorry."

"Because you were fast?"

"Yeah, sometimes it's quick, other times, it takes eighty-four years."

Mabel leans down and kisses me. "I'll make it last later when I get my mouth on you." She pops out of bed, stark naked, breasts bouncing. "Let's go eat." She bends over and gathers her panties and the Star Wars T-shirt. This version of Mabel is literally all I ever wanted. She's sure of herself, of who she is and who she wants. And now it seems I'm the one who's not sure of who she is or wants.

It's possible that I could be happy without Olive. Isn't it?

Goddammit, it has to be.

❖

Olive

Well, that was awkward.

I had an ominous feeling that I was going to walk in on something. Part of the reason I knocked instead of my usual throwing open the door and jumping onto Eleanor's bed to wake her up.

Jealousy flares inside me. And anger. Toward myself more than anything but also toward Mabel. How dare she waltz in here and take my best friend from me in every possible way?

Wait a second. These feelings I'm having, am I worried about being replaced as a best friend? Or is it something else? I don't have feelings for Eleanor, do I? She literally sat and told me she does—or did—and at the time, I was filled with dread. But now? Now I can't stop thinking about her. But maybe I do have feelings for her? I love her. I love everything about her.

The idea of sharing her, or worse, losing her, has me tied in knots. I assumed we'd grow old together, and we would both be happy *existing*. The physical side has never been something I need in order to feel fulfilled.

Maybe that's why Paul was distant in the final years. He was different from the man I fell in love with and married and spent a great deal of my life with. He was closed up and insecure and barely spoke to me about anything important. The Bears and the Cubs were hardly topics I cared about, yet I learned as much as I could just so I could talk to him. I'll never forget the last time I asked him to talk about whatever was bothering him. The middle of August, a sweltering day in Chicago, a stack of papers on his desk, client folders and deposition notes, and I found him staring out the window, tears streaming down his face. I begged him to tell me what was going on, and he wiped his face, looked at me, and told me he loved me more than anything in this world.

The next day, he was dead on the Dan Ryan, his motorcycle fifty feet behind him.

Would things have been different if I had talked to him? Would he have realized none of this was his fault? That I'm wired differently? That I loved him as much as I could. That all I wanted was for him to be happy again.

That was the *only* reason I was going to divorce him. Because I couldn't make him happy anymore, and it was clear that he knew it, and so did I, but I was too stupid and scared to talk to him. I was too embarrassed.

So here I am.

An overweight, confused, controlling, possibly asexual bisexual who lies when the truth is too hard.

What a fucking catch.

No wonder Eleanor hates me. I don't blame her. Thank God she let me go and found comfort in the arms of someone who broke her heart. At least Mabel is skinny. And beautiful. And successful. And has her head on her shoulders instead of in the past feeling guilty over everything I've done to get to this place. Mabel is clearly the better choice.

Clearly.

And Sunny is a good choice for me. She's kind and caring and has no idea what a fucking shitshow I am. And her saying she wants to get to know me? God. I want to tell her to run for the hills. Don't turn back. Just keep on running. I'm not nearly as put together as I appear. I'm a hot mess, and the more these layers are pulled back, the more starts to show. Sometimes, I feel like an antique, an old necklace hanging on by a thin chain. It's only a matter of time before that chain breaks.

Sunny doesn't seem to be fazed by anything new she learns. Last night, I told her about my childhood and my parents and losing my mom, and I cried, and she sat there and listened and reacted when needed. She held me and kissed my forehead. She told me about her past and her parents, too. About growing up wondering who she was and finally figuring it out when she was fifteen in the back seat of an old Mercury Sable. Living an out life seems freeing for her. She doesn't speak of regret. She doesn't speak of guilt. Her stories are happy, even when she suffered heartbreak at a young age. She finds the silver lining in everything. Her gratefulness over finding acting and being able to be passionate about it is a breath of fresh air. When she recalled a memory of her very first audition, I felt as if I was standing right there with her, in awe of her then as much as I am now.

She is nothing at all what I thought I'd find in this lifetime. She's stable and beautiful and doesn't need me to take care of her. I try too hard to take care of people, especially when they don't need it, as if I know better what someone needs or wants. I barely know what I want. How the hell can I know what someone else wants?

Sunny is cooking scrambled eggs while the four sex-addicted women upstairs pull themselves together. Her hair is a mess, and it's adorable that she hasn't even tried to fix the spiky parts. She has her jeans on from last night, but the sleeveless T-shirt is Harriet's. She looks like she belongs here making eggs, making me *happy*. I want to touch her, the back of her neck, wrap my arms around her and ask her to stay.

Forever.

Because tomorrow, she leaves, and she will undoubtedly take a piece of my soul with her. It will hurt. I will be sad, yes, I will also be so excited to watch her be successful. Even from afar. I'll go from being the object of her affection to being a fan. A no one. Someone she might remember when she meets a new woman in a bar or on the set of her next movie. Will she recall the nights we spent together, when she helped me learn to be okay with the person I have become? Or will I be the only one with memories of lingering touches and hazy stares?

I lean against the counter next to the stove. "What?" I ask because her lips have a grin on them, and she shrugs. "Tell me."

"I like being here with you. You make me happy. I feel at peace."

"I was thinking the same thing about you. I'm very happy I met you."

"I'm thrilled you met me, too," she says, and her righteousness has me chuckling. She leans in and kisses me on the cheek. It's the most intimate thing she's done, and my heart skips a beat. When she pulls away, she must see the shock on my face because she says, "I'm sorry."

"Stop." I place a hand on her cheek and run my thumb along the softness. "Kiss me."

"Are you sure?"

I nod. "Yes. I am sure." I close the distance because the desire to feel her lips is too strong to fight. Our lips touch, and I can feel her trembling. I put my other hand on her face and deepen the kiss. Her hands are on my waist. I silence the small voice inside my head that likes to remind me of my weight.

"The eggs are getting cold," she mumbles against my lips.

I chuckle between kisses. "We should have done this last night." We should have. I have yet another regret now.

She pulls away the tiniest of amounts. "We still have tonight." She's right, but the way she says it causes my heart to clench, and my eyes tear up. "Olive." Her voice is a whisper. "Don't think about tomorrow. Just be present with me now. Okay?"

I nod as I hold back my tears. "Okay, okay."

"Are we interrupting something? Or should we go back up to the room?"

I roll my eyes as Harriet and Judy breeze into the kitchen. "You mean how you two interrupted us all night long?"

"Oh, good one. Good one." Harriet shakes her head, and Judy blushes ten shades of red. Harriet is wearing pajamas like she's trying to fool us into thinking they slept at all. We know better. We *heard* better. Judy has one of Harriet's T-shirts on and her chinos from the night before. They're holding hands. They look incredibly good together. As much as I hated the idea of Harriet hooking up with this woman when they first arrived, I am glad to see Harriet happy. I don't know if I've ever seen her this way before. In all the years of us being friends, how is it possible that she has never looked this happy?

"Where are the other two?"

"We're coming right now," I hear Eleanor shout down the stairs.

"Am I the only one holding back a snide comment?" I look at Sunny, Judy, then Harriet. "Yes?"

Sunny moves the eggs to the center island where the pancakes, bacon, and the fruit bowl are waiting. "No, I'm holding it back, too."

"I don't think I'm allowed to make any snide comments about sex right now." Harriet shrugs. "Totally worth it, though."

Judy leans into her and kisses her on the cheek. "It was most definitely worth it." I'm not nearly as uncomfortable as normal while watching their display of affection. Maybe understanding myself is going to be good for a lot more than only my inner peace.

"Okay, okay, we're here." Eleanor rushes into the kitchen looking like she's been ridden hard and put away wet. Mabel is wearing her favorite Star Wars T-shirt and her yoga pants, and yep, there's my old pal jealousy, flaring his nostrils inside my chest.

"Well, well, well, don't you two look—"

Judy finishes Harriet's sentence with, "Gently used."

"Ha, ha, ha, very funny." Eleanor heads toward the dining room with a full plate, but I catch the dramatic eye roll. "You two are not allowed to say a word about how we look this morning. We could barely sleep with all the racket coming from your side of the house."

"Seriously," I say. Sunny and I take seats across from Eleanor and Mabel, who hasn't said a word yet except a very small good morning. "Can ya keep it down tonight? I mean, good for you both, but goddamn."

Judy shakes her head. "Well, I'm sufficiently embarrassed."

Harriet pulls Judy's face to hers and kisses her. "Don't be. You were amazing." And I swear, I can see the embarrassment literally leave Judy's body. It's as if Harriet pulled it right from her.

"We have a very long day today. I'm hoping we can get going in the next hour and head to the welcome center. Can you two be ready by then?"

"Absolutely. I need to shower."

"Yeah, same here." Eleanor's small smirk is too much. Why can I handle the thought of Judy and Harriet and not Eleanor and Mabel? What does this mean?

"Okay, great. And we'll see you three later? At the event?"

"Absolutely. I am looking forward to it," Mabel says, and while she's looking right at me, as if she senses and understands something that I don't, she slides her hand around Eleanor's shoulders. When she breaks eye contact, she kisses Eleanor on the cheek, and Eleanor's face softens, her shoulders relax, and…it hits me.

"Wonderful." I've lost her.

CHAPTER TWENTY-THREE

Harriet

"Okay, Hattie? The food is prepped, the linens are going on around half-past three, right?" Eleanor, who is not acting right, but we don't have the time to unpack whatever the hell is going on with her, asks as she slows her walk to an abrupt stop. Her nerves are on display for the entire staff to see. I want to tell her to settle the fuck down, but that won't go over well.

"Yes, and the place settings will be out right before the party starts. The crew should finish a half hour before we start letting people in at five." I motion between myself and Eleanor. "That's what we discussed, remember?"

"Perfect, yes. That'll be great. Then people can come in, visit the bar, mingle, enjoy hors d'oeuvres and live music." Eleanor spins, the venue in all its beautiful glory stretched out in front of her. She breathes in deep and holds it. "It's going to be great," she whispers.

I do the same. There are six rows built into the rocks. They're all wide enough that we can put chairs up if needed. Our original plan for the venue was for weddings and parties. Concerts were an afterthought, but I feel like the addition of live music is part of the reason the event sold out. Of the eighty round tables, every seat is purchased. And the standing-room-only tickets sold out when we opened them up a week ago.

I'm pleasantly surprised by the excitement. "I mixed up the menu a bit. I hope that's okay," I say. Olive's eyes widen. "Don't worry. Nothing crazy, but since the dress code is now casual, and it's a concert, I made more dishes that can be enjoyed without a table." My reasoning seems to calm her. "Appetizers are caprese skewers, prosciutto-wrapped shrimp, crab cakes with roasted red pepper cream sauce, and macaroni and cheese stuffed jalapeño poppers with my buttermilk ranch dip. For dinner, I did brisket, pulled pork sliders, and chicken and waffles. I'm also serving roasted vegetables over cheesy polenta, bacon-wrapped asparagus, and wilted leaf lettuce salad with warm dressing."

"Holy fuck, my mouth is watering." Eleanor groans. "I was too nervous to eat this morning."

"All of that sounds amazing, Hattie." Olive takes a deep breath. "This is going to be good. Isn't it?" She's begging for reassurance.

I grab her by the shoulders. "Ollie, baby, this place looks amazing. It's going to go exactly how we want it to go."

"We got this," Eleanor adds, and her voice has a weird level of finality to it. Her words still seem to help relieve Olive's stress. Her shoulders relax instantly. This reprieve will be brief. She's going to be a borderline lunatic the rest of the evening. Eleanor and I will be the ones who get to wrangle her. That's our number one job.

"And," Eleanor starts, "during those amazeballs appetizers, we'll have live music with The T's, which will be perfect, nice and easygoing. Then at six, after everyone has arrived and mingled, we'll start the event." She walks backward to the stage and spreads her arms wide. "I'm emceeing. I'll do my little ditty, welcome everyone, make 'em laugh, then introduce you, Olive. You can do the speech you've been working on. And voilà. The party starts. We have the Jackson Quartet playing Sinatra throughout dinner. And after that, Grace and the Night Blossoms will go on."

"I still cannot believe Grace and the freaking Night Blossoms are coming here," Olive says. "She's so popular now. They won a Grammy, didn't they?"

"Whoa, whoa, whoa," I say as I butt in. "*I'm* the one who booked them. Remember?" I went to high school with Grace and her sister, Ginny. It was a great win for me. "And all three bands confirmed last week."

"Oh, Hattie, you're right. Credit where credit is due." Olive takes a deep breath. "Actually, I want to take this moment, right now, to express my deepest apologies to you both. I've been a royal pain in the ass, and I don't know how you both didn't walk out on me. Numerous times. Especially you, Hattie." She bounces a little on her toes. She's wearing Adidas and capri yoga pants and a sanctuary zip-up hoodie.

Her laid-back outsides do not match her insides, I'm sure of it. "I also want to say—"

"You really don't have to say anything else." I try to stop her from going on because I am not in a good spot emotionally, and her going on and on, saying all the right things, will have me blubbering in no time. And I do not want or need to cry.

"No, listen, please. I need to say this." She adjusts her dark-framed glasses. "You have done so much for this event. I can't even begin to tell you how much I appreciate you." She puts her hands on my shoulders. "You are very important to me. You know that, right? Like, I could not do this without you. You are everything this place needed. Everything." Her eyes are welling with tears. Ugh. That's not good. Seeing tears summons *my* tears. "You're young, hip, adorable, and fucking talented."

My eyes are starting to burn. "Ollie, don't you dare cry."

She pulls me into her, arms wrapping around me, and when I bury my face in the crook of her neck, it starts to happen. "Thank you." I pull away and sniffle. *Shit.* I'm crying. I wipe at my eyes as I turn away.

"Are you crying? Oh my God, you're crying!"

"Holy shit!" Eleanor spins me around, amusement peppered with her own happiness layered in her tone. "Olive, you made her cry."

"I hate you both," I say as Eleanor pulls me into a hug. She's crying now, too, and for the first time in a long time, I feel good. Every aspect of my life feels amazing, including this part, which was starting to suffocate me.

"Also," Eleanor says softly. "I'm chopped liver."

"Ellie, don't even start with me—"

Eleanor raises her hand to stop Olive. It's in this moment that I realize something has happened between them that I am not supposed to be aware of. "I was kidding, Olive." Eleanor starts to walk away, hands held in the air in mock defeat.

But defeat of what?

❖

Olive

The welcome packet materials Eleanor's team put together are perfect. They went above and beyond. The packet is complete with a pricing sheet, the menu for events, as well as discount codes for rooms. I am blown away at how everything has come together. And now, the Charm Amphitheater will be the hottest venue this side of the Mississippi. Or at least on the Western Slope.

"Ellie, these came out perfectly."

"Sondra is a goddamn genius." Eleanor shrugs. "I have a great staff. What can I say?"

"Is Celine ready to be even busier? Once people see this place, they're going to want to book it." We're sitting on one of the rows of the Amphitheater, taking it all in. Eleanor's hair is pulled back, and wisps are around her face. She has her black-framed glasses on. Something about the way she pushes them up the bridge of her nose by nudging the underside of the left lens makes my chest ache.

"Yes, she's prepared. As long as we get out of the red, I'll be able to hire an assistant coordinator if need be. She said she knows someone who could start whenever." She clears her throat. "We'll handle it, either way."

Harriet leans into Eleanor's shoulder. "You doing okay?"

Eleanor's eyes are filled with tears in an instant. "Yeah, yeah. Just, y'know, missing my mom. This is something she would have loved to see." She sighs, her shoulders slumped. "I feel like we did the right thing by creating this place, but damn, sometimes it's hard not to be able to share this with them." She pushes her glasses to the top of her head and wipes her eyes. "Y'know what I mean?"

"Boy, don't I ever." The desire to comfort her is too strong, so I take a chance and wrap an arm around her shoulders. To my surprise, she doesn't pull away. In fact, she kind of melts into me. "I'd give anything for my mom to be here, too."

"Yeah, same here." Harriet's voice cracks. "Goddammit," she says softly. "I am not going to cry in front of you two again."

We all start to laugh through our tears. "This is exactly what I wanted when I thought about doing this all those years ago." I take a deep breath. Eleanor's perfume has infiltrated my surroundings. "I wanted this. Exactly this. With you two. And we have it."

Without warning, Eleanor gently places a hand on my upper thigh. My entire body starts to overheat. I look at it, at the gold ring on her ring finger, at the gold beaded bracelets, and she flips her hand over. "Take my hand," she says softly. Then does the same to Harriet. When I'm holding one hand and Harriet is holding the other, she squeezes tightly. "I don't want to lose either of you."

"You're not going to," Harriet says. Her voice is so quiet. "I don't want us ever to split up."

"We're in this together, ladies." I squeeze Eleanor back. "Forever."

"Yes. Forever." And something about the way she says forever has me wondering if she really means it.

Within an instant, my brain is hijacked by my pessimism. She's going to leave. I open my mouth but realize the employees are starting to arrive for the staff meeting. Eleanor hasn't moved, is still holding my hand, and there is sadness in her eyes. I need to know what's happening inside her mind.

The employees have gathered now, waiting patiently for us to start the meeting. We don't have time to figure this out, but I still say, "Eleanor?" I squeeze her hand again. "Will you talk to me?"

"Everything is fine," she whispers.

"I don't believe you."

"I love you," she says very softly. "I love you so much. You know that, right?"

"Ellie—"

"Okay, everyone, let's start the meeting." Harriet stands while Glenda passes out the agenda.

I look back at Eleanor. "You have to talk to me."

"Don't worry about me. Okay?" She releases my hand and stands. "Thank you, everyone, for getting here early and for making it to our meeting on time. What an accomplishment." A peal of hilarity rolls through the crowd. "I'm impressed. Now, let's see if you can impress me for the rest of the afternoon and evening…"

The rest of what she's saying is lost as my brain continues to overanalyze every word she mumbled to me. I know she loves me, but that wasn't a normal I love you. That was more. That was…everything. She meant every syllable. And I'm stuck sitting here, wondering what the fuck I'm supposed to do now.

Eleanor

"After the event, clean-up is key." I look out over the staff. "I want this place cleaned and ready to go for anyone who sets up a tour tomorrow. Is that clear?"

"Crystal, boss!"

"And please, remember that you will be representing the sanctuary tonight. That means everyone needs to be in their uniforms. Dark blue jeans, navy blue button-downs, floral ties, and the hummingbird tie clips. Is that understood?"

There's a collective yes.

"If anyone doesn't have part of the uniform, please get with Celine after the meeting. Celine, raise your hand so they know where you are." She does as asked. "Everyone say, 'Hi, Celine!'"

"Hi, Celine!"

"Perfect." I take one more look at the crowd of employees. "This is the biggest event of the entire year. We have a Grammy Award–winning band coming. We have over four hundred people in attendance. We are going to be packed to the brim. The most important part, though, is what?"

"Remember to have fun," they say in unison.

"Exactly. Now, break and go get ready. Celine, what time do you want first shift people here?"

Celine stands and addresses the crowd. "Please be here by three. Second shift, I would like you here by eight."

"What if we want to stay and work second shift?"

"You are more than welcome to stay and enjoy yourselves after your shifts are over," I say. "Okay, that's all I have. I'm turning you all over to Celine." I turn and walk toward where Olive and Harriet are waiting. Olive looks like I dropped the worst possible news ever on her. I have, essentially. I haven't revealed the entire truth yet, whatever that truth is. I'm going to start something with Mabel, or I'm not. I'm mad at Olive, or I'm not. I'm leaving, or I'm not. There's this nagging feeling that keeps reminding me how Mabel isn't staying, and at the end of the day, I don't think I want to leave.

Everything we've built together? This amazing sanctuary dedicated to our mothers? Do I really *want* to leave?

"That went well," Harriet says. "I think this is going to go very smoothly."

"Aw, man, you jinxed it. You know that, right?"

"Shit. You're right. I mean, I think this is going to go horribly."

"Well, you can't say that!" Olive smacks her arm. "How do you not know this?"

"Because I don't believe in that shit. You get back what you put out into the universe. If I've learned anything from you, Ellie, it's that."

I place my hand on my heart. "Oh, Hattie, that's sweet."

"I swear, Hattie," Olive starts, "you've become a different person in the past six months. You know that?"

"I do." Harriet beams. "I want to ask you both something."

"Oh, Lord," I say softly. "What is it?"

"So." Harriet takes a deep breath and holds it for a few seconds. When she lets it out, she says, "Judy wants to marry me."

I gasp. "What?"

Olive sucks a breath in so fast, she starts to cough. Harriet starts to pat her on the back. "Are you okay?"

Through coughs, Olive nods. "Yeah, just choking on the shock."

Harriet groans. "I don't know what to do."

"What do you want to do?"

"I truthfully don't know." Harriet shrugs. "I really love her. She makes me, like, crazy happy. I feel like a whole new person with her. It's, yeah, it's incredible."

It is lovely to see her like this. "But?"

"I don't think there is a but. I have never wanted to get married before. Like, what am I supposed to feel?"

"Excited?" I shrug. "Happy?"

"I am those things. For sure."

"What did you say?" Olive's voice is drenched with worry. I fear her worry is selfish because not only is she worried she'll lose me, but she could also lose Harriet. She'd be hard pressed to find a new general manager and executive chef.

"I didn't answer her. Then she basically did a take back and said she was kidding."

"You didn't answer?" Olive asks, and she lets out a small laugh. "Hattie, you're joking, right?"

"Serious as a heart attack. I swear, I am a magnet for uncomfortable situations."

"You need to decide what you're going to do," I say.

"That's all the words of encouragement you have for me, eh?"

"I mean, you got this?" I give her an enthusiastic thumbs-up.

She shrugs. "She did say she'd move here."

"She would?" My mouth falls open. "Are you serious? Doesn't she have kids?"

"Yep. She's not worried about it." Harriet jumps from her seat on the edge of the stage. "I gotta go meet Talula and Taryn. They're coming early to check in, and then they'll want to set up." She pushes her hands into the pockets of her ripped jean shorts. "And just so you both know, I think I'm going to say yes."

"Hattie," I whisper and yank her into a hug. "I love you, and I want you to be happy. Whatever that means. If Judy makes you happy, I'm all for it. And I know a wonderful venue."

I hear Olive start to laugh and then feel her arms wrap around us. "And it will all be taken care of. Whatever you need from us, Hattie, you got it."

"I love you both," she says, and she pulls away and heads toward the exit.

Olive is standing there watching Harriet leave, and she seems completely dumbfounded. I feel similar, taken aback but strangely happy. "Well, that was unexpected."

She sighs. "Was it, though? She's been so caught up in Judy since they arrived. Sometimes love hits different." Olive's expression moves from happy to worried in a flash. I've only seen this look once before. And it was right after she told me about Paul's accident. "Are you going to leave me?"

Her question breaks my heart. I want to tell her *no, oh my God, no, of course not.* But I don't know what I'm thinking or doing, and to say that without being one hundred percent sure is stupid. "Olive…"

"Please, are you leaving me? You need to tell me."

"I don't know." The words seem to smack her across the face, but they shock me, too. And I want to take them back. I want to grab them and put them back in my mouth and swallow them until they aren't real any longer.

"Is she really who you want?"

"Olive—"

"No, Eleanor, listen to me. Is she who you want? Do you want this version of Mabel Sommers? Or will you perpetually be in love with the eighteen-year-old Mabel from your past?"

"I don't know."

"That's a child's answer. You know that."

She's not wrong, but I have no rebuttal.

"If you leave, what happens when it doesn't work out? Do you come back? Do you expect me to lick your wounds?"

"What the hell, Olive?" I try to step around her, to avoid this conversation at all costs, but she moves in front of me like an agile cat. "What do you want from me?" She doesn't answer quick enough, so

I add, "Seriously, what the fuck do you want from me?" I move past her this time, past the anguish in her eyes, the bewilderment written all over her face.

When I'm four steps away, I hear her say, "I want you."

"Excuse me?" I flip around, and Olive shrugs, shrugs while standing there in her stupid yoga pants and stupid hoodie, and I'm speechless.

"I don't want to lose you."

"That's not the same thing." My voice cracks. "And you know it."

"Ellie, please, don't leave. Don't leave with her."

The anger inside was building before, but now that she's let her true feelings into the world, I let my anger bubble over. "You have got to be kidding me." I walk toward her because I don't want to shout, but I need her to hear me. "You said you didn't want me. You said you didn't love me the way I love you. You did this. You didn't want me." I place a hand over my heart and pat myself hard so she fucking gets it. "Don't stand there and tell me you don't want me to leave because you're jealous. That's not fair."

"I didn't realize that what I was feeling for you was this. I didn't know a lot about myself. I am finding out—"

"Olive...I. Don't. Care." My words seem to physically crash into her because she takes a step backward. I hate myself. I do care. I care so much. I adjust my glasses and turn, storming away as fast as possible.

CHAPTER TWENTY-FOUR

Olive

I've never been great at admitting when I'm wrong. Not because I don't know when I'm wrong. Admitting defeat, though? Admitting that I overreacted or misspoke or anything like that? That's where I crumble because it means I'm weak, so much weaker than I ever thought or have ever wanted people to see me.

Pride is ridiculous. We're told to take pride in our work, in ourselves, in what we do throughout our lives, but when pride keeps us from admitting when we're wrong, it stops being good.

I'm filled with regret, too. Regret that I didn't tell her about Paul sooner. Regret that I didn't realize what I felt for Eleanor was deeper than friendship. I should have never said what I said to her and certainly not like that, before our event, in a fit of fear-induced jealousy. I'm sick about it. I misspoke. I was wrong, wrong, wrong. I shouldn't have let jealousy win, but unfortunately, I gave up and let it storm the castle. And now we are in ruins because I couldn't keep my mouth shut.

This is not the way I wanted this evening to go. I wanted us to be a united front. I wanted to greet the guests together. I wanted us to be unwavering and steadfast, together. Instead, she won't look at me. She won't speak to me. She has done everything in her power to not get near me.

We're almost through the Jackson Quartet setlist. I'm nervous as hell as I stand off to the side of the stage, waiting for Eleanor to grab the microphone and introduce me. Will she do it? Or will she make Harriet do it? I hope to God she doesn't pull something like that.

"You look nervous."

I hear Sunny's voice so I turn. Her dark eyes are unwavering, but her presence surrounds me with a tentative sadness. I wasn't prepared for that. "Hi," I say as I grab her hand. "Thank you for finding me."

She squeezes my hand gently. "Are you okay?"

I shake my head, lick my lips, and look at the stage as the final notes of "Luck Be a Lady" ring out. "Not really."

"What's going on?" Sunny slides her hand along the small of my back. Her touch is comforting, and I want to sink into her. But I can't. "You can talk to me."

She looks sharp in her mauve and violet floral button-down and dark blue jeans. I place a hand on her chest, on her navy necktie, right over her sternum. "Sunny," I say as softly as possible. "You are amazing. You know that, right?"

She shrugs, a very small smirk. "I don't know about that."

"Well, you are." I let the words fall before I hear Eleanor's voice filling the space between us.

"Welcome, welcome, everyone, to the grand opening celebration and concert for the Charm Amphitheater, our newest and most elegant event venue here at the Hummingbird Sanctuary."

The crowd erupts, clapping like crazy, hooting and hollering, which makes me think the free bar has been a big hit.

"It will come as no surprise to anyone," Eleanor starts, wrapping the cord of the microphone around her hand as she walks across the stage. She was born to perform. "But Olive Zyntarski, the mastermind of our amazing sanctuary, has been dreaming of opening this venue since we broke ground three years ago. I remember the first time she walked over to this part of the property and said, 'We need to put a venue in, something that will be welcoming and interesting and will make people feel like they belong here.' And she made sure it happened. But…" Eleanor finds me in the crowd. "She welcomes people into her heart and hopes they feel like they belong." I realize when tears start streaming down my face that I'm blubbering like a fool. Why is she saying all this? And why does she have to look fantastic up there? Black blazer, black slacks, cream-colored top, and dammit, she looks breathtaking. Her hair is down; her makeup is perfect. "The sanctuary is our gift to women everywhere. We want you to know that if you need to take a breath, we're here to offer the oxygen. And without further ado, I'd like to introduce you all to Olive Zyntarski."

Once again, the crowd goes wild, and I realize there's a standing ovation when I make it to the stage. My heart is in my throat. Eleanor stops me with a gentle touch to the arm. She holds out the microphone, but I seem to have lost my muscle function. She squeezes my bicep very softly and gives me a soft but encouraging smile.

"Knock 'em dead," she whispers when I finally take the microphone.

I can't seem to wrap my brain around what's happening. I never expected this sort of reception. "Wow." It's all I can say as everyone starts to settle and take their seats. "Wow. Thank you all." I place a hand on my heart, nervousness causing it to beat like a bass drum. I take a deep breath. "This is…wow. You're all incredible. Thank you." Once everyone has quieted, it's my turn to speak. And all I have to do is… *Speak to the crowd, Olive. Like a normal human being.* And hope to God that my speech is well received.

❖

Eleanor

Look at how great she looks. That amazing purple blouse with those navy slacks? She looks in control and beautiful. She's in her element. Or at least, it seems that way.

I hate being this mad at her. I wanted to throw the microphone at her and leave, but that would have gone over horribly. I can't stay mad at her forever, either. After going over everything in my head a thousand times, I get why she was scared to bring up the note. I get why she kept that secret. And enough time has passed that we need to bury that information and hope it never sees the light of day.

But on top of all that, how am I supposed to handle this brand-new information? I'm finally feeling things again. Feeling feelings other than the ones I was holding on to for her. I'm making headway on a real relationship again instead of settling for the crumbs Olive gives me.

This isn't fair, I want to scream at her. And tell her how stupid she is and how she missed her opportunity and how this ship has sailed. But then I think about her, her heart and remarkable soul. And I want to cry. I want to tell her that I'm sorry, that I will never stop loving her, that I don't know what to do or who to turn to.

And I'm right back to the beginning.

This time, it isn't Mabel breaking my heart. It's Olive. I never gave her the opportunity to break me before because I knew I wasn't who she wanted. I knew it was a one-way street.

And now everything I knew is what? Is it false? Have I been wrong this entire time?

"This has been one hell of a journey," Olive says, her words pulling me out of the depths of my despair. She's fidgeting with the microphone cord, and when her eyes land on mine, I take a deep breath and make it as obvious as possible. Maybe she'll take the hint and do the same.

She gives me a small smile and nods. "I wouldn't have been able to do it without my best friends and co-owners, Eleanor Fitzwallace and Harriet Marshall." Her voice is shaking, and I can't tell if it's from nerves or from the apparent emotion bubbling beneath the surface. "These two women are why the sanctuary is what it is." She seems to relax as she finishes her sentence. "A lot of people over the years since my mom's passing have said that every day, things get a little easier, days go by a little quicker, the sun starts to shine a little brighter. I'd love to say all of that is absolutely true because that would make everything easier, wouldn't it?" Her small laugh washes over the crowd. She needs to land the plane. She's losing them. "And while all these things could be true, everything got a little easier to handle once we poured our hearts and souls into the Hummingbird Sanctuary."

She pauses and looks around. The Edison lights are all lit, and the grounds look absolutely breathtaking. The sanctuary is perfect. "And until my friends, who I love more than anything in the entire world, reminded me that we are all in this together, I didn't fully understand the magnitude of this place. We have all lost our mothers. We know what it's like to ache to hear our mom's voice again, even if it's to tell us we went overboard on the resort and probably overspent, but hell, what are you going to do?" The crowd laughs. "The sanctuary is everything special and important and exciting about our mothers poured into the beauty of Colorado's Western Slope, poured into the peace of Colorado's *soul*."

My throat tightens as I hold back the emotions I absolutely do not want to let out right now. It's one thing to get a little teary-eyed but to bawl in front of everyone? Not a good plan. Mabel sniffles next to me. There's a pull inside me to comfort her, but I am frozen in place for some reason.

"So if I could have everyone raise their glass and take a minute to honor all of the mothers, wherever they are." The staff is passing out glasses of champagne to anyone who doesn't already have one. I take the one Glenda passes to me. "Eleanor, Harriet?" Olive says, raising her own glass. "I love you both. And I have never been happier that we are doing this together. I'm sad we had to lose our mothers, but I am honored that you both chose to continue their legacy here." Olive holds her champagne flute higher to the sky. "I love you, Mama. And I'll miss you every single day of my life. Until we meet again."

I can't take my eyes off Olive. I am bowled over by her in most moments, yes, but especially in this one. What am I supposed to do now?

I go to sip my champagne and feel Harriet lean into me. "What are you doing?" Her voice is smooth, low, and I have a feeling I know what she means, but I'm not positive.

"What?"

"You're going to leave, aren't you?"

I don't say anything, just stare into her eyes, and she shrugs.

Her expression falls, and she looks away, leaving me mentally grasping for a rebuttal. "I had a feeling," she says before she drinks. "You're going to break Olive's heart."

"Excuse me?"

"You heard me." She drinks the rest of her champagne and sets it on the tray of the staff member who breezes by. She slips her hands into her pockets, and her gaze never wavers from the stage, where Olive is shaking hands while the band sets up. "Olive can't do this without us."

She's not wrong. "So? Why is that my problem? I'll give up my shares."

She whips her head toward me. "Are you fucking kidding me?"

I force myself to swallow a rather large lump, but my efforts are pointless. I take a drink, hoping it helps, but even it has a hard time going down.

"You are going to break her if you leave."

"That's not fair."

"No, it's not." Harriet turns to leave, but I grab her arm and pull her so she stays.

"Hattie, this isn't...I don't know what I'm doing yet. You can't say anything."

"Say anything to who about what?"

Fuck. That's Olive's voice asking that question. I let go of Harriet's arm. "Nothing."

"She's going to leave."

I groan, anger flooding my entire body. I am going to throttle Harriet. "You fucking asshole."

"Ladies."

"What?" we both say in unison.

"This is not the time or the place."

Olive is right. We cannot do this now. But my mood is fucked. I will never be able to have fun. I swear to God, I should have never done this with friends. It never works out. Cecily was right. I don't say a word as I push between them and head through the crowd. When I hit the edge of the Amphitheater, I hear Grace and the Night Blossoms start to play my very favorite song, "The Truth Always Stings," and I wonder if whatever higher power is in charge is fucking with me.

I stand at the edge of the crowd. I'm trying to calm down. I don't want to be a complete bitch the rest of the night. After all, I still have Mabel to think about.

Christ. Mabel. What the fuck am I doing?

She's standing fairly far away, her cell phone pressed to her ear. Her brows are furrowed, her right index finger shoved into her free ear. She stomps and looks at the night sky. God, I do love her. She's my Mabel.

But am I in love with her? Is she worth losing all of this?

Are my feelings for her worth losing Olive?

Is anything worth losing Olive?

Harriet

"I fucking knew it, Judy. I fucking knew it."

Judy has a hand on the small of my back. We're standing far away from everyone, nestled in a little alcove because I had to get away from the crowd. "She didn't confirm anything."

"She has never been completely happy here. She misses Chicago. The big city." I shake my head. "She begged me to come out here, and I did, and she's the one who fucking leaves? I don't fucking think so."

"Hattie, honey, you need to calm down." Judy places her hands on my cheeks. "Everything will work out."

"I don't know."

Judy sighs, and her hands fall from my face. She folds her arms. "Would it make you feel any better if I told you something that will probably help? Something I'm not supposed to tell you?"

"Um, yes. Tell me, please."

She sighs again. "Dammit," she says under her breath. "Mabel is going to kill me."

"Judy, spill the tea."

"Mabel is leaving after this trip. She took a job with *The Washington Post* as a foreign correspondent. She's moving overseas. This is her last article for *On the Verge*."

I feel myself blink once, then twice, then a third time, as if my eyelids are having a hard time digesting what they just heard.

"Unless Eleanor plans on moving to London with her..." Judy shrugs. "I doubt this is going to last."

"Well, shit." My stomach is filled with lead. I want to run to Eleanor right now and apologize and tell her how stupid I am for forever getting judgmental over matters of the heart. I am so, so stupid.

"Yeah, go easy on Eleanor. She may be struggling with something, but I doubt she's going to leave. And if she does, it's not going to be *for* Mabel. I don't know her well, but I don't think she wants to leave." Judy touches my forearm, and the heat from her skin soothes my frazzled nerves.

"Well, shit."

"You can't tell her before Mabel does."

"I—"

"Hattie, you cannot tell Eleanor. I'm serious."

I shake my head. "No, no. I won't. I promise. I'm just like, bowled over or whatever, like, Mabel has been pushing Eleanor only to leave her again?"

"Believe me, she's not in a good spot for that very reason." She pushes the left side of her hair behind her ear and breathes in. I am so attracted to her that I literally have to tell myself to concentrate on the conversation we're having. I'm terrible. "She's going to tell her tonight. She..." Judy pauses and folds her arms again. My eyes are drawn to her cleavage. "God, I'm the worst friend ever. She made me promise not to tell, and here I am blabbing." She groans. "She has to leave tonight and take a red-eye to DC."

"Well, shit again." There is this desire inside me to do exactly what Judy asked me not to. But it is not, nor will it ever will be, my place to break Eleanor's heart. Apparently, that's still Mabel's place. I'm the one who will be here to quietly pick up the pieces. "This is going to break her heart."

Judy smiles, then lets out a small laugh. "Hattie."

"What?" I furrow my brow. "What's so funny?"

"Eleanor is in love with Olive. Can't you see that?"

"Girl, what are you talkin—" I stop abruptly when Judy tilts her head and arches an eyebrow. There's no use trying to lie to protect Eleanor. "Yeah, you're right."

"That's what I thought." She pulls me closer. "Mabel is not the long-term love. Her career comes first."

"Wow. Sounds like someone else I used to know."

"I assume you mean yourself?"

"Sure do." I wrap my arms around Judy's waist. Her body pressed against mine has me feeling all types of turned on. "Until you came along."

"And flipped your whole world upside down." She leans in and kisses me, then presses her forehead into mine. "Don't worry about Eleanor, okay? I have a feeling she'll be fine."

"I like how you barely know her, and you're like, oh, she'll be fine. Like, how the fuck do you know that?"

"Because." She kisses me again, quickly at first, then softer and longer. "I'm very intuitive, like a mind reader."

"Is that right?"

"Oh yes. For instance, I know exactly what you're thinking."

"And what is that?" I rub her backside and cup her ass cheeks over her maroon dress.

She leans next to my ear. "You're thinking that you've never loved someone as much as me."

"That is very true."

"And you're thinking that you want to take me home and fuck me."

I chuckle as I pull her dress, hiking it higher and higher, the left side over her thigh. "I don't need to take you anywhere to fuck you," I whisper as I slide my finger toward the front of her panties, but my search comes up fruitless. "Um."

Her eyebrows rise, and she licks her lips.

"Ma'am, you're not wearing any panties."

"No, I'm not."

"My word."

"You were saying?"

I look over my shoulders, checking to make sure we're still hidden. I capture her lips as I press my fingers against her. When she spreads her legs, I let my fingers go where they're being called. And once I dip inside her wetness and hear her moan my name, I realize that this is the best I have ever felt in my entire life.

❖

Eleanor

"That concert was seriously the best I've ever been to."

I lie back on the top row of the now dark and empty Amphitheater. The sky is plastered with stars. I will never get over how many stars are visible when the light pollution isn't an issue. This is exactly how I imagine the rest of my days. Being able to see these stars and smell this clean air and gasp in awe when I see wildlife in the actual wild.

Mabel mimics my position, then I feel her hand as she intertwines her fingers with mine. And for the first time since seeing her again, I feel like I'm cheating on Olive. I'm sick to my stomach because that is not the case at all. That is my twisted and confused mind making up reasons why this could never work between Mabel and me. If self-sabotage was an Olympic sport, I'd be the reigning champion.

"I am still so blown away by this place."

"Mabel?"

"Hmm?"

"What are we doing?"

She lets out a very small puff of air. "At this very moment, we're talking."

I groan, exasperated, as I sit up. "You know what I mean, Mabes."

She does the same and crosses her legs at the ankles. Her head is bent, and her hair has tumbled over her shoulders in big, loose curls. I have a mind to ask her what's so interesting about the Chuck Taylors she's wearing. "I know what you mean. And, truthfully, I haven't been able to stop thinking about us. About you. And everything that happened since I saw you standing there with Lizzie, pants covered in golden retriever fur." She sighs. "I'm fucking torn. I don't know what to do."

"Why don't you talk it out with me?" I'm impressed with the level of clarity it sounds like I possess, when in actuality, I have been a hot mess since the second I saw her, and I am still a mess. Maybe lukewarm now but nevertheless. My eyes are drawn to the line of her neck, the slope of her bare shoulders, and the goose bumps that have littered her skin from the cool mountain air. Her beauty has always taken my breath away. From the moment I saw her in fifth grade to right now and every other moment in between. Falling for my best friend at such a young age was maybe the worst thing that could ever happen to me. Inseparable isn't necessarily the best foundation to build a relationship on. I wonder now if time and distance and age have made it so we'd be trapped together yet held apart by some kind of invisible barrier. "Mabel?"

"I have to tell you something."

As much as I'd like to act cool, the apprehension in her voice makes my stomach drop. "What is it?"

"I'm leaving."

"I know. You're leaving tomorrow. This isn't a breaking news story that you've got the scoop on."

"No, Eleanor," she says, then groans, then shakes her hands before balling them into fists. "I'm…leaving tonight." She looks at her watch. "The helicopter will be here in, *fuck*, a little over an hour."

I realize after a few seconds that my mouth is hanging open. I snap it closed. "Wait. What? What are you saying?"

"I haven't been honest with you."

Imagine that. She is going to be the death of me. I just know it. "Oh, you have got to be *kidding* me. You're just going to walk away again?"

Her face twists, and she rolls her eyes. "That's not fair."

"Fair?" I laugh, a single *ha.* "Mabel, I swear to God, this better be the best fucking reason I've ever heard, or I'll show you fair." My insides are on fire. Even behind my eyeballs is roaring fire. I am at the end of my rope here. Olive and Mabel are going to kill me. I just know it. I'm going to die a single lesbian because neither of the women I love want me. What the actual fuck?

"No, please, listen." She scoots to the edge of the row and stands, as if standing gives her an advantage. "I didn't expect any of this to happen. I didn't expect that I'd come all this way and stumble into you, of all the people in all the world. I didn't realize this was going to happen." Her words are dripping with sincerity, and I believe her. I don't want to, but I do. "I don't think you realize exactly how much I hate myself for everything that happened between us. I don't think you get it."

"I get it."

"Do you?" She wipes away tears. I hate seeing her cry. It makes me so very weak. "I haven't had a real relationship in…God, I can't even remember. College? I don't know. But every single time I had a chance to be happy, I ruined it. I let my career get in the way because maybe that's my one true love. I don't know." She laughs through her tears. "And here I go again, letting my career win." She reaches for my hand, and I don't fight her. Hell, I already gave her my heart again. "I took a job with *The Washington Post* the day before we flew in. And then I saw you, and we…we did all of this, and I've gone and fallen back in love with you, and now what? Because I have to be in DC tomorrow. Not in two months like I was planning because I'm flying to London on Tuesday."

Is this really happening? I try to blink away my confusion. I hear every word she's saying, but I also feel like I'm in a nightmare. "I'm confused."

"Please don't make me say it again."

"But…London?"

Her shoulders fall. "I'll be a foreign correspondent. I'm…I'm moving."

"Mabel."

"I should have told you sooner. I didn't expect any of this. You or me or us, and I didn't think this was real. Like, after all these years, and then, bam, I run into you, and God, all the feelings I had for you then were still there and then, then, then…"

"You need to breathe. Take some breaths." She is two seconds away from full-on hysterics, and while I can handle it because I deal with those myself, I don't know if she can. It's clear she's not used to feeling this much.

"I thought maybe this wasn't real or that we weren't going to feel the same way, and then last night happened. And it was so good. But then I got a call tonight, and now I've gone and fucked everything up all over again." She lets out a frenzied whine as she drops my hand and pushes her fingers into her hair. "I am always fucking things up with you. I hate myself right now." She's sobbing, pulling on her hair, and I thought I was dramatic. This is horrible. All of it. But for the first time, she is much more of a hot mess than I am, and it's a little comforting. "I am such a bitch."

Her tone breaks my heart all over again. "Mabel, baby, come

here." I pull her toward me, take her hands from her hair and hold them. She's shaking like a leaf. "Listen, I'm not mad at you."

"You aren't?" she whispers through a tear-stained voice.

"Oh my God, no. Not at all." The weight sitting on my chest is starting to crumble. "I am…" I'm pulling my words together as fast as possible, but it feels like it takes a lifetime. Perhaps because the words I'm about to say have taken almost an entire lifetime for me to have the courage to say. The opportunity to close this chapter of my life…I'm finally ready to move on. The shock and dismay coursing through me feels how I suspect holding a bolt of lightning would feel. "I'm very happy for you."

"What about us?"

"There will forever be an us, Mabel." I wipe the tears from her face. "You will always have a place in my heart."

She smiles through her tears. "I don't want to leave you."

"I don't want you to leave. But you were always leaving, weren't you?"

She shrugs.

"You weren't moving here. And as much as I sometimes want to escape, I'm not leaving. This is my home"

"You could." She places a hand against my cheek. "You could come with me, and we could be happy together."

"In London."

She shrugs again. "Anywhere."

I sigh. I'm positive that if I'm pushed too hard in any direction, I'm going to crumble into a million pieces. "I love you."

"But?"

I pull her next to me on the row. She leans into me, head on my shoulder, as I wrap an arm around her. "But you don't want me to come."

"I do."

"Seriously? You're picking your career right now over everything. And that's fine. But that's how it would always be. And I'm way too sensitive to be second in your life."

"You have never been second." She's crying so hard now that her words come out in gasps. "Even when you felt like you were, you weren't."

"We can be the very best of friends. Isn't that okay?"

"Friends with benefits?"

I start to laugh.

"Because you're really good. Like, the best I've ever had."

"You are ridiculous."

She leans into me harder. "I love you so much."

"You have been everything I needed right when I needed it. I doubt that'll ever change." I kiss the top of her head.

"Will you come visit me?"

"I will."

"You promise you don't hate me?"

I tilt her face toward me. "I have never hated you. Even when I should have, I couldn't." I kiss her softly. She tastes like salt, and even though it makes no sense, she also tastes like hope, like maybe my life isn't over this time. I spent so much of my past running from these feelings, not wanting closure because it would mean reopening the wound. Every relationship I have ever been in has succumbed to my inability to admit that time and space really did heal me. All I needed was the opportunity to finish the chapter. And now it's time to start living again. "Do you hear me?"

She nods as she kisses me again and again and again. "I miss you already," she whispers. "I love you so much. I hope you know that."

"I do," I say against her lips. I do know that. But at the same time, underneath the fact that I am going to miss her all over again, I'm not hurt this time.

I am happy.

Finally.

And somewhere deep inside, I'm also relieved.

CHAPTER TWENTY-FIVE

Olive

"You remembered to pack everything?" I motion to Sunny's suitcase from my spot on her bed. We spent the night together again. Completely clothed. The entire night. And nothing happened, which, honestly, is fine. Even though she's the most understanding and patient person I've ever been around, I have to wonder what kind of restraint it took to never once try anything with me. She never pushed for more, and oddly enough, I was ready to give more. I found myself needing the sweet release of sex and being touched. I guess ultimately, I'm the one who didn't push her.

I'm not filled with any sort of regret regarding Sunny, and it's refreshing, albeit not normal for me. Usually, in any situation, I always wish I would have done at least one thing differently. But this time, I'm at peace.

She crawls across the bed and presses her forehead against mine. "I wish I could pack you, too."

"I'm going to miss you."

Her lips are soft when she presses them against my cheek. "I feel the same."

"What's next on your agenda?"

She places a hand on my thigh and rubs lightly. "I start filming a new movie in a month. Another indie film. I'll be a straight woman this time, a therapist being stalked by an ex-patient. Not sure how I feel about that."

"Yeah, I can only imagine."

"I meant the straight part."

"That's what I meant, too." And we both laugh as she playfully smacks my thigh. "You as a straight girl seems like a great way to work on your range."

Again, her laughter surrounds us. "Would you be cool if I came back to visit you?"

A small part of me wishes she could stay. We wouldn't work as a couple, that much has become clear. But it'd be nice to have someone to keep my mind occupied. I want her to remind me that I'm not only okay when Eleanor loves me. I'm okay all the time. "I would love it."

"It's settled then." She sounds as if she believes that, but a part of my heart knows this is the end of the road.

"Let me get dressed, and I'll walk you to the pad."

❖

Harriet

"You're sure you're okay with this? It'll be two weeks. And then I'll be back." I grab Olive's hands and squeeze. "I promise, I'm coming back."

"I know you are. I'm very happy for you. I want you to know that."

"Thank you, Ollie." I pull her into a hug. "I'll miss you."

"It's only two weeks. You'll be fine." She laughs as she smacks my ass. "Now, get going so you can get back."

I release her and look over at Eleanor. She's standing a few feet away at the helicopter pad. She looks good for someone who probably got her heart broken last night. I walk over and put my hands on her shoulders. "Are you okay?"

She nods. "I'm good. I promise."

"How's your heart?"

"It's good." She shrugs. "For the first time in a really long time."

"I'll be back, okay?"

"You'd better come back, you jerk." Eleanor places both hands on my face. She kisses me on the lips. "Go meet those kids. They're gonna love you."

I take a deep breath. "You sure?"

"Yes, I'm sure. I've never been more positive about anything in my entire life." She kisses me quickly again. "Get going."

I turn to walk toward the helicopter where Judy has already boarded.

"Are you leaving Mabel here?" Olive asks.

I turn back to Eleanor. "Did you not tell Olive?"

"Tell me what?"

"Mabel left last night. She had to catch a red-eye to DC."

Olive's head snaps toward Eleanor, who seems to be avoiding eye contact at all costs.

"What the fuck is going on with the two of you?" I ask and point at them both. "Huh?"

"Nothing." Eleanor's answer is too quick. "Get out of here. They're waiting." And she waves as she starts to walk away.

"Olive?"

"Don't worry about her, Hattie. Everything is fine."

"You're a horrible liar." I wave. "You know that."

She smiles back at me. "Tell Sunny I'll miss her."

I nod, but my heart is telling me that leaving these two like this isn't good. I have to take care of myself this time, though. I need to. For the first time in a long time, I have a future with someone. I can't let anything get in the way of that. I head over to the helicopter and board as quickly as possible. When I sit next to Judy, she puts her hand right above my knee and squeezes.

"You good?"

"I've never been better." I lean in and kiss her quickly. "I love you."

"I love you," she whispers right before the pilot starts the engine.

"Sunny?" I shout, and Judy hands me a pair of headphones. I put them on and speak into the microphone portion. "Sunny?"

"Yeah?"

"Olive says she'll miss you."

A small grin appears on Sunny's face. I lean back, seat belt buckled, and take a deep breath. I'm starting my life. Finally. And it feels fucking good.

CHAPTER TWENTY-SIX

Eleanor

Since yesterday, I've managed, with superb success, to avoid Olive. I don't know how exactly, other than I snuck into the house last night like a cat burglar, without a peep, and I somehow made it out of the house before six this morning, showered and ready for the day. It helps that I wasn't at all tipsy last night. And once I said good-bye to Mabel, my night was pretty much over.

I thought I'd feel a lot emptier than I do. I've dissected the events of the past four days over and over again. How is it possible to love her but not be sad that she left? Is this what being a fully functioning adult feels like? Not allowing heartache to dictate every single part of my day? Not crying at the drop of a hat? Not worrying that I'll never find love again?

I'm more upset about everything that went down between Olive and me than I am about Mabel. And I'm scared to admit it to anyone but myself.

I'm in love with Olive. I have been for years. That much is clear as day. What I don't understand is what happened to her that made her finally see me?

And now I'm stuck here at the sanctuary, all alone with Olive in that big house, scared out of my mind that I'll never find the courage to tell her exactly what I'm thinking and feeling. Because what would I tell her, exactly? My capacity to form coherent sentences seems to have waved bye-bye for now. For once, can something work out in my favor?

I'm hiding in my room, lights low, chill music on, incense burning because I'm trying to find my Zen that's been missing since Thursday afternoon. I'm also hoping that my door being closed means Olive won't try to talk to me. In the world of childish things to do, I have cornered the market. I'm sure this whole situation of me avoiding her is totally going to work. Totally sure.

And that's when there's a knock on my door.

Well, that was short-lived. Guess this is not the something that is going to work out in my favor.

God. I'm an idiot.

"Ellie?"

Ignore her. Ignore her, Eleanor. "Come in." *You absolute buffoon.*

The door opens slowly, and in pokes Olive's head. "Can we…can we talk?"

Nope. Absolutely not. "Sure." *Oh, for fuck's sake, Eleanor!*

And before another second passes, she's crossed the room and is sitting cross-legged in front of me. My heart is pounding like a bass drum. She grabs my hands, not allowing me to even think about pulling away. "I love you."

I sigh, roll my eyes because now I'm irritated. I'm sitting here, meditating my life away, trying to figure out a way around what happened with Mabel, with Olive, and she waltzes in here and tells me she loves me? Who does she think she is? Why do the higher powers want to play games with me? Why? "Olive—"

"No, Ellie. You don't get to talk right now. I'm sorry."

I'm torn between wanting to hate her for commanding my emotions and wanting to love her for knowing when I need an emotional intervention.

"I love you. You. I think I am *in* love with you. And I don't know how I missed it or why I missed it, or even if maybe I didn't miss it, but I was too afraid to admit it. I don't know." She's rambling. My heart is aching because I secretly love when she rambles. She is so human and real in these moments. And getting to see her like this is an honor. "I should have never waited. At the very least, I should have talked to you about what I was going through."

"I can't argue with that."

She smiles. "And I should have told you about Paul. Everything. I promise, I will never keep secrets from you again."

I nod.

"Also, and I just gotta say this. I know you love Mabel, and that's okay. I won't try to stop you or get in your way. Or I guess, get in her way. She…she doesn't deserve you, but you? You deserve to be happy. And if it's not with me, I have to be okay with that."

Something comes over me, and I start to laugh.

"What?"

My laughter is offending her. It feels good to express a different emotion than sadness. "Olive," I say after I've composed myself. "You're so fucking dense sometimes."

"Excuse me?"

And in one quick movement, I'm kneeling in front of her, hands on her face, leaning into her space, and placing my lips on hers. Is it cliché to say my entire world shifts when I feel her lips? Because it does. She doesn't kiss me back at first, but I still know it was the right thing to do. I pull away. "I'm here, aren't I?"

She blinks, licks her lips, then nods.

"Then stop talking," I whisper. "And kiss me." And she does. She pulls me into her, her lips crashing into mine as if she can't get them on me fast enough. She's kissing me like this is what we should have been doing for the last fifteen years, like she should have left Paul for me, like we were made to do this together. It's freaking me out the tiniest of bits because why does this feel better than anything I experienced with Mabel? Why did we wait so goddamn long? What happens if this doesn't work? What happens to us, to the sanctuary, to everything?

And then I remember that life is too fucking short. And right now, I am enjoying this far too much to care.

❖

Olive

Well, that didn't go as planned.

Eleanor is next to me on her bed. She's sleeping and has been for the past two hours, and my mind has been running that entire time. I didn't mean for any of that to happen. I feel a little dirty, like, I spent the entire weekend with Sunny, and now I'm kissing Eleanor?

Eleanor. When she sleeps, she has always reminded me of a body of water on a calm day, when the surface resembles glass. One tiny pebble being tossed in will disturb everything. She's gorgeous. Her eyelashes rest against the soft skin under her eyes. She has a small mole halfway between her nose and lips, and I have always loved it and never understood why.

God, I'm stupid.

Her lips are swollen, her skin is completely clear of makeup. I can barely look at her now without my heart beating like crazy. I'm mad at myself for not realizing this sooner. How dumb am I that I didn't put two and two together? I have always had these intense feelings for her, and I assumed it was normal.

It was normal to think she's the most beautiful person I've ever seen in my entire life. It was normal to love the way her body looks in a bathing suit. It was normal to enjoy touching her, her back, her arm, her shoulder. It was normal to think about her when I was alone and normal to wonder about her and…

Jesus.

Everything makes sense now.

Every. Single. Thing.

The ceiling's exposed beams have my attention now because if I keep gawking at Eleanor, I'm going to have to wake her up.

It's never too late to find the person who makes me excited to be alive, who reminds me on a daily basis that life is worth living. And she has never once made me feel self-conscious. Not once. Not when we first met. Not now. She has made me feel beautiful.

Is it okay that it took me being taken by Sunny to finally realize that all my feelings, doubts, and insecurities were because I had no idea how I felt about Eleanor?

Or does it make me a horrible human being?

No, it makes sense. It makes total sense because I never felt completely comfortable with Sunny. I loved how she made me feel, but I was waiting for the other shoe to drop. I knew she was leaving. I knew she was going to go on and only remember me occasionally. And at the end of the day, I was only invested because I was too afraid to lose Eleanor.

Maybe that's what makes me a horrible human being.

"It's a good thing I can't hear your thoughts."

I let out a small chuckle. Eleanor's eyes are still closed. "I thought you were asleep."

"I was, but I could feel that you're over there freaking out, so it woke me up." She smiles as her eyes slide open. "Are you okay?"

"I am. I'm very okay." I roll toward her and put my hand on

her face. "Maybe that's what is worrying me. I never feel this okay about…" I sigh. "About stuff like this, about being intimate."

"I'm right here for whatever you need or want." She places a hand over mine and moves it so she can kiss my fingers. "I'll let you drive the car. Like normal."

"Are you trying to tell me I'm controlling?"

"No, not at all," she says, sarcasm coating her words. "You know I don't love making decisions. It works."

"Very, very true." I move closer and kiss her. "That is going to take some time to get used to."

"Kissing me?"

"No," I whisper. "Being able to."

"Well," she giggles, "by all means, don't stop."

"I won't." I lean in and kiss her again. "I won't ever stop."

And I don't plan on it.

CHAPTER TWENTY-SEVEN

Olive

The two weeks that Harriet has been gone have flown by. Tomorrow is Monday, and I cannot wait for her to be back in action. I can say with certainty that our restaurant cannot survive any longer without her. Glenda is hanging on by a thread. Nothing bad has happened, but "I am not cut out for this every single day. I better get a vacation when Hattie comes back" is something I've heard a few times. I love Glenda, and I get why Harriet needs her, but damn, she doesn't hold back at all. I guess I should feel happy that she is comfortable enough to voice her opinions.

And I am crazy stressed about whatever is happening between Eleanor and me. I need to talk to someone about it, and it can't be Keri, the only other person at the sanctuary I feel close to. Or Juan. I don't think that's the kind of stuff he wants to help me with.

We sleep in the same bed, not because we start that way but because I find myself missing her and end up sneaking into her bed at night. And she holds me, and I love every single second of it. And she smells fresh and clean, like fabric softener and face cream and the minty sweetness of Crest on her breath. There is something so sensual about being close enough to smell her. Goddamn.

These feelings are hard to understand. I have never felt like this before. Never. Is this menopause? Is it that spectrum of asexuality? Where I actually do want sex with someone? I'm confused and, yes, scared because what the fuck is going on with me?

But I've been thinking about her more than I thought was possible. It's frightening. I imagine doing things to her, seeing her head leaned back and her neck exposed. And knowing that I'm the one making her do those things. The thoughts cause my heart rate to speed up and my breathing to become erratic and…and…*and goddamn.*

I grip the railing as I climb the stairs to go to bed. I should go to her bedroom right now. Shouldn't I? I need to start the night with her and see what happens. It's not that I don't want to go through with it. *Go through with it?*

That makes it sound like a procedure that I'm dreading. I'm not dreading it. I'm worried about it. Because it's been a long time, and Eleanor is, well, everything to me. Maybe that's why I've never wanted to admit this to myself before. Losing her would be the worst thing I have ever gone through. Even worse than losing my husband.

Her door is open. It's never open. I creep over and peek inside. Her bedside lamp is on, and she's in bed, propped up, reading *The Seven Husbands of Evelyn Hugo*, glasses on, hair in messy curls, and I realize that this feeling happening inside me? Yeah, this is what I have never had before. This strange cocktail of fear, excitement, happiness. I clear my throat, and she lays her book down, a lazy smile spreading across her lips. Add desire to the cocktail because she's wearing a black silk tank top, and I'm, well, I'm speechless.

"Hi," she says softly.

I can't even say hi back. I open my mouth, and no sound comes out. I don't know if I've ever been speechless before.

"You coming to bed?"

I can only nod as I walk over. Every move she makes is mesmerizing. She's closing her book, setting it on the bedside table, sliding her glasses off, folding the arms in, placing them on top of the book. Quite possibly the simplest movements and it's as if I'm watching an Oscar contender. She pulls the covers back on the side of the bed where I've been sleeping, and the way she does it exposes a full side view of her body, and I see that her tank is actually a nightgown, and why is that even sexier? I'm in a sleep shirt and shorts, and she looks like a model, for Christ's sake. When I slip between the sheets, she rolls onto her side. She knows. She fucking knows, and it makes me happy and mad. Happy because she knows me so well but mad because I hate being this transparent. And I hate being this nervous. I'm a fifty-year-old woman. I shouldn't be nervous like this about sex. Or at least the possibility of it.

"Olive?"

My head snaps toward the sound.

"You realize that I will be fine if you never want to have sex with me."

My heart breaks. That's not it. God, that's not it. It's not that I don't want to.

"I'm okay with having this much of you. I survived on way less for years." She lets out a small laugh, as if she's laughing at an inside joke. "I'm a big girl. I'll, um…I'll survive."

And that tone, the way her voice swaddles the word *survive*, is when I say fuck it and decide life is too fucking short. I lunge at her, and my lips crash into hers. Our teeth knock, we start to giggle, and it feels so amazing. "I'm sorry," I whisper against her lips.

"It's okay."

"No, not that, Ellie." I'm breathless. "I'm sorry, but I can't be the reason you merely survive. I want to be why you thrive."

"Olive," she whispers, and her eyes are filling with tears. I kiss her again and again and again as I find the bottom of her nightgown and start to yank it up, up, up until she's lifting her hips, then breaking from our kiss so she can pull it over her head. I've seen her naked one other time. We had moved into the residence only days earlier, and we were all drinking, talking about anything and everything, enjoying the incredible space we created. She was drunk and decided on a whim to cannonball into the pool in her clothes. It wasn't until she got out and stripped that I saw her. It was quick, and only her backside was showing before she wrapped a towel around herself. But the image haunts me. The line of her back, the way her waist curved into her hips and her ass. It's funny how the past is visiting to show me I'm not crazy now, and I wasn't crazy then. I was in love with her.

If the vision of her backside haunts me, the sight of her frontside will comfort me. Her tan lines accentuate her breasts. She's wearing light pink cotton panties. I can't handle how adorable she is. I'm caught between wanting to soak up every ounce of her with my eyes to wanting to memorize every inch of her with my hands. Once she tosses her nightgown over her shoulder, she finds my lips again, her hands on my face, my hands on her hips because she's managed to top me. It's not surprising. She is always in control, and her being in control during sex isn't shocking. It's comforting because next to the space where my excitement resides, my nerves are waving at me, reminding me that I'm clothed and chubby and what if…what if she doesn't like what she sees?

"Sit up," she says softly as she rocks back onto her knees and grabs my hand to pull me. I do as she says. Even if I wanted to argue, I don't have the brain capacity. My eyes are glued to her hands, to her slender fingers, to the gold ring she never takes off her left hand, to the hair tie around her wrist, as she reaches forward to the hem of my sleep shirt. "Look at me." Her voice is velvet, calming my fears with its softness. "Don't worry."

"Ellie…"

"I've loved you and your body since the moment I saw you at that fundraiser." Her sincerity is the most heartwarming thing I have ever experienced. My hesitation starts to drift away as soon as she says that. I reach down and take my shirt off. Her hands are on me, on my breasts as she leans in and kisses me. "You forgot how long I've loved you, didn't you?"

I pull away. "I think I forgot how much I love *you*." I take her face in my hands. "Let me remind us both." I kiss her and push her backward gently onto her back, a giggle bubbling from her, and my entire body feels as if it's on fire. Something has come over me. Is it desire or love? I don't know, but I want to taste every single part of her body. I kiss her, run my tongue along her jawline, nip her neck, bite her earlobe, hear her moan my name, keep going until I'm on her chest. I take one of her nipples into my mouth and lick it until it starts to harden. I bite down gently, and she moans again. I do the same to the other one, and once again, she's moaning my name, her back arching into me. "I have half a mind to think you like this."

"Yes." Her voice is low and so, so very sexy. "I love that."

"So if I…" I suck hard on her nipple and hear her groan loudly. "Do that, it's something you like?"

"Yes, yes, yes."

"And if I bite down here?" I bite the side of her breast. She yelps, and I giggle against the soft flesh. "I'm sorry."

"No, you aren't." She has her head lifted from the mattress and is chuckling softly, which is causing her breasts to jiggle, and I am shocked at how much I love every second of this.

I place kisses along her sternum to her flat belly, to her navel. She's breathing hard, her belly moving with every intake and exhale. Every part of her is different than mine. She is toned, barely a stretch mark, tanned. In this moment, I'm not feeling self-conscious, though. I am excited that I'm getting to see her like this. Not naked, although that is fucking incredible. I'm getting to see her vulnerable and excited in ways I've never seen before. "You are beautiful," I say. She raises her head and locks her eyes on mine. "I should have told you before. I should have told you every single day."

"Olive," she whispers. "Don't." She sits up, hands on my face, and pulls me closer. "Don't say that." She kisses me deep, so deep I wonder if I've ever felt something filled with this much passion before.

I break apart. "Take these off." I pull on the waistband of her pink panties, and she lifts her hips, and I slide them off. Her abs flex, and the sensation it causes inside me is undeniable. That flare in the pit of my stomach? That's the ravenous desire I've never felt before. I thought it was a myth, but here I am, filled with so much desire that I might combust. "Jesus *Christ*."

She starts to laugh again. "What?"

"You." I shake my head. "You're perfect."

"Oh Lord. I am so far from perfect."

I'm trying to gather my words, but my eyes land on the deep-sea green of hers, and I'm rendered speechless.

"Olive?"

"Hmm?"

She is still propped up with her hands, and her hair is a bit wilder than it was when I first came into her bedroom. But she looks sexier, if that's even possible. "If you don't finish this, I'm going to start on you, and I guarantee, you won't be able to form a coherent thought after."

"Well, then. I guess I better stop stalling." I lunge for her, and we fall back onto the bed, my breasts colliding with hers. We fit together in the most perfect of ways. I move my hand down her body while kissing her, feel her stomach, the apex between her thighs, her soft, slick folds before I slide two fingers gently inside her. She gasps into our kiss. I break apart and watch as I push my fingers into her slowly. She leans her head back, exposing her neck, and I see her jaw muscle flex when she clenches her teeth, a strained moan coming from deep inside her.

It's interesting because obviously, I know what to do. I mean, don't all women sort of know what they want? I'd like to think we do. But I've never felt this comfortable in my knowledge before. Even on myself, I would fumble and fight against my orgasm, as if I didn't deserve to feel good. But hearing the way she sounds while being pleasured, while I'm pleasuring her? Wow. *Wow, wow, wow.*

"I'm so close," she whispers.

"So if I stopped, that'd be a problem?"

Her eyelids fly open. "Um, yes. That'd be a huge problem."

"Like, I shouldn't pull my fingers out like this?" I slide them out, and she groans.

"Olive."

"What about this?" I slip them back in and pull out as slow as humanly possible. She lets out another low groan. "And what if I do this?" I move a bit to brush her clit with my thumb as I thrust slowly. She spreads her legs a little wider. My hand is sopping wet. The feeling of it is such a turn-on. "Is that what you don't want me to stop?"

She digs her nails into my back. "Don't stop, please."

I place my lips on her chin, then her lips as I pull out and focus all my attention on her clit. Within seconds, I feel her entire body tense and shake. I keep massaging her as she comes. I don't want to stop. I want her to beg me to stop. Her thighs are clamped around my hand, but I can still move just enough. Without warning, she rolls to the side, away from me, and my hand is no longer between us.

"Fuck," she says between breaths. "Fuck, fuck, fuck."

"Are you okay?"

"Fuck." She laughs. "Yes, I'm okay. Holy *shit*, Olive."

I lean over and kiss her shoulder before she rolls back to me. "Not bad for my first time with a girl?"

"I mean, you did all right."

It's my turn to laugh as she pulls me down, kissing me. I want to do it all over again. I want to make her feel good again. I want to put my mouth on her and make her scream.

What is happening to me?

Eleanor

I don't even know how to explain what is happening. I never expected this. I never in a million years thought this would ever happen to me. I spent so much of my life hating how Mabel broke my heart that I forgot to find real love with someone else. And then I met Olive and fell hard and fast and knew it would never happen. I pined and pined because she was unattainable and safe. Olive was never going to break my heart because I was never going to tell her how I felt. I was going to love her from afar and take it to my grave.

And then.

Then Mabel happened. And Sunny happened. And I realized that

I was never going to get over Olive if I didn't tell her. I needed to tell her, and she would say exactly what I needed her to say. That it was never going to happen. Then I could finally take a breath and move the fuck on.

But that isn't what happened. I tried to let all of my love for her go, and it was as if she caught it and gave it right back to me. Now here I am, my heart beating so hard for her that I can barely breathe.

"You know, I can still fuck you even with those shorts on." I motion to Olive's pajama bottoms. "But if you're not comfortable, we can stop."

The look on her face is undeniable. She's nervous about taking them off, as if seeing her completely naked is going to be a huge turn-off for me. She has no idea that I have always found her so fucking sexy. Everything about her. From her hair, her eyes, her dimples, to her breasts, her hips, her thighs. I don't want to make it sound like I stare at her and try to control myself because that's not it at all. It's that I have never once looked at her and not seen someone I could spend the rest of my life loving.

"Olive?"

"I'm...I need a second." She is leaning against the headboard, a pillow clutched to her chest to cover her.

"Do you really think I don't find you attractive?" I kneel in front of her, stark naked, bite marks on my breasts and sides from her. I clasp my hands and rest them in my lap. I don't want to force anything on her. I want her to know I'm serious. Everything about me is serious about her. I can imagine it'd be difficult to know that I am serious when we were in what seemed to be such different spots two weeks earlier.

"I think you don't want to hurt my feelings."

"Olive—"

"No, you have to understand why I'm self-conscious, though. Like, look at me." She moves the pillow and exposes herself, her breasts, her stomach.

"You want me to see what you see?"

"Yes, but what do you think I see?"

"I think you think you're ugly. That you're not worth being stared at. That you aren't worthy of being worshipped."

She nods.

"But all I see, all I have ever seen, is beautiful curves and soft skin and a delicate heart and a delightful soul." I shrug. "You take my breath away." I place my hand on her outstretched leg. "You are *gorgeous*.

Everything about you." The words seem to wash over her, and I wait patiently to see what her next move is. "I will never make you do something you don't want to do. I hope you know that."

She hooks her thumbs into the waistband of her shorts and starts to move them down her thighs. I don't help. I want her to make these first moves because if she doesn't want this, I am not going to push her. She's been struggling with who she is and what labels she thinks she needs to apply to herself. The numerous conversations we've had in the past two weeks have made me fully aware that she is scared, nervous, not sure if she's ready or if this is really what she wants.

I get her hesitation. I do. Because two weeks ago, there was Mabel and Sunny and confusion. And we both seemed to be heading in different directions. But we came back together, as if we're both magnets that only feel complete when together. I have to think that maybe that's part of what stopped us from doing anything. We both assumed that if we weren't everything to each other, then we couldn't be anything to each other. As if it would never work if that wasn't the case. But life isn't all things from one source. It's a little of this and a little of that, and we do what we need to do to survive.

But she wants me to thrive.

What does that even mean? I've only been surviving for as long as I can remember. How do I thrive?

"I need you to do something for me." Olive's voice is soft as she tosses her shorts to the floor.

"Anything," I say as she fidgets, as if she's deciding whether or not to grab the pillow to cover up or to allow herself to *be* in her own skin, comfortable or not.

"I need you to promise me that you will never stop your heart from doing whatever it needs to be okay."

I blink a couple times. It's as if she was listening to my thoughts. "What do you mean?"

"I mean." She takes a deep breath, and my eyes are drawn to her very full breasts, the light pink of her areola and nipple, and the way they hang a bit lower than mine because of the size. I want to bury my face in them. "I mean, I'm a lot to handle, and right now, I want this, I want you…but I don't know what I'm going through or what my body wants and if you…" She breathes deeply again, bites her lip, then shrugs. "I will never hold you back from needing more than I can give you."

"Wow." I try to hold back my emotion because it's boiling right to the surface. "Is this how adults speak to each other?"

She sighs, nods, and smiles. "I'm being honest and real with you, Ellie. Because I love you, and I don't want to lose you because of who I am"—she pats her heart—"in here."

I reach forward and place my hand on hers, over her heart. "Okay."

"Okay," she whispers. "Now kiss me and have sex with me, please."

I can't help the laugh that springs out of me. "Your wish is my command." I lean into her and nudge her nose with mine. "I love you, too, by the way."

"Good."

And I capture her lips and kiss her with as much love as I can bestow. I want her to know how much I need her, how much I care for her, how much I appreciate every word she said. She is so much more to me than a best friend or a lover. She is my partner, my other half, the reason my heart beats and beats and beats.

She's lying on her back now, and I hold myself up with one hand as I continue to kiss her, my other hand on her breast, massaging, rolling her nipple between my forefinger and thumb until it's taut. I straddle her left thigh and access the other nipple. She presses her thigh into me, and I grind into her as I start to tweak both nipples. She moans into our kiss, and goddamn, that is one of my favorite feelings in the whole world. The vibration of a moan against my lips, my tongue. Fuck. I pinch her nipples again and am rewarded with another moan. She breaks apart this time and leans her head back, and I latch on to the soft skin of her neck. Her skin is so soft, like honey, and I am so very grateful that I finally get to taste her. I want to get my mouth on her.

"Eleanor?"

I hear her say my name, low, seductive. "Yes?"

"Thank you."

"For what, my love?"

She has her eyes shut and her head leaned back. "For being patient with me." Her voice is strained.

I lean down and kiss her cheek, then her lips. "I've heard patience is a virtue."

"Yeah, well," she says softly before she moans again and wraps her arm around me, then drags her nails down my back. "Let's see if I have the same virtue."

"Trust me. You won't have to be nearly as patient with me." I start to kiss my way down her body, across her chest, her stomach, her pubic area where she has trimmed tidy hair. I drag my tongue down her bikini area, down, down, to the soft skin of her inner thigh. I spread her legs and place my mouth on her without warning and hear her gasp. I don't want to wait any longer. I want her to come hard, right in my mouth.

I push my tongue inside her before I replace it with two fingers. I suck her clit into my mouth and start to flick it with my tongue. She is breathing hard, her moans low, guttural, and I am enjoying every single second. I thrust into her very softly, never completely pulling out. She's moving against my tongue, pushing into me, so I start to flick her harder and faster. It doesn't take long before I feel her orgasm. She clenches around my fingers and arches her back, but I don't stop. I keep flicking, hold her legs open with my free hand, and before long, she's coming again and again.

"Eleanor, you…you have to…stop." Her plea is said between breaths, and when I look up at her, she has her hands on her face. I do as she begs and start to pull my fingers from her. She moans my name. "My God," she says, breathless, panting.

I move up the side of her body and settle next to her. "You okay?"

"That was…" She opens her eyes and looks at me. "That was amazing."

"I'm glad you enjoyed yourself."

She rolls toward me. "Um, yes, I absolutely enjoyed myself."

"Wanna go again?"

"Actually," she says before she leans in and kisses me. "I do want to go again. But I think it's my turn to taste you."

I lift my head from the bed and sit upright. I salute her. "Reporting for duty."

A laugh pours from her as she pulls me down to her. When her lips land on mine, I realize that I haven't thought about the past for the first time in a really long time. And it feels amazing.

Harriet

It feels a little weird driving up to the sanctuary at night. Before I go anywhere else, I want to check at the restaurant and make sure nothing crazy happened while I was gone. It was nice to disconnect from the stress of everything, even if only for a minute. I love my job, I love Olive and Eleanor, but it's been three years since I've had a break, and distancing myself from all of it was much needed.

Judy's kids are amazing. I say kids, but they're almost grown. Grace is a sophomore at UCLA in their business program, and Joseph is gearing up to go back to Chicago to attend Columbia College for animation. Conlon is the youngest, and he'll be out of the house in a couple years. He was definitely the most talkative of the three, too. Although Grace was definitely the happiest that her mother had finally found someone who made her happy.

Hanging out with them, learning how each of them interacts with their mom and trying not to stick out like a sore thumb was a little difficult at first. I mean, I'm black. And they're very white, and even though I don't see Judy as different than me, I knew it would eventually be an issue. And it was. Not because I wanted it to be but because it simply is. Nothing bad happened. We had numerous conversations, though, about what it means to be in a mixed relationship. And why it won't always be easy and why her white privilege can be such a dealbreaker. I'm thankful for Judy's ability to listen, and she never once tried to explain anything from her point of view because honestly, her point of view is skewed. I love her, and I want to be with her. But we needed to put it all on the table and sort through it. Especially if we want this to work. At the end of the day, we're as happy as we were when I jumped on the helicopter to leave with her.

The restaurant is bustling when I enter. Not a single table is empty, but the dinner rush is almost up. An hour or so and it'll be time to stop seating people. I rise on my tippy-toes and look around for Glenda. She's talking to a couple at the bar. It makes me happy to see her enjoying the leadership role. It took a minute for her to feel comfortable, but she's gotten the hang of it.

I don't touch base with anyone. I don't even go into the kitchen. The second I do, vacation is over, so I sneak out the entrance and head to the residence. I don't think Eleanor and Olive are expecting me until tomorrow, but I figure it'll be nice to surprise them.

When I open the front door and head inside, there are lights on in the kitchen. As soon as I turn the corner, I feel my eyes just about bug out of my head. "What is going on?" Eleanor jerks away from kissing Olive, and what the fuck did I miss while I was gone? "I was only gone two weeks." They're both standing at the island, nightshirts on, no shorts, hair messy. "I mean, right?" I rush to the calendar hanging on the wall.

Eleanor is the first to start laughing. "You're home early."

"Only by a day."

She rushes over and grabs my hands. "We have some news."

"Yeah, good news." Olive is all smiles. "Not that this should surprise you."

I shake my head. "Are you two serious? You're, y'know, together?"

Eleanor shrugs. "I guess you could say that."

"We're seeing how this goes." Olive wraps her arms around Eleanor and kisses her cheek.

I am absolutely floored. "No more Mabel? And no more Sunny?"

"So many questions," Eleanor says. "Let's get you a snack and a glass of wine, and we can talk."

"I'll take a vodka on the rocks, please."

Eleanor moves to the liquor bar and starts pouring Tito's into a rocks glass. Olive is looking at me as if she is silently begging me to understand. "I don't even know what to say."

"Say you're okay with it," Olive says softly as she takes my hand with both of hers. "I think we both want and need your blessing."

Eleanor whisks back over and hands me my drink, the ice clinking. "At the very least, it'd be cool if you could be understanding."

I take a drink of Tito's and let it sit in my mouth for a second before swallowing. "My blessing, hmm?"

They nod, and I chuckle at the looks on their faces, at the clear display that they've been going at it for most of the evening. "You two aren't going to kill each other?"

"Well, I mean, maybe?" Eleanor laughs, and Olive smacks her on the ass. "But we've talked—"

"A lot."

"And we are on the same page."

"The exact same page."

"Which is?" I point at Olive, then Eleanor. "Because I'm not going to be okay with this if you two are going to fight and bicker and make working here miserable."

"Let's just say we know what we need and what each other wants, and that's all that matters."

I tilt my head and twist my face. "That sounds ominous."

"Yeah, well, don't worry, okay?" Eleanor's tone is soothing. I know I should listen to her. "And tell us about your trip."

"Will you both put some pants on first?"

Olive rolls her eyes and shakes her head. "Like you've never seen our legs before," she says as they follow each other out of the kitchen and upstairs.

I pull a stool from the center island and sit, taking a sip of vodka as I wait for the two people I never thought in a million years would settle down together. In fact, my money was on Eleanor leaving to be with Mabel. I can't believe how the past month has unfolded. It started with us being completely worried sick about the *On the Verge* article, to us being completely enamored with the VIP threesome, to me finding the love of my life, and Eleanor and Olive finding happiness together.

Nothing about what happened is ordinary, but that's exactly why it's special. And that's exactly why the Hummingbird Sanctuary is special, because it's so far from ordinary. I am excited about the future, and it's because I took a chance on this place with my two best friends. And I have never felt more loved and more encouraged.

Looking forward to the future is something I try to do because life is short. But I've never been the person to count down the days for something. And now here I am, counting down the days until Judy moves here with Conlon for his last year of high school that he swears he'll be fine with online. I'm scared. Nervous. But most of all? I am happy.

And when Eleanor and Olive join me at the bar, talking over each other as they tell me the story of how they ended up in bed together, I realize that they're happy, too.

And happiness?

That's the entire reason we started this ride to begin with—to find happiness.

We found it.

Finally.

EPILOGUE

Olive

For the first time in years, the Western Slope has escaped the summer fires. The front range was burning, but for some reason, we have been lucky and haven't had a single spark this far west. It has thrilled me because dealing with fire season is never fun. I'm constantly on edge, and we are usually fairly slow. This entire summer has been different, though. It seems we escaped not only the fires but also any threat of having to close. Business is booming, and the constant fear that resided in my chest has finally dissipated. Thank God.

"Keri, I have to get home. Is there anything else?"

"Yes! One second." Keri fumbles around with papers until she finds a large envelope. She hands it over. "This came for you. I meant to give it to you earlier, but I completely spaced."

I swallow the nervousness that sprang to life inside my throat. "This came today?"

"Yeah, ugh, I suck. We were so busy, and I got sidetracked—"

"No, no, Keri, it's fine." I finally take the envelope. There's a heft to it, and for some reason the weight seems to drag my shoulders down. "Thank you. Is that, um, is that all?"

"Yep. Marco is going to take over for me, and then I'll be over there."

"Sounds good." I turn to leave, exiting the welcome center as quickly as possible. Once outside, I stop and look at the envelope again. I slide my index finger under the flap, gently pry it open, and pull a magazine out. "Wow." Staring back at me is a picture of me, Eleanor, and Harriet on the cover of *On the Verge*. We are sitting outside the

Amphitheater. I remember when Mabel snapped the picture with Eleanor's camera. It was after I told Eleanor I loved her and before she started talking to me again. But we all look good together. Eleanor's hair is perfect, Harriet's black hat is so sharp, and the purple of my blouse is beautiful against the greens and browns of the backdrop, and across the bottom are the words *Women in Charge*. I realize that, when a tear lands on the magazine, I'm crying. I flip the magazine open to a Post-it on the page where the article starts.

> *Eleanor, Olive, and Harriet,*
> *Please know that I think you are all the most incredible women I have ever had the privilege of knowing. Enjoy the fame. You deserve it.*
> *Love, Mabel*

I close the magazine, hold it next to my chest, and take a deep breath.

We did it. We really freaking did it.

❖

Eleanor

My hand is shaking as I hold the magazine. Olive handed it over, gave me a kiss, then turned and left. It was as if she knew I needed to be alone with it, with Mabel's words, with the soft lines of her cursive handwritten note.

I'm holding the envelope in my hand when a card falls from it. I see my name scribbled across the small white envelope. After picking it up, I open it with delicate fingers and pull the card from it.

> *Eleanor,*
> *I hope you are happy. And I miss you every single day.*

I'm crying, and it makes me mad at myself. It's not the time to cry. I'm going to smear my makeup, and if I sit down and sob, I'm going to wrinkle my dress, and that's not okay. I set the magazine on the table in my bedroom, then pick up my phone. I quickly type out a text.

> *Got your note. I miss you, too. Please stay safe and come home in one piece.*

The text takes a second to send, and every time that happens, I start to worry that something has happened to her.

There's a knock on my door, and I look over at Olive standing there, holding her dress. "Can you help me with this?"

She's in her bra and panties, and it makes me happy that she is comfortable enough to do that now, walk around like that, and not worry that someone is judging her. Because all that exists inside me is love for her. And that's all that will ever exist.

❖

Harriet

I've never been so nervous in my entire life. I look in the mirror and smooth my hands over the sides of my hair. My eyes find Eleanor's as she stares at me, too. "Yes?"

"You okay?"

"Nope. I'm freaking the fuck out." I groan. "I'm doing the right thing, right?"

"Oh, Hattie, yes, a thousand times, yes. You are doing the right thing," Olive answers from across the dressing room. "You've wanted this almost since day one."

"Yeah, but is this the right—"

"Yes." Eleanor pushes her arms around me from behind and hugs me. "You've never been like this before. You've never wanted something this much."

"You're right."

"Obviously. I'm always right." Eleanor loosens her grip and spins me around. She straightens my floral tie, runs her hands over the shoulders of my blue blazer, and holds me by the biceps. "You are gorgeous."

I can feel heat filling my cheeks. "I love you, Ellie."

"And I love you, too."

"And I *also* love you." Olive breezes over, a red rose boutonniere in her hand. She takes my lapel and attaches it with ease. She looks into my eyes and places her hands on my cheeks. "You deserve this happiness. I hope you know that."

"It's time."

I look at Eleanor, then back to Olive. "Thank you for everything."

"Stop. You're not going anywhere." Olive leans in and kisses my cheek, then moves across the room to the double doors.

"You ready?" Eleanor nudges me.

"I am."

"Then let's get you married."

When we walk out of the doors, I look over to my left and see Judy standing there in a beautiful dress, flowing cream lace, and a crown of flowers on her head. The sight of her takes my breath away. All I can think is that I am the luckiest person in the entire world.

And when I meet her at the altar, and Eleanor stands before us, I realize that this love was what my heart was waiting for.

And it was all worth it.

On the Verge
July 2021

"Lost Love and Finding Salvation at the Hummingbird Sanctuary"
by Mabel Sommers

The sun is high in the Colorado sky when I sit with Olive Zyntarski, part owner of the Hummingbird Sanctuary, which is nestled in a valley along the western slope of the Rockies. Olive is impeccably dressed in a navy tailored suit, her dark brown hair in loose curls around her face. A gold bracelet with a hummingbird pendant hangs limply around her right wrist, and a gold ring resides on her right hand. Her entire aura is striking, and being in her presence has me feeling some type of way. She commands my attention in a nonintrusive way. She reminds me of a summer morning, fresh, clean, and ready to take on anything, and I want to get up and experience that summer morning, regardless of how early it is.

Olive stirs her Earl Grey, the cream transforming from cumulus clouds to overcast within seconds. She drags the spoon against the rim of the teacup and places it gently on the saucer. "The sanctuary means more to me than simply a resort to make money."

I feel as if I've offended her with my question, "Why a resort?" I raise a hand so I can correct myself, but she continues.

"As a woman, I'm sure you will understand this because life for us seems to sort of get in the way, but sometimes, we need to get out of something or away from somewhere, and we just don't."

The way she emphasizes certain words makes something deep, deep inside me clench. It's as if she knows firsthand what it feels like to be trapped in a situation and not know how to escape. She's right, though, even if she isn't speaking from experience. As a woman, I do understand the feeling of feeling trapped and needing out. All women can understand that. Life does get in the way, but so do abusive partners or children whom we must put first or our inability to put ourselves first for even half a second. It starts to add up, and when it becomes too much, instead of taking a minute to find ourselves, within an instant, we often lose complete sight of ourselves.

"The other owners, Eleanor and Harriet, we all have mothers who have passed away," Olive explains. She is pulling gently on the hummingbird pendant. "And each of us was very close to our mothers before they passed. When we first started talking about the possibility of starting a business, I remember saying I wanted it to be an homage to our mothers, to their sacrifices and attention to detail that made us who we are." Olive picks up her tea, pinkie slightly in the air, and sips. She was born and raised in Rangely, Colorado, a tiny blip on the map that you might miss if you weren't looking for it. She moved to Chicago for college and eventually married. When she speaks of her husband now, it's with remorse and a tinge of something else, maybe guilt, as he has since passed away. "I know he would have loved what we've done with the place." She's gazing at the lush grounds of the sanctuary, and it's clear from her carriage and demeanor that she is pleased with how everything has turned out.

And she should be. Not only are the grounds spectacular, but the accommodations are even more so. I was thoroughly impressed with everything from the complimentary toiletries, all locally sourced, to the bedding and decorations, all natural and organic cottons, to the immaculate housekeeping that goes into each room.

"We wanted to make sure that everything we love about Colorado made its way into the overall theme. It's not meant to be overbearing or hoity-toity. Every detail is so the guest is immersed in the beauty of our surroundings, in the beauty of nature."

I learned a lot about each owner while I visited the sanctuary, as they so lovingly refer to the resort. It's interesting because as someone who had her reservations about anything that was promised to change my life, I really rolled my eyes at first. A hummingbird sanctuary? I've been hardened by the cruel concrete jungle that is Los Angeles, so there was no way I was going to be moved by this place. Sure. A sanctuary. I doubted very much that it would feel at all like however a sanctuary is supposed to feel.

But I was wrong. Fully and completely.

If LA is the city of angels, then the sanctuary is the city of peace.

Learning about Olive through numerous conversations made me realize exactly why they decided on that name. Not only do hummingbirds have a much deeper meaning than I realized, but anyone who comes to the sanctuary leaves feeling refreshed and relaxed, and dare I say, safe? As a writer, I should never say that I have a hard time describing the safeness I felt while I was there. Or even after, when I was on the helicopter that took me away from much more than a resort. How is it possible that a vacation changed my life?

Olive Zyntarski is a beautiful and calm woman who not only exudes happiness but lives her life in such a way that makes you want to also be happy around her. She has this way about her that instantly relaxes you. I felt honored to be in her presence, and I was thrilled when she opened up to me, explaining how the hummingbirds bring a blanket of calm every spring. I have always thought of myself as more spiritual than anything. Olive made me realize that it doesn't take a lot to believe in the spirit of a tiny hummingbird.

As the days turned into nights, I was able to spend time with Harriet Marshall, the general manager and executive chef for the bar and restaurant at the sanctuary, aptly named the Feeder and Bird's Eye View, respectively. Hattie grew up in Chicago and was snatched away from her restaurant there to start up the sanctuary. She speaks about her friends with a love I've never seen before. I am impressed and moved by her, especially when she says, "Olive and Eleanor are exactly the kind of soulmates you want when you're trying to create something worthwhile." Her words sort of slam into me, and I feel breathless in their wake. Her style is unique, and everything around her embodies that uniqueness. She is coolness personified, and I was so happy to be able to sit and speak with her. She cooked for me and made me feel as if I had never really had food before. I didn't think that was possible. "Food should be an experience. Every single time," she said as she finished plating one of the two meals she made for me. And let me tell you, she did not disappoint. Every single dish she prepared was an experience. One that I'd also describe as spiritual.

She also reminds me of why it's so important to stop and take a breath every now and then. "Life moves so fast, and most of the time, we're so busy with the minutiae that we forget to actually live." She speaks with the voice of someone who has gone through a lot in her thirty-some years, and I feel grateful that I've been given the opportunity to experience her. Harriet's calm demeanor is exactly what a relaxing resort restaurant needs, and it's exactly what the sanctuary has received with her.

And the last of the owners is Eleanor Fitzwallace, marketing extraordinaire. Eleanor, who graduated with honors from Northwestern with an undergrad in marketing and the University of Chicago with an MBA, is hands down one of the most interesting people I have ever been around in my entire life. She not only has a passion for marketing, but she also has a passion for women and the unique experiences they have. As a woman, I haven't ever really sat and thought about all the different things we all go through. But Eleanor has. And she has made sure to address many of those things at the sanctuary. She genuinely cares about the sanctuary's guests. And I can see it in every single word she says about her work for the resort.

Honestly, there is so much that I could say about this insanely talented woman. I could go on and on about her attention to detail, her ability to take an excursion around the property and make it the most exciting bike ride I've ever been on, her drive and desire to make sure every single guest has something to rave about when they leave. "Sure, the sanctuary is aimed at women, and while that was done intentionally, I also think it was done because at the end of the day, women and their friendships and their connections and their love for others is why we are all here, present, and accounted for," Eleanor said to me over drinks. She is so right. "Women are powerful and exciting and sexy, and if we can actively encourage every single woman to remember that, to take control of their lives, well, then I think that means we have succeeded."

And succeed they have. The Hummingbird Sanctuary is one of the only places I have ever been where I literally felt my entire life change, my world shift back onto its axis. Love and laughter were found again. And I was reminded that life is too short to constantly obsess about the past, to worry about the future, and not focus on the present. Life happens all around us: nature and wildlife and, yes, even the hummingbird. We have to stop caring about the loves we lost, about the friendships we didn't cultivate, about the people who are no longer with us. We have to start honoring them and the way they have helped to mold us into the people we are today.

Life-changing seems so cliché, but it's the truth. My life changed at the sanctuary. And I know I am not the only one. We need to thank women like Olive, Harriet, and Eleanor. They are creating places where we can feel safe and invigorated and, yes, loved. So, thank you, my dears. You are quite simply doing God's work.

Mabel Sommers is a contributing columnist for On the Verge *and an international correspondent for* The Washington Post.

About the Author

Erin Zak grew up on the Western Slope of Colorado in a town with a population of 2,500, a solitary Subway, and one stoplight. She started writing at a young age and has always had a very active imagination. Erin later transplanted to Indiana where she attended college, started writing a book, and had dreams of one day actually finding the courage to try to get it published.

Erin now resides in Florida, away from the snow and cold, near the Gulf Coast with her family. She enjoys the sun, sand, writing, and spoiling her cocker spaniel, Hanna. When she's not writing, she's obsessively collecting Star Wars memorabilia, planning the next trip to Disney World, or whipping up something delicious to eat in the kitchen.

Books Available From Bold Strokes Books

The Business of Pleasure by Ronica Black. Editor in chief Valerie Raffield is quickly becoming smitten by Lennox, the graphic artist she's hired to work remotely. But when Lennox doesn't show for their first face-to-face meeting, Valerie's heart and her business may be in jeopardy. (978-1-63679-134-0)

Cold Blood by Genevieve McCluer. Maybe together, Kalila and Dorenia have a chance of taking down the vampires who have eluded them all these years. And maybe, in each other, they can find a love worth living for. (978-1-63679-195-1)

Greener Pastures by Aurora Rey. When city girl and CPA Audrey Adams finds herself tending her aunt's farm, will Rowan Marshall—the charming cider maker next door—turn out to be her saving grace or the bane of her existence? (978-1-63679-116-6)

Grounded by Amanda Radley. For a second chance, Olivia and Emily will need to accept their mistakes, learn to communicate properly, and with a little help from five-year-old Henry, fall madly in love all over again. Sequel to Flight SQA016. (978-1-63679-241-5)

The Hummingbird Sanctuary by Erin Zak. The Hummingbird Sanctuary, Colorado's hottest resort destination: Come for the mountains, stay for the charm, and enjoy the drama as Olive, Eleanor, and Harriet figure out the meaning of true friendship. (978-1-63679-163-0)

Journey's End by Amanda Radley. In this heartwarming conclusion to the Flight series, Olivia and Emily must finally decide what they want, what they need, and how to follow the dreams of their hearts. (978-1-63679-233-0)

Secret Agent by Michelle Larkin. CIA agent Peyton North embarks on a global chase to apprehend rogue agent Zoey Blackwood, but her commitment to the mission is tested as the sparks between them ignite and their sizzling attraction approaches a point of no return. (978-1-63555-753-4)

Something Between Us by Krystina Rivers. A decade after her heart was broken under Don't Ask, Don't Tell, Kirby runs into her first love and has to decide if what's still between them is enough to heal her broken heart. (978-1-63679-135-7)

Sugar Girl by Emma L McGeown. Having traded in traditional romance for the perks of Sugar Dating, Ciara Reilly not only enjoys the no-strings-attached arrangement, she's also a hit with her clients. That is, until she meets the beautiful entrepreneur Charlie Keller, who makes her want to go sugar-free. (978-1-63679-156-2)

With a Twist by Georgia Beers. Starting over isn't easy for Amelia Martini. When the irritatingly cheerful Kirby Dupress comes into her life, will Amelia be brave enough to go after the love she really wants? (978-1-63555-987-3)

The Witch Queen's Mate by Jennifer Karter. Barra and Silvi must overcome their ingrained hatred and prejudice to use Barra's magic and save both their peoples from not just slavery, but destruction. (978-1-63679-202-6)

Business of the Heart by Claire Forsythe. When a hopeless romantic meets a tough-as-nails cynic, they'll need to overcome the wounds of the past to discover that their hearts are the most important business of all. (978-1-63679-167-8)

Dying for You by Jenny Frame. Can Victorija Dred keep an age-old vow and fight the need to take blood from Daisy Macdougall? (978-1-63679-073-2)

Exclusive by Melissa Brayden. Skylar Ruiz lands the TV reporting job of a lifetime, but is she willing to sacrifice it all for the love of her longtime crush, anchorwoman Carolyn McNamara? (978-1-63679-112-8)

Her Duchess to Desire by Jane Walsh. An up-and-coming interior designer seeks to create a happily ever after with an intriguing duchess, proving that love never goes out of fashion. (978-1-63679-065-7)

Take Her Down by Lauren Emily Whalen. Stakes are cutthroat, scheming is creative, and loyalty is ever-changing in this queer, female-driven YA retelling of Shakespeare's Julius Caesar. (978-1-63679-089-3)